Meet the Shaughnessy Brothers

Made for Us

"Chase grabs readers by the heartstrings and reels them right into the antics of the lively Shaughnessy family... gratifying and realistic; it's an uncluttered, perfectly paced look at two individuals trying to move forward after tragedy."

—*Publishers Weekly*

"Delightful...heartfelt...classic romance."
—*RT Book Reviews*, 4.5 Stars

"Elegant prose and honest dialogue...a heartwarming story that sizzles with passion."
—*Fresh Fiction*

"A classically styled romance...filled with sweetness, humor, and heartfelt emotion. *Made For Us* is a winner."
—*Long and Short Reviews*

"A beautiful perfection of a read...I will treasure the first Shaughnessy brother forever and can't wait to be a part of the rest of this dynamic family and their love stories."
—*Romancing Life*

Also by Samantha Chase

Love *Walks* In

SAMANTHA CHASE

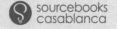

sourcebooks
casablanca

Published by Sourcebooks Casablanca, an imprint of Sourcebooks, Inc.
P.O. Box 4410, Naperville, Illinois 60567-4410
(630) 961-3900
Fax: (630) 961-2168
www.sourcebooks.com

Printed and bound in Canada.
MBP 10 9 8 7 6 5 4 3 2 1

Prologue

Seventeen Years Ago…

Why wouldn't everyone leave?

Hugh Shaughnessy stood in the corner of his living room, glaring at the masses. They came. They saw. They said their condolences. Wasn't that enough?

Everywhere he looked, there were people. He glanced at his watch and shook his head with disgust. Four thirty. Didn't anyone realize someone needed to start preparing dinner at five? Every night the family sat down for dinner at exactly six fifteen, but if someone didn't start moving these people toward the door, it wasn't going to happen.

Schedules.

It was all about the schedules.

There was no room for spontaneity—no room for straying from the norm. He'd learned that the hard way. And there were at least a hundred people milling about to witness the lesson he'd been forced to learn.

Turning his back on everyone, he thought of the conversation he'd had only days before with his mother.

"Do you have any idea what time it is?" Lillian Shaughnessy asked her second oldest son as soon as he'd walked through the front door.

Hugh took off his letterman jacket, hung it on his

designated peg on the wall, and shrugged. "I don't know. Nine?"

His mother's eyes narrowed as she looked at him. "It's after ten. Where were you that you couldn't call to say you were going to be late?"

Not really in the mood for a lecture or an argument, Hugh walked toward the kitchen to get something to eat. He made it all of three steps before his mother—who was almost a foot shorter than him—grabbed him by the arm and forced him to look at her. "What?" he snapped. "I went out with a couple of friends after school. I lost track of time. It's not a big deal. I'm almost eighteen. Don't you think it's time I stopped having a curfew? I mean…really. Can't a guy go out once in a while without it turning into a big deal?"

But it was a big deal. Lillian Shaughnessy ran a tight ship in her home. With six kids, she had no choice. There were chores to do, meals to cook, homework to be checked, and without a routine—a schedule—things could easily fall apart and break down into chaos.

"You know the rules, Hugh. You had chores to do this afternoon—chores Quinn had to take on because you weren't here."

"So? I'll do his chores tomorrow."

Lillian looked up at her son, her expression firm. "That's not the point and you know it. You broke the rules. Again. You didn't come home on time and you didn't call. Again. This is the third time this week." She held out her hand. "Give me your keys."

"What?" Hugh cried. "But…that's not fair!"

She shook her head. "No driving for a week. You'll

have to take the bus to and from school. If one of your friends drives you, you'll still need to be home on time. No extra stops, no excuses."

Hugh wanted to argue, but he knew it was pointless. Without a word, he put the keys in his mother's hand and turned to go to his room.

"Your dinner is in the microwave," she said, still standing where he'd left her.

"I'm not hungry," he mumbled and went to his room.

For the next two days he was the model son—he came home on time, did his chores and his homework all without saying a word of complaint. On the third day, he came home miserable. It was storming and the walk from the bus stop had left him soaked to the skin.

"You'd better get changed before you catch a cold," his mother warned, but she looked distracted.

"What's going on?" Hugh asked.

"Darcy has an ear infection. I've got to pick up a prescription for her." She looked out the window and frowned. "I had hoped the rain would let up by now. I can't wait any longer."

It was on the tip of his tongue to offer to go for her, but he remembered his punishment. And for a moment, he wanted to be mean—to show her how her stupid punishment affected her too. "Well, if I was allowed to drive, I'd go. But since it's so important for me to learn my lesson..." He let his words die off.

Lillian merely gave him a tight smile. "You can be mad at me all you want. You broke curfew...for what? To go joyriding for an afternoon? Was it worth it?" She reached for her coat and slipped it on, her eyes still on Hugh.

Her expression softened. She reached out and cupped his cheek. "Sweetheart, there's nothing wrong with wanting to have some fun once in a while. It's just… well, you didn't call. You had no consideration for your family and our rules. I don't think your father and I are strict, we don't ask too much…"

"I know, Mom. But—"

"But," she interrupted, "maybe next time you'll think twice before being so impulsive."

Hugh wasn't so sure, but he kept it to himself.

"I'll be back in a little while," Lillian said. "Darcy's finally sleeping so I want to get to the pharmacy and back before she wakes up. Quinn is staying after school and Riley and Owen will be home soon."

Yeah, yeah…Hugh knew the drill. The schedule. No surprises.

Lillian walked out the door into the storm.

And never came home.

That wasn't on the schedule, Hugh kept telling himself. It wasn't something any of them were prepared for.

And it certainly wasn't what any of them wanted.

For all the times he'd mocked the schedules and the routine and the flat-out boringness of their lives, right now Hugh would give everything he had to have it all back.

To have *her* back.

At five o'clock, he moved into the kitchen. Luckily no one was in there. Their guests had finally started to leave, and it was remarkably the one quiet room in the house.

"Hugh?" his father asked as he came into the room a few minutes later. "What are you doing?"

"Making dinner. It's spaghetti night."

Ian Shaughnessy stood with tears in his eyes as he watched his son get out the ingredients to make dinner. "Hugh," he began, "there's enough food out in the dining room to feed a small army. I don't think we have to make dinner tonight."

Hugh stopped and looked at him. "But...it's Thursday. We always have spaghetti on Thursday." He turned and pointed to the chalkboard his mother kept in the kitchen. "See? Thursday. Spaghetti." Then he went back to getting out the large pot his mother used to cook pasta in.

He filled it and put it on the stove and when he turned back around, his father was right there in front of him. "Hugh..." he said gruffly, right before he wrapped his son in his arms.

Something inside of Hugh broke. "She always..."

"I know," Ian said.

"She would want..."

"I know that too. But for tonight, we'll let the menu slide." He pulled back and smiled sadly. "Tomorrow will be soon enough to get back on track with dinners. Although I think we have about twenty casseroles over-flowing from the freezer just in case."

Hugh wiped away the tears streaming down his cheeks. "I just want..." He swallowed hard.

Ian stopped him. "I know, Hugh. I want it too."

They stood there in silence for a long time, and Hugh decided then and there that he would honor his mother by doing things the way she wanted—he'd follow the rules. Never again would he act impulsively or without conscious thought.

He couldn't afford to.

Not ever again.

Chapter 1

IT WAS COMPLETELY UNACCEPTABLE.

"I don't think I understand."

Hugh Shaughnessy straightened the cell phone that sat on his desk until it was completely in line with the rest of the items there—all while keeping eye contact with his assistant Dorothy. "I said," he began slowly, "it isn't going to work for me. It's unacceptable. Tell her no."

Dorothy shifted nervously. "Um…I don't think that's an option, Hugh. You…you can't exactly…" She hesitated, clearly trying to choose her words. "What I mean is, I don't think you get a say in this."

He arched a brow at her. "Really?"

"I could see if it was a request for time off or for vacation, but…"

"Technically, she is asking for time off," he said reasonably.

"No. What she's doing is quitting," Dorothy stated in the same tone.

A sigh of frustration escaped before Hugh could stop it. He rose and crossed the office to stare out the open window. "Tell her we require a minimum of two weeks' notice or else."

"Or else what?"

Looking over his shoulder, he replied, "Or there'll be no letter of recommendation. If anything, I'll make sure she never works in the industry again."

"Don't you think it's a little harsh?"

Turning and walking back to his desk, Hugh sat down, clearly restless. "Don't you think it's a little harsh for Heather to quit—with no notice—because she fell in love and wants to run off and get married in Vegas?"

Dorothy chuckled, quickly stopping when she noticed the glare on her boss's face. "Personally, I think it's romantic."

"Vegas? That's romantic for you? We run some of the most beautiful and romantic resorts in the country—hell, the world!—and you're choosing Vegas?" he snapped.

"Now I didn't say that, Hugh." She bristled. "What I said was how I thought the whole *thing* was romantic— meaning the relationship. Heather and Dave have waited so long for this and with his military service coming to an end, they can finally get married. And they're going to have a baby and—"

"She's pregnant?"

"She really hasn't told anyone, but clearly you can see why they're anxious to get married."

Honestly, he didn't. People had babies all the time without rushing out and getting married. He didn't agree with it, but that's the way it was. The fact that his special events coordinator was deserting him on such short notice to do it? Well, it just added fuel to the fire.

Folding his arms on the desk, Hugh looked at his assistant pleadingly. "Dorothy, we are getting ready to start a very busy season at our resorts. We've got full calendars. And on top of that, you know I've been courting a new wine distributor. He's due here tomorrow. Heather is supposed to sit in on those meetings and come up with a presentation to convince him to do business with us. Can't you convince her to stay through the end of the month?"

"Hugh, you're not listening. Heather's gone. She wasn't giving us a heads-up, she wasn't giving us an option. She stopped by earlier—with her bags packed, loaded, and waiting in a cab—and said good-bye. She's probably at the airport right now waiting to board a flight. Face it, we have to come up with a plan B."

"You'll have to sit in on the meeting and come up with the presentation. You know what we're looking for. You can just—"

"Hold it right there, chief," she said sternly, holding out a hand to stop him. "That is not going to happen."

"Excuse me?"

"There are many things in my job description, but party and event planning isn't one of them. From everything you've told me, this guy is a little high maintenance and demands perfection. My idea of a party consists of inexpensive wine, cheese and crackers, and a deck of cards."

Hugh rolled his eyes. "Dotty…"

"I'm serious, Hugh. I'm from another generation. I don't understand yours. My friends and I enjoy going out for a quiet dinner and then playing mah-jongg. We're not into music or the latest trends. Trust me, having me work on this would not help you in any way, shape, or form."

Unfortunately, Hugh knew she was right. He just hated being in a jam like this, and having Dorothy's help would have simplified everything. Scrubbing a weary hand across his face, he looked back at her. "Any suggestions then?"

"Off the top of my head? No. But give me a few hours to make some calls and I'll see what I can do."

"This is a nightmare," he grumbled.

Reaching across the desk, Dorothy patted his hand. "It's definitely not the greatest thing to have happened, but it's far from the worst. We'll make it work. We always do." With an encouraging smile, she turned and walked out of the room.

With a curse, Hugh reached for the phone and began scrolling through his contacts. Surely he had to know someone who could take over the position on short notice. Hell, right now he'd even consider letting his sister come and do it. Darcy was in her first year of college back in North Carolina and he needed someone right here in California, but maybe she could get school credit for this. While she didn't technically have any experience, she was young and social and in touch with the latest trends. Hell, her vivacious personality alone would be an asset.

"Now I know I'm getting desperate," he muttered. Pulling his eighteen-year-old sister out of school was not the solution to this. Although…

The buzzing of the phone in his hand brought him out of his reverie. His brother Aidan's face showed up on the screen and Hugh almost wept with relief. A distraction was exactly what he needed right now.

"Aidan! What's up, man? You don't normally call midday."

"You know, you use that greeting on me no matter what time I call," he replied with a chuckle. "Is there a time slot when I'm supposed to call that I don't know about? Did I miss the spreadsheet?"

Hugh couldn't help but smile. He knew Aidan was right. He should be thankful for a friendly voice on the phone and not nitpick about when it came. "Sorry, bro. You just always seem to catch me off guard."

"Maybe let your guard down every once in a while. Live a little."

"Ha! This coming from the king of control. Nice!"

"Yeah, yeah, yeah…once upon a time that was me. Clearly I've passed the torch on to you."

"Whatever. So what's going on? Everyone okay?"

"Yeah, everyone's fine. I wanted to talk to you about…um…well, Zoe and I were thinking of having a destination wedding. And the more we talked about it, the more we figured who better to get advice from than you. So? What do you think?"

"Wow! So you're ready to start making plans? That's great! I didn't realize you were there yet."

"If it was up to me, we'd be married already. Zoe wanted us to settle in and spend time getting to know each other more, and get her business off the ground before we started planning a wedding."

"So she's ready to branch out on her own? What about Martha?"

"She's still going to do stuff with Martha, but it's going to be more like a partnership. Martha deals more with commercial accounts and Zoe really enjoys doing residential. They've been playing around with the idea for a while, and they're going to give it a trial run."

"How do you feel about it?"

Aidan chuckled. "I want Zoe to be happy and she's much happier being her own boss and choosing her own clients. So we'll see how it all goes. But that's a story for another time. We want to talk to you about options for the wedding. We want to meet with you and your event person and figure out which resort fits our needs and what the availability is. I think it would be great for the family."

"What do you mean?"

"Hugh…when was the last time Dad went anywhere?"

Too long ago. "Okay, stupid question. Sorry. So this is your way of forcing him to break out of his rut."

"He's been making progress since Darcy left for school but…baby steps. He goes bowling with the guys once a week, he went fishing last weekend with the same group."

"For him, it's huge. At least he's spending time with friends."

"Yeah, but it's still… He's still sticking close to home. You travel. Riley travels. Hell, even Owen travels. But Dad?"

"And you."

"Fine. I don't travel either. So it will be good for a few of us. Happy?"

Hugh laughed. "Extremely."

"Okay, so who do we need to talk to and what's your schedule like? Zoe and I are open to flying to wherever you are so we can talk in person."

"Here's the thing—I'm happy for you guys. I really am. You've just caught me at a bad time."

"Oh, I'm sorry. I didn't realize you were busy. Why didn't you cut me off? You can call me later or—"

"No, no, no. That's not what I mean. I mean it's a bad time—my events coordinator just quit and I don't have a replacement lined up."

"Is that all?"

"Is that all?" Hugh repeated incredulously. "It's huge! We have a lot of events scheduled and without someone overseeing them, it could be a disaster!"

"She wasn't your only event coordinator, Hugh. I mean that would be…"

"Shut up."

"She was your only events person? You own twelve resorts, Hugh! How is that possible?"

If there was one thing Hugh hated more than chaos, it was being questioned on how he managed his business. "Look, Aidan, you run a construction business. You have no idea how to do things in the hospitality business. I know I have twelve resorts, but they're small. Intimate. We're like a family. Each resort has someone who acts as an assistant to Heather, but she was the go-to on all events."

"That's just weird. And probably not the smartest managerial decision you've ever made."

"And we're done here."

"Okay, okay…I'm sorry. Look, give me a call when the smoke clears so we can set up a meeting. Like I said, Zoe and I aren't in a huge rush and we're willing to meet you wherever you are."

"I appreciate it, I do. But you're going to have to give me something to go on here. Are you thinking beach? Mountains? Do you want to stay stateside? Or were you thinking of Australia?"

"Get things settled where you are, Hugh, then we'll talk. Trust me, Zoe and I can wait until you're ready."

"Thanks, man. I'll give you a call soon."

Hugh placed the phone back down on his desk and sighed. Yeah, maybe it wasn't such a great idea to have one main events coordinator, but Heather had been the best. She oversaw her staff and managed to make every event unique. Now he had to figure out how to move forward and find a replacement.

Fast.

He looked up when Dorothy knocked and poked her head back through the door. He knew immediately the news wasn't good. It was written all over her face. "What? What's happened now?"

"Your wine guy? William Bellows?"

Hugh nodded.

"He's arriving today."

"No. He's arriving tomorrow."

She shook her head. "His assistant just called. He's on his way now. He wrapped up his other business early. She called to make sure we would have a suite ready for him."

Cursing, Hugh stood and kicked his chair out of the way. "This is unbelievable! I can't catch a break today!"

"I did manage to tell her you would be tied up in meetings and would have to stick to your original plans with him. She said it would be fine."

"Lucky me."

"Okay," she began, stepping farther into the room. "Again, it's not an ideal situation but it's not a catastrophe either. We'll make sure his suite is ready, we'll arrange for spa services and dinner and keep him pampered like a VIP. In the meantime, we'll continue to figure out who you're going to use as a replacement for Heather."

"Where's Josie? She's worked as Heather's assistant here. We'll use her as a temp."

Dorothy shook her head.

"What? Why not?"

"She's on vacation. Two weeks."

"So call her in. Tell her it's an emergency."

"Already tried. She's in Europe."

"Has everyone stopped working?" Hugh yelled. "How is it possible all of this fell into place like this?"

"Bad timing?"

He glared at her. "Not the time, Dotty."

"Can I ask you something?"

He nodded even as he rubbed his temple to ward off the headache that was building.

"Why are you freaking out so much about this meeting? I've never seen you like this before and you've done business with people from all over the world. What is it about this guy that has you so overwhelmed?"

Hugh dropped his hands into his lap. "He's a little… eccentric. Unconventional."

Dorothy quirked a brow at him. "Unconventional in what way?"

"He's not the kind of guy who follows any kind of plan. He tends to go with the flow and follow his gut instincts…that sort of thing. One time, he was on vacation in Italy and hired a guy to handle sales of a particular wine here in the U.S. just because he liked his shoes! And the guy didn't even speak English!"

"The guy he hired or Mr. Bellows?"

"I'm glad you're having fun with this," he said in a near growl. "The guy he hired! Then Bellows hired a tutor to teach the guy English!"

"And? How did it turn out?"

Hugh raked a hand through his hair. "He's the top salesman in the company."

"Oh dear," she murmured. "And you want to do

business with him? You're his complete opposite! How are you going to handle working without any structure? You know how much you hate that."

"I know, I know." He sighed. "Honestly, I'm hoping if I present a completely well-thought-out plan to him, he'll simply agree to go along with it. There won't need to be any gut instinct or flowing because I'll have it all covered."

She chuckled, and when Hugh glared at her, Dorothy quickly placed a hand over her mouth. Clearing her throat, she continued, "You're not counting on that, are you?"

Hugh straightened in his seat. "As a matter of fact, I am. That's why this presentation has to be flawless!"

"Oh, Hugh…"

"Look, I'm getting it all worked out. It's not the way I envisioned but…"

"You're just going to go with the flow?" she finished and then smirked.

"Cute."

"Let's take a walk. We'll go over to the suite we're preparing for Mr. Bellows, check on the grounds. Sometimes a change of scenery can help us brainstorm. What do you say?"

"I'd say you're talking to me like I'm a moron, and I don't like it."

She smiled at him sweetly. "But are you coming with me?"

Dammit. Without a word, he strode from his office and waited for his assistant to catch up.

An hour later, Hugh strolled back to his office. His mind was still scrambling for a solution to his current crisis, but his eyes were fixed on the immaculate landscaping along the path between the resort buildings.

He had chosen every tree, every plant. He had worked with a team of electricians to ensure guests would be able to see at night without seeing the lights. There had been dozens of meetings to find the perfect combination of mulch and stone and brick. He'd made every decision. He'd solved every crisis.

But for the life of him, he didn't have a clue how to solve this current one.

A soft breeze blew as the sun was going down in Napa. It was a beautiful time of day—very peaceful. Very tranquil. And nothing pleased him more than seeing the beauty around him. The blue oaks were in full foliage, the lawn was perfectly manicured, the hot-pink suitcase accented the...

Wait. *What?* The hot-pink suitcase? "What the hell?" Hugh muttered as he looked around to see if any guests were wandering around. "Who would leave a suitcase in the middle of the lawn?" Stepping closer to it, he continued to scan the area. Sometimes guests got caught up in the scenery and stopped to take pictures on the way to their room.

It was a hideous piece of luggage. Neon pink with white polka dots, hard-shelled...it was an eyesore. There were no tags on it and while he knew he should be suspicious, his first thought was getting rid of it so the grounds could go back to looking like they normally did.

Lush. Beautiful.

Free of blinding pink baggage.

There was no time to call a bellhop. He was on a schedule and there was still so much he had to do. With a huff, Hugh grabbed the suitcase and rolled it behind him to the main building, hoping whoever owned it would come looking for it.

Soon.

There were guests checking in at the front desk when he arrived, and rather than interrupt, he took the offensive luggage back to his office, making a note to call the concierge and let him handle it. Unfortunately, his phone started ringing as soon as he closed the door and for the next thirty minutes, he did his best to sort through the short list of assistants who might be able to fill in for Heather.

By the time he put the phone down, it was after six and Dorothy had gone for the day. He'd managed to decide on flying one of Heather's assistants in from Montana. With any luck, Marnie would arrive in the morning and they could have an hour to go over what he was going to need from her in great detail.

He stared at the computer screen in front of him. The only special event going on tonight was a small wedding. Hugh frowned at the screen. Very small. Apparently it was a spur-of-the-moment thing and the concierge was handling all of the details. A bride, a groom, no guests.

"Weird," he said with a shake of his head. Why did people elope? Wasn't part of the getting-married process having a big, obnoxious wedding? Hell if he knew. It didn't seem to be the direction Aidan and Zoe were going in, but most of the weddings Hugh had attended had bordered on the ridiculous.

Hugh knew—if given the chance—he'd opt for the low-key wedding himself. Not that he was looking to get married. At least not right now. Eventually he would.

He'd find someone suitable—someone with common interests and morals—and settle down. He wanted kids—maybe three—and would maybe cut back on his traveling a bit. Deep down, he knew it sounded more like a business transaction than anything else, but it was basically what he wanted.

After witnessing his own father's devastation after losing Hugh's mother, there was no way he was going to allow himself to experience the same thing. Ever. Loving someone as completely as Ian Shaughnessy had loved Lillian was not something Hugh ever intended to do. Love made you weak, and if there was one thing Hugh prided himself on, it was being strong. All the ridiculous wedding hoopla and messy feelings might be fine for some—like Aidan and Zoe—but not for him.

This particular wedding happening tonight seemed to be under control—nothing about it should cause any issues. They'd have their ceremony in the garden, then they were having dinner delivered to their suite. Seemed like a no-brainer to him.

And yet...

"Dammit," he muttered, knowing he'd want to walk by the gardens and make sure everything was up to his expectations. It was normally something Heather would do. Or Josie. Or Dorothy. But apparently tonight it was up to *him* to handle it personally. It was one more thing to add to his plate.

So much for relaxing tonight.

Besides checking on the garden, there was no way Hugh could possibly go to his suite and relax when there was so much to do to prepare for his meeting with Bellows and making sure Marnie came off as professional and knowledgeable. Luckily he'd been keeping detailed records and files and already had his own pitch ready. He just hoped Marnie would be able to come up with something on the fly to persuade Bellows to give them a chance.

Scanning his files, he quickly composed an email and sent it off to Marnie for her to read in preparation for tomorrow. He'd rather send her as much information as humanly possible—even if it overwhelmed her—rather than have her come off sounding ill-prepared. There was nothing more irritating to Hugh than feeling like he was wasting his time with a client or customer because one of them didn't have all the necessary information.

Some would call it obsessive. Hugh preferred to think of it as being considerate.

Standing and stretching, he caught sight of the ugly suitcase. "Shit," he muttered. Yet another thing to add to his list—dealing with the mystery luggage. Not wanting to waste any more time, he shut down his computer, collected the rest of the files he was going to need for the night along with his phone, and walked out of the office, locking the door behind him.

At the front desk he stopped and left instructions with the concierge regarding the suitcase.

"I'm sorry, Mr. Shaughnessy, but there hasn't been any inquiry regarding it. I've asked around and no one remembers checking anyone in with that color luggage." Tim had been with the resort since the beginning, and Hugh knew the man paid special attention to just about everything that went on. Guests loved him because he had a knack for listening to everything they had to say and then making sure their stay was everything they wanted it to be. So if Tim didn't know who the luggage belonged to, Hugh wasn't sure what to do.

"Well, if anyone does come for it, I've left it in my office. I trust you—and only you—to go in and get it. If you're not here, have someone call me and I'll be here in a matter of minutes."

"Yes, Mr. Shaughnessy. I'll make sure it's handled. Thank you."

"Have a good night, Tim."

"You as well, sir," the man said with a smile.

Hugh smiled back but his mind was already spinning. It seemed odd that no one had come looking for it and for a minute, paranoia got the better of him and he considered calling in the local police and having the bag scanned for a bomb.

"I'm seriously losing my mind," he grumbled as he walked away from the desk and out the front door.

At each of the dozen resorts Hugh owned, he kept an apartment. It made life easier. Each was designed and decorated to his exact specifications and it gave him a sense of continuity—a sense of home. This particular resort had only one building with more than three floors and he had taken the top-floor suite as his own.

Stepping out into the evening air, he looked around and couldn't help but feel a sense of pride again. It never got old. This was his. All of it. He'd worked hard, invested well, ran a tight ship, and knew his limitations. Sure, he could have expanded on most of his properties, but Hugh liked a more intimate atmosphere—a place where couples could come and relax. Let the bigger names compete for acreage and the most amenities. What he had accomplished with his resorts was in a class by itself.

The walk to his suite normally would have him turning to the left, but Hugh took the path to the right, toward the gardens. He was restless. Within the hour he'd have dinner brought to his suite and he'd be alone with his thoughts. Not that it was an unusual scenario, but tonight it felt a little more…lonely.

Luckily he had a trip home coming up. It had been almost six months since he'd been back. The last time had been for Darcy's birthday and even that had been nothing more than a quick weekend.

Or maybe he needed a date.

It had been about three months since he'd last spent a weekend with a woman, and while it certainly wasn't a record for him, it was amazing how fast the time had gone and how it hadn't occurred to him until right this minute. As he strolled toward the back of the main building, Hugh tried to picture his date's face in his mind and couldn't.

That couldn't be a good sign. No matter. It was what it was. Note to self—after closing this deal with Bellows and finding a replacement for Heather, he needed to relax with the family. Then it hit him—maybe he should call Riley. Hell, his little brother was one of the biggest rock stars in the world. If anyone could hook him up with someone for a weekend fling, it would be Riley.

Problem solved. With a renewed pep in his step, he turned the corner and saw some movement up ahead. Guests didn't usually come around to this part of the resort. It was the back of the main building—there weren't any signs to stop them or warn them away, but it was mainly parking spaces, a couple of small storage buildings, and trees. Nothing to see.

Slowing his pace, he saw someone peeking into one of the windows. Odd. Doing his best to stay out of sight, without losing sight of what was going on, he heard some rustling in the bushes lining the back of the building. Some were taller than others, and now from where he was standing, he couldn't tell what was going on.

With no other choice, he stepped back out into the open and walked toward this potential…what? Peeper? Perpetrator? Seriously, he had no idea what it was he was about to confront.

"Dammit," came a muttered voice, and Hugh decided it was definitely female. *That* piqued his interest. He stopped just on the other side of the tall bush shielding her from his view and realized the woman was looking in *his* window! The window to his office! What in the world?

Not a minute later, he was appalled to see she was sliding the window open! How had he managed to lock the door to his office and not the window? Dammit, he'd opened it earlier in the day because the temperatures had been so mild and sometimes he just needed to smell the fresh air when he was cooped up in his office.

It wasn't likely to happen again after what he was currently witnessing.

The window squeaked, and it snapped him back to the present. Great, he was so busy obsessing about fresh air he had forgotten about the person trying to break into his office! Stepping around the shrub and ready to haul off and give this person a piece of his mind, Hugh immediately stopped short, his jaw hitting the ground.

There, right in front of him, were two of the longest

legs he'd ever seen and quite possibly the world's most perfect female bottom.

In nothing but a hot-pink thong.

His throat instantly dried and his heart rate kicked up. He stood—mesmerized—as her sexy bottom wiggled back and forth. He couldn't tear his eyes away.

Or move.

In that instant, it didn't matter that she was trespassing. It didn't matter that she was clearly breaking and entering. All that mattered was watching the movement of her body.

Then she disappeared through the window and into his office.

It took a full minute for Hugh to realize he was staring at nothing but his window before he shook his head to clear it and made his move. In a flash he was silently through the window, and his sexy intruder hadn't noticed. She was looking around the dimly lit room, and unfortunately he couldn't get a good look at her.

Standing in the corner, he continued to observe. If she was going to try to steal something, he wanted to be certain to catch her in the act. In a perfect world, he'd hit the lights as soon as she took something that clearly didn't belong to her so he could press charges. He hated people touching his belongings—especially when they so blatantly held such little regard for his privacy.

But who was she? Why was she here in his office?

"Finally," he heard her mutter. Stepping closer to his desk, he reached for the small lamp there and turned it on. A small scream escaped her at the intrusion of light.

"Is there something I can help you with?" Hugh

asked with a calmness he didn't feel. As soon as his eyes adjusted to the light, he felt as poleaxed at the sight of her face as he had at the sight of her climbing through the window.

The first thing to register was the fact that she was wearing more than the hot-pink thong. She had on a strapless white dress. It hit mid-thigh and showcased a curvy body and tanned limbs. Her hair was long and blond, and she looked like some sort of beach goddess.

Huge blue eyes stared back at him. One hand covered her heart as the other covered her belly. "Who…? What are you…?"

"Doing in my own office?" he supplied. "I believe that's what I should be asking you. How about explaining why it is you're in here and why you decided to climb in through the window? Some call it breaking and entering." Hugh watched the play of emotion on her face as she lowered her hands to her sides. He expected tears. He expected apologies. He certainly didn't expect attitude.

"You stole my suitcase," she snapped at him.

"Excuse me?"

"You heard me," she said, crossing her arms over her chest and cocking a hip. "That suitcase right there? It's mine. You had no right to take it."

Hugh was stunned speechless. He owned the damn resort—didn't this woman realize that? "You left it out in the middle of the property. I brought it here to keep it safe. Anyone could have grabbed it and taken off with it. I was simply making sure nothing happened to it."

She rolled her eyes. "Yeah, yeah, yeah. Whatever. It wasn't your responsibility. I left it there for a reason."

He cocked a brow at her. "Oh really? And what was it?"

"None of your business," she said evenly, then looked at the watch on her slim wrist. "Look, are we cool here? Obviously the luggage is mine so...can I go?"

Was this woman for real? "Actually, it's not obvious the luggage is yours. There's no tag on it, no identification. And if you knew it was in here, why didn't you go to the front desk and ask for it?"

A little of her bravado seemed to fade. "They were busy and...and...I needed to get it so I can go."

"Leaving already? Were you even a guest here?"

She nodded. "I really need to go. What's it gonna take to prove to you this suitcase is mine?"

The resort was small enough that Hugh normally recognized his guests. He didn't recognize this woman, and God knew she was attractive enough that had he seen her before, he definitely would have remembered. "I don't believe you."

"About what?" she asked incredulously.

"About being a guest. I know all of our guests. I never saw you before."

She rolled her eyes again. "We just checked in this morning. What are you, resort security?"

"No," he said smugly. "The resort owner."

Those blue eyes went wide again. Slowly she composed herself. "Okay, Mister Resort Owner. What happens now?"

"You said 'we just checked in.' Who's 'we'?"

"It doesn't matter. I checked in with someone and now I'm leaving. It's not a crime."

"No...but breaking and entering is."

"You stole my suitcase!" she cried.

"Okay, we're going around in circles here, Miss...?"

"Burke. Aubrey Burke."

"Do you have ID?"

"In my purse."

Hugh looked at her expectantly.

"It's outside in the bushes."

Without a word, Hugh hopped out the window and looked around. Tucked under one of the shrubs was a pair of white sandals and a purse. He scooped them both up and climbed back in through the window again. And mentally cursed himself for having to behave like this.

He didn't hand the small white clutch to her—he opened it and pulled out her driver's license, inspecting it. Aubrey Burke of Raleigh, North Carolina. He placed the card back inside her purse before handing it to her, along with her shoes.

"Now can I go?"

"It doesn't prove the bag is yours."

"Oh, for crying out loud. Are you for real?" When Hugh didn't answer, Aubrey let out a sigh of agitation. "Okay, fine." She took a step away from the luggage. "Open it up. Inside you'll find a white bikini with a matching cover-up, a white silk nightie, a red dress, a black dress, and a blue one." She stopped and thought for a moment. "There's also a cosmetics case, a small pouch with some jewelry, and my laptop. And six pairs of shoes."

"Six?" he asked with a smirk.

"I couldn't decide which ones I wanted to wear so I brought a selection."

Unable to help himself, Hugh walked over, crouched in front of the suitcase, and opened it. He should have just let her go. After all, who would lie about owning

this hideous piece of luggage? Curiosity got the better
of him and soon he found himself up to his elbows in all
of the items Aubrey had listed.

And some she hadn't.

"Oh yeah...and several pairs of panties," she said
with a smirk of her own. "Forgot about those."

Hugh never would.

They were lacy and tiny and in every color imagin-
able. An image of the hot-pink pair she was currently
wearing flashed through his mind and he had to stifle a
groan. When he realized he was still touching the lingerie, he quickly dropped it, slammed the suitcase closed,
and stood up. He cleared his voice before he could
speak. "Um...so...yeah. I guess it's yours."

"I told you it was."

"It still doesn't explain why—"

"I know it was wrong to go through the window and
all, but I was in a rush. And now, thanks to this little
game of cops and robbers, my cab is probably gone and
I've most likely missed my flight."

It was on the tip of his tongue to apologize, but he
quickly remembered he wasn't the one in the wrong here.

"I'm sorry about that, but you have to understand—
you broke into my office. I can't simply overlook that."

Aubrey's eyes began to well with tears. "I'm sorry,"
she said, her voice shaky. "I really am. You have to
know I've never done anything like this before. I just... I
needed..." She paused. "I never should have come here."

"To my office?" Hugh asked.

She shook her head. "Here. To Napa. The resort.
Everything."

Something about her whole demeanor began to make

Hugh uncomfortable. The situation was bizarre, to say the least, but Aubrey was clearly someone looking for a quick escape. "Are you in some kind of trouble?" he finally asked.

She shook her head and met his gaze. "I really need to leave. Please."

Her plea was a mere whisper, and damn if it didn't make him feel a tightening in his chest. He should be furious with this woman—he should be ranting and raving about her invading his privacy and pretty much pitching a fit because she had messed up his schedule. But one look at those big blue eyes and the slight tremble of her lips and he just couldn't do it. Any of it.

Shifting uncomfortably, Hugh said, "I'm sorry about your flight. Is there anything I can do?"

Aubrey wiped a stray tear away and straightened. "It was the last available flight out of San Francisco tonight. I'll have to see what I can find tomorrow."

He nodded. It wasn't any of his business anyway. "Well…for what it's worth…I hope you get home safely."

"Thanks." Her words were soft, quiet. She turned and secured her suitcase, slipping on her sandals.

"If it's all right with you, I'd prefer you leave through the door rather than the window," Hugh said, hoping to lighten the mood with a little humor. He was relieved when Aubrey smiled.

"That would be nice. Thank you."

Hugh followed her to the door and admired the soft sway of her hips and the way her short skirt swished as she moved. His throat went dry again. Aubrey looked curvy and soft and…he made a mental note to call Riley as soon as he got to his suite.

Reaching around her at the door, he opened it and was about to wish her well when she immediately stepped back, bumping into him right before slamming the door closed. "I can't go out there," she said, her gaze a little wild.

"What? Why?"

"I...I can't. Please. Can I just stay here? For a few more minutes?"

His curiosity was beyond piqued, but he nodded and put some space between them. "Of course." He motioned for Aubrey to sit down on the sofa set up against the wall. "There's some water and soda in the mini fridge in the corner. Help yourself. I'll be right back." Hugh saw her nod but also noted she was looking around the room as if planning her escape. He walked over to the window and closed and locked it. "Promise me you'll wait until I get back, okay?"

Aubrey grimaced. "Fine."

"Thank you." With a nod of approval, Hugh strode from the office and out to the lobby. Tim was standing at the desk talking with a guest. Standing back for a moment, he listened to the conversation.

"You must have seen her. She would have had to come here to get another room!" the guest snapped.

"I'm sorry, sir, but we haven't had any requests for a room from any walk-ins," Tim said with a smile.

The man sighed loudly. "She wasn't a walk-in. She arrived with me. Blond. In a white dress. Pink luggage."

Hugh stiffened. This was the *we* Aubrey had mentioned? The guy sounded like a total ass. Unable to help himself, he walked over to the desk. "Is there something I can help you with?"

Tim seemed to sag with relief while the other guy seemed to bristle. "Who the hell are you?"

"Hugh Shaughnessy. I own the resort."

"Finally," the man grumbled. "I'm looking for the woman I arrived here with. She took off and I need to find her."

"I'm sorry," Hugh began, "and you are?"

"Paul Hollingsworth." They shook hands. "Aubrey and I checked in this morning and now she's gone. This is a real inconvenience and I demand to know where she is."

"Tim?" Hugh said with a serene smile. "Have you seen Mr. Hollingsworth's guest?"

Tim shook his head. "No, I haven't, sir. Which is what I've been trying to tell him."

Hugh turned back to Hollingsworth. "My employee has no reason to lie to you. Are you sure she didn't go shopping?"

"No," Paul snapped. "All of her things are gone!" He threw up his hands and took a few steps away while he muttered, "Inconsiderate bitch. I knew I should have asked someone else."

The statement filled Hugh with rage. "Wait…did you say she had pink luggage?"

Paul nodded and came back to stand in front of him. "She did."

"Long blond hair? White dress?"

Again Paul nodded.

"Right, right. I remember her now. I helped her get a cab. She said she was going to the airport."

"What?" Paul yelled. "And you let her go?"

Hugh shrugged. "It wasn't my place to stop her," he

said mildly. "Guests request cabs or town cars to take them to the airport all the time. Is there a problem?"

"Damn woman," Paul muttered. "I'm going to need a car to take me to the airport too. I need to collect my things." He turned to Tim. "Get a bellman to help me transport my luggage immediately." Then he was gone.

"Yes, sir," Tim said. "Right away."

Hugh watched until Paul was out of sight before he turned to look at Tim. "Make sure he gets everything he needs and he leaves the property. Close out his bill and if he comes back, we don't have any vacancies, understand?"

Tim looked at him curiously but nodded. "Understood."

There was no doubt in Hugh's mind Tim wanted to know what was going on. Hell, so did he. Why had he lied for a complete stranger? Why did he get involved? "Let me know if there's any further issues, Tim."

"Yes, sir," he said pleasantly and turned to take care of his task.

For a minute, Hugh stood rooted to the spot, torn about what to do. There was work to do, meetings to prepare for—it's what he had scheduled for the evening. He was already behind thanks to this current drama, and it seemed as if he was going to remain so.

Looking toward his office door, he sighed. "Okay, Miss Aubrey Burke, let's find out what's really going on."

Chapter 2

AUBREY SILENTLY SHUT THE OFFICE DOOR AND LET out a breath she hadn't realized she was holding. On shaky legs, she walked back over to the sofa and sat down. This was so not the way she had imagined things going. Not in any way, shape, or form.

A quick glance at her watch showed it was nearly seven. In a few minutes she was supposed to be getting married. *Married.* Just the word was enough to make her stomach clench. What the hell had she been thinking? Paul Hollingsworth was not the man she pictured living happily ever after with.

And that explained the runaway bride stint she was currently living out.

When she'd opened the door and seen him in the lobby, she'd panicked. And when she'd looked out a few minutes later and seen...hell, what was his name? All he'd said was that he owned the resort. He'd never given her his name.

Well damn.

Anyway, when she'd looked out the door and seen Mister Resort Owner talking to Paul, Aubrey had a strong urge to flee out the window and into the night. But somehow she had stood her ground and watched as whatever Paul was hearing made him more and more furious. It wasn't until he'd walked away that Aubrey had closed the door.

Now what? What was she supposed to do now? It was too late to get a flight and she'd have to find a place to stay for the night. Preferably someplace far from here where she wouldn't run into Paul.

It wasn't that Paul was a mean person, but he did have a tendency to talk over her and make her feel small and more than a little incompetent. That's how she'd ended up here. It had been Paul's idea for them to get married. They'd been in San Francisco on business when Paul had brought up the idea. Aubrey still couldn't believe she'd let him talk her into it, but here they were.

They'd never really dated and if she were completely honest, she didn't particularly like him. But…like most of the people in her life, Paul had played on her one insecurity and used it to his advantage. He was business partners with her father—a man who barely acknowl- edged her anymore—and Paul had convinced her this would be a way to get back in her father's good graces.

It wasn't until she had mistakenly overheard the two on the phone that she realized it didn't matter if she was in her father's good graces or not. There was no way she could possibly go through with the ceremony. Paul's smarmy, condescending tone as he'd talked about finally getting Aubrey to fall in line had really sealed the deal.

So while he talked and thought she was taking a nap, Aubrey had packed her suitcase and thrown it out the second-story window. Once it was on the ground, she was ready to crawl out after it when she'd spotted Mister Resort Owner picking it up and carrying it away! In her entire life, Aubrey had never been a tomboy or one who climbed trees, and yet she had shimmied out the window and down the side of the building as if she had been doing it for years. She'd followed the man all the way to the main building and then had to find a way in without drawing attention to herself. The fewer people who saw her leaving, the better.

Clearly that didn't go as planned.

Now she was stuck in this office, trying to figure out where to go from here.

No doubt Paul was furious. And probably on the phone with her father right now telling him what she'd done. It couldn't be helped. Aubrey hated it, but right now, it was the least of her worries.

The door to the office opened and Mister Resort Owner walked in. He closed the door and offered her a small smile. She studied him. He was tall—easily over six feet—and reminded her a little bit of Thor…or Chris Hemsworth. He was definitely movie star material, and for a minute she wished they had met under different circumstances. Right now she was certain he was anxious to get rid of her, probably still a little annoyed at finding her in his office in the first place.

"Are you okay?" he asked softly as he came to stand in front of her.

She could have handled his annoyance or arrogance, but she wasn't prepared for his obvious concern. It wasn't something she was used to, and all she could do was nod and stare.

"I told your…companion…you'd left for the airport. He's packing up and getting ready to head there. No doubt he's going to look for you." He took a seat beside her on the sofa. "Care to tell me what's going on?"

Aubrey took in his strong features as her eyes scanned his face. The strong jaw, the sandy-brown hair that matched the color of his eyes. He had a five o'clock shadow darkening his jaw, and she thought it made him look beyond attractive.

Whoa, girl. Stop thinking like that right now! she admonished herself. Tearing her gaze away, she cleared her throat. "Who are you?" It came out before she could stop it. "I mean, other than the owner of the resort."

His features softened a little at her inquiry, his smile growing, and Aubrey noticed the dimples and almost hummed with appreciation. Unable to help herself, she smiled back and waited. And waited. And waited. If she wasn't mistaken, he seemed as interested in looking at her as she was with him.

"Hugh Shaughnessy," he finally said, holding out his hand.

Aubrey didn't hesitate to reach out and shake it, but as soon as she did, she gasped. His hand seemed to swallow hers. It was warm and hard and so…masculine. Wow. "It's nice to meet you, Hugh Shaughnessy," she said shyly, but didn't make a real effort to take her hand back.

And he didn't seem in a hurry to release it.

Growing a little uncomfortable with the silence, Aubrey reluctantly removed her hand from his and asked, "Why did you cover for me?"

He shrugged. "Honestly? He was being a major jerk and harassing my employee. I figured if you were so anxious to get away from him that you climbed through a window to get in here unseen, combined with the way he was talking to Tim…well, it seemed like the thing to do."

"Oh. Thank you." Aubrey tucked a long strand of

hair behind her ear and shifted. "So…um…once Paul's gone, I guess I'll need a cab too."

"Where are you going? I thought you missed your flight."

"I did," she began, "but I'll still need a place to stay tonight. I don't want to sleep at the airport—or risk running into Paul—so…"

"We have a room for you here," Hugh said.

Aubrey was a little taken aback. How could she possibly explain that while she appreciated the offer, this resort was a little out of her comfort zone? Well, not her personal comfort zone but her wallet's comfort zone.

"That's very nice of you, but I think I've outstayed my welcome here." She rose and walked over to the mini fridge he'd referred to earlier, helping herself to a bottle of water. "I think it would be better for everyone if I found someplace else to stay."

From his spot on the sofa, Hugh continued to silently study her. Aubrey took a long drink of water, and when he still didn't say anything, she found herself starting to fidget. "Thank you for the offer though. I mean, if I were you, I would be happy to see me getting in a cab and driving away. I'm sure I messed up your evening—you must have had other things to do than apprehending a luggage thief. Well…not really a thief…it really is my luggage and I was simply getting it back. I didn't notice if there were other hotels nearby, but I'm sure I can use my phone to Google the area and find something appropriate for the night and—"

"Aubrey?" Hugh interrupted.

"Hmm?"

"You're rambling." His smile deepened. Those dimples were back and Aubrey's knees went weak.

"I... I know. You just make me a little...nervous."

"Me?"

She nodded.

"Why?"

Oh God. Was he really asking that? "Well, to be honest, you're a little intimidating."

He chuckled. "Really? Because I thought the same thing about you."

The very idea made her laugh and she quickly covered her mouth to try to control it. "Me? I'm not intimidating to anyone!"

Hugh stood and walked toward her. "You broke into my office and had the nerve to make me feel like *I* was the one doing something wrong," he said, and soon they were both laughing again.

"It was...what do they call it...false bravado. Trust me, this is not something I normally do."

"Good to know I'm not harboring a fugitive."

Her brows rose at his teasing tone. "Very funny. But seriously, I need to find a place to stay. Can you maybe check and see if Paul has left?"

With a nod, Hugh walked over to his desk and picked up the phone. He spoke quietly and Aubrey did her best to keep calm. The sooner she could leave, the better for her peace of mind. Hugh Shaughnessy was definitely messing with that right now. The last thing she should be doing after climbing out a window to escape marrying Paul was getting all cozy and flirty with the sexy resort owner.

"The cab is waiting and Paul is on his way down with a couple of bellhops, so he should be gone within the next fifteen minutes," he said. "You'll probably want to wait a little bit after he leaves to make sure he's really on his way. Can I interest you in some dinner?"

This was bad. Bad, bad, bad, bad. And yet…

"I shouldn't," Aubrey forced herself to say.

"Why? Are you one of those women who doesn't eat dinner?" he asked lightly, and Aubrey couldn't help but giggle again.

"Absolutely not," she replied. "I'm one of those women who seriously enjoys a good dinner."

"So why not let me—"

"Hugh, I appreciate all you're doing. I do. But I've intruded on your evening enough. By now you probably would be at home having dinner with your family. I promise not to climb through any more windows. You can go on home and I'll stay out of trouble." She made a cross over her heart.

"By now I would be home reading reports and waiting for room service to bring me my dinner," he said simply. "Not the most exciting way to spend the evening."

"Oh."

"But…you're probably right. I do need to go. I'll take you out the back door and you can sit by the lounge or the pool, or have some dinner. I'll let Tim know you'll be needing a cab in about an hour. Will that work?"

She couldn't believe his kindness. His considerateness. Unable to speak due to the lump in her throat, she merely nodded.

"Okay then. Why don't you grab your luggage and we'll head out. Once you're on your way, I'll go to the desk and talk with Tim. He'll take care of you and help you find a place to stay if you need it. But we do—"

"It's okay, Hugh. Really. You're being beyond generous, considering what I did here today."

"You were in a bad situation and needed help." He paused. "You'll notice I haven't pressed you for details on what exactly that situation is."

She couldn't help but smile. "Yes, I did notice and I thank you."

He looked like there was more he wanted to say, but didn't. Instead he walked over to the door and held it open for her. Together they silently walked down a hallway labeled Employees Only and out a door leading to one of the many gardens.

"If you take this path to the left, you'll get to the pool area. There's a lounge there and they offer drinks and appetizers. If you want dinner, you go to the right and there are two restaurants to choose from. The Vine is a five-star French restaurant that I highly recommend. Then there's also Lillian's—you can get everything from soup to burgers to steak there. They specialize in comfort food."

That one intrigued Aubrey, but she didn't comment on it. Instead she said, "I do want to thank you for everything, Hugh. I appreciate all of your help. And kindness."

"You're welcome, Aubrey. I hope… I hope everything's okay."

She forced a bright smile. "It will be. Thank you." And with that, she picked up the handle of her suitcase and let it roll behind her as she walked away.

———

He should have been relieved. After all, now he was free to resume his schedule and get down to the business of preparing for his meeting with William Bellows tomorrow. Hugh watched until Aubrey turned a corner out of sight.

He sighed.

Riley. He needed to call Riley and see if he could hook him up for a weekend. Just the thought of it suddenly made his stomach turn. This was what he was reduced to? Asking his own brother to act as some kind of pimp? Okay, scratch that. Don't call Riley. But pencil in some personal time where he could hopefully meet someone and maybe work off some of this...tension.

And if she happened to be a curvy blond with big blue eyes and a thing for lacy thongs, who was he to complain.

"I'm seriously losing it," he muttered. "I need to focus on the present. Blonds...or...women with any color hair will have to wait."

With a renewed sense of purpose, Hugh turned and walked back into the main building, toward the front desk. He found Tim standing behind it with a smile on his face. "Later on, Miss Aubrey Burke will be coming up here to speak to you."

Tim looked at him expectantly.

"She'll need you to get her a cab and maybe help her find another place to stay."

"She doesn't like her room?"

"She no longer has a room and I get the impression she couldn't afford one on her own."

"I don't think I understand."

"She's the owner of the pink suitcase," he said, and chuckled at the image of it as it popped into his mind.

"I thought you said you had put her in a cab to the airport earlier."

Oops. "It's a long story."

Tim chuckled. "Apparently."

"Did Mr. Hollingsworth leave?"

"Yes, sir. I put him in the cab myself."

"And did he behave while he was getting ready to leave?"

Tim chuckled again. "Define behave."

Hugh laughed. "Unbelievable. I don't understand some people. It wasn't our fault his companion bailed on him. Maybe he should be taking a closer look at himself rather than putting the blame on us."

"Well, in his defense, they were supposed to get married tonight."

"*What?*" Hugh said loudly, then stepped closer to the desk and lowered his voice. "What do you mean?"

Tim nervously fidgeted with his tie. "Well…um…he and Miss Burke were the couple who were supposed to get married in the gardens tonight."

Son of a bitch! And then it hit him—the white dress, the white negligee, the white bikini. Dammit! "So the bride got cold feet," he forced himself to say, but his throat felt tight. "It's still not an excuse to take it out on you or the staff." His mind was reeling—he couldn't believe Aubrey hadn't said one word about it. "Did he… did he mention what happened?"

Tim studied him for a moment. "He really didn't speak directly to us."

"Oh."

"However…I got the impression this was not a marriage based on love."

"Why not?"

"Because he mumbled several times about how he should have asked Kristen."

"Who's Kristen?" Hugh asked.

"I don't know, sir. Like I said, he really wasn't talking to me. By the time we got to his suite, he was on the phone and David and I waited by the door for him."

"Did you hear any of the phone conversation?" Hugh hated to sound like a fourteen-year-old girl, but he had to know.

"I could only hear part of it and…"

"*And?*"

"I feel really weird about this."

"What do you mean?"

"We're gossiping."

Hugh looked at him incredulously. "And?"

"And…it was you who trained us all to not gossip about our guests."

Well…damn. Tim had a point. "You're right. I'm sorry. I shouldn't be doing this. The whole situation really… It was all a little bizarre and dramatic and I guess I needed a distraction more than I thought."

"If you'd like I can tell you what I heard," Tim offered.

"No. No," he said more firmly. "I'm going to my suite. If you can, have the kitchen send my dinner over in about thirty minutes."

"Tonight's special at The Vine is Blanquette de Veau. I hear it's spectacular."

Hugh shook his head. "It's Thursday, Tim. Call the chef over at Lillian's. He knows what to do." With a smile and a nod, he turned and walked away.

—∿∿—

Three hours later, Hugh's mind was still reeling. Married. Aubrey had come here to get married and had essentially run away from her wedding. He snorted with disgust. It made perfect sense after meeting her fiancé, but something about the whole thing still didn't sit right with him. And there was no way for him to get any answers because by now Aubrey was gone and he had no way of contacting her.

And really, he shouldn't.

Or shouldn't want to.

The thing was, finding Aubrey Burke climbing through his window—and flashing her spectacular ass at him—was probably the most exciting thing to happen to Hugh in months. He was in a rut. Stuck in his routine. And that's the way he normally liked it. Only now…it felt sad. Empty.

Depressing.

"Fresh air. I need some fresh air," he said as he rose from his sofa and stretched. The remnants of his spaghetti dinner were still on the table, but he didn't have the will to care. He'd ditched his dress slacks and shirt earlier and was currently in jeans and a T-shirt. Casual. Comfortable. "And I'm not in a rut," he mumbled, although he knew he was lying. While he didn't always change into casual clothes at the end of the work day, it wasn't completely unheard of.

With no specific destination in mind, Hugh left his suite, deciding to see where the night took him. The weather was warm for a May evening and as soon as he stepped outside, he felt himself relax.

On the path he waved to a few guests, picked up a couple of stray pieces of trash—a straw wrapper, a napkin—and soon found himself approaching the pool and lounge area. Since the temperatures were mild, one wall of the lounge was fully open, and he smiled at the sound of the music playing and people laughing.

Deciding he could use a drink, he wandered over and smiled at his bartender Nick.

"How's it going, boss?"

"Can't complain." Hugh looked around at the small crowd and smiled again. "It looks like you're having a good night here."

Nick nodded. "Definitely a nice crowd for a Thursday night. I was just thinking—" His words were cut off by a boom of laughter coming from the corner of the room. Both Hugh and Nick turned. "That has got to be one of the loudest guys I've ever heard."

Hugh chuckled. "Has he been drinking a lot?"

"No. He wasn't impressed with our wine selection—made some snarky comments about it—and he's been nursing a beer for the last hour." Then Nick smiled. "But he's certainly one lucky SOB."

"Why?" Hugh craned his neck, trying to see who this guy was.

"He came in alone, but he managed to snag a beautiful woman and she's been sitting with him ever since. All she's drinking is water." He shrugged. "I'm not going to Hawaii on those tips, I can tell you that." He slid a beer over to Hugh—the same beer he always drank.

"Thanks. See you later, Nick." The bartender waved and Hugh decided to get up and see who this loud—and lucky—guy was.

"Hugh!"

Hugh heard the man before he saw him, and when he made his way through the throng of people, he found William Bellows sitting at the corner table.

"William, hey! I heard you arrived early. Having a good time?"

"Please, we're off the clock and we're casual. And besides, I prefer to be called Bill."

This was news to Hugh, but he'd go with it. "So, are you having a good time, Bill?" he asked with a smile, and laughed when Bill toasted him with his half-empty bottle of beer.

"I'm having a great time. The massage was amazing, dinner was fantastic, and…" He motioned to the woman sitting across from him—whom Hugh hadn't noticed— "this lovely lady has been laughing at my jokes and regaling me with stories of her uptight family." He laughed. "It's been a great night."

Hugh felt as if he'd been punched in the gut.

Aubrey.

Her expression was a little bit bashful and a little bit defiant, and Hugh said the first thing that popped into his mind. "You didn't leave."

She shook her head. "No, I didn't leave."

"You were supposed to get married today." He hadn't meant to say it, but it was out before he could stop himself.

"How…? Who…?"

"Holy crap!" Bill yelled. "You were supposed to get married today? Did the groom leave you at the altar?"

Without breaking eye contact with Aubrey, Hugh answered, "No. She left him."

"*That* is freaking awesome," Bill said with a laugh. "Bartender! Champagne! We're celebrating!"

"No," Aubrey said, trying to keep her voice down. "No, we're not." Her eyes strayed to Bill's as she said it, but immediately went back to Hugh's. "I would appreciate it if you wouldn't go announcing that to everyone."

He knew she was right, and yet it angered him how he had offered her dinner, a room for the night—not his—and she had turned him down, only to find her sitting here with...Bill.

"So how'd you do it?" Bill asked. "Did you wait until the preacher asked you to repeat your vows or did you just not show up?"

"I really don't want to talk about this," Aubrey said, suddenly sounding very prim.

"Oh, come on! I've never met a real runaway bride before! You've got to give me something!"

Hugh had never seen this side of Bill before. They'd only met in person once and most of their interactions had been over the phone. Right now he found him incredibly obnoxious. "Bill..." he began but was ignored.

"How long had you been dating this guy? Or...or been engaged to him? Did you leave him a note? Did you have a fight?"

Unfortunately, Hugh wanted the answers to all those questions too, and he found himself leaning in a little bit closer in hopes of finding out what had really happened.

Aubrey looked helplessly from one to the other before her shoulders sagged. With a sigh of resignation she said, "Fine. We weren't together very long at all. No engagement. It was a spur-of-the-moment thing and... and I chickened out. I threw my suitcase out the window and shimmied out after it." Then she focused her eyes on Hugh. "And you know the rest."

Yeah. He knew the rest. And he felt even more unsettled now that he knew the beginning. Why would you impulsively agree to marry someone and then back out? Hugh couldn't understand it.

Maybe he had at one time in his life, but not anymore. Being impulsive only led to bad things. Maybe Aubrey understood that. Maybe it was why she backed out. But did she love that guy Paul?

"If you two will excuse me," Aubrey said as she rose from her chair and turned to walk away.

"Hey, come on, Runaway Bride!" Bill called after her. "Don't go!" But Aubrey was halfway across the bar by then.

"She has a name, dammit!" Hugh sneered at Bill before going after her. He caught up with her next to the pool and noticed she had her suitcase with her. "Aubrey! *Wait!*"

She rounded on him, her eyes wide, her expression sad. "What? What do you want, Hugh? Do you want to humiliate me in front of more people?" She looked around the deserted pool area. "Well, there's no one here. Now if you'll excuse me, I need to find Tim and get a cab."

Hugh reached out, placing a hand on her arm to stop her. "I'm sorry," he said. "I...I didn't think. I was surprised to see you, and all night I've been wondering about what your story was and... I acted like a jerk. I'm sorry."

She stood silently and seemed to consider his words. "I didn't realize it had gotten so late. I really need to find a hotel."

"No, you don't need to. Stay here tonight. The room's on me. It's the least I could do."

"Hugh... I don't think..."

"Please, Aubrey. What I just did in there was..."

"Reprehensible?" she supplied.

He nodded. "Yes. Please let me do this for you. I'll arrange for a town car to take you to the airport tomorrow when you know what flight you'll be on." He could see the war going on inside her head and felt horrible about his behavior. That was not his thing. He couldn't remember the last time he had done something so stupid.

"Okay," she finally said.

"Really? You'll stay?"

"It's only one night and it is getting late."

Hugh couldn't help but smile. "Thank you." They stood there in the moonlight for several silent moments before he remembered to speak again. "Come on. Let's go to the front desk and we'll find you a room."

"Are you sure it won't be a problem?"

"You may end up with the same room you had earlier with Hollingsworth. Will that be a problem?"

"Are you fishing for more to the story or are you genuinely concerned?"

He deserved the jab so he took it. "Genuinely concerned."

"It will be fine," she said with a small smile.

"Okay. Good. But I'll ask Tim if anything else is available—just in case."

"Thank you."

Together they made it to the lobby, where Tim looked up and quickly hid his surprise with an easy smile. "Good evening, Mr. Shaughnessy. I didn't expect to see you back this evening." Then he turned to Aubrey. "And it's good to see you, Miss Burke. Are you ready for me to get a cab for you?"

"Tim," Hugh began, "we are going to provide a room

for Miss Burke this evening. Can you tell me what we have available?"

"Yes, sir," he said pleasantly as he searched his computer screen. "We currently have two rooms available. One is the room Miss Burke had earlier and the other is"— he paused and looked up at Hugh—"in your building."

"We'll take that one," Hugh said, then realized how he'd worded it. "I mean *she'll* take that one. Not we. She. Alone." *Oh, for the love of it, just shut up!*

Tim smiled at Aubrey. "Give me one minute and I'll have your key for you."

"Thank you," she said as the two of them shared a smirk at Hugh's obvious embarrassment.

Five minutes later, Tim had her checked in. "Do you need help with your luggage, Miss Burke?"

"I'm fine, Tim. But thank you. Have a good night."

"You too, miss."

Hugh took the suitcase and led the way out of the building. "I'll show you the way since—obviously— I'm going the same way."

Luckily Aubrey didn't rib him about his faux pas and together they walked silently toward the back of the property.

"This is all really beautiful, Hugh. You've created something stunning here."

He stood a little taller with pride. "Thank you. This one is one of my favorites."

She turned her head and looked at him. "You have more than one?"

Nodding, he said, "Twelve. But this one is my newest and it's probably the one I've put the most personal touches on."

"Wow. I can't imagine what that's like—owning twelve luxury resorts. Where are the rest of them?"

They were approaching the building but Hugh stopped at a bench just beside it and sat down. When Aubrey looked at him questioningly, he said, "I hope you don't mind. I thought we could at least sit down while we talk."

With a smile, she sat down beside him and kicked off her sandals. "They're killing me. They look great but they're not made for walking."

"Now that's a shame," he said with a wink.

Aubrey blushed. "So…um, your other resorts?"

"Oh, right. Okay, so we're here in Napa, and then we have one down south in San Diego. We've got one in Hawaii and one in Montana. We have more on the East Coast. There's Maine, upstate New York, Michigan, Vermont, and South Carolina. Then we cross the pond"—he chuckled—"for one in London, and the farthest one is in Sydney."

"Australia?"

He nodded. "I don't get there as much as I'd like, but it's beautiful. Very different from what we have here, but it takes my breath away every time."

"Wow. That's amazing. Do they all look like this?" She motioned to their surroundings.

"No. Each of them is different. The only common thread is how I keep them small. I don't want big, sprawling properties with hundreds of rooms. I like a smaller, more intimate surrounding. I like guests to think of my resorts as a true retreat—a respite from their everyday lives. Someplace they can come and relax and go home refreshed."

"It sounds fabulous," she said wistfully. "You must be very proud."

"I am. I always wanted to do it, but I never thought it would be on this scale. I'm very blessed."

"So where's the next one going to be?" she asked, sounding genuinely curious.

"My family has been hinting—loudly—how they'd like me to build one close to home so they'll see me more."

"It sounds nice. Do you have a big family?"

"There are six of us kids," Hugh said with a grin.

"Oh my goodness!"

"How many siblings do you have?" Hugh asked.

Aubrey looked at the ground and combed her hair back behind her ear. "I'm an only child."

Hugh couldn't imagine what that must have been like for her growing up, but chose to keep it to himself. "Well, we are a big crowd when we get together."

"Does everyone still live close to home? Is that why they want you to build a resort there?"

The question gave him pause. She had a point. Most of his siblings were either on the move or not living close to home. Why were they giving him grief about needing to build in North Carolina if they weren't going to be there?

"Hugh?"

"What? Oh, sorry. My mind wandered for a moment. We're all scattered. My dad is still in the house we all grew up in, and my oldest brother—Aidan—he lives a couple of miles away. He's going to get married soon but I think he and Zoe are going to stay in the area. My brother Quinn is still in the area, but he owns a chain of auto shops that specialize in restoration and he travels a lot. Then there are the twins—Riley and Owen. Neither of them live close to home and they both travel with their jobs."

No need to announce that Riley was one of the biggest rock stars in the world. He'd found out the hard way—and more than once—that once you mentioned Riley Shaughnessy was your brother, women tended to fixate on it and chose to keep on hanging around in hopes of meeting him.

Lesson learned.

"Your poor mother. All those boys!"

Hugh smiled sadly. "Yeah. We gave her a hard time, but she finally had her little girl. My sister Darcy is the baby of the family. She just started her first year of college. She's only a couple of hours from home and we're not sure where she'll want to go after she graduates. I have a feeling she'll be a traveler too."

"I couldn't imagine growing up with five older brothers. You all must have scared away every boy in a twenty-mile radius!"

"More like a thirty-mile one," Hugh said. "But she does all right and she knows if she ever needs anything, we're all here for her."

"That's nice." A yawn escaped before she could help herself. Looking down at her watch, she said, "I know this may sound lame, but it's getting late and it's been a long day."

Hugh stood and held out a hand to help her to her feet. He lingered for a moment, enjoying the feel of her hand in his before letting go. "Your room is on the third floor. Come on, I'll walk you up."

"Tim said you stay in this building too."

"It's the only building with a fourth floor. I took the whole floor as my apartment."

Aubrey nodded. "I'm sure it's beautiful."

It was right there—the opportunity to invite her up—and God knew he wanted to. But then he looked at her white dress and it all came back to him.

Her wedding.

Hollingsworth.

No, he might be attracted to Aubrey, but there was no way he was going to act on it. She may have said she and the guy hadn't dated long, but it had still been only a few hours since they'd broken up and he had no intention of being someone's rebound.

No matter how much he wanted that right now. Especially after sitting here in the moonlight and simply enjoying their conversation.

They walked into the building and waited for the elevator. Once inside, Aubrey turned to him. "I want to thank you—again—for all of this. I appreciate the room tonight and not having to drive around looking for a place to stay."

Hugh stuck his hands in his pockets to keep from reaching out and touching her. "Like I said, it's the least I could do."

"I guess we both did some stupid things today—to one another. I suppose we're even now."

Is that what she thought? "Aubrey, I didn't say those things as a way of getting back at you for what happened earlier in my office. You have to believe me. It was just me putting my foot in my mouth."

"I believe you, Hugh. I do. Sorry. I didn't mean to make you defensive."

"Okay. Good."

The elevator came to a halt on the third floor, and Aubrey took the suitcase from his hand. "I think I've got it from here." She stepped out and turned to face him. "Good night, Hugh."

"Good night, Aubrey." She turned to walk away, and Hugh put his hand on the door to keep it open another minute. "Stop in before you leave tomorrow. Let me know when your flight is, okay?"

She nodded. "I will. Good night."

Hugh let the door close and leaned back against the wall. "Yes it was," he said. "Yes it was."

―∿∿∿―

Once inside her room, Aubrey tucked her suitcase out of the way and immediately walked over to the window to look at the view. The night was clear, the moon was full, and for the first time in a long time, she felt…hopeful.

This afternoon she had been dreading her future and thought all was lost. But now… Now it didn't seem all that bad. She'd walked away from Paul and his ridiculous proposal plan and the sky hadn't fallen. The world had continued to spin. Of course she had shut her phone off, so tomorrow things could be very different, but for right now, everything was all right.

For the next thirty minutes she went through her nighttime routine to get ready for bed, adding a nice hot shower to the mix. After climbing in and out of a couple of windows and crawling through the bushes, she was surprised she didn't look worse.

Wrapped in a towel, she went through her suitcase and frowned at the white negligee. What the hell had she been thinking when she'd purchased and packed that thing?

That you were hopeful for a normal wedding night?

Not hardly.

There wasn't a doubt in her mind Paul had expected her to sleep with him—and she would have—but to dress the part of the blushing bride was just foolish on her part. Aubrey didn't have a choice but to wear it; her options were that or nothing, and she didn't enjoy the au naturel thing.

Slipping into the white silk, she studied her reflection. And frowned. It was a beautiful garment, but no matter how much she adjusted the straps and fidgeted, it wouldn't cover her the way she wanted it to. Not that it mattered. There was no one here to see her. Still, she couldn't help but trace a finger over the scar on her chest with a sigh.

"And you should be thankful for it," she said to herself as she turned off the bathroom light and walked into the large bedroom. The king-size bed looked absolutely wonderful and she realized how tired she was.

Pulling back the blankets and situating the pillows, she climbed in and made herself comfortable. It wasn't hard to do. The sheets felt wonderfully cool against her skin and the pillows were the perfect firmness. It was almost as if someone has picked everything out just for her.

Turning off the light, she thought about Hugh Shaughnessy. Did he pick out things like the bedding and linens for his resorts? When she closed her eyes, it wasn't hard to conjure up his face in her mind. He was one of the most attractive men Aubrey had ever met. Handsome, sexy, funny…and did she mention sexy?

Yes, Hugh Shaughnessy was all that, and even though he'd had a moment of jerkiness, overall he seemed to be a good guy. He'd gotten rid of Paul and given her a place to stay when she'd needed it. And he hadn't thrown her out or had her arrested when she'd broken into his office.

So for a day that had started out seemingly bleak, it had ended fairly well. But where did it leave her? What happened tomorrow when she had to leave Napa? Aubrey knew she couldn't leave her phone turned off forever, and there were going to be consequences for the way she'd handled things with Paul. But what else could she do? Where could she go?

It was times like this she envied people like the Shaughnessys. What she wouldn't give to have a sibling to turn to. Someone to support her and have her back. Someone who understood how unreasonable her parents were and could offer advice on what she was supposed to do with her life now.

There were no immediate answers. Every scenario she imagined involved going home and letting Paul have his temper tantrum, quickly followed by a lecture from her father on what a disappointment she was before he went back to ignoring her again.

Not exactly the kind of thing that made a person want to go home.

This time there were no windows to climb out. No escape route. No plan B.

Her eyes felt heavy and her limbs were starting to relax. She was just about to give in to it and go to sleep when she realized she hadn't bothered to look for a flight for tomorrow. After Hugh had left her the first time, she had gone to the lounge and had a bite to eat, then met up with Bordeaux Bill. She chuckled. That's how he'd introduced himself. Then he'd talked nonstop about the wine business—it had been all Aubrey could do to keep up.

And then Hugh had shown up.

Was it any wonder she hadn't had time to book a flight?

She racked her brain and realized by turning on her phone, there was a chance she'd be tempted to listen to any voice mails. Then she'd get upset—or angry—and any hope of sleep would be shot to hell.

"I'll do it in the morning," she said around a yawn. Feeling like she'd found the perfect solution, she rolled onto her belly and got comfortable. Now that she thought about it, she'd go to the concierge desk and see if they could help with a flight. Then she could keep her phone off even longer.

Now *that* sounded like a plan.

Or maybe she could "accidentally" drop her phone in the pool.

That sounded like an even *better* plan.

Chapter 3

IT WAS NEARLY ELEVEN A.M. WHEN AUBREY ROLLED over and looked at the clock. With a muttered curse, she kicked off the covers and jumped from the bed. What time was checkout? She went in search of the papers Tim had given her the night before. Finding them on the desk, she sagged with relief when she saw he'd noted a late checkout time of one o'clock for her. God bless that man.

Still, she knew she needed to get herself together and find a flight home. Her purse was sitting there staring at her like a ticking time bomb. All she had to do was open it, pull out her phone, and... Well, then the reality of what she had done yesterday would surely come blasting straight at her in the form of text messages and voice mails.

"And the purse stays put," she said and walked over to the window. It was another beautiful day in Napa, and as she pulled the curtains open wide, Aubrey couldn't help but smile. She couldn't imagine being able to wake up to such a spectacular view every day. Not that Raleigh wasn't a nice place to live, but it didn't offer views of lush gardens and vineyards like this.

At least, not where she lived.

Knowing staring at the scenery was just a way of delaying the inevitable, she stepped away and went to take a shower. The one the night before had been more about cleaning herself off and washing the day away. This time she intended to make it a long, hot one where she could let herself relax.

Twenty minutes later, Aubrey felt like a new woman. The shower had been exactly what she'd needed. The luxury skin care products were positively decadent. And the white fluffy robe was definitely getting tucked into her luggage to take home! The only downside to what was starting out to be a great morning was her wardrobe.

With the initial plans for the trip focused on business, Aubrey had packed light. Paul had told her they didn't need any casual clothes because there wouldn't be any down time during the trip. Their slight detour to Napa had been a spur-of-the-moment addition.

Shuffling through the luggage, she thought about her options. She couldn't fly home in the bikini, and she'd already worn both the blue and black dresses...so the red dress it was. It wasn't a bad dress, but right now, she would almost kill for a pair of comfortable jeans and a T-shirt.

After slathering on some body lotion, she pulled on a pair of panties and slipped the dress over her head before getting to work on her hair and makeup. Knowing there was a good chance she'd be spending the bulk of her day traveling, she went with minimal effort on both. Her long, straight hair—once it was dry—got twisted up in a sassy little updo, and with just a bit of mascara and lipstick, she was good to go.

With nothing left to do—and hating how her dress clashed with her luggage—Aubrey looked around the room and made sure she hadn't forgotten anything. Her stomach growled loudly and it made her smile. Checkout could wait until after she grabbed some lunch. Leaving her luggage, she picked up her room key and decided to head over to Lillian's to get a bite to eat.

Even though she knew she was doing it again—simply delaying the inevitable—she couldn't force herself to care. At the elevator she thought of Hugh. Was he still upstairs in his suite, or was he well into his workday and already at the office? She had a feeling he was probably in his office and felt a wave of disappointment. He really did seem like a nice guy, and in other circumstances she probably would have pursued the obvious attraction between the two of them.

Unfortunately, this was the wrong place and time.

"Story of my life," she muttered and stepped into the elevator.

Ten minutes later, she was seated at a lovely table at Lillian's with a view of a small pond. It was relatively empty and Aubrey figured it was because it was too late for breakfast and maybe too early for lunch for some people. She mentally shrugged. Noon was the perfect time to eat—especially when her stomach was being so vocal about needing food!

"Hey, Runaway Bride! How are you?" Aubrey looked up to see Bill standing next to her table with a big grin on his face. She wanted to be annoyed by the ridiculous nickname, but his infectious smile made it impossible.

"I'm good, Bill. How are you today?" she asked pleasantly.

"Mind if I join you?"

"That depends."

He looked at her quizzically. "On what?"

"On whether you're going to call me Runaway Bride

all through lunch," she said saucily and was rewarded with a loud laugh from him.

"Sweetheart, I love a woman who isn't afraid to speak her mind!" He pulled up a chair and got himself situated before he looked at her again. "It's a pleasure to see you again…Aubrey."

Her own smile grew. "Thank you."

They each picked up a menu and began to scan it. "I know I monopolized the conversation last night," Bill began, "so why don't you tell me a little about you?"

Hugh paced his office like a caged animal and checked his watch for the tenth time.

Bill was late.

Where could he be? It wasn't as if this was an early morning meeting! It was after two in the afternoon, for crying out loud! Marnie was sitting on the sofa with her tablet and seemed perfectly content to wait.

Not Hugh.

With a huff of agitation, he stormed from the office and out to Dorothy's desk. "Any word from Bellows?" he snapped.

She shook her head. "I'll call Tim and see if anyone's seen him around the resort today."

Rather than go back to his office, Hugh waited while she made the call and listened to her end of the conversation. When she hung up, he looked at her expectantly. "Well?"

"He hasn't come to the desk for anything, but Tim is sending a couple of the boys out to check all the usual areas—his room, the pool, the lounge, and the restaurants."

"I can't believe he would be late for our meeting because he was hanging out by the pool," Hugh grumbled. "I mean, he's a businessman. He came here specifically for this meeting!"

"You said he was a little unconventional," she reminded him. "Maybe he just took your appointed meeting time as a suggestion." When she noticed the tightness of Hugh's jaw and the way his face was slightly reddening, she quickly amended, "I'm sure there's a perfectly reasonable explanation," she said evenly, clearly doing her best to try to calm her boss down.

"Somehow I doubt it." Hugh was never late for a meeting. It made a bad impression. And right now, his impression of William Bellows wasn't particularly favorable. Why couldn't everyone just be considerate? He'd worked his ass off for this meeting and had spent three hours coaching Marnie on everything. And now they were sitting around waiting.

The desk phone beeped and Dorothy quickly answered. A minute later she hung up and looked at Hugh. "He's over at Lillian's. Do you want them to remind him of your meeting?"

Hugh cursed under his breath. "No. I'll go over there myself and see what's going on. Thanks." Without a word to Marnie, he stalked from the outer office and made his way to the restaurant, fuming the entire way.

When he stepped into the restaurant, the hostess took one look at him and almost shrank back. "Can I help you, Mr. Shaughnessy?" she asked nervously.

He was about to answer when he heard Bellows's laughter. "Son of a..." he muttered, looking at the hostess and forcing a smile. "No, thank you. I think I found who I'm looking for."

Walking across the restaurant, he found Bill sitting at a corner table.

"So the next thing you know," he was saying, "I'm standing on the top shelf in the warehouse and the guy drives off with the pallet truck!"

Then Hugh registered the female laughter.

Aubrey.

What the…?

"Hugh!" Aubrey said with surprise when she spotted him. "How are you?"

How was he? He was furious! This was supposed to be one of the biggest meetings for his resorts and it wasn't happening because Bill was having lunch with Aubrey? He wasn't sure who he was angrier with!

"Hey, Hugh!" Bill said as he stood and shook Hugh's hand. "We're supposed to meet up in a little while, right?"

"Actually," Hugh began, "we were supposed to meet thirty minutes ago."

"What?" Bill said loudly. "Seriously?" He looked at his watch and at least had the good sense to look embarrassed. "Sorry, man. I completely lost track of the time."

Now wasn't the time to argue, so Hugh plastered a smile on his face and said, "It's all right. Why don't we head over to my office and…?"

"No need," Bill said and gestured for Hugh to take a seat and join them.

"Maybe I should go," Aubrey said.

"No, no," Bill said, stopping her. "You need to be here for this."

Hugh sat down and looked quizzically from one to the other. "I don't see why."

"The reason I lost track of the time is because this young lady is a genius," Bill began, soldiering on before Hugh could speak. "I ran into Aubrey, invited myself to join her for lunch, and we got to talking. I asked her what she did for a living and got to know her a little. Turns out, she's exactly what you and I need."

"Excuse me?" Hugh sputtered. "What the hell are you talking about?"

"I told her about our meeting and all the things we'd been discussing, and Aubrey had some fabulous ideas."

"Really?" Hugh asked with a hint of sarcasm as he looked at Aubrey and back at Bill. "I'm sure she did, but if we can go back to my office, Marnie and I have some great ideas for how we can launch your products at our resorts and—"

"You're not listening, Hugh. I'm telling you what Aubrey suggested is what I want. And...I want her handling it."

"*What!?*" Hugh cried as he stood up. "She doesn't work for me, Bill! Hell, before yesterday—when she broke into my office—I didn't even know her!"

Bill laughed and looked at Aubrey. "You broke into his office?"

She shrugged, looking more than a little embarrassed. "It's a long story, but basically, he stole my luggage and I went in to get it."

"I did not *steal* your luggage. It was in the middle of the lawn and sticking out like a sore thumb!"

"And I told you I was handling it!" she snapped back.

"And how was I supposed to know that? It's not

every day someone tosses their ugly suitcase out the window and shimmies out after it!"

"Okay, kids," Bill interrupted. "Time out. I can see this is a sore subject for you both. Why don't we just skip over what happened yesterday and focus on the here and now. And the future." He put his focus on Hugh. "I'm telling you, Hugh, the girl's a genius. I've been racking my brain for weeks on what I wanted to accomplish with you, and in a matter of minutes, Aubrey had a plan that hit the nail on the head!"

Hugh glared at Aubrey for a moment before returning his attention to Bill. "Tell you what, why don't you come with me to my office and talk with me and Marnie, and we'll try to incorporate some of Aubrey's ideas."

Bill studied him hard for a solid minute. "Hugh, do you know how many resorts, hotels, and restaurants I deal with?"

Shit. Hugh knew right then and there he was very close to losing Bill. "I do," he said calmly.

"I deal with big companies and small ones, but do you know what they all have in common?"

Hugh shook his head, suddenly feeling very nervous.

"I handpicked them all. If I don't like them, I don't do business with them." Bill's earlier jovial tone was gone and now he was almost deadly calm. "I've been approached by some of the biggest resorts in the country—in the world—because I can get wines no one else can, thanks to my exclusive contracts with so many vineyards and wineries. So when I sit here and tell you if you want my business, this is the way I want it, you need to pay close attention and listen."

His gut instinct was to tell Bill Bellows to take his

wine and his exclusive contracts and shove them, but unfortunately, Hugh couldn't do it. This deal was the final thing he wanted for his existing resorts. It was the icing on the cake.

He just wanted to ink the deal on his own terms.

Swallowing hard, he put a smile back on his face. "Okay," he said evenly. "I'm all ears. Tell me what the two of you have come up with."

Bill relaxed back in his seat and grinned at Aubrey. "You're on, sweetheart."

Hugh looked over at Aubrey and forced his smile to stay in place. "Yes, please, *sweetheart*. I'm anxious to hear all about your ideas."

Aubrey squirmed in her seat. "Um…I really didn't think it would come to this," she began nervously, looking at Bill for assistance. "I'm not good at presentations and…"

"Nonsense," Bill said. "Just say it like you said it to me."

She took a steadying breath. "Okay." Turning, she faced Hugh. "Bill told me about you wanting to put his wines in all of your resorts."

"That's right," Hugh said.

"And you were planning a launch event here in Napa."

Hugh nodded.

"I think it's a bad idea."

His gaze narrowed, hardened. "Why?" he asked through clenched teeth.

"You're in wine country. One of the things I'm sure your guests love about this particular resort is how you showcase local wineries and vineyards. By making a big production out of acquiring new wines from Bill, you're essentially thumbing your nose at the very people who have made *this* resort so successful."

She had a point, but Hugh kept silent and let her go on.

"My idea is that you don't do one launch, you launch at each resort. You make it an event where you invite your VIP guests, the media, trade magazines and newspapers. You create a special menu showcasing the wines Bill is bringing to the table. You do heavy marketing and PR and make sure each event is different. You go with the geography—what's popular in the area—so it also draws in the locals without making it seem hokey or clichéd." She looked at Bill and smiled.

But when she looked at Hugh, her smile fell. He was not amused, and it must have shown.

Bill broke the silence. "We've already started talking about ideas for some of the locations. If it's all right with you, we'll save Napa for near the end. Like Aubrey said, we don't want to offend anyone, and I think we'll generate more buzz with your other resorts." He paused and took a drink. "I'm telling you, Hugh, I think this is going to be very beneficial for both of us. None of my other clients turned our contract into an event. We'd be putting both of our businesses on the map in a big way."

Hugh worried it might be too big. He didn't want to be forced to grow. He liked the way his resorts operated now. Small. Intimate. Private. Would this campaign ruin that for them?

"You don't look convinced," Bill said finally. "Is it because this isn't your idea, or do you have other concerns?"

"Honestly, I think it all sounds great. I think it's completely doable."

"But…?"

"But," Hugh began, "the appeal of my resorts is their intimate settings. The privacy. What we're suggesting could be a media circus."

"No, no, no," Aubrey interrupted. "We can totally keep it small and intimate. We can control the guest list and if anything, by keeping it exclusive, it will make people more interested in getting a reservation—even for a later date. I think you'll find in the weeks if not months afterward, you'll have an increase in reservations and occupancy."

"I want final approval on all ad campaigns and guest lists," Hugh said.

"Done," Bill replied. "Once we agree on a few key things, the ball is in your court on that end. We can hammer out products and dates together as we go so they fit with each resort's needs. But the campaign itself, I want you and Aubrey to handle. It's not my area of expertise or interest. Just make it lucrative for the both of us and I'm happy."

"Bill, I'm sure Aubrey has a job back home—"

"She doesn't."

Hugh looked at Aubrey skeptically. "Do you have any experience with this sort of thing? I mean, basically I'm being asked to hire you because you had an idea. It doesn't mean you know how to carry it all out."

She looked hurt by his words and tone. "I can assure you I've done this sort of thing dozens of times before. I've been organizing fund-raisers and charity events since I was a teenager."

"And yet you currently don't have a job," Hugh said mildly.

Now it was her turn to glare. "Let's just say I'm in between jobs right now."

"Does it have anything to do with your impromptu wedding yesterday?" he asked with a hint of sarcasm.

Aubrey turned and looked at Bill. "Maybe this isn't a good idea. I'm sure Hugh has a staff who is perfectly capable of handling this. I can go over our ideas with them and be on a plane by tonight."

"You still haven't booked your flight home?" Hugh interrupted. "I thought you would have by now."

Ignoring his question, Aubrey stayed focused on Bill. "I appreciate your wanting to help me, but I don't think working with Hugh is going to work."

"Nonsense. You can still work with his staff, but I like the way you think," Bill said. "You managed to do what no one else I've been working with has. You got in my brain and pulled out the ideas I couldn't communicate. You're the perfect person for this job." Then he turned to Hugh. "You'll make this work, right?"

With only a slight hesitation, Hugh nodded.

"Okay then," Bill said, standing. "I'm going to relax by the pool. Hugh, I want you to work on a list of what products you want for each resort and the dates you want to start shipping. Once we get that out of the way, we'll get our legal teams working on the contracts. Keep me posted on the progress of the campaigns and the launch event dates, and whether you'll need any promotional material from me."

"Bill, I really think we should go back to my office and discuss all of this together and—"

"I think we're off to a good start here and we don't need to beat it to death. I'm here through the weekend. Why don't we have dinner tonight after you've had a chance to talk with Aubrey, and the three of us can chat about this some more?"

Somehow Hugh had lost control of the entire situation and his head was spinning. Before he could voice another concern, Bill shook his hand and left the restaurant. "What the hell just happened here?" he asked out loud to no one in particular.

Aubrey stood and straightened her dress. "Hugh, you have to know... I didn't plan—"

"Don't," he interrupted. "Do you have any idea what you've done?"

She shook her head.

"I have been working on this deal for months, and you just undid everything I had worked on."

"I didn't know!" she cried. "I had no idea Bill was going to—"

"Whatever. It doesn't matter. It's done. I just... I need a little time to process it. Meet me in my office at four and we'll talk about it some more."

And with that, he was gone.

———

Aubrey wasn't sure if she should high-five or kick herself.

This was an incredible opportunity—everything she had been hoping for career-wise. And all done without the help of her family connections.

That was the best part.

There wasn't a doubt in her mind that she could do it. Right now her brain was simply swirling with

ideas even though she had never seen any of Hugh's
other resorts. Just knowing the locations and having the
opportunity to make each event new and different and
exciting was more than she had ever hoped for. Hugh
would certainly see…

Hugh.

The image of the carefully banked anger on his face
was etched clearly in her mind. How could she have
known a simple conversation with Bill would transpire
into all of this? It was obvious Hugh had some strong
opinions regarding her running out on her wedding, and
this whole situation wasn't going to help. By now he
probably had her categorized as a major flake—or a
royal pain in the butt.

It couldn't be helped. Well, the wedding part could
have been helped. She never should have agreed to
marry Paul. It was a stupid idea and completely child-
ish. At twenty-six, she was too old to keep trying to seek
her father's approval. If she hadn't earned it by now, she
never would. And it was his loss.

*Keep telling yourself that and maybe someday you'll
believe it.*

And as for the whole thing with Bill… Well, she had
just been making conversation. There was no way she
could have known Hugh had been working on this deal
or for how long. Aubrey knew she was many things, but
a mind reader wasn't one of them and he was going to
have to deal with it.

And Aubrey had a feeling she was going to have to
get used to dealing with Hugh. It wasn't a bad thing, per
se, but she couldn't quite shake the feeling they were
going to butt heads the entire time she worked for him.

That caused her to pause. What exactly was this going to entail? Her life was back in Raleigh. Hell, she was wearing the last of the clothes she had packed. Was she going to be able to work remotely? Immediately she shook her head. In order for her to get a feel for each of the events, she was going to have to travel.

Yippee! her inner voice cheered. Oh, it was going to be so good to break away and finally start to live! For far too long Aubrey had let other people's ideas and watchful eyes dictate the things she did, and she was tired of dodging those looks and opinions. This was going to be her time—time to prove to everyone she could make it on her own. That she was smart enough. Strong enough.

Good enough.

With her inner pep talk done, she finally rose from the table and went to pay the check. "No worries, Miss Burke, it's been taken care of," the hostess told her.

"But...by who?"

"Mr. Shaughnessy."

She hated that Hugh had done so much for her and she had kind of ruined his business plan. Aubrey knew she'd be able to make it up to him by hitting this campaign out of the park and making it a success. But it was going to take a while. And she had a feeling Hugh Shaughnessy was not big on patience.

It was already pushing three in the afternoon. Looking down at herself, Aubrey knew her little red sundress was not the type of thing she should wear to a business meeting, and no matter how unconventional this all was, meeting with Hugh constituted a business meeting.

Turning back to the hostess, she began to formulate a plan. "Excuse me, is there a boutique anywhere on the property where I could get a couple of outfits that aren't quite so…"

"Casual?"

Aubrey nodded. "Exactly. I'm not looking for bathing suits or T-shirts. I need something more put together than what I'm wearing now."

The girl nodded, took out a map of the resort, and showed Aubrey where to go. "They have clothes for just about every occasion, so you should be set."

With a word of thanks, Aubrey took the map and headed off in the direction of the boutique with a little spring in her step.

Hugh Shaughnessy may not think he needed her on this project and he may not want her on it, but by the time she was done, he was going to be damn glad about it.

—◦—

"Miss Burke is here to see you," Dorothy said to Hugh over the phone, and Hugh looked at his watch.

She was five minutes early.

He almost smiled at the fact that she quite possibly was on the same wavelength as him where work was concerned, but then he remembered how she had all but ruined the presentation he had worked so hard for.

The fact that her ideas blew his out of the water was beside the point.

Hugh knew enough about business to realize the presentation he had put together would not have impressed a man like William Bellows. It would have come off okay but uninspiring. What Aubrey had managed to think of in such a short amount of time was really impressive.

But still annoying.

"Give me five minutes, Dorothy, then you can send her in."

"Yes, sir," she said and hung up.

Relaxing back in his chair, Hugh tried to figure out what he was supposed to do with Aubrey. When he'd come back to the office after meeting with her and Bill, he had found Marnie still sitting there waiting. It had been awkward explaining she wasn't going to be needed for this particular project, and then apologizing for wasting her time.

He did find out, however, she was not interested in filling Heather's position, so he was still back to square one on that front.

The obvious choice at this exact moment was to offer it to Aubrey. It would solve a lot of problems, and since she was going to be on the payroll for this project, it just made sense. Unfortunately, he knew this project was going to demand a lot of time and attention to pull off successfully, and he didn't want her distracted by any other events.

So again, back to square one.

His cell phone rang and he was about to hit ignore when he saw his brother Quinn's face on the screen. Two brothers in two days? What were the odds? "Hey, Quinn, what's up?"

"Dude, when are you coming home again?"

"I'm fine, seriously, thanks for asking," Hugh said dryly.

"Yeah, yeah, yeah…you're fine, I'm fine, blah, blah, blah. I'm serious, man. When are you coming home again?"

"I…um…two weeks. Why? What's up?"

Quinn let out a breath—loudly. "There's some property that's recently been brought to my attention that I think would be perfect for one of your resorts."

"Oh no. Not you too."

"What? What do you mean not me too?"

"Dad's been harping on me to put my next resort in North Carolina, Aidan's mentioned it, and he got Zoe in on the whole thing. Hell, even Darcy's mentioned it as a way to tell me she'd be open to moving back home if she could work there."

Quinn laughed. "Did she say work or was it implied? Because I have a feeling Darcy would be more interested in socializing and hanging out by the pool than doing actual work."

"I don't remember. So how'd you find out about this property?"

"Anna's taking a real estate course and…"

"Wait a minute. When did that happen? I thought she loved working at the pub?"

"She does, but suddenly she felt she was in a rut. So now she's thinking real estate could be interesting. Personally, I think it's boring as shit, but I'm not the one who has to do it."

"Can't you talk her out of it? I mean, she's really good with the pub. And you know old Steve is going to retire in the next couple of years—I always thought she'd take it over. She's a phenomenal cook and we all know she's basically running the place now."

"Look, you don't have to tell me. She's got it in her head she needs to make some changes in her life. Don't ask me why, must be a girl thing."

"What are you, twelve?"

"Shut up."

Hugh chuckled. "Okay, so I'm guessing Anna found out about this property and you think it would be good for me...why?"

"Prime location, Hugh. It's closer to the sound than the ocean, but you've got over two hundred acres."

"Is there anything on it now? Any structures?"

"No. It's a clean slate. The listing hasn't gone public yet but Anna thinks..."

"Would Anna get the commission?"

"I would imagine so. She takes her test next week so she should have her license not long after."

It was the last thing on Hugh's mind—building a resort in North Carolina—but he had to admit knowing there was property available was pretty damn appealing. There was a soft knock on his office door and he looked up as Aubrey walked in.

Talk about appealing...

"Look, Quinn, I've got a meeting starting now. Send me the information and some pictures and let me think on it."

"Oh man! Really? Are you seriously thinking about it?"

"Slow down. I'm not making any promises, but if you look at it and think it looks solid and Anna's involved, I'll definitely give it some serious thought, okay?"

"Deal. And Hugh?"

"Yeah?"

"Thanks."

Putting the phone down on his desk, Hugh motioned to Aubrey to have a seat. He immediately noticed that the red dress she'd had on at lunch was gone and in its place was a more sensible ensemble—cream skirt and blouse and low heels. It wasn't nearly as appealing as the red dress, and yet she still looked stunning.

Reel it in, Shaughnessy, and focus on business. And for the love of it, don't think about what color thong she's wearing today!

Easier said than done.

"Hugh," she began before he could say anything, "I want to apologize for the way things went earlier. I had no idea Bill was going to propose this arrangement to you. Had he talked to me beforehand, I would have bowed out."

"Are you saying you don't want to do this?"

"Oh no. I want to do this and I know I can do an amazing job with it. I just don't want you to…you know…hate me because of the way it all came to be."

He studied her for a moment. She was nervous. She was fidgeting. And he'd made her feel that way. Hugh was a serious businessman who held everyone who worked for him to a high level of expectations, but he never liked to make someone uncomfortable. Sighing, he tried to make himself relax.

"Look, I'm not going to lie to you, Aubrey, this was not the way I envisioned my meetings with Bill going. You took me by surprise with your ideas and how much Bill liked them and… I'll get over it. I promise I won't let it interfere with our working relationship."

She visibly relaxed. "Oh. Okay. Good." And then she smiled at him. "Which brings us to the first topic—my working for you. I'm not really sure what it's going to entail. I mean, as of right now, I don't have a place to stay except back home in Raleigh."

"What happened to your room?"

"I checked out. It was only for the night."

"Oh, right."

"So I'll need to know what you're going to expect from me and where I'll need to be and when. I'll obviously have to go home and take care of some things there—I hadn't planned on being gone this long."

"You weren't going on a honeymoon?"

She sagged in her seat. "Okay, I'm going to say this once and that's it. My relationship with Paul was a mistake. We weren't in love, we barely dated. I'm not proud of how I was willing to marry someone under those conditions, but there it is. I would appreciate it if we could move on from it. I feel like you keep bringing it up and I don't understand why."

Neither did he, but Aubrey kept looking at him expectantly. "Curiosity. I never knew anyone who walked away from their own wedding." He shrugged, trying to sound casual.

She sighed wearily. "I don't want it to keep being a…a thing, you know? I don't want you to define me by this one act."

"It was a hell of an act, Aubrey. It's not every day I find a woman so desperate to get away from the man she's supposed to marry that she's willing to climb out windows."

She stood abruptly and took a step toward him. "You know what? This isn't going to work. I thought maybe it could—hoped it would—but I don't think it can. For whatever reason, you're stuck on this one point and it's something I'd like to forget."

"Forget?" Hugh cried. "Sweetheart, it happened less than twenty-four hours ago! Cut me some slack here!

It's how we met! I'm not likely to forget that a beautiful woman flashed her ass to me as she climbed through my office window!"

"Flashed my…!" She let out a little shriek of frustration and blushed furiously. Turning away, she picked up her purse and stormed toward the door.

Hugh was on his feet in an instant and ran after her, slamming his hand against the door before she could open it. Aubrey was trapped between Hugh and the door, and they both seemed to instantly still. Without conscious thought, he leaned in until they were almost touching. He could smell her shampoo, her perfume, and as those scents wrapped around him, Hugh was powerless to stop a small groan from escaping.

"Hugh," she said softly, but he heard the tremble in her voice.

And immediately stepped away.

Mentally cursing himself, he took a few more steps away from Aubrey, but noted she hadn't moved. Hugh knew he had to get his head on straight before he spoke. Taking a steadying breath, he forced himself to turn around and face her. "I'm sorry."

Aubrey looked over her shoulder at him. "I meant what I said," she began, her voice softly shaking. "This won't work if you're going to keep throwing yesterday back at me. I've had to deal with that sort of thing my entire life and I'm done. I won't tolerate it from you—or anyone else."

He nodded. "I understand and again, I'm sorry. I'm not perfect, Aubrey, and I can't promise it will never happen again, but I do promise to do my best. Please. I want us to work together on this. Bill wants us to work together on this. If I promise to try to act as if we're meeting for the first time—right here, right now—will you stay?"

She was silent for so long, Hugh thought she was surely going to tell him to go to hell and storm out the door. Then, with nothing more than a slight nod of her head, Aubrey walked back into the room until she was standing right in front of him.

"Good afternoon, Mr. Shaughnessy," she said with a bright smile. "I'm Aubrey Burke. It's a pleasure to meet you." She held out her hand and Hugh shook it.

"Thank you for coming to meet with me on such short notice, Miss Burke. Please…have a seat."

And just like that, they were ready to start anew.

—◆◆◆—

An hour later, Aubrey had finally finished outlining all the ideas she had so far. She was mentally exhausted.

"I think if you can give me a couple of days, I can have a formal draft of all of this. Right now it's mostly me talking off the top of my head. I wasn't prepared to come in and do a full presentation."

Hugh nodded. "It shouldn't be a problem." He looked at his watch. "But it is getting late and there are some things we need to address right away."

"Such as?"

"I know you mentioned needing to go home, but I'd like it if you stayed through the weekend so we can meet with Bill another time or two."

"It shouldn't be a problem, except I checked out of my room. It's Friday, which means you probably have all of the rooms booked, so I'll need to find a place to stay."

With nothing more than a nod, Hugh picked up the phone and had Dorothy check their availability for the weekend. He hated the thought of sending Aubrey to stay someplace else when she didn't have a car to get back and forth.

Sure, that's the reason, he mocked himself.

Who was he kidding? If there weren't any rooms available, Hugh's apartment had four bedrooms—there would be plenty of room for her. He always made sure his on-site apartments were large enough so his family could come and stay with him at any time. Most of them had never taken him up on the offer, but Hugh felt better knowing the space was there should he need it.

Having Aubrey stay there, however, was probably not the smartest plan he'd ever had. For starters, he barely knew her. And yet he was wildly attracted to her. Maybe it was because he hadn't had a date in months, but Hugh had a feeling it was more than that. He saw beautiful, single women walking around his resorts every day and none of them had caused the kind of kick-in-the-gut reaction Aubrey had.

Too bad the timing sucked.

Hanging up the phone, he looked at Aubrey. "Dorothy is going to check on a room for you. And once she's done, I'll have her work on your flight home on Monday. We'll need to discuss how long you'd like to be home for, then I think our best course of action would be to take a bit of a whirlwind trip to at least four of the resorts. This way you can start working on the campaign. I'm sure seeing them in person will help with the creative process."

"Absolutely," Aubrey replied. "But if you can give

me any brochures and web addresses for them, I can at least get started. Have you thought about where you want to hold the first launch?"

He had. Unfortunately, she had shot the idea down. Rather than comment on it, he stopped and pondered it. "We're approaching the summer season, and I think I'd prefer to stay out of the south and wait until the cooler temperatures set in. We want our guests to be able to enjoy each of the resorts and the amenities without the possibility of the heat ruining their experience."

"Sounds like a plan. So we start up north." She stopped and considered her options. "If it's all right with you, I'd like to maybe save Vermont and Maine for the fall. I think we can really play on the foliage."

"Agreed. But if it's what we're going to do, we might as well put our upstate New York resort in with them and do a whole northeast blitz, right?"

"There are pros and cons to it…"

It amazed Hugh how easily they bantered back and forth, and how in sync they were with one another on the direction of the campaign. Clearly she was an intelligent woman, and while it was a plus for their working relationship, it just made him all the more intrigued about who Aubrey really was. And no matter how hard he tried, the same questions kept coming to mind: Why had she agreed to marry a man she didn't love? Why wasn't she working right now? Why was she so willing to take on a job with him on such short notice, one that would keep her traveling and away from home?

Eventually, Hugh knew he'd have the answers.

"So what do you think?" Aubrey asked, her face full of excitement and expectation.

Crap. He'd totally zoned out while she was talking and now he felt like a complete idiot. Between the barbs about her running out on her wedding, sniffing her hair, and now not paying attention to her ideas, Hugh was certain she was going to throw in the towel and tell him what a colossal tool he was.

And he'd completely deserve it.

"Hugh?"

He was about to apologize when Dorothy knocked on the door and came in. *Whew!* He'd never been so thankful to see another person in his life. Smiling brightly at his assistant, he asked, "So? What did you find out?"

"We're booked solid for the weekend," Dorothy said, turning to smile sympathetically at Aubrey. "I'm sorry. If you'd like, I can see what's available in the area for you and we can arrange car service to take you back and forth, if it's agreeable to you?"

"Oh…um…" Aubrey began.

"Dotty, give us a few minutes. In the meantime, can you please see about making travel arrangements for Aubrey to fly back to Raleigh on Monday and return…?" He looked at Aubrey for confirmation.

Her blue eyes went wide at how quickly things were moving. "I…I guess I could be back here by next weekend if that's all right. Or I could come back sooner? I don't really have a lot to do. I just need to check on some things and pack properly."

Dorothy shook her head and looked at Hugh. "You're leaving for Florida on Wednesday, then you were going up to Hilton Head for the weekend, and then we have you penciled in for some time with your family the week after."

Hugh looked at his assistant and let his mind consider all of the things that needed to be done. They could take this weekend for Aubrey to study this particular resort. Maybe it would be best for her to travel with him to Florida and South Carolina, then she could go home while he was with his family. Plus, he'd get the opportunity to tour the property Quinn had told him about.

Yes. This was a schedule he could definitely work with. He clapped his hands together and smiled, looking from Dorothy to Aubrey and back again. "Okay, let's plan on Aubrey going home to Raleigh on Monday and, if you're agreeable," he said to Aubrey, "you can meet me down in Palm Beach and travel with me to Hilton Head." Without waiting for her response, he turned back to Dorothy. "Check with both resorts and make reservations for Miss Burke."

Dorothy nodded and instead of leaving, she turned to Aubrey. "Before we begin, is this all okay with you? It's a little bit of a whirlwind and it's very short notice."

Aubrey smiled gratefully. "It will be fine. I'm looking forward to getting started."

They chatted for another minute on logistics and travel times, and Dorothy wished them both a good night and a good weekend before she walked out the door.

"She's very efficient," Aubrey said once the office door closed.

"She's a godsend. I don't know what I'd do without her." He paused. "She'll have all of your travel itineraries ready for you before she leaves."

"Wow! She works fast."

He chuckled. "She does this sort of thing all the time. I'm pretty regimented on my travel schedule—it's rare I have to do something on the spur of the moment. But we deal with a lot of VIP guests and several business clients like Bill, so Dorothy's a pro at doing the travel stuff."

"Well, that's good." She folded her hands in her lap and looked around nervously. Hugh noticed she tended to nibble on her bottom lip when she was nervous. He was just about to ask what was on her mind when she spoke again. "So...about a place to stay this weekend?"

Damn. Was there a way to offer her one of the rooms in his apartment without coming off as weird and creepy? As of now, they were technically employer/employee, and it might be considered inappropriate. With a shake of his head, Hugh knew what he had to do. Picking up the phone, he buzzed through to Dorothy.

"Yes?"

"I know you're busy with the flight reservations and all, but we'll need to find Aubrey a room in town for the weekend. Maybe you can get Tim to help you?"

"No problem. Give me a few minutes."

Looking up at Aubrey, he smiled apologetically. "I know it's not ideal, but..."

She held up a hand to stop him. "It's fine. Really. You've been beyond generous already. I don't expect you to turn away guests with a reservation so I'm not inconvenienced."

While he appreciated her good attitude, it didn't make him feel any better. "I guess we'll wait and see what Dorothy comes up with. I can drive you over to check in and then we'll meet Bill for dinner. What do you think?"

Aubrey sagged a little. "Honestly? He's exhausting."

Hugh laughed out loud. "Oh, thank God. I thought I was the only one who felt that way!"

"Are you kidding? When I met him last night in the lounge, I thought it was the alcohol making him so loud and chatty, but it turns out it's just his personality!"

"It wasn't so noticeable over the phone, but once he arrived here, I was a little surprised. He's a great guy and an amazing businessman but…"

"Definitely not quiet and reserved." They both laughed, then fell into companionable silence until Dorothy knocked on the door.

She walked in and handed Aubrey a folder. "In here are all your travel documents. I was able to coordinate it so you'll be arriving in Palm Beach within fifteen minutes of each other, so you'll both be able to take the town car to the resort. Then you'll be driving with Hugh up to Hilton Head."

"Driving?" Aubrey asked in surprise.

Dorothy nodded. "Every once in a while, the boss prefers to drive. It takes longer, it's less efficient, but he's quirky like that."

"Hey! I'm right here."

Dorothy smiled at him serenely. "And it's nothing I haven't said to you before. I understand why you like to do it, but I still think you're crazy to want to drive up I-95 when you can be flying first class."

"Maybe because I don't get to drive as often as I'd like. Have you ever thought of that?"

"Of course I have. You say it to me every time we have this conversation."

"And yet we're still having it." But he grinned at her. He liked how Dorothy wasn't afraid to speak her mind to him—and how she was genuinely concerned for him in a maternal way.

"I do have some bad news, however."

"Uh-oh," Aubrey said quietly.

"There's a big music festival this weekend. It normally doesn't affect us because our guests come here just to relax, but the rest of the local hotels are all booked. I called around and had Tim and the boys at the desk do the same—there isn't a room to be had within a fifty-mile radius." She looked at Aubrey apologetically. "I'm sorry." Then she looked at Hugh. "Maybe we can—"

"Aubrey can stay with me," Hugh blurted out.

"What?" both women said in unison.

"I've got an entire apartment with four guest rooms. It's just for the weekend and at this point, it's the only option. I'm not going to make her sleep here in the office, for crying out loud." He stared at his assistant, as if daring her to argue. "Do you have another suggestion?"

She silently shook her head.

Hugh looked over at Aubrey and saw the telltale nibbling of her lip. "It's not ideal, I know. And I feel very bad about putting you in this awkward position, but there's plenty of room and you'll have lots of privacy. It's only for two nights. We'll be so busy during the day with new-hire paperwork and getting things in motion for the campaign, it won't be a big deal. I promise."

Her eyes went from his to Dorothy's as if seeking the older woman's approval. "It really is a huge space," Dorothy said. "And believe me when I say he's hardly ever there."

Aubrey still didn't look convinced.

Hugh wanted to put her mind at ease. "I'll sleep here in the office then, if that's what it takes to make you feel okay with the situation. You can have the entire apartment to yourself." It was the last thing he ever thought he'd offer.

Idiot.

"Oh no. I couldn't let you do that, Hugh. I'm being silly, right? I mean, we're adults. I'll have my own room. What's the big deal?"

Dorothy looked from one to the other. "I'll leave it to the two of you to work out." She looked at Aubrey. "I'm looking forward to working with you, Miss Burke, and if you have any questions about your travel plans, please don't hesitate to give me a call."

"Thank you, Dorothy. I appreciate all your help."

"Boss, I'll see you on Monday."

Hugh nodded. "Have a good weekend."

When they were alone, Aubrey spoke first. "I'm sorry I seemed to freak out. I don't know why I did. I feel bad intruding on your personal space, and no matter how much I genuinely try to leave you alone, the universe keeps throwing us together."

That was one way of looking at it. "Like I said, it's not ideal, but I think we can handle it for the weekend. Besides, if we're going to be traveling together next week and working together closely on this campaign, it makes sense for us to get used to hanging out together now."

"I suppose." But she didn't sound convinced.

Hugh stood and stretched. "Come on. It's getting late. We should probably freshen up and call Bill to see when he'd like to meet. I probably should have done it already, but my head was spinning after our earlier meeting."

Aubrey chuckled. "Join the club."

"Where's your luggage?"

"Tim's holding it at the front desk for me. I wasn't sure what to do with it and I was getting tired of lugging it around."

Together they walked out to get it, wishing Tim a good evening before stepping out into the evening air. It was another mild night, and the walk to Hugh's apartment was spent largely in silence. Hugh was lost in his own thoughts. How was he going to manage not only having Aubrey in his apartment, sleeping in the next room, but traveling with her all next week? Clearly he was a glutton for punishment.

They entered the building and rode up in the elevator quietly. When the doors opened, Hugh let her go first, then stepped out and took his key card from his pocket. "I have extras inside. Remind me to give you one so you can come and go as you need to without having to wait on me."

He had a feeling he'd be locking himself in his office for the majority of the weekend.

"I assume we'll be working together all weekend, but I appreciate the offer."

"You don't have to be on the clock the whole time," he said lightly, opening the door for her. "You should take some time to enjoy the pool or something. No use in both of us being cooped up in the office all weekend. The weather's supposed to be beautiful."

She nodded, stopping in the middle of the living room. "Oh, Hugh. This is wonderful." Looking over her shoulder, she smiled at him.

And Hugh knew he was in over his head.

Chapter 4

AUBREY WAS IN TROUBLE.

Big, serious trouble.

It was near midnight and she and Hugh were walking through the door of his apartment. Dinner with Bill had been loud and lively and exhausting. Bill had teased her mercilessly because she didn't drink. He carried on about how difficult it was going to be for her to put together a wine campaign without knowing what it tasted like. Luckily, Hugh had come to her rescue and assured Bill one had nothing to do with the other.

It was the first time Aubrey could remember someone coming to her defense.

Ever.

She needed space—Hugh made her feel too many things. She turned to him and said, "It's been another long day. I think I'm going to get ready for bed. I'll see you in the morning."

Hugh nodded, then called her name before she could open her door. "Don't let the things Bill said upset you. You don't need to drink the product to be able to do your job. We have chefs and sommeliers who handle that end of the event. You're going to do a great job."

All she could do was nod. Emotion clogged her throat and she quickly walked into her room and shut the door before letting the first tear fall.

Why did she have to meet Hugh now? Why, when

her life had pretty much hit a new low, did she have to meet a man who was kind, compassionate, and giving? She wiped the tear away and almost chuckled. He was also a little arrogant, opinionated, and bossy, but all in all, with his incredible good looks and sexy body and... never mind. She groaned and sank to the floor.

Now what? Looking around the room, she couldn't believe it was really hers to use. It had a king-size bed, a spa-quality en suite, and a balcony overlooking another pond. It was so peaceful and beautiful.

Her eyes stopped on her purse. She had left it—and her phone—in the room earlier because she didn't need it.

"It's time," she said quietly and rose to walk across the room. Taking the phone out, she turned it on and waited to see how many voice mails and text messages there were. Much to her surprise, there weren't many.

There were three texts from friends and two voice mails from Paul. The first one was nothing but his ranting and raving and calling her names—she'd expected it—but his second one was much calmer.

"Aubrey, you know why I thought our getting married was a good idea. However, it was more beneficial for me than you, and it wasn't fair of me to make you think otherwise. Anyway, when I got home, I explained my situation to Kristen and she has agreed to be my wife. We're going to Vegas on Saturday. I didn't want you to hear about it from anyone else. I hope things won't be awkward for you when you come home. Take care."

She threw the phone down on the bed. "Son of a *bitch*!" she hissed. *She* had wanted to simply go to

Vegas, but Paul had called her tacky. God, how could she have been so stupid? So trusting?

Scooping up the phone, she was about to delete both messages when it started to ring. The sound startled her and the phone flew from her hands. Taking a deep breath, Aubrey reached for it, surprised to see her father's face on the screen. It was after midnight on California time. Back in North Carolina, it was three hours earlier. "Hello?" she answered nervously as she stepped out onto the balcony.

"Aubrey, it's about time you answered your phone. Where are you?"

"It's awful late, Dad. Is everything okay?" She was hoping he didn't notice her diversion tactics.

"I'm aware of the time, Aubrey. If you're still in California—which I have a suspicion you are—then you're aware of the time difference."

"Yes, Dad."

"Had you had your phone turned on, I wouldn't have to do this at such an ungodly hour."

She wanted to mention he could have left a message, but held her tongue. "Yes, Dad."

For the next ten minutes she listened to him rant about how irresponsible she was and how humiliating it was for Paul to come home without her. Aubrey was about to point out that Paul had clearly gotten over his humiliation, but figured her father wouldn't appreciate the observation.

The entire time he talked, she stood looking out at the property. The sky was clear, there was a gentle breeze, and if it weren't for the harping on the other end of the phone, she would almost call it a perfect night.

"I'm tired of your behavior, Aubrey," her father was saying. "It was understandable when you were younger, but enough is enough. I'm tired of making excuses for you."

Hadn't she told Hugh earlier she was done with people talking to her like this? "No one's asked you to make excuses. There is nothing wrong with me," she said firmly. "And you know what? I am sick and tired of you making me feel like something is."

"Maybe you're forgetting—"

"I'm not forgetting anything," she interrupted. "Maybe it's *you* who needs to forget. I'm a disappointment to you—I get it. I don't need you calling just to remind me of it. If I'm so horrible and such a letdown, then why don't you do us both a favor and stop calling."

"How dare you talk to me like this!"

"No. How dare *you*," she hissed. "A parent is supposed to love their child unconditionally. That's never been the case for you, and you know what? I'm tired of having to prove myself to you. I'm never going to be what you want me to be, so let's just call it a day and move on, all right?"

"Aubrey…" he warned.

"No, I'm serious. I'm sorry you wasted your time calling tonight. Should you want to talk to me like a normal parent, I would love to hear from you, but if you're only calling to point out my shortcomings, please don't. I'm done." He said her name again but Aubrey ignored it. "Good-bye, Dad." She hung up the phone.

And turned it back off.

Well, that had gone well. She leaned on the balcony railing and took several deep breaths to try to calm her racing heartbeat. After a few minutes, she straightened and looked up at the stars in the sky, hugging herself as she began to cry.

—⁓—

Hugh knew he should have gone inside the minute he heard Aubrey talking on the phone, but part of him couldn't turn away—especially after hearing the pain in her voice.

From the side of the conversation he could hear, her father sounded like a major jackass. Hugh couldn't imagine what it must be like for her to have to deal with such disapproval. In all his life, Hugh couldn't remember a time when his father hadn't backed him up and cheered him on. Hell, Ian Shaughnessy was probably one of the best dads in the world. Hugh realized now how lucky he was.

Did they agree on everything? No. But Ian had never been one to remind his kids of their faults or their mistakes—and there had been plenty. Hugh's heart squeezed as he couldn't help but remember what his mistakes had cost his family. And yet…his father had never said one unkind word to him about it.

Sometimes he wished he had. It would make the guilt a little easier to deal with.

Pushing those thoughts aside like he always did, Hugh leaned against the French door leading out to his own balcony and sighed. The sound of Aubrey's sobbing was killing him, and he was completely torn. He didn't want to embarrass her by stepping out into the open and admitting he'd heard her conversation, but at the same time, the need to comfort her was nearly overwhelming.

"Aubrey?" he said quietly, walking out onto his own balcony so she could see him.

She quickly wiped her tears away as she faced him. "What… What are you doing out here?"

"I came out to get some air and I heard you crying. Are you all right?" He expected her to politely lie and wish him a good night.

"No," she said softly. "I'm really not."

Hugh gauged the distance between the two balconies and knew he couldn't simply jump over. It would have been cool as hell, but he'd be no use to her if he misjudged the distance and fell. Instead he walked back through his room and the living room, letting himself into Aubrey's room. She hadn't moved from where she was, so he strode out onto the balcony and took her in his arms.

And simply held her while the last of the dam broke.

She cried as if she were brokenhearted. She clutched at his shirt as if she had needed to do this for far too long. He didn't have any words. He wouldn't have spoken if he did. For now, this was what Aubrey needed— someone to hold her. Someone to comfort her. Someone to simply accept her.

—∾∾—

Aubrey woke up the next morning and instantly groaned when she realized last night wasn't a dream. She had cried all over Hugh until she had practically collapsed. Then he had carried her to her bed and gently put her down, kissing her forehead. And just when she thought he had taken his chance to escape, he was back with a glass of water for her. He made sure she was comfortable, kissed her gently again, and then he was gone.

Ugh. The poor man must be wishing he had just let her rob his office and not interfered. She was a mess. A stinking hot mess. How in the world was she supposed to face him this morning, knowing he must think the same thing of her? Aubrey eyed the balcony, but it was too high to escape that way.

"No more running," she murmured as she climbed from the bed, still wearing last night's clothes. It wasn't particularly early—eight a.m.—but she wasn't sure if Hugh was an early riser or not. Hopefully he was already down at the office. She'd shower and get herself feeling human again before seeking him out.

Thirty minutes later, dressed in one of her new outfits—black capris and a sky-blue sleeveless blouse— Aubrey stepped out into the living room. And froze.

Hugh was sitting at the breakfast bar drinking a cup of coffee and reading the paper. "Good morning," he said. "I wasn't sure if you were big on breakfast, so I had them send up an assortment of food—fruit, cereal, muffins, that sort of thing. If you'd like something hot like eggs or pancakes, we can have them sent up, too."

He wasn't asking her to leave.

He was offering her breakfast like everything was completely normal.

Nervously tucking her hair behind her ear, she straightened in her spot. "Listen… Hugh, about last night…"

He waved her off. "Today is a new day," he said with a sincere smile. "Okay?"

There were so many things Aubrey wanted to say, but she took the lifeline he extended, returning his smile. "Okay." She walked over to where the breakfast tray was. Her practical side told her to have some of the fresh fruit, but the other side urged her to have one of the giant muffins.

"There's banana nut, blueberry, and chocolate chip," Hugh said as he watched her.

"As much as I would love the chocolate chip one, I don't think it's quite right for breakfast," Aubrey said, sighing as she picked up the plate of fruit. Before she knew it, Hugh was beside her, taking the plate from her hands. "What are you doing?"

He leaned in and spoke to her in an exaggerated whisper. "You're technically on vacation. It's okay to have chocolate for breakfast. Besides, I won't tell."

She looked at him and couldn't help but giggle. "It just feels so wrong."

Now it was Hugh's turn to chuckle. "It's okay. Live a little." Without a word, Hugh put the muffin on a plate, handed it to Aubrey, and took her by the shoulders, directing her to the breakfast bar. "Sit. Eat."

And she did. It was quite possibly the best muffin—or breakfast—she'd ever eaten. It felt completely decadent, and it wasn't until she was halfway through it that she realized Hugh was staring at her. Swallowing the last bite, she looked at him. "What?"

His face was resting in his hand and he was smiling—he seemed to do that a lot. At least, he always seemed to be smiling at her.

"It's good to see you enjoying a meal."

Aubrey looked at him quizzically. "What are you talking about? I always enjoy my meals."

Hugh shook his head. "I know I can't speak for how you normally eat, but since you've been here, you've been very reserved while you ate. This muffin? It was a completely different experience."

She wanted to be a little bit offended by his observation, but couldn't. "If you can believe it, that's the first time I've ever eaten baked goods for breakfast. It was never allowed."

Hugh's shocked expression was almost comical. "How is that possible? What about bagels?"

Aubrey shook her head.

"Donuts?"

"Definitely not."

"Toast?"

She laughed. "That's not a baked good."

"Technically, it is. Bread is baked, therefore toast is a baked good."

Aubrey rolled her eyes. "Okay, then to be clear, I've never eaten the kind of baked goods one would find in an actual bakery for breakfast."

"That borders on child abuse."

She had to agree. "My parents were very regimented and sticklers for rules. They didn't believe in indulging in things that weren't good for you."

"Is that why you don't drink?" he asked, suddenly serious.

"No. I just never acquired a taste for alcohol—any alcohol." She shrugged. "I was the permanently designated driver. It wasn't a bad thing."

"So you don't drink, you don't indulge in sweets—"

"Correction," she interrupted, "I don't indulge in sweets for breakfast." With a giggle she added, "My parents weren't aware of the other times."

Hugh laughed out loud and emptied his cup of coffee.

"You're a rebel, Aubrey!" He stood and walked to the sink to rinse out his mug before placing it in the dishwasher. "So I was thinking we'd head down to the office and finish up your employment paperwork, and while you're doing that, I'll gather all of the files and brochures I have handy on the other properties so you can start studying them. What do you think?"

"I think it sounds like you have everything in order."

He frowned. "You make it sound like it's a bad thing."

"No. No!" she said more adamantly. "I just meant you're very organized and you know exactly what needs to be done. Being organized isn't a bad thing, Hugh. If anything, it's going to be very helpful to me."

Her response seemed to satisfy him, because he visibly relaxed and nodded. "Let's head to the office."

<center>~~~</center>

Two days later, Aubrey was on a flight back home. The weekend had been so much more than she ever could have imagined. She and Hugh were in sync in so many ways and so far, they worked very well together.

The campaign was already taking shape. After they had worked in the office on Saturday, Aubrey had spent the bulk of the day Sunday thoroughly exploring the resort and talking to employees and guests to get a firm understanding of what people were looking for and what would work when they held the launch there.

Hugh had given her access to everything she asked for—VIP suites, private rooms, the kitchens—and Aubrey had no doubt he was going to do the same at each of his locations. The thought of going to other places as luxurious as Napa was enough to make her giddy. This was her time. This was her chance to finally break out of the sheltered life she'd been living.

All Aubrey knew was that she was going to make this campaign a success. By the time they were done, people would be seeking her out for more than just the local charity functions and fund-raisers she had been doing for years. It wasn't that she didn't enjoy organizing them—she did—but it was time to branch out and do something more.

For the first time in days, Aubrey didn't completely regret flying with Paul to Napa. If it hadn't been for that one decision, she never would have met Hugh or Bill or gotten this job.

Silver linings.

Once she was back at her town house, she immediately sprang into action. There was laundry to do and clothing to sort through. This time she would be certain to have an outfit for every occasion and not get caught having to shop at the resort boutiques just to look presentable. Aubrey may have been out of work—not by choice—when she left for Napa, but she still had a fabulous wardrobe.

It didn't take long to have everything sorted and coordinated. There were dresses, skirts, slacks, jeans, sandals, stilettos, and lingerie.

Her obsession.

She blushed as she remembered how Hugh had dug through her suitcase less than a week ago. Now that she thought of it, she had packed a ridiculous amount of underwear. But in her defense, she was supposed to have been on her honeymoon, and though she wasn't particularly attracted to Paul, Aubrey had hoped by at least dressing sexy she'd feel motivated to have a real wedding night.

Now the thought of it made her stomach turn. She was so thankful she hadn't followed through.

And more so since meeting Hugh.

Now there was a man Aubrey wouldn't need any additional motivation to get physical with.

She blushed at the thought. She had to stop thinking of him like that. He was her boss now. There was no way she could get involved with him. Ever. This job with him was temporary—but a long temporary—and quite possibly it might turn out to be only part-time. After all, once she toured all the resorts, the remainder of the work wouldn't take very long. She would implement all of the plans and then his staff would take over.

She pictured the Montana launch, doing a big "I told you so" dance in front of her parents. That one made her laugh. Ultimately, she knew no matter how things panned out with this campaign, she would still need to find other work. She couldn't possibly drag this out indefinitely, but it would open doors for her. Who knew? Maybe eventually she would consider moving away from her hometown and finally making it on her own.

That was the dream.

Part-time, temporary, it didn't matter. The fact was she had a job doing something she loved. And no matter how long it lasted, Aubrey was grateful she had something to look forward to.

She'd just have to learn to look at Hugh as if he wore a big "hands off" sign.

How hard could it be?

Hugh was not having a good day.

As he stalked off the jetway, he mentally cursed every person in his way. The flight to West Palm Beach from San Francisco had been delayed, there'd been a crying baby and a loud drunken man seated in first class with him, and he hadn't been able to get a damn thing done on the entire flight.

He'd like to blame it all on the airline, but unfortunately, his day had started off crappy. There had been a delivery error from their produce carrier, which meant The Vine was going to have to make some last-minute changes to their menu for the next couple of days. There was a stomach bug making its way through the staff and they were short-handed in nearly every area: reservations, front desk, concierge, housekeeping. Everyone was scrambling to cover the extra shifts, but Hugh wasn't happy about how this would affect the overall level of customer service they offered their guests.

He was supposed to hold interviews for Heather's position while he was here in Florida, but none of the applicants seemed impressive. All of the scheduled events were being covered, but Hugh knew it was only a matter of time before something new was booked that no one knew how to handle.

And on top of it all, Riley had called and told him he was going to be in Miami this week and planned on driving up to West Palm to see him. Normally, Hugh would have loved that, but this was not the week for it. For starters, he was too distracted with business, and secondly…there was Aubrey. Hugh wasn't ready to let her meet his rock-star brother.

While Hugh was aware Aubrey wasn't his and there wasn't anything going on between them, he also wasn't ready to dangle temptation in front of her in the form of his swaggering little brother.

He'd have to find a way to keep the two of them apart.

By the time he was down in baggage claim, he felt mildly more in control. Since he had arrived late, he assumed Aubrey had taken their reserved town car and gone on to the resort. Hugh was fine with it—he could easily grab a cab and get there on his own. As soon as he had his luggage he'd—

"Hugh!"

Turning around, Hugh saw Aubrey smiling and waving as she walked toward him. He wasn't sure if he was happy to see her or if this was just more of today's bad luck. She looked so hopeful and excited, probably happier than he'd ever seen her.

And sexy as hell in a black pencil skirt and matching stilettos.

He'd bet a small fortune there was a black lace thong as part of the ensemble, and cursed himself for letting his thoughts go in that direction.

She stopped in front of him, grinning from ear to ear. "Hey! Glad you got in safely."

"What are you doing here?" he asked, confused. "I thought you left here hours ago with the car Dotty reserved."

"She called to let me know you were delayed and told me I could go on without you, but…I didn't want to. I'm a bit nervous about getting started, so I thought it would be better if we showed up together and you introduced me to everyone."

Hugh noted she was speaking a little bit faster than normal—another telltale sign she was nervous. "And the car?"

"I just texted the driver to let him know you arrived. He should be here in fifteen minutes."

Hugh wasn't sure if he should be impressed by her ability to take care of a situation or annoyed that she'd made changes to the itinerary without anyone's permission.

He opted to be impressed. He was tired of being in a bad mood. Maybe for a few minutes he could let himself relax and hope that when they arrived at the hotel, he wouldn't be met with the same kind of issues he'd just left behind in Napa.

"Sounds great," he finally said. "I was just going to call a cab to take me over to the resort." The luggage turnstile buzzer rang out and Hugh walked over to wait for his bags.

"So I did a lot of research while I was home, and I've already mapped out the preliminaries for each of the events based on the information you gave me. I was thinking we could—"

Hugh chuckled and held up a hand to stop her. "Aubrey, take a few minutes to relax. You're not on the clock yet and we'll have plenty of time to talk about it. It's been a hell of a morning and if it's all right with you, I could stand to talk about anything else, as long as it's not work related."

"Oh, okay. That's fine. I just didn't want you to think I'd been slacking off."

"You were home and on your own time. I didn't

expect you to spend every waking moment working on this project." He leaned over and grabbed his first bag before looking at her again. "You're entitled to have time to yourself. So did you get everything taken care of at home? Someone watering your plants? Checking the mail, that sort of thing?"

She nodded. "There wasn't too much to do. I pretty much have a black thumb so all of my plants are artificial, and the mail is taken care of. I left my itinerary with some friends and…here I am."

He noticed she didn't mention anything about her family and that had his curiosity piqued. It would certainly be their topic of conversation on the car ride to the resort. Reaching for his second bag, Hugh straightened and looked at Aubrey. "That's everything." He looked down and noticed she only had one large suitcase with her and thankfully, it wasn't hot pink. "Is that your only bag?"

She nodded.

"I'm impressed. It's been my observation most women travel with multiple pieces of luggage."

"Oh, I was tempted, believe me. But I also am a champion at consolidating and maximizing what I can fit in my bag. Looks can be very deceiving. Inside this one piece of luggage is a whopping twenty-one outfits."

"Your last suitcase contained mostly shoes," he said with a grin. "Did you cut back this time?"

That made her laugh. "Kind of. I stuck to the basics I'd be able to use over the course of the week."

He eyed her, still grinning. "How many pairs?"

"I think our car should be here by now," she said, stopping when she realized Hugh wasn't following her.

She turned and saw him standing five feet behind her, his luggage on the ground. "What?"

"Come on. Out with it. How many pairs of shoes did you bring?" Why he felt the need to tease her like this, he didn't know. All he knew was he was enjoying it. He spent his time surrounded by people—Dorothy, his employees—but he never found someone he enjoyed this silly, carefree banter with. It was a nice feeling.

She rolled her eyes. "Six."

"Six pairs of shoes?"

She nodded.

"You know you're only going to be gone for eight days, right?"

"Then technically, I'm two pairs short," she replied saucily. "Now come on, chief. The car is probably out front and we shouldn't keep him waiting."

And damn if he didn't follow her command like some sort of trained puppy.

Only Hugh was fairly certain puppies didn't focus their attention on the soft sway of a woman's hips as she led the way.

Thankful for the distraction of the car's arrival and getting settled in, Hugh felt slightly more in control by the time they pulled away from the airport. For a few minutes he was content to simply sit and watch the scenery go by, but then he remembered he wanted to get to know her better.

"So," he began, breaking the silence, "you're not missing out on anything by being away for another week?"

Aubrey shook her head. "Not really."

"Tell me about your work—I mean, the work you were doing before coming to Napa."

She sighed. "There's not a whole lot to tell. I've done a lot of work organizing charity events and fund-raisers in the community. I've worked with a lot of nonprofits close to home."

He looked at her oddly. "How did you support yourself? Working for nonprofits certainly wasn't paying your bills."

"I had been on the payroll of my father's company. He's kind of a big deal in the world of finance. His work bores me to death, but there was always a need for parties and galas and whatnot. I was cheap labor and he knew I'd follow his instructions to a T."

Daddy issues. Great. "You said you 'had' been. You quit?"

She nodded. "I hit a point where I couldn't stand putting on the same party over and over and over. To be honest, this isn't my first career choice. But things happen and…here I am." She met his gaze evenly. "I'm very good at what I do, don't get me wrong, and I'm not settling. I know I may have made it sound that way, but it's not. I…I don't want you to think I'm going to be phoning this in."

He never would have thought it. "So what was your first choice?"

"Excuse me?"

"You said this wasn't your first career choice. What was?"

Aubrey looked away and focused on the passing scenery. "It was nothing more than a silly childhood dream. It doesn't matter. This sort of fell into my lap and I enjoy it."

Hugh knew enough about people to know when they

were trying to convince themselves of something. He knew he was going to have to go the long way around if he was going to get an answer out of her. "When I was a kid, I used to dream of being a surfer."

Her eyes widened before she broke out in a fit of giggles. "A surfer? Like a professional one?"

He shrugged. "Sure. Why not? I thought I was so awesome at it, people would come to the beach and pay to watch me."

"And how old were you when this was your dream?"

"Fourteen." He sighed. "I really was good. Everyone said so."

"So what kept you from going pro?"

Life, he admitted to himself. "I realized I enjoyed being inside and wearing dry clothes rather than being out in the hot sun in wet shorts all day." Resting his head back against the seat, he turned to look at her. "And the sand gets to be a real nuisance after a while."

It made her giggle all the more. "I can only imagine."

"So come on… I just shared my failed claim to fame. What did you want to be?"

Aubrey shook her head, her laughter fading. "No. It's too… It was nothing."

Nudging her with his elbow, he pleaded. "Come on. No one outside my family knows about my surfer dreams. They all thought I just did it for fun. I won't tell anyone, I promise."

She rolled her eyes. "Okay, fine. I…I wanted to be a dancer."

He straightened in his seat as his brows rose at her. "A dancer? That's pretty damn cool. What kind of dancing? Ballroom? Ballet? Modern?"

"I was trained in ballet. I started dancing when I was three." She chuckled at the memory. "In most of the pictures from my childhood, I'm wearing a tutu."

Hugh smiled at the imagery. "So what happened? Injury?"

A sad smile played across her lips. "A dancer's life is very regimented. If you step away from it for any length of time, it's hard to get back in. The hours of practicing are brutal. I…I guess I didn't want it bad enough."

He had a feeling there was more to it, but when Aubrey grew silent and turned her attention back out the window, Hugh let the topic go for now and simply relaxed with the silence for the remainder of the drive.

Once they arrived, relaxation quickly became a distant memory. Hugh's management team was waiting for them. As soon as they were out of the car, introductions were made and they were immediately swept up in resort business.

Hugh assigned the resort's assistant event coordinator, Elaine, to give Aubrey a tour and show her to her room while he dealt with some issues that needed his immediate attention. He had meetings planned with the head of each department—it was what he always did. He liked to be informed on how everything was operating, and offer his staff the opportunity to have one-on-one time with him to voice their concerns.

By the time he had his office to himself, it was after eight in the evening and he was starving. Picking up the phone, he called the front desk and asked to be connected to Aubrey's room. All of the tension of the last four hours seemed to ebb away at the sound of her voice.

"Hey," he said with a relaxed sigh. "Did you get settled in all right?"

"Oh my goodness, the staff here is wonderful! Elaine showed me around. I didn't think I'd like anything better than Napa, but I'm seriously starting to reconsider. This entire place is beautiful, Hugh! How do you do it?"

"Have you eaten dinner yet? I know it's late, but…"

"I just got back to my room a few minutes ago. I was so wrapped up in looking around and talking to everyone, I completely forgot about it."

"Would you like to meet me for dinner?"

"That sounds fabulous. I didn't realize I was hungry until you said the word dinner." She chuckled. "Which restaurant?"

The thought of the noise and having to socialize with anyone else was not appealing in the least. Most of the time when Hugh was at a resort, unless he was meeting with a client, he ate in his apartment. Which was what he said to Aubrey. "It's been a really long day. Would you mind if we just ordered dinner to my place? I'd like to hear about what you saw today and what ideas you've come up with, and we can do that a lot easier in the apartment than we could in one of the restaurants."

"I don't mind at all. If you can believe it, I'm pretty much done smiling and being social for the day. It's exhausting."

"Well, I hope it doesn't mean you're going to frown and be quietly grumpy while we eat," he teased, smiling when he heard her laugh.

"You know what I mean. Sometimes it's nice to step away from the crowds." She paused. "You don't mind if I change into casual clothes, do you?"

If she had said "something more comfortable," he might have groaned at the image, but "casual" was a little less tantalizing. "Go right ahead. Give me about thirty minutes and come on over. Do you know how to get here?"

"Elaine gave me a map," she replied. "What are we having for dinner?"

Wednesday was fried chicken night. Hugh wasn't ready to let her in on his OCD about meals, so he simply left the option up to her. "Whatever you want. I can have the kitchen prepare whatever you're in the mood for."

"What are you having?"

"Me? I think…" He pretended to consider his options. "I think I'm in the mood for a little comfort food. Maybe some fried chicken and mashed potatoes."

"Ooo…that does sound good. Same for me, please!"

"You got it. I'll see you in thirty," he said before hanging up the phone.

―――∾―――

Aubrey stood outside Hugh's apartment for a solid five minutes trying to calm her nerves. Everything about the day had been perfect—the people, the resort, her room—and as much as she didn't want to admit it, having a little bit of time away from Hugh had been a blessing. The man had a way of distracting her whenever he was near, and having the afternoon to work with other members of his staff meant she accomplished everything she had hoped for on her first day.

Looking down at herself, she felt a little self-conscious. She was basically one step above wearing her pajamas—black capri-length yoga pants and a white T-shirt. It was far from glamorous and even further from the business attire she'd been in all day. Looking down, she wiggled her toes and smiled at her hot-pink flip-flops with the giant flower on the top. She'd seen them in one of the resort shops earlier while being shown around and couldn't resist buying them. Besides being adorable, they were very comfortable, therefore a practical purchase. Even if they were a little bright for a business dinner.

Yeah, maybe she'd gone a little too casual. Maybe she could run back to her room and…

The door opened and Hugh stood there, magnificent in a pair of well-worn jeans and a T-shirt with some sort of logo faded from many, many wears. "I was wondering if you were ever going to knock on the door. Is everything okay?"

"What?" she croaked, then cleared her throat. "I mean, yes. Sorry. I guess my mind wandered there for a bit and I lost track of the time."

Standing back, he motioned for her to come in. "Cute shoes," he teased as she started toward him. "I seem to recall us selling some almost exactly like them down in the boutique."

Busted. "I…um…I was just doing my part to support the company and all. Some would call it being a good employee."

"Or some would say you have a shoe addiction." His tone was light, his grin big as he waited for her to walk through the door.

When she did, Aubrey made it all of five steps before she froze. Everything was exactly the same as it was in

Napa. Everything. The layout, the furniture, the decor…
it was as if she was transported back to California.

Hugh shut the door and walked around her, seemingly unaware of her dismay. "Dinner arrived a few
minutes ago. I've got it set up at the table. We can set
up the files over there if you'd like, or we can wait until
after dinner." He was standing next to the dining room
table when he finally noticed Aubrey hadn't moved.
"Are you all right?"

What could she possibly say? "I think I just had a
moment of déjà vu," she managed to say with a nervous giggle.

Hugh looked around the place. "Oh, the decor. Yeah.
I get it. I pretty much live at my resorts. I don't have a
place of my own, you know, off property."

"What about by your family?"

He shrugged. "When I go home to visit, I stay with
my father, and sleep in the bedroom I grew up in."

And the weirdness continued. "Don't you…maybe
want a place of your own that isn't at a resort?"

Holding out a chair, Hugh motioned for Aubrey to
join him. "I don't know. I would never be there. Believe
it or not, the resorts keep me busy, and while I'm not
always stopping in and problem solving, there are times
when I stay for a month or so and just enjoy the sim-
plicity of the day-to-day stuff. It's not a bad way to
live." She sat and then Hugh took his seat. "It never
seemed like a necessity or a smart choice financially to
purchase a place I would only live in a month or two
out of the year."

"Maybe you wouldn't spend so much time at the
resorts if you had a place to live. You could set up a

home office to oversee the day-to-day stuff and then space out your travel time so you wouldn't have to be gone for such long amounts of time."

Reaching across the table, Hugh lifted the lid off her plate and then did the same for his own. "I don't know. I don't even know where I'd want to live."

"Where does your family live?"

"Everywhere," he said with a chuckle.

"No, I'm serious. Where is your dad?"

"Coastal North Carolina."

"Seriously? Don't you think it's a coincidence we're both from North Carolina but met in Napa?" she asked with a hint of excitement in her voice.

"Well, to be fair, North Carolina is a pretty big state…"

"Oh, you're no fun," she teased and then looked down at her plate. It was piled high with large pieces of fried chicken, a mountain of mashed potatoes, and glazed baby carrots. Looking up at Hugh, she asked, "Is all this for one person?"

He laughed. "Don't feel obligated. I told the chef to make two plates and I guess he figured they were either both for me or at least for two guys. Just promise you won't pick at it. I want you to enjoy it."

From the scents rolling off the plate, Aubrey had no doubt she'd be enjoying it. Tomorrow her clothes might not appreciate it, but for now, she was pretty much in heaven. It was obvious Hugh was waiting for her to take the first bite before he would start eating, so she didn't hesitate to dig in.

The first bite was nearly orgasmic.

"Oh…my…God," she moaned. "Whoever the chef is, I want to marry him."

Hugh smiled and began to eat. "I take it that means you like it?"

"Like is too mild a word. This is love, pure and simple. I may never eat another salad ever again."

They ate the rest of the meal in silence. Aubrey made it through half her portion before crying uncle. "I hate that I'm full, but it was way too much for one person." Then she looked over and saw Hugh had pretty much devoured every last bite. "Or for this particular person," she teased.

"I'm a lot bigger than you," he said and leaned back in his seat. "And I'm used to eating like this."

"I think I'll have to stop eating with you because if this is how you do it, I'll need a whole new wardrobe."

"Everything in moderation," he said with a wink as he stood up and began clearing the dishes.

"Please, let me help." Together they loaded dishes in the dishwasher, and when they were done Aubrey looked around curiously.

"What are you thinking about now?" Hugh asked.

"If one of the restaurants brought up the food, why are you doing the dishes? Couldn't you just leave it on a tray outside your door like your guests do?"

"I do leave them outside the door. After they're clean. I can't stand the thought of dirty dishes sitting on my doorstep. It looks bad." He wiped his hands on a dish towel and then rubbed them together. "Now, why don't you show me what you accomplished today? It sounded like you had a pretty full day yourself."

Aubrey set the files out on the table and took her tablet out of her satchel, bristling with excitement. "I was so inspired! Everywhere I looked, something would catch my eye and the next thing I knew, I had a clear picture in mind for how I envisioned the launch party."

Hugh could not only see, but feel her excitement. She was so animated when she spoke and there was such passion behind her words; he was absolutely captivated. "Where do you picture us holding the event? We do have a banquet room for special events that would work…"

Aubrey shook her head. "No. Anyone can do a banquet room. We'll utilize the amazing landscape and do this outdoors."

"What about the weather? You can't control whether it's going to rain."

"I understand that, so we'll use tents. It's a little more invasive to the property and might detract from the beauty you've created, but my plan is to bring some of it into the tent. We'll do white, twinkly lights on the ceiling and—weather permitting—we'll leave the sides of the tent off so guests can wander the grounds and really appreciate all you've done here."

He nodded in approval.

"Once you give me a list of wines you'll be focusing on for each resort, I'll work with the chefs on the menus. They're already aware of what we're doing, and I want to give them ample time to create something new and different that's not already on any of their menus. We want this to be an event even your regular guests will want to come to because everything will be exclusive to the night."

"And what about drinks? Are you thinking of having an open bar or simply offering Bill's collection?"

"Bill's collection is the star of the show. We'll let it be known—discreetly—that other beverages are available, but this event is meant to showcase the wine. What we don't want to do is exclude anyone who isn't a wine drinker."

"Like yourself?" he asked lightly.

"Even if I did drink, I wouldn't on the night of an event. I'll be walking around overseeing everything, so it's a nonissue."

They sat silently for a moment, and then Hugh was ready to start picking her brain on the resort—not just from the campaign standpoint, but as an overall impression. They talked at great length about the strengths and weaknesses, the challenges of having a small, exclusive destination when it was surrounded by much larger, less exclusive ones.

"This is a fairly big vacation area. I know a lot of people think I'm foolish for keeping things small, but not everyone is looking for a big, loud family vacation," he said after a while.

"For a man who grew up in a big family, you seem pretty intent on not catering to them. If anything, I would have thought you'd be a little more sensitive to that demographic."

"One has nothing to do with the other. I am sympathetic to families who search for places they can travel to without breaking the bank, but it's not who I felt called to cater to. I like the privacy, the quiet. I grew up in a form of controlled chaos. There were six of us kids, so there was always noise and commotion. When we did go on vacation, it was to the same place because it was what we could afford and it was filled with other families just like us. I didn't realize it at the time, but as an adult looking back, it really wasn't a vacation for my parents." He paused and smiled sadly. "They deserved to have a little time for themselves. A little peace and quiet." He sighed. "They never got it."

Somehow Aubrey knew without asking that his mother was gone. "When did your mother pass away?"

"When I was seventeen," he said quietly. "My mother lived for the six of us and she never had the chance to do anything for herself."

"I think she did," Aubrey said, her tone soft. "She loved all of you and that's what made her happy. I bet her best moments were watching all of you grow and the achievements you made."

Hugh studied her for a moment. "I don't know. Is your mother like that?" His tone was still low but held a hint of curiosity, as if what she was saying was completely foreign to him.

Aubrey shook her head. "Just the opposite. But I spent a lot of time surrounded by other mothers and saw how it could be. How it *should* be."

"I'm sorry," he said and then gave a sad chuckle. "I think you're right, though. Mom was everyone's cheerleader. It didn't matter if you did well on a spelling test or if you made the touchdown that won the game, she made a big deal out of it. We had a wall of pictures because she made sure she captured every accomplishment and hung it up for everyone to see."

"She sounds amazing."

Hugh nodded. "She was." He looked down at his hands folded on the table and then nodded again. "She was that and more."

Unable to help herself, Aubrey placed a hand on top of his and gently squeezed. There was nothing she could say. She had no idea what it was like to physically lose a parent, but from watching Hugh, she knew it must be devastating.

While Aubrey's parents were both still alive, they hadn't been part of her life—particularly her mother—in a long time. At least, not in the way she'd always thought a parent should. Maybe it was her own issue. Maybe she wasn't realistic in her beliefs on how a parent should act or feel or behave. But sitting here looking at Hugh, she wasn't so sure.

"I didn't mean to make you sad," she said softly, still touching him.

Hugh straightened in his seat, his eyes meeting hers. "It's just... I miss her. I don't often let myself say that or feel it, but sometimes..."

"You can't help it. She's a part of you. She's always going to be a part of you."

He nodded but didn't speak. His eyes scanned her face as if studying it, committing it to memory. Shifting, he put his other hand on top of hers and Aubrey reveled in the heat of it, the difference in size and texture.

Something was happening here—something she knew she wouldn't be able to stop. It may have only been days since they'd first met, but it felt as if she'd known him forever. She sensed Hugh felt it too.

Why was she fighting it so hard? There was clearly a connection here. She felt it from the moment she first saw him. True, there had been other things on her mind, but good Lord, the man was every temptation brought to life! The fact that his pulse seemed to be beating as erratically as hers told her she wasn't imagining things.

Did he just move closer?

Oh boy. It had been so long since Aubrey had felt passionate about anything, or anyone. And in the last week, Hugh Shaughnessy had proved to be the person she needed to bring passion back into her life. He challenged her, made her laugh, made her angry, made her... feel. Oh God. It was so good to feel again!

She inched closer.

He whispered her name as his head slowly tilted toward her. She heard the pain and plea in his tone. She knew he was battling his own demons, and while this could complicate everything, Aubrey didn't have it in her to care.

A million questions raced through her mind, and yet the only thing to escape her lips was a hushed, "Yes."

Closing the distance between them, Hugh hesitated, his lips hovering above hers, and Aubrey sighed, hoping to encourage him. Her eyes closed, her heart raced, and then he was there, his lips against hers. Softly. Gently. Tentatively. Aubrey was ready to throw caution to the wind and simply crawl into his lap when a sound by the door pulled them apart.

"Hey, big brother! I guess you forgot I was coming."

Aubrey looked at the man in the doorway and then back to Hugh. "Is this... Is he...?"

Hugh nearly growled as he raked a shaky hand through his hair and stood. "Aubrey Burke, I'd like you to meet my younger brother Riley."

Chapter 5

HUGH HAD NEVER BEEN MORE FRUSTRATED IN HIS entire life. While he was always happy to see one of his siblings, Riley's timing was the worst.

He'd finally caved. Finally said screw it and took a chance to taste Aubrey's sweet lips, and his brother chose *now* to show up? Why the hell hadn't he called first?

Hugh introduced them as Riley stepped forward—all six-foot, lean, rock-star inch of him—and took one of Aubrey's hands in his and kissed it.

Hugh wanted to kill him.

"It's a pleasure to meet you, Aubrey," Riley said smoothly, a knowing smile on his face.

"It's nice to meet you too," she said shyly before taking her hand back. She looked from Riley to Hugh and back again. "Are you in the resort business too?"

Riley let out a full throaty laugh as he looked at her with disbelief. "Are you serious?"

Aubrey nodded. "Hugh didn't mention what the rest of his siblings did for a living. I was just curious."

Now Hugh looked at her like she was crazy. "Aubrey, don't you know who he is?"

"Of course. He's your brother Riley. Why?"

In an instant, all of the anger left Hugh's body as he started laughing too. He looked over at Riley, who suddenly didn't look quite so cocky. His trademark smirk was gone and in its place was a bit of a pout.

"I...I don't understand," Aubrey said, trying to be heard over Hugh's laughter. "What's so funny?"

"Sweetheart," Hugh began, taking a deep breath to get his laughter under control, "don't you listen to the radio?"

Looking at him as if he were speaking another language, she frowned. "Why? What does that have to do with anything?"

Now it was Riley's turn to step forward. "What kind of music do you listen to, darlin'?"

"Classical. Jazz." She stopped and considered for a moment. "That's it."

And Hugh started laughing all over again.

"I don't see what's so damn funny," Riley snapped.

"Little brother, I do believe we just found the one person in the world who doesn't know who you are!"

"I still don't understand. What do you do, Riley? Are you on the radio? Like a disc jockey or something?"

With a growl of frustration, Riley walked over to the kitchen to grab something to drink, muttering the whole way about how he had a song in the top ten in the country.

Aubrey blushed and looked at Hugh apologetically. "I'm sorry," she said, scrambling to get her files together. "I really should be going. Thanks for going over all of this with me, Hugh."

Snapping out of his amusement, Hugh helped her collect her things. When he was right next to her, he murmured in her ear, "Don't worry about Riley. It's good for him to be humbled every once in a while." Then, because he couldn't help himself, he nuzzled closer.

"Hugh," she whispered right before she moved away. "I should go. It... It's late and..."

They both straightened and faced each other, and Hugh skimmed a hand down her cheek, marveling at its softness. "I'm sorry the night ended like this."

She shook her head. "Maybe it's for the best."

"What do you mean?"

Sighing, she met his gaze. "This… Things could get complicated. I'm working with you on this campaign and…well…"

"Aubrey," he said softly, "the campaign is the last thing on my mind. What just happened here has nothing to do with work and everything to do with what's been destined to happen since I first saw you."

"You mean when you first saw my bottom climbing through your window?"

Hugh knew she was trying to make light of the situation, but damn if the image of her in that thong didn't make all the blood in his body rush south. Luckily, he was able to keep his focus on her face and silently prayed she wouldn't notice his body's reaction to her. "I'm not going to lie to you. It was an amazing sight, but it's this face that keeps drawing me in," he said, still caressing her cheek.

"Oh," she sighed.

"We'll talk more about this tomorrow," he forced himself to say. Out of the corner of his eye, Hugh could see Riley glaring at them from the kitchen. "Why don't I walk you back to your room?"

"I'd like that."

They gathered the rest of her things and headed for the door. Riley stood and watched them from the kitchen. "It was nice to meet you, Riley," Aubrey said, still embarrassed by her earlier faux pas.

"You too, Aubrey," he said politely. "Maybe I'll see you around."

"I'd like that. Hugh and I will be here for a few days," she said, and then seemed to realize how it sounded. "I mean… We'll be here *working* and I'm working on a new campaign for him and—"

"Aubrey?" Hugh interrupted. When she looked at him, he teased, "Stop talking." Then he looked at Riley. "I'll see you in a bit."

Riley merely nodded and watched them walk out the door.

The elevator ride was silent and Hugh contemplated leaning in and really kissing her. One look at Aubrey, however, and he knew immediately she was struggling with everything that had just happened—the kiss, the interruption, his brother.

Once they stepped outside and started walking on the dimly lit path toward her building, she spoke. "I really didn't mean to insult your brother. I feel so bad about it. I hope I don't run into him again. I think I'd die of embarrassment."

"It's not a big deal. Like I said, it's good for Riley to realize he isn't the center of everyone's universe."

"Maybe. But I'm sure he expects people—even if they're not fans—to know who he is. I guess I'm a little more out of touch than I thought."

"Nonsense. You like what you like. There's nothing wrong with it. I'm sure he doesn't know any of the jazz musicians you listen to."

Aubrey chuckled. "I doubt I'd recognize most of them either."

"You get the point," Hugh said and boldly reached

for her hand. He smiled when she didn't resist or pull away. "Don't worry about Riley. He'll survive. His ego could use a couple of knocks."

"I just wish I wasn't the one to do it."

He squeezed her hand. "Trust me. He'll survive. And you will too." They reached her building and stopped at the entrance. "What are your plans for tomorrow?"

"Elaine's going to take me around the city to get a feel for it. We're going to look at our competition a bit and shop a little for VIP gifts. I think everyone we invite to the party should have a gift bag waiting for them in their rooms. It will be filled with some items exclusive to the resort, but I'd also like to find items from local businesses, you know, something with the local flavor." She paused and looked at him. "What do you think?"

"I think it sounds like you're going to be very busy. When will I see you?" Slowly, giving her time to accept or reject what he was doing, Hugh pulled her in close until they were toe to toe with one another.

With a sigh, Aubrey relaxed into him. "Mmm… I don't know. I'm meeting her in the lobby at ten and I figured we'd be out until mid-afternoon. What are you doing for dinner tomorrow night?"

Hugh shook his head. "That's too long to wait. Promise me you'll stop by my office when you get back." He leaned in and placed a gentle kiss on her lips. Aubrey immediately melted into the kiss, and he had to fight for control. Now wasn't the time to take this any further, and he didn't want it to feel like he was rushing her. No matter how much he wanted to. Lifting his head, he rested his forehead against hers. "Feel free to use the door this time," he teased lightly and laughed when she smacked his arm playfully.

"Jerk." It was all she got out before Hugh swooped back in for one last kiss. Sighing, Aubrey looked up into his eyes. "I'll see you tomorrow."

"Yes, you will," he said and it was a near growl. He watched Aubrey enter her building, waving to her before she turned away and the door closed behind her.

He took the path back to his own building at a slow pace. His mind was reeling and he was beyond annoyed with his brother. While he knew—realistically—Riley had no idea he was going to be interrupting something, it didn't make Hugh feel any less irritated. If Riley hadn't walked in when he did, there wasn't a doubt in Hugh's mind he and Aubrey would be getting to know each other a lot better at this very moment.

Dammit.

Now he was going to have to walk back into his apartment and tippy-toe around his brother's fragile ego while dodging questions about Aubrey. No doubt Riley would give him a hard time about the whole situation and they'd suddenly turn into twelve-year-olds.

This was so not the way the night should have ended.

Hugh looked up at the star-filled sky and sighed. He didn't want to be alone, but he didn't feel like hanging out with Riley.

He wanted Aubrey.

Luckily, Hugh was a realist. It wasn't going to happen tonight. Maybe not even tomorrow night. They would have their time. Soon. But right now there was no point in standing here staring at the sky and dreaming like a teenage girl. He'd wasted enough time. This was the real world, and it was time to go back to his apartment, spend time with his brother, and try to focus on whatever had brought Riley here.

And not let his mind wander to Aubrey and what she was doing.

———

"I didn't think I'd be seeing you again tonight," Riley said when Hugh walked through the door.

"I told you I'd be back."

"Yeah, but I figured you were saying that so I wouldn't ask any questions or make any comments about you getting lucky," he said with a grin. He was sprawled out on the sofa, a bowl of popcorn in his lap and an open beer on the coffee table. A replay of a hockey game was on the TV.

Hugh kicked off his shoes and sat down beside him. Wordlessly he reached for a handful of popcorn and together they watched a couple minutes of the game.

"You didn't need to come back, you know," Riley finally said.

With a shrug, Hugh looked at him. "Yeah, I did."

Riley chuckled. "Why? Is the blond playing hard to get?"

Hugh silently counted to ten before answering. "No. I am."

Riley laughed out loud. "Yeah, right. What are you doing? Holding out for a ring?"

"Very funny. It's all just…new. Aubrey works for me now—I didn't orchestrate or want that—but she does, so it has the potential to get complicated. And we've only known each other for a week, so like I said, it's new."

"Huh. So are you really into her?"

Was he? Stupid question. "Yeah. I am."

"Damn, not you too. I can barely stand all of the domestic bliss Aidan goes on about. For crying out loud, we all know Zoe's great. Why can't he shut up about it once in a while?"

Hugh chuckled. "You're sounding a little bit jaded there, bro. What's the matter? A decline in fan club membership?"

"Screw you," Riley muttered. "All I'm saying is maybe there are other things to talk about. It doesn't all have to be the wonders of Zoe."

"So what do you want to talk about? The number of panties that landed on stage at your last show? How many naked girls always seem to find a way into your secured hotel room?"

Riley glared at him. "Is that what you think my life is like?" he snapped. "That I'm so freaking shallow I have nothing else to talk about?"

And for the first time, Hugh realized something wasn't right in his brother's world. Maybe that was why he'd showed up here tonight. "You're right. I'm sorry. I'm being very judgmental."

Standing, Riley put the bowl of popcorn on the table and picked up his beer, finishing it off. "Yeah, you are." Then he shook his head. "Forget it. It's nothing."

"Clearly it's something, Ry. What's going on?"

For a minute, Riley ignored him, putting all his attention on the television. When the game went to a commercial, he was shocked when the TV went blank. He turned and looked at Hugh. "What'd you do that for?"

"Because last I checked, neither of us were big on

hockey. You drove all the way here, you didn't call to let me know you were on your way. I think something's on your mind, so spill it."

He shook his head again and walked to the kitchen to put his empty bottle in the recycling bin. "Don't you ever just feel the need to be…home?"

"I'm heading there next week. Lately, I've been feeling it."

"It's easy for you," Riley began, sitting back down on the couch. "You're your own boss. You can pretty much choose when you want to take a break. I can't."

"Um…yes, you can. Last I checked, you were the one pushing for such a lengthy tour. It's got to be coming to an end soon. Why don't you take time at the end of the schedule and go home? You know Dad would love it if you did."

"Yeah, and I know I would enjoy it too—to have the chance to settle in and relax rather than a quick weekend or something. But…" He paused and then sighed wearily. He looked Hugh in the eyes, his expression bleak. "Do you really think I'm shallow?"

Well, crap. Hugh had known he might have to stroke his brother's ego a little bit when he got back here, but he'd thought it would be over Aubrey's reaction to him, not Hugh's. "Dude, I already apologized. I didn't mean…"

"No, that's not what I'm talking about. I mean in general. Do you think I'm shallow because I don't give a shit and I basically let my management team manipulate me so that I keep up an image?"

"Where is this coming from? Did someone say that to you?"

There was a slight hesitation before Riley replied. "It came up recently. I was supposed to be interviewed for one of those music industry documentaries, but the producers declined and pulled me off the project because they didn't think I had enough substance. I mean, what the hell does that mean? And who is saying this crap?"

"Did you try talking to them? Or having your manager talk to them?"

Riley shrugged. "You know Mick. He's a great manager but he hates confrontation. He told me to forget about it and focus on other projects. The only problem is, I can't. It's like I'm obsessed with doing the damn documentary! I can't write… I'm stuck in my own head right now and seriously doubting myself."

"And you think going home will help?"

"I don't know. Maybe. It might be nice to surround myself with people who don't think I'm crap."

"No one thinks that, Riley."

"Obviously somebody does. And that person—or persons—cost me the opportunity to be part of a project I was really looking forward to!"

Unable to help himself, Hugh yawned. It was late and it had been a long and tedious day. "Sorry."

"Don't be. I'm damn near exhausted too." Standing back up, he stretched. "I'm sorry I interrupted your time with Aubrey tonight."

Hugh stood and squeezed his brother's shoulder. "I'm not gonna lie to you, I wanted to beat the crap out of you when you walked in. But I know you didn't do it on purpose."

"Yeah, not like when you had Mary Kate Miller in

the basement when you were sixteen and Owen and I crept down and hid in the closet, right?"

"You jumped out and scared the crap out of us." Hugh chuckled. "And yeah, I pretty much wanted to beat the crap out of you then too."

"If I remember correctly, you chased us up the stairs and right out of the house. Owen ran for three blocks before he realized you'd gone back inside."

"He never takes chances."

"Sure he does," Riley said defensively. "He's a scientist, always trying to disprove whatever theories are currently out there in hopes of making a name for himself. If you ask me, Owen's the bravest of all of us."

Hugh couldn't help but be a little envious. Riley and Owen were fraternal twins and as different as night and day, and yet they had a bond stronger than any of the other siblings. "Make sure you tell him that next time we're all together and he's having a panic attack because a woman looked at him."

Riley couldn't help but chuckle. "He can't help that he's shy."

"Makes him all the more irresistible to the ladies," Hugh teased.

Together they walked to the kitchen. Riley ditched the rest of the popcorn and put the bowl in the sink. Hugh immediately took it out and placed it in the dishwasher.

"Unclench once in a while, Hugh. No one ever died from leaving a dirty dish in the sink."

"That's beautiful, man. Maybe you can write a song about it."

A colorful curse came out of Riley's mouth as he turned toward his bedroom. "Screw you."

"So poetic," Hugh taunted.

At the door to his room, Riley turned. "What ungodly time do you get up in the morning?"

"Around eight. I like to be in my office at nine. Why? Plan on getting up with me?"

"Hell no. Just curious if you were going to be around."

"What about you? How long are you staying?"

"Anxious to get rid of me already?"

Hugh smiled and shook his head. "No. Just curious. I'm only going to be here until Saturday and then we're heading on to Hilton Head."

"We?" Riley said as he waggled his eyebrows. "You and the blond?"

"Her name is Aubrey," Hugh said through clenched teeth.

Riley rolled his eyes. "Fine. Aubrey. Is she the 'we' you were talking about?"

"As a matter of fact, she is."

"I'll probably leave here Friday afternoon then, if it's okay."

"Where are you off to? Another show this weekend?"

"Yeah. Texas. I told Mick I'd meet him for lunch Friday here in town and then we'd fly out together."

"How many more dates until the tour is done?" Hugh was leaning against his own bedroom door frame. He was mentally and physically exhausted, but more than anything, he was worried about his brother.

"Fifteen."

"How long will those take?"

"Eight weeks."

"Damn."

"Exactly." Riley yawned widely. "Look, we're

almost to the point of grunting because we're both so damn tired. Go get some sleep and I'll catch up with you at some point tomorrow. I plan on sleeping as long as humanly possible and then ordering some food to the room before I sit by the pool for a couple of hours."

"Try not to cause a riot." And before he turned away, Hugh added, "I'll let security know you're here. Call me when you're heading down and I'll make sure you're not disturbed."

"Dude…" He yawned and pointed. "Best."

"Right back at ya."

———

Aubrey felt completely inspired. Invigorated.

Her outing with Elaine had been exactly what she needed to fill in the gaps regarding the West Palm Beach launch. They arrived back at the resort a little after one and after waving good-bye to her new friend, Aubrey immediately headed for her suite. While she knew she'd told Hugh she'd stop in and see him when she got back, she was too wound up with excitement and needed to get all of her ideas down on paper before the inspiration fled. Besides, they were back earlier than she had thought. She'd seek him out in an hour.

At least that had been her plan.

The weather outside was downright perfect—blue skies, sun shining, a gentle breeze—and all Aubrey could do from her desk in her suite was keep looking outside. Commending herself on at least trying to stay inside and work, she ran and changed into a pair of shorts and tank, gathered her laptop and notebook, and fairly skipped out the door.

Once outside, she contemplated where to go—one of the gardens or the pool. She could get something to drink and have a little more space to spread out by the pool, so she headed that way.

Since all Hugh's resorts were geared for couples and not families, there weren't any loud noises in the pool area. The few people who were there were simply enjoying the sunshine and keeping to themselves. Aubrey spotted an umbrella-covered table off to the side of the concession/bar area and made a beeline for it. The sun felt glorious and she kept an internal dialogue going with herself on the benefits of being outside.

Stopping briefly at the bar, she ordered a glass of lemonade and settled in at the table. With her laptop open and her notes spread out, Aubrey took a deep breath, ready to get to work, when...

"Not a bad spot for an office. I mean, if you've got to work, why not make it someplace tropical, right?"

Looking up, she saw Riley Shaughnessy smiling down at her.

And wanted to crawl under the table and die.

All night she had beaten herself up over not knowing who he was and insulting him. She had hoped to avoid seeing him while he was here and cursed her impetuous decision to work outside. She smiled at him. "Oh...hi, Riley."

If he sensed she was nervous, he didn't let on. Instead, he pulled up a chair and sat down next to her. "What are you working on?"

Nervously, she cleared her throat. "Oh, um... It's a campaign I'm working on for Hugh."

He nodded. "A campaign, huh? What for? Is it only for this resort?"

Studying his face, Aubrey realized he wasn't just making small talk. He was genuinely interested. "It's for all the resorts. He's working on a deal with a wine distributor. We worked out the preliminaries, and now it's up to me to flesh out the ideas and do a presentation to seal the deal, so to speak."

Riley relaxed a little in his seat. "So you get to come up with an idea for what—an advertisement? Brochures? Slogans?"

"There's more to it than that. We'll be hosting launch parties at each of the resorts with a VIP guest list—the entire event will focus on the new wines. We'll have special menus to complement them as well."

He nodded. "So you have to come up with the party plan and theme and then…what? Clone it? Get the footprint—so to speak—to each of the resorts to carry out?"

"No, we're going to make each one its own personalized event. They'll be customized based on their locations, local cultures, foods, and such. Your brother is going to go through the extensive list of wines and choose which ones he wants for each resort location, and then we'll work on the menus and what sort of theme we want for the party. It's going to be a lot of work to pull it all together, but when we're through, it's going to be amazing."

A wide smile crossed Riley's face. "So you do this sort of thing for a living?"

Aubrey blushed and broke eye contact, suddenly embarrassed. "Um…sort of. I used to do a lot of charity events and fund-raisers for my father's business.

I always wanted to branch out and do more, but...it wasn't necessary."

"So how did you land this gig then?"

"Honestly? Right place at the right time," she said with a small laugh. "I happened to meet the wine guy and we struck up a conversation. I had no idea who he was or that your brother was looking to do business with him. He bounced some ideas off me and I gave him my thoughts and the next thing I knew, he was telling Hugh he wanted me to work on the project! It was...surreal."

Riley's eyes narrowed a little. "You could have said no."

Aubrey had met enough people in her years of working with the public to know when someone was fishing for information. There was a hint of suspicion, if she wasn't mistaken, and she wasn't the least bit offended by it. Aubrey had no doubt there were many people who would question how she came to land this position.

Rather than get defensive or argue with him, she simply agreed. "You're right. I could have said no, but after talking with Bill, I had a clear vision of what I could do with this campaign. Hugh was angry about it, and I was ready to just step back and say 'thanks but no thanks.'"

"But..." Riley prompted.

"But...Bill told Hugh the only way he was going to agree to do business with him was if I worked on the campaign."

Riley laughed out loud. "Seriously? Hugh must have pitched a fit! He hates it when people stray from the plan."

She tucked that bit of information away for a later

time. "Well, I didn't see him pitch anything, but he let me know he wasn't pleased with the turn of events." Aubrey paused, sighing. "I really didn't intend to make things difficult for Hugh. I was just having a conversation with a guy in a restaurant." She shrugged. "I didn't seek out this job, but I'll be damned if I'm going to give it up. I'm good at what I do and I know I can make your brother proud."

Riley seemed pleased with her answer. Looking over his shoulder, he motioned for the bartender to bring him a drink. Once the club soda and lime was placed in front of him, Riley thanked him and turned his attention back to Aubrey. "So tell me, what have you got planned so far for these one-of-a-kind events? Or are you keeping them a secret for now?" His tone was low, almost a whisper, as if they were in cahoots with one another.

Aubrey giggled. "I'm sure you have other things to do than sit here and listen to my party ideas."

Taking a sip of his drink, Riley shook his head. "Nope. I'm all yours."

A girl didn't need to know exactly who Riley Shaughnessy was to know his brand of charm could be lethal. How many women would kill to have him make such a statement to them? Aubrey could only imagine. Looking around the pool area, she was amazed no one was bothering him. There were several bikini-clad women lounging around and yet none of them were pestering Riley. How was it possible?

"Security," Riley said.

She turned her attention back to him. "Excuse me?"

"I said security. I see you looking around—you're probably wondering why no one is hovering around, making a nuisance of themselves." He shrugged. "Hugh arranged for his security people to alert the guests that I'm not to be disturbed—or hounded."

"Oh," Aubrey said and began shuffling her things together. "And here I am yammering on about my work. I'm sorry. You were probably wanting a little time to yourself and I'm disturbing you." She stood. "I never should have—"

Riley reached out and placed a hand on her arm to stop her. "In case you've forgotten, I approached you. So if anyone's guilty of disturbing anyone, it's me for disturbing you. You were all set to do some work and I invited myself to sit down." He flashed her a boyish grin. "That would mean I owe *you* an apology."

"Oh." She blushed again. "It's okay. Really. I…I just wanted to work outside. The weather is perfect and I never get to do this."

"And I can't blame you. Like I said when I came over, it's a great office space." He smiled at Aubrey and they both relaxed back in their seats. "Hey, listen… Are you hungry? I haven't had lunch yet so I'm going to order a burger. Would you like something?"

"Thank you, but I had lunch a little earlier."

He shrugged. "So? That doesn't mean you can't have a snack. Are you hungry? What did you have for lunch?"

"A salad." At the look on his face, Aubrey quickly added, "It was a pretty big salad. It had chicken and lots of veggies and…"

"And it's rabbit food. C'mon. Have a bite to eat with me. You can bounce some ideas off me while we eat. What do you say?"

"Well…" She stopped to think about her options. "I

guess it wouldn't be the worst thing to have a snack. Maybe some fruit or—"

Riley held up a hand to stop her. "Uh-uh. If you're going to sit here and have a snack with me while I'm eating a gourmet burger and fries, you're going to need to eat something with a little more substance. How about I get the burger and we'll split an order of cheesy fries? What do you say?"

Her inner voice, who rarely got to have any fun, was doing backflips at the thought of having such a decadent snack. Fries? With cheese? Um…yes, please! But then the other little voice—the one who sounded suspiciously like her mother—chimed in, making a tsk-ing sound. Aubrey immediately felt herself tense up. Greasy snacks—especially between meals—were always big no-no's when she was growing up. Even though she knew she was an adult capable of making her own decisions, Aubrey still had a problem when it came to breaking from how she was raised.

To be good?

Or to be bad?

Riley watched her expectantly. "I mean, don't get me wrong," he began, "I could totally eat both by myself, and if you're not hungry, I'm not going to force you to eat cheese fries. Or a milk shake."

Aubrey's ears perked up and she saw the mischievous twinkle in Riley's eyes. "Milk shake? You mean like a real ice cream milk shake?"

He leaned in close, all devilishly handsome and bad-boy charm. "Vanilla or chocolate?"

Was he serious? With a wicked smile of her own, Aubrey leaned in too. "Chocolate."

Riley broke out laughing and called the bartender back over to give him their order. Once the man was gone, he leaned back in his seat, still smiling. "Aubrey, I think you and I are going to get along just fine."

———

Hugh looked at his watch for the tenth time and frowned. Where was Aubrey? It was almost four o'clock and she hadn't shown up. Was it really possible she and Elaine were still driving around town?

"It's not possible," he muttered and picked up his phone to call Elaine's extension.

"Hello?"

All the tension he'd been feeling started to leave his body. "Elaine, it's Hugh. Is Aubrey with you?"

"No," she said pleasantly. "Last I saw her was about three hours ago and she was heading back to her suite to do some work. Have you tried calling her there?"

He hadn't. "No. But thanks. I'll try her there." Hanging up the phone, Hugh mentally chastised himself for not calling her room first. "Idiot," he murmured and dialed Aubrey's room. After leaving her a voice-mail message, Hugh hung up and cursed. "Where the hell is she?"

Rising, he paced his office a few times and realized he wasn't going to get anything done until he knew where Aubrey was—and why she didn't stop by and see him like they had planned. Lately, it seemed no one could keep a meeting time. This was the second time in a week he was having to chase someone down.

Maybe she was purposely avoiding him. He stopped in his tracks. Maybe she was uncomfortable after their kiss last night and was having second thoughts about the two of them. "Well damn," he said, grabbing his cell phone from his desk and leaving the office. Whether Aubrey was having second thoughts or not, they still had to work together, and she'd told him she'd stop by the office and update him on her progress. She hadn't. As her boss, it was his responsibility to remind her of her commitment to this campaign.

He hoped she wasn't having second thoughts. It would be fine if she had simply lost track of time because she was working, but he'd have a problem with anything else.

Hugh never allowed himself to get involved with a member of his staff. It was never an issue before—no one had ever tempted him the way Aubrey had. Now that he had a taste of her, he knew he wanted—*needed*—more.

Once outside, Hugh had to stop and say hello to guests and even took a minute to talk to one of the landscapers about the shape of some of the tropical plants. He was on a mission, but it was also important to take the time to talk to people and address issues regarding the resort. He was walking by the pool area when he stopped short. And listened.

Aubrey.

He may not have known her for very long, but he already knew the sound of her laughter. Turning around, he walked through the gate and looked around. Her laughter rang out again and Hugh spotted her at a table far in the corner.

And she wasn't alone.

Why was it that every time he stumbled upon her, she was talking to a man? Did she ever sit by herself?

It wasn't until he got closer that he realized who she

was sitting with, and everything in him went hot…and then cold.

Riley.

Son of a… Hugh felt as if he'd been punched in the gut, but he refused to let it show. By now he should be used to this. Women were attracted to him until his rock-star baby brother showed up. Normally it wasn't a big deal, but with Aubrey, it was. Last night she didn't even know who Riley was. No doubt she had Googled him and realized what a big star he was.

No wonder she'd blown him off today. Riley Shaughnessy was a much bigger fish, and apparently women were into that sort of thing.

He'd thought maybe Aubrey was different.

Better.

His.

It took a minute for Hugh to collect his thoughts and get himself under control. If this was how it was going to be, he'd deal with it. Alone. Without any witnesses. There was no reason for Riley to see how betrayed he felt or for Aubrey to see she'd hurt him. He'd dealt with worse and he'd survived. With a steadying breath, he made his way around the pool toward them.

"So there I was, about a hundred people staring at me, and I knew I was completely screwed!"

Aubrey laughed. "What did you do?"

"I had to make a choice—I could admit I'd lied to get the gig and risk getting thrown out, or I could pretend to pass out and hope it was enough of a diversion to get me out of there."

"Please tell me you chose fake passing out!"

Riley laughed and shook his head. "Hell no! I knew a

little bit of Spanish and somehow managed to convince the crowd to sing along with me...in English! It was probably the most off-key, mispronounced sing-along in the history of music, but at least I didn't have to look like a fool! I played the super-extended version—it lasted about fifteen minutes—and by then, my time was up!"

"Oh my goodness! That's awesome! I can't imagine..."

"Well, well, well," Hugh said pleasantly as he strolled casually up to the table. "It's been a long time since I heard the old cantina karaoke story." He plastered a smile on his face while fighting the urge to punch his brother in the face. Not only had he stolen his girl, but he was doing it with cheesy, outdated stories!

"Hey, bro," Riley said, saluting him with his drink. "You finally breaking out of the office for the day?"

Hugh looked at him and then at Aubrey, who looked beautiful and carefree and...hell. Just looking at her made his chest hurt. "I wanted to check in with Aubrey about her meeting today with Elaine. You were supposed to give me a progress report. The only way we're going to stay on track and get things done is to discuss where you're at."

Aubrey looked at her watch and gasped. "Oh! Hugh, I am so sorry. I came out here to work because it was so beautiful out and then Riley came over and we got to talking and—"

"It's fine," Hugh interrupted. "I'm in between meetings right now, so why don't you give me a brief rundown and then send me an email with a detailed report." His tone was cool, impersonal, and a little bit firm.

"Dude," Riley said. "Ease up. She's not on a deadline to cure cancer, it's a party, for Pete's sake."

"She's being paid to work, not sit poolside playing groupie with you," Hugh snapped and then cursed himself. His brother was no idiot. He was going to know Hugh was pissed and he'd instantly lost the upper hand. Dammit.

Aubrey shuffled some papers around and cleared her throat to get his attention. She gave him a rundown of the sights she had seen with Elaine and how she was going to incorporate some of the local flavor into the party in West Palm Beach. "I'm meeting with your chef over at Patrice's in the morning to discuss some menu options."

"Make sure you're not interrupting his prep time," Hugh said.

"Hugh, seriously, what is your deal?" Riley asked. "This girl is a genius. She's been telling me about her ideas and honestly, they're brilliant. Just relax and let her do her thing."

That was it. Hugh had hit his limit. "This really isn't any of your concern, Riley," he snapped. "I don't walk around backstage at your shows telling you or your entourage how to do things, and I would appreciate it if you showed me the same courtesy."

Riley looked ready to argue but kept his mouth shut.

"I... I um... I let Jacques tell me what time would work for him," Aubrey began meekly. "And I let him know if anything changed or came up, we could talk at a later date. I was just excited about the opportunity to speak with him."

Hugh nodded silently and mentally counted to ten. "Anything else?"

Aubrey looked through her notes, then straightened up and smiled brightly. "Yes. So…um…Riley and I were talking and after we covered the food and the decor, we started talking about entertainment. After checking his calendar, he said he would be able to perform at at least one of the launches! Isn't that great?"

Her smile was so bright and hopeful, but all Hugh could see was red. "You did *what*?" he asked through clenched teeth, directing his attention at Aubrey.

"Hugh…" Riley warned.

"I… We just…" She cleared her throat. "I'm not sure what the problem is."

"You asked my brother to perform at one of the launches? Do I have that right?"

"He offered," Aubrey said weakly, confusion written all over her face.

"He offered," Hugh repeated, glaring at his brother. "So now you're in the habit of doing little private parties?"

Riley stood calmly. "I'm not going to do this with you here," he said. "If you have something to say to me, I'll meet you back at your place." Turning, he smiled down at Aubrey. "Can I walk you back to your room?"

"We're not done talking, Aubrey and I," Hugh said tightly.

Ignoring him, Riley kept his focus on Aubrey. "My offer still stands."

She shook her head. "Thank you, but like Hugh said, we still have things to discuss."

He nodded. "Thank you for having lunch with me. I hope to see you again before I leave." Then he took one of her hands in his and kissed it. "Take care,

Aubrey." He shot Hugh an angry glance before walking away.

It wasn't until he was out of sight that Hugh finally looked at Aubrey again. "Let's get one thing straight, I do not use my family for any of my business endeavors."

Aubrey sighed loudly. "Riley offered, Hugh. I did *not* approach him or ask him about it. It was his idea!"

He waved her off like he didn't believe her and then turned to walk away. "Either way, forget it. It's not happening. Email me your report and…"

"Hey!" she called after him as she came to her feet. Hugh turned slowly and faced her. "I don't know what just went on here, but I'm telling you now, I don't like it."

Hugh arched a brow at her. "Oh really? You don't like it? Well, that's too bad."

She came around the table and advanced on him. "I don't think so. If you have a problem with me, then say it. Don't come out here and insult me and talk down to me. Especially after kissing me last night!" She took a deep breath and let it out. "Now I'll admit I mismanaged my time today, but it's not a crime. If you're having second thoughts about what happened last night, at least have the decency to say it. Don't attack me for something ridiculous to get yourself out of it."

For a minute, Hugh wasn't sure what to do or say. She thought *he* was having second thoughts? Seriously? He took a deliberate step closer to her, his eyes never leaving hers. "You were supposed to meet with me when you got back. It's very important to me that people keep their word. When you tell me you're going to be somewhere or do something, then I expect you to do it."

Now it was Aubrey's turn to cock a brow at him. "You *expect* me to do it? I'm sorry," she began sarcastically, "I didn't think I was behaving like a wayward child. I messed up, Hugh!" she cried with frustration. "News flash, most people do. Nobody's perfect!"

Part of him had to respect the fact that she wasn't backing down, and part of him was so completely turned on and overwhelmed with the need to touch her that it was almost painful. Then he remembered how cozy she'd looked with his brother and it was like a bucket of ice water being dumped over his head.

"I get it, but if you want to hang around playing groupie to my brother, do it on your own time." He turned and strode away.

And this time, he didn't stop or turn back when she called after him.

He was at a crossroad—literally. If he took the path to the left, he would be back at his office. The path to the right led to his apartment.

And Riley.

"Screw it," he muttered. He wasn't ready to deal with his brother just yet. He had work to do. Or he could find work to do. Either way, Hugh planned on holing up in his office for the next several hours until he got his emotions under control.

Walking through the lobby, his head concierge, Ricardo, called out to him, but Hugh ignored him. He just needed to get to his office. To shut the door. Lock it. And sit and wallow or fume or whatever he needed to do to get his head back on straight.

Nearly tearing the door from its hinges, Hugh stepped into his office and slammed the door before locking it.

"Did that make you feel better?"

Son of a bitch. Turning around, Hugh faced the very person he was trying to avoid. "What the hell do you want?" he grumbled, walking over to his desk and sitting down.

"I want to know what your problem is," Riley said, taking a seat facing Hugh.

"Right now? I have too much work to do and I had to waste time traipsing around looking for Aubrey because she blew off our meeting."

"For real? That's what you're going with?" He leaned forward, his elbows resting on his knees as he stared Hugh down. "We don't lie to one another, Hugh, so cut the bullshit."

Hugh's eyes narrowed to slits. "You don't want to go there right now. Trust me."

"I've got nothing else to do," Riley said and gave him a cocky smile. "I can sit here all night and wait. Try me."

Hugh wanted to unleash all his anger and frustration on Riley right then and there, but didn't want to show his weakness. Didn't want his brother to know his insecurities. And most of all, he didn't want his pity.

Ever.

So he simply ignored him. Facing his computer, Hugh pulled up a couple of financial reports and studied them. He sent off a couple of emails to various resort management teams regarding the reports. He even managed to make a few phone calls.

All while Riley sat and stared at him, looking for all the world like he was completely comfortable sitting there silently.

It pissed Hugh off even more.

After an hour, Hugh shut everything down and straightened his desk, still pretending Riley wasn't there. Sure, he felt like a twelve-year-old, but for the life of him, he couldn't seem to stop himself. Collecting his things, he made his way to the door and felt more than heard Riley behind him.

"Are you done yet?" Riley finally asked as they walked out the door.

Hugh ignored him.

They walked out of the lobby and stepped outside. "That's cool," Riley said. "This has been the most relaxing time I've had in months. I'm really enjoying myself."

If it was possible, Hugh felt his blood begin to boil.

Together they took the path back to Hugh's apartment. Riley kept up a running commentary the entire time about everything they saw—the trees, the flowers, the lighting—he even tried to engage Hugh in a conversation about a lizard that crossed their path.

Silence.

By the time they reached the elevator, Riley had given up on talking and started humming and whistling, which he knew bothered his brother. When Hugh turned and glared at him, Riley simply grinned and whistled with a little more enthusiasm.

Inside the apartment, Riley closed the door and broke out in a full chorus of his latest song. Hugh slammed his keys down on the dining room table and went to the kitchen to grab himself a beer, certain he was going to go insane any minute if his brother didn't shut up.

Beer in hand, he turned and ended up face-to-face with Riley.

"I can keep this up all night, bro," Riley said, still

grinning. "You forget, I sing for a living. I'm used to spending hours at a time on stage or in the studio. I don't tire easily." When Hugh still didn't utter a sound, Riley leaned in until they were almost nose to nose and began to sing "Ninety-nine Bottles of Beer on the Wall."

"That's it!" Hugh shouted, shoving Riley away to put some distance between them. "I can't stand it anymore! Just shut the hell up already!"

"No can do. I'm going to keep going until you tell me what that was all about by the pool. I get you're all uptight about…everything, but there was no reason for you to be such a complete jackass. To me and to Aubrey."

Hugh gripped the neck of the bottle so tight he feared he'd break it. "You and Aubrey? How nice."

With a nod, he followed Hugh into the living room. "Oh…I get it. You're not pissed Aubrey didn't come to your office, you're pissed she was hanging out with me." He laughed. "Seriously, Hugh, what the hell?"

"Don't you get enough women on your own? I mean, you're a freaking rock star. Women chase you all over the world! Clearly that's not enough for you, because you had to go make a move on Aubrey. Why? Did it tick you off because she had no idea who you were? Was it so big of a blow to your colossal ego that you needed to make sure she got to know you?"

All of the lighthearted, good-natured ease Riley had been sporting for the last hour disappeared. His eyes narrowed and his voice was almost deadly calm. "Let's get one thing straight: I did not make a move on Aubrey. You told me how you felt about her and I would never do that to you. Hell, I would never do that to anyone. I was sitting by the pool and saw her come out to work.

I went over to say hello. I thought it might be nice to get to know her—especially if she's someone special to you. I figured there had to be something about her if you were so head over freaking heels this fast."

Riley took a deep breath and rolled his shoulders to ease some of the tension he was feeling. "Contrary to popular belief, I don't need my ego stroked. I don't walk around thinking everyone in the world should know who I am. I'm okay with who I am and what I do, and that's the second time in as many days you've gone there with me and I'm sick of it." He started to say more, but gave up. Throwing his hands in the air in defeat, he stalked toward his bedroom.

"Where the hell are you going?" Hugh demanded.

"I'm packing. I had no idea you thought so little of me." Looking over his shoulder, he almost looked sad. "Good to know how you really feel, Hugh." Then he slammed the door.

Hugh stared at the closed door for a solid minute before he could make himself move. Shaking his head with disgust, he knew he had to make things right. With a muttered curse, he walked over to Riley's door. He didn't bother knocking, he just walked in and found Riley putting his suitcase on the bed.

"I don't feel like that," Hugh said, his voice low.

"Seems to me you do."

"Yeah, well… I'm just out of sorts right now and you're a convenient target."

Riley turned. "That's bullshit and you know it. You know what I think? I think you're angry and frustrated and so damn scared to do the wrong thing you're almost paralyzed. You want Aubrey? Then go get her! It shouldn't matter that you just met. It shouldn't matter that she works for you! You're into her, she's into you, and all you're doing is making yourself and everyone around you miserable while you map out every move so you can feel safe."

"It's not that easy!"

"Then make it that easy!" Riley fired back. "God, Hugh. What the hell is wrong with you? Both you and Aidan are so careful and cautious and it's almost painful to watch! He almost lost Zoe because of it and you're going to do the same thing!"

"It's not the same thing, Riley. You have no idea, so don't go there."

Folding his arms across his chest, Riley simply glared at him. "What would happen if you just walked across the property to Aubrey's room and knocked? What do you think could possibly go wrong if she opened the door and you took her in your arms and kissed her?"

Hugh's heart started to pound and he felt a wave of anxiety wash over him. "I…it's…she would probably…"

"She'd probably kiss you back. Then she'd probably invite you in. And then, if you're lucky, she'd ask you to stay." He threw out his hands. "Dude, what have you got to lose? Women love a man who can be spontaneous! Don't be the guy who has to pencil in sex on his calendar because you're too uptight to simply go with what you're feeling!"

How could he possibly explain to his brother why he felt the way he did? How could he put into words that his spontaneous behavior was the reason their mother was gone? The reason his five siblings lost their anchor?

He couldn't.

Hugh understood what Riley was saying—he truly did—and while he knew the likelihood of something bad coming from going after Aubrey was slim, he just didn't know if he was willing to take the chance.

He'd never second-guessed himself with a woman. Maybe it was because he'd never felt quite this strongly about one before. It scared the hell out of him even more.

"Okay, fine," Riley said with disgust. "Sit there and work it all out in your head like you always do. But know this—Aubrey is a pretty fantastic woman. I can see why you feel the way you do. She's smart and funny and beautiful. But if you noticed it, so will somebody else. So while you're sitting here making graphs and charts in your head and working out the perfect timeline, some other guy is going to swoop in and make his move." He stopped. "Not me. But someone else will. If you keep parading her around all of your resorts introducing her to people, she's going to catch someone else's eye, and you'll be all but forgotten. You'll be her boss and nothing more. Is that what you want?"

With his heart racing, his palms sweating, and his throat dry, Hugh knew he had to make a decision. Fast. He looked at his brother, who was smiling smugly. He shook his head. "No. No, that's not what I want."

Riley's smile softened and he crossed his arms over his chest. "What do you want then?"

"Aubrey. I just want Aubrey."

"Then go get her, bro."

And for the first time in seventeen years, Hugh Shaughnessy did something impetuous.

He went after the girl.

Chapter 6

RESTLESS.

Aubrey couldn't sit still. It had been several hours since Hugh had left her by the pool, and she was still bristling with anger and frustration. She was having a hard time believing his complete turnaround toward her was all because she had lost track of the time. And if that was the case, then she had seriously misjudged him.

And it was a shame, because she felt a connection to Hugh Shaughnessy she'd never felt with any other man.

Ever.

With a sigh, she walked over to her desk and sat down. Her laptop was open and her email program was up, waiting for her to compose her stupid report to Hugh. A report. He wouldn't even talk to her—he'd simply relegated her to employee mode and walked away.

Jerk.

She slouched slightly in her seat. It didn't seem right. Hugh was *behaving* like a major jerk, but Aubrey couldn't believe that was who he really was. He was nice. He was considerate and he could be funny.

And he kissed like a dream.

She groaned.

All night she had tossed and turned—all she could think about was kissing Hugh. If Riley hadn't shown up when he had, Aubrey had no doubt she would have practically begged to spend the night with him. It had been a long time since she'd been intimate with a man and even though she had thought she could have gone that route with Paul—and at the time didn't think it would be a big deal—she realized she couldn't have gone through with it. It had taken just one kiss from Hugh and Aubrey had known she had been missing out on something amazing. A connection—a connection paired with a damn-near perfect kiss that was like nothing she'd ever experienced before.

Hot.

Wet.

Consuming.

Even now, she began to shift uncomfortably in her seat. Damn Hugh Shaughnessy for getting her all hot and bothered and then turning into a jerk! Straightening, she began to type furiously. "He wants a report, I'll give him a report," she muttered as her fingers pounded the keyboard.

With all her experience typing inquiry letters, thank you notes, and reports for fund-raisers and charity events, this was a no-brainer. The only difference with this one was she was making it as cool and clinical as she possibly could. No banter, no personal comments, just the straight business facts and figures.

When she was done, Aubrey sat back and read her work. Everything was there, itemized and written in a clear and concise manner so it would be easily understood. It was boring as hell to read but it wasn't her problem. She was about to hit send when there was a knock at the door.

Frowning, she rose and walked across the room, wondering if it was Riley coming to check on her. He was a nice enough guy and she enjoyed talking with him this afternoon, but for all of his sex-symbol status, Aubrey didn't feel a damn thing. No attraction, no need to get flirty with him—he was simply a nice guy who was easy to hang out with.

And he wasn't Hugh.

There was enough of a resemblance you could tell they were related, but their personalities and mannerisms were unique to each of them. Aubrey was certain if she mentioned to her friends she had eaten with Riley Shaughnessy, they'd be green with envy. She shrugged. Just a nice guy.

Without bothering to look through the peephole, she pulled the door open and felt her heart skip a beat at the sight of Hugh. He looked...rattled. Every time she had seen him, he was completely composed and put together—never a hair out of place. And right now he looked disheveled, nervous, and as much as it pained her to admit it, sexier than she'd ever seen him.

His arms were bracketed in the door frame, and he stared at her with a dark intensity that made her shiver. For all she knew, he was here to yell at her some more—or fire her—but she couldn't find the strength to care. His name was a whisper on her lips before she could stop it.

Their eyes locked on one another. Aubrey began to tremble. This was a side of him she didn't know—not that she knew him at all—but the way he seemed to barely be holding on to his control told her that whatever brought him here, he wasn't happy about it.

Unable to stand the silence for another minute, Aubrey opened her mouth to speak.

She never got a word out.

In an instant, Hugh's hands reached out and cupped her face as he claimed her lips with his. Aubrey barely had time to think, to register what was happening, but she immediately went up on tiptoes and raked her hands through his hair, pulling him close.

If she'd thought last night's kiss was hot, it was nothing compared to this. He backed her up and then kicked the door shut. Once he had her against the wall, he simply devoured her.

Aubrey thought she heard herself whimper, but she was too caught up in the sensations. His hands were no longer on her face—they were moving, touching her, exploring her as his body pressed in so close she could feel his heart beat.

When his lips left hers, Aubrey drew in a breath and let it out slowly. The things Hugh was doing to her with his hands and his lips had her moving restlessly against him. With her hands still anchored in his hair, she whispered, "I thought you were mad at me."

Hugh nipped at her collarbone and shook his head. "No. Not you," he said breathlessly, seemingly unwilling to let his mouth leave her skin. "Me."

He was mad at himself? For what? But before she could let that thought take hold, his mouth was back against hers. And then she couldn't think at all. Only feel.

Shamelessly she rubbed against him, needing more, wanting more. His erection pressed up against her belly and although Aubrey wouldn't have minded staying locked like this forever, she knew it would only get better if they left the entryway. Trying her best to convey what she was feeling without breaking their kiss, she ran one foot along the back of his leg and almost cried out when Hugh rocked against her.

"Hugh...please," she panted, moving her lips from his briefly.

She didn't need to say anything more. His hands immediately traveled down her back and cupped her bottom, gently squeezing before he lifted her. Aubrey wrapped her legs around his waist and sighed with relief.

This was really happening.

Hugh was really here. With her.

He swiftly carried her across the room, gently placing her down on the bed and immediately following her down. But he wasn't kissing her. His hands weren't moving. Instead, he was looking at her—really looking at her.

"My God, you are so beautiful," he said, his voice a husky whisper. Aubrey felt herself blush under his gaze. "I didn't plan this. I didn't intend to come here and...and..."

"Pounce?" she said softly, a slow smile crossing her face. Relief flooded her when he smiled too.

"Exactly. I swore I'd go slow. I promised myself I'd have some self-control and take the time for us to get to know each other."

"Hugh?"

"Hmm?"

"Stop talking." Her arms wound around him to pull him down closer. "There are many ways to get to know one another," she said, leaning up to trail kisses along his jaw before she gently bit down on his earlobe. "And I think what we're doing now is a great way to start."

Hugh went completely still and Aubrey felt a moment

of panic. Maybe she was being too forward? Maybe he didn't like it when she took control? Maybe...

That intense gaze was back, and it took every ounce of control she possessed to not move when all she wanted to do was feel him everywhere. Now.

"I need to know," he began, one hand trailing up to gently skim across her cheek, "that you're sure. I don't want to rush you. I don't want you to have any regrets that I came here and...pounced."

She smiled, knowing she would never forget this moment. This man, who was confident in every aspect of his world, suddenly seemed a little uncertain. A little vulnerable.

Slowly, Aubrey shifted and let one of her hands mimic his, skimming down the side of his face. She loved the scratchiness of his skin as she cupped his cheek. "Hugh Shaughnessy, I knew as soon as I saw you in your office that this was where I wanted to be."

"It wasn't that long ago," he said, still giving her time to think about her actions. Time to change her mind.

"Sometimes time doesn't matter. Sometimes you have to just go with what feels right." She sighed happily. "And this? This feels right."

Relief seemed to wash over his features.

"I don't want you to leave," she said, her voice a little stronger than it had been moments ago. "And I don't want you to slow down."

A sexy smile crossed his face. "Sometimes slow is a good thing, sweetheart."

She couldn't help but smile back. "Oh, absolutely. But sometimes," she said slowly, rocking up into him, "things are too good to take slow."

Hugh leaned forward and ran his tongue along the slender column of her throat. "Maybe I just want to take my time and savor you. Every. Inch. Of. You."

Oh my. Gently, Aubrey placed her hands on Hugh's shoulders and put some space between them. "That's a lot to consider. But maybe this will help." Then she crossed her arms in front of herself and pulled her tank top over her head, revealing her black lace bra. The shirt went flying as she relaxed back against the mattress, inwardly smiling at the look of naked desire on Hugh's face as he took in the sight of her.

"You win," he said.

When Hugh opened his eyes later on, the room was dark. He was curious about the time but didn't have the energy to lift his head from the pillow. How it was possible to be so completely exhausted and exhilarated at the same time, he wasn't sure, but it was exactly how he felt. Hell, if Aubrey rolled over and told him she wanted him again, he'd be completely on board.

Damn. The woman had simply blown his mind. While he knew he'd had great sex before, what he'd just experienced with Aubrey—twice—was completely different. There was something about…everything. Everything about her—the way she looked, the way she talked, the way she gave herself so completely to him— made Hugh's chest tighten.

It's too soon.

It wasn't the first time the thought had entered his mind. If he were honest, he'd admit he wanted Aubrey from the moment he saw her—thong viewing aside.

He fought it, telling himself it was too soon—it was impossible to be feeling this strongly for a woman he'd just met. And yet...here they were. And they were physically compatible almost to the point of spontaneously combusting.

He was already getting hard again just thinking about it.

In his arms, Aubrey started to stir. She stretched, her bare bottom brushing up against him. The arm he'd banded around her waist tightened as he pulled her closer, loving the feel of her. Unable to help himself, he placed a gentle kiss on her temple, wishing she'd wake up.

Sighing, Hugh forced himself to be patient. Besides, there were a lot of things racing through his mind, mainly about the mystery that was Aubrey. In the short time they'd known one another, he knew she was smart, articulate, and creative. He knew she had a complicated relationship with her parents and never willingly talked about them.

He wanted to know why. He wanted to know about her childhood, where she grew up, what her dreams were. He wanted... Hugh stopped and mentally cursed. He wanted it all.

Shit.

Hugh wasn't an expert on these things, but even he knew when something was more than a fling. This wasn't about sex or getting Aubrey out of his system.

He was falling in love.

He could argue it was too soon until he was blue in the face, but it didn't change a thing. He wanted to take Aubrey home to meet his family, and he couldn't wait to show her all of his resorts. Hell, he wanted to show her his world. All of it.

He wanted them to be together.

"Hugh?" Aubrey whispered, turning around in his arms so they were face-to-face.

He placed a soft kiss on her forehead, her eyelids, and the tip of her nose before landing on her lips. It was one of those lazy, drugging kisses and they both sank into it. Hugh pulled back first. "Hey, you," he said softly.

"Hi," she said with a sigh. "Sorry I fell asleep."

"Nothing to be sorry for. Are you hungry?"

"Mmm… I think I am."

"Do you want to go down to one of the restaurants or would you like to order in?"

"In." She stretched, causing her entire body to rub against his. "Definitely in." Aubrey shimmied a little until her face was level with Hugh's chest. She rained tiny kisses along his collarbone and pecs, and her tongue traced lazy circles around his nipple.

It could have been a groan, it could have been a growl. Whatever it was, all Hugh knew was he never wanted Aubrey to stop. His hand anchored itself into her glorious mane of blond hair. He whispered her name as he sighed with pleasure. "You're killing me."

"Well, I think it's only fair. You made me feel like that…multiple times."

He chuckled. "Sweetheart, if you don't stop, dinner will be a thing of the past. The next opportunity you'll have for a meal will be breakfast."

Aubrey's actions slowed slightly before she pulled back and looked at him. "You can think of food at a time like this?" she teased.

The twinkle in her eyes was quickly becoming addictive. Tucking a finger under her chin before letting his hand skim across her cheek, he returned her smile. "Maybe I'm just making sure we both have enough energy to get us through round two."

"Round two?" she repeated. "I thought we had that already."

Hugh shook his head. "Oh no. That was just the beginning. We have a long night ahead of us. Now we've napped a bit and we'll have something to eat."

Aubrey looked at him as her smile grew. "I really like the way you think, Shaughnessy."

"As much as I hate to move, let me get up and call in an order for us. What would you like?"

"Whatever you're having will be fine."

Hugh sat up. "Are you sure? You're not in the mood for anything in particular?"

"I'm learning you have excellent taste in food, and after last night's fried chicken, I'm willing to bet that whatever you order, I'm going to love it."

In his mind, Hugh knew what day of the week it was and what he normally ate. But suddenly, it wasn't what he wanted.

He'd taken a big leap of faith today—he'd broken one of the main rules he lived his life by. Maybe it wouldn't be a bad thing to go a little rogue one more time.

"What about pizza?" he asked with just a hint of hesitation.

"Ooo...can we eat it in bed? I've always wanted to just be a little decadent and eat pizza in bed." She let out a feminine giggle, covering her mouth with her hand before she went into a full-blown laugh. "Oh gosh! I'm sorry. How ridiculous did that sound? I mean, how is pizza in bed decadent?" And then she laughed again.

Her laughter was infectious and Hugh found himself hugging her to him as they both laughed uncontrollably. "It feels good to laugh with you," he said. Looking over his shoulder, he saw the clock on the bedside table read nine-fifteen. "Let me call in our order so we can eat." Releasing her, Hugh picked up the hotel phone and then looked over at Aubrey. "Any special topping requests?"

She shook her head. "I'm good with whatever you're having."

Hugh made the call but watched as Aubrey rose from the bed and walked across the room to get a robe from her closet. It was a shame she wanted to cover up. He was all for the decadent pizza-in-bed option—especially if it involved Aubrey naked. Once he placed their order with the kitchen, he rose and picked his pants up from the floor, pulling them on.

Slowly, he made his way across the room to where Aubrey was looking out on the small balcony with a view of one of the tropical gardens. Stepping in close, Hugh wrapped his arms around her from behind. "You okay?"

"I am," she said and leaned back into him. "How long until the pizza gets here?"

"Thirty minutes. The chef is making it special for us so it takes a little longer."

She looked over her shoulder at him. "I would have been fine ordering from a local pizza place. You didn't need to make the chef go crazy. I don't want to interrupt his time," she said with just a hint of sass.

"Okay, I completely deserve that one," he conceded.

"Yes, you do," she said seriously, turning to face him. "I hate to bring up a topic that has the potential to ruin this night but—"

Hugh placed a finger over her lips. "I'm sorry. I was a complete jackass earlier and I know it."

"Why? I just don't understand."

Lying to her or making excuses wasn't an option. "I was jealous."

Aubrey's eyes went wide with disbelief. "Jealous? Of what?"

"Riley."

She rolled her eyes. "Are you serious? That's what put you in a mood?"

"The fact that you didn't show up at my office started the whole thing. I was really looking forward to seeing you and…" He stopped and touched her cheek, then ran the pad of his thumb over her lips. "And kissing you again. I was thinking about it all day; it's what got me through my morning. When you didn't call and didn't show up, at first I thought something was wrong. I was heading to your room when I found you by the pool with Riley."

"Do you really think I'm the kind of woman who'd kiss you one night and then go after your brother the next day?"

"He's one of the biggest rock stars in the world."

"And I had no idea who he was!" she cried.

"That was last night," he replied reasonably. "Don't tell me you didn't come back here and do a Google search on him."

"I came back here and thought about you."

Hugh studied her face and knew she wasn't lying.

Slowly, deliberately, he pulled her in close and rested his forehead against hers. "And what were you thinking?"

Aubrey purred. "I was wishing you had come up here with me and we'd spent the night making love."

In a flash, Hugh scooped her up in his arms and strode back over to the bed. He dropped her down and reached for the sash on her robe.

"Hugh!" she cried. "What about dinner?"

"Don't worry," he said with a wink, "I promise we'll be done before it arrives."

———

The pizza was gone.

Most of the blankets were on the floor.

And Aubrey was beyond content.

Hugh's hand was tracing lazy circles on her shoulder while her head rested on his chest. Yeah, life was good. Maybe even perfect. She sighed softly and placed a kiss on his chest.

"Are you full?" he asked. "Should we order dessert?"

She shook her head. "I have everything I need right here."

They stayed like that in companionable silence for several long moments before Hugh spoke. "Can I ask you something?" Aubrey raised her head and nodded. "Do you need to rush back home after we get done at Hilton Head?"

She looked at him oddly and shook her head again. "No. Why?"

"What about your family? Do you need to check in with them? Or check on your place and pick up the mail?"

Aubrey pulled out of his arms and sat up beside him, pulling the sheet up to cover herself. "Everything is taken care of and I don't need to check in with anyone. What's this all about, Hugh?"

Sitting up straight, Hugh propped himself up on some pillows and raked a hand through his hair while he searched for the right words. "I guess I'm just wondering about your life. You've heard about my family and my business and you've met one of my brothers, but I don't know about yours."

Her eyes went a little wide. "That's what you want to talk about right now? Families?"

"I don't know. Maybe. Like I said, I'm curious about you—your life, what you like or don't like, your hobbies…"

Aubrey ran a hand through her hair and let out a sigh. "But…now?"

He shrugged. "I don't see why not."

"It's kind of weird for post-sex conversation."

"Is there a normal kind of post-sex conversation?" he asked with a smirk. "Are there rules?"

She rolled her eyes at him. "No. It's just…okay, maybe there is. Normally, post-sex talk is 'Was it good for you?' or 'Hey, do you want to do it again?'"

"And was it? Do you?" he teased and then laughed when she playfully smacked his arm.

"Now you're just making fun of me," she said with a pout as she reclined against her own pillows.

Hugh leaned over and placed a kiss on her forehead. "I'm not. I promise. I just want to get to know you."

This time her sigh was a bit louder. "Okay. Fine. What do you want to know?" She wasn't deliberately trying to be difficult, but there were so many other things she'd rather be doing than answering questions about her life.

Obviously her tone and lack of enthusiasm weren't enough to deter Hugh. He placed an arm around her and tucked her in close to his side. "Tell me about your family," he said softly.

"I'm an only child and my parents divorced when I was eighteen. They waited until the day after my high school graduation to tell me."

"Wow. That had to come as quite a shock."

She shrugged. "Not really. It was almost a relief. They never got along, barely spoke most of the time. Although why they felt the need to wait until that point in time, I'll never understand."

"I think a lot of people do that. They want to wait until their kids are grown. Maybe they felt you'd be able to handle it better."

"Maybe. I don't know. Honestly, I wish they had talked about it more, because I would have told them to give it up years ago."

He kissed the top of her head. "I'm sorry."

"Yeah, well… It happens. I'm not the only kid whose parents divorced."

"Are you close with them?"

"Who? My parents? Um…no." When Hugh just stared at her, Aubrey knew she'd have to elaborate. "They were never the warm, fuzzy type. Not nurturers in any capacity. Basically, I'm a disappointment to them. Never measured up to their expectations." It was impossible to hide the hurt and bitterness, but she hoped Hugh would take the hint that this was a sore subject.

"Where did you go to college?"

"Meredith. All-girl school." She looked at him and couldn't help but laugh at the shocked look on his face. "It wasn't so bad. It was local and I had a lot of friends there. I studied business and communications." Then she shrugged. "And I graduated."

"Any pets?"

She smiled sadly. "I had a dog once."

"What kind?"

"A yellow Lab." She sighed. "We didn't keep him very long. My mother was allergic. I always wanted another one but…it just never happened."

"What was his name?"

"Promise not to laugh."

He crossed his fingers over his heart.

"Abercrombie." She could tell he was trying very hard to stay serious.

"May I ask how you arrived at that name?"

"Honestly, I don't remember." She smiled at the image of her little puppy in her mind. "It just seemed to fit." Then she shrugged. "He was from a litter of ten and I wanted him and two others, but my parents put their foot down."

"Three puppies? Why would you do that to yourself?"

"One in each color—yellow, chocolate, and black. I'd have the complete set."

"Okay then." He shifted to get more comfortable. "Hobbies?"

Was he serious? Didn't he realize this was the most unromantic way to recover from hours of making love? "Shopping."

"For shoes, no doubt," he teased. "Seriously, what

do you enjoy doing that doesn't involve the use of your MasterCard?"

"I enjoy swimming and tennis. I read an average of three books a week, and if I go to the movies, I want to laugh. Nothing serious. No dramas. No action flicks."

"You mentioned dancing the other day. Do you still do it from time to time?"

She shook her head.

Hugh sat silently for a moment, resting his head on top of hers. Aubrey hoped the interview portion of the evening was over. She was just as curious about him as he was about her, but this wasn't the time to get into it. She imagined long talks over dinners or on their drive up to Hilton Head. Right now she wouldn't mind simply going to sleep.

Out of the corner of her eye, she looked up at him and yawned. Loudly. And hoped he'd take the hint.

"One more," he said softly. Reaching out, he tugged the sheet down a bit and traced the scar near her heart. "Tell me about this."

He spoke so quietly, his touch so soft and gentle that for the first time in her life, she didn't mind talking about it.

"I had cancer as a teen."

To his credit, Hugh didn't speak. There were no obligatory apologies or gasps of shock. He simply held her, his head still resting on hers, waiting for her to share her story.

"I had been training in ballet since I was three. My parents were obsessive about it and it was the only time they really took an interest in me. Don't get me wrong, I enjoyed it and I was good at it. At least, that's what all my instructors told me." She paused and did her best to push the bitterness aside.

"When I was twelve, I began to struggle. I couldn't keep up. I was so tired, and there were times I would barely make it through my classes and practices. My parents accused me of being lazy, of not wanting it enough. My teachers would say the same thing. I began to think I was crazy. I mean… I was young, I was healthy, and—to my knowledge—nothing had changed."

She waited a minute to see if he'd comment, but he didn't. His hand was softly skimming up and down her arm and it felt…soothing. Comforting.

"There was a big recital coming up and there were going to be scouts there for several large ballet companies. My parents kept harping on me about the importance of being perfect for the show. When I told them I was doing my best and reminded them I was tired and didn't feel quite like myself, they said I was trying to sabotage my career. I was *twelve*!" she cried with emotion. "I was a child and they were trying to make me plan my entire life at that point!"

Clearing her voice, she snuggled a little closer to Hugh. "Two days before the recital, I collapsed at rehearsal. Completely passed out. I was rushed by ambulance to the hospital and I remember hearing the doctors and nurses commenting that I was probably anorexic because I was so thin. It was a miracle one of the ER doctors on call that day happened to be familiar with childhood cancers. They ran bloodwork and did all kinds of tests, then they sat me and my parents down and said they were checking for leukemia." She wiped away a stray tear, still remembering how numb she'd felt at hearing those words for the first time. But she refused to cry. Crying meant weakness. Another gift, compliments of her mother and father. "My parents never even looked at me. They sat there in silence for what seemed like forever, and suddenly my mother asked if it would still be all right for me to dance in the recital."

Hugh stiffened beside her.

"They didn't get it. They refused to understand the magnitude of what was happening. Once the diagnosis was confirmed, things happened so fast. I was in the hospital for weeks at a time and when I was home, I was completely isolated. I had private tutors and nurses who came in to take care of me." She shook her head. "I wasn't allowed to go back to school—even when the doctors said it was okay. It was as if they were afraid I'd contaminate the place."

"Maybe they were worried the germs would harm you," he said carefully.

"No. They told me no one would want me at school. That the other students shouldn't have to worry about their health." In her mind, Aubrey could still hear the disdain in their voices. "I reminded them no one can *catch* cancer, but they'd just went on with their business as if I hadn't said a word. Then they left me in the care of those nurses and tutors while they went to Paris because they needed a break. Their words."

A muttered curse under his breath was Hugh's only response.

"It took three years for me to go into remission. The day we received the news, my mother called my ballet instructor and asked her to start working with me again. I was really excited about the possibility—I'd

finally be allowed to socialize again and do something
I enjoyed."

"But…"

She gave a mirthless laugh. "By then, my body had
started to change. The years away from the daily rou-
tines and exercises and practices left me out of shape.
I no longer had the body of a dancer, and we were told
it was too late for me to go back. My career as a dancer
was over." Her voice was completely devoid of emotion. "They never forgave me."

Then she waited. It wasn't often that Aubrey shared
this much information about her life—it was too painful.
When she did, she would receive pity, condolences, and
maybe a bit of outrage on her behalf. She appreciated
the effort, but it didn't do much to help heal what was
broken inside of her.

Slowly, Hugh laid her back down. He leaned over
and kissed her softly on the lips, then traveled farther down to her throat and placed a kiss right on
her port scar.

At his gentle touch, Aubrey let her tears fall freely.
And Hugh was there to wipe them away.

—⁓—

The next day Hugh stepped back into his apartment with
a huge smile on his face and a new outlook on life.

And he was whistling.

He took his shower, put on fresh clothes, and sat
down at the dining room table with his tablet to go
over his schedule for the day. It was their last day in
Florida—they were scheduled to drive out in the morning for Hilton Head.

It was barely eight thirty and Hugh felt as if the day was already dragging. He and Aubrey had slept for only a few hours and when his alarm went off at six, the plan had been to order breakfast.

They'd made love instead.

The next time he'd looked at the clock, his OCD had refused to let him linger any longer, no matter how big of a temptation Aubrey was. He'd kissed her good-bye and promised to see her for lunch.

He looked at his watch again and frowned. Damn day was going to last forever.

The plan for the day wasn't particularly full. This resort had one of the best management staffs out of all of them, so his presence here wasn't really needed. It just made him feel better to oversee things for a little while and keep everyone on their toes. He closed out of the calendar and went to the kitchen to make himself a cup of coffee. While waiting for it to brew, his mind wandered to the previous night and a slow smile crept across his face.

It wasn't just the sex fogging his brain—although it was amazing—it was all the things he'd learned about Aubrey. *Cancer*. He was still thrown by the revelation. He had a million questions he wanted to ask her, but knew it was a sensitive subject and didn't want to overwhelm her. He eyed his tablet. Maybe he'd do a little research on his own just so he could have a conversation with her and know what to ask without sounding completely ignorant.

The image of her as a young girl, going through so much without the love and support of normal parents, filled him with rage. Hugh knew he was luckier than most—his parents had always put their children first no matter what. He couldn't remember a time when they weren't encouraging all of them in whatever endeavor they were involved in. He cursed the fact it wasn't that way for Aubrey. No wonder she'd talked to her father the way she had the other night.

There was no way he was going to be able to function if he kept focusing on the negative. He needed to remember that, and be supportive of Aubrey no matter what. She'd dealt with negative and unsupportive people her entire life. All he wanted to do was take some of the hurt away.

He'd felt her tears last night—felt the moment when she finally let herself feel. He'd kissed them away and then made love to her slowly, tenderly. He'd wanted her to feel loved, cherished...like she was everything.

Because she was.

Grabbing his cup of coffee, he mentally smacked himself. "I'm practically ready to cry myself," he muttered.

Walking back to the dining room table, he heard a door open and turned to see Riley coming out of his bedroom. His hair was completely disheveled and his eyes were mere slits. "Little early for you to be up, isn't it?"

Riley grunted and went to help himself to the coffee. "I had a weird dream that woke me up."

"Weird? What was it about?"

"I dreamt I was sleeping and someone—who clearly got lucky last night—came home whistling." He glared at Hugh. "Why do I get the stink eye when I whistle, but you're allowed to do it?"

Hugh grinned. "My house. My rules."

"Yeah, well…screw you."

It would have been easy to gloat, but Hugh was in too good a mood and decided to take pity on his little brother. "What time are you out of here today?"

"Anxious to get rid of me?"

"Dude, stop being so sensitive. I'm just asking about your schedule. Thought maybe we could have breakfast together before you left."

Riley looked at the clock on the wall and then his brother. "Isn't this a little late for you to still be hanging around the house? Aren't you usually in your office by now?"

"Light schedule today," Hugh said easily, sitting down. "C'mon. I'll order us some breakfast and we'll hang out until you have to go. What do you say?"

Riley looked at him suspiciously.

"What? What's the matter? Do you not remember what breakfast is because you sleep until noon most days?"

"Ha-ha. Very funny." He took a sip of his coffee. "You're being nice."

"I'm a nice guy."

"No," Riley said, coming to join him at the table. "You're being weird nice. You never skip time at the office. You're always working. Why are you suddenly so willing to play hooky this morning?"

"Are we really having this conversation? Do you want breakfast or not? Because, personally, I'm starving."

And then Riley relaxed and grinned knowingly. "I bet you are." He took a sip of his coffee. "So I take it things went well with Aubrey and she didn't kick you in the nuts or something because you were a jackass yesterday?"

"Yes, things went well and no, she didn't kick me."

Hugh felt the sappy grin coming on and there wasn't a thing he could do to stop it.

"Oh, for the love of it," Riley moaned. "You're one of those."

Hugh looked at him oddly. "One of what?"

"You're one of those guys who gets all girly and emotional and…and…whistles and sighs after sex. Damn. I thought you were a little manlier than that."

"Excuse me, there is nothing wrong with my…manliness. And I'm not getting all girly. It was a good night and…and that's it. It just made me smile."

"So…what? Now you're dating? You're sex buddies? I mean…what?"

Rather than answer, Hugh called the restaurant and ordered their breakfast. He knew waiting for his answer was killing Riley, but it was just a perk now. When he was seated again, he took a long sip of his coffee before looking at his brother.

"Seriously, dude," Riley snapped.

"Breakfast will be here in twenty minutes," Hugh said with a grin.

"Okay, fine. Be that way. Don't tell me what's going on with Aubrey, but remember this—if it weren't for me, you wouldn't have that stupid grin on your face. You'd be moping around here all frustrated and uptight, worrying about your stupid schedule."

It was on the tip of his tongue to argue, but Hugh knew he'd be lying. "Okay, fine." He relented. "You were right. You're the reason all is right with the world. Happy?"

Riley grinned. "I'm getting there." He finished off his coffee. "But seriously, things are good with the two of you? You apologized for being an ass?"

"I did." Hugh nodded.

"Good." They sat in companionable silence for a few minutes. "So...was it crazy monkey sex or boring, normal sex?"

Hugh stood up, smacking him in the head as he walked by. "None of your damn business."

With a roar of laughter, Riley got up and helped himself to another cup of coffee.

———

"Knock, knock." Aubrey peeked her head inside Hugh's office with a smile. "Is this a bad time?"

He couldn't help but smile back. "It's the perfect time. Come on in."

She stepped in and closed the door behind her, walking toward Hugh's desk. He met her halfway and immediately took her into his arms and kissed her breathless. "Oh my," she said when they broke apart. "That's quite a greeting."

"Get used to it." He took her by the hand and led her over to the sofa. "How was your morning?"

"It was good. Jacques was amazing. He was very open to my menu suggestions. He's going to work on it and we'll keep in touch via email to finalize everything. He's very sweet."

Hugh knew he was blessed with some of the finest chefs, but he'd never heard anyone describe Jacques as being sweet. He was moody, temperamental, and could be out and out indignant at times. But clearly, Aubrey knew exactly how to handle him. "I'm glad. I can't wait to hear all about it."

"How about you? Are you okay?"

He looked at her quizzically. "Yeah. Why?"

"Well, Riley left. I know the two of you don't get to spend a lot of time together and this was a really short visit. I wanted to make sure you were all right."

He leaned in and kissed her again. "I'm fine. This is how it normally goes. Out of all of us, Riley's schedule is the hardest to work with. The fact that he took the few days he had and came here was great. I think he just needed the rest more than anything. It isn't often he gets to step out of the spotlight and just chill out."

Aubrey squeezed his hand. "It's pretty awesome you can do that for him. He's lucky to have you."

"Would you mind telling him that the next time you see him? Because he seems to think we're all lucky to have *him*."

"I'm sure you all feel you're the MVP of the family at one time or another." She rested her head on his shoulder. "Not that I would know, but it would be my guess."

"You're pretty much spot-on there." He turned and simply inhaled. Damn, he even liked the way she smelled—like clean clothes and sunshine. Maybe sex did make him act a bit girly.

"So, ready for lunch?" he asked.

"I'm famished. Jacques may have been open to talking with me and sharing ideas, but he would not let me taste anything."

"He's like that. Don't take it personally."

"Oh, I didn't. I'm not normally a big breakfast person. I had some yogurt before I went over there, but I am definitely ready for something better now."

Hugh stood and helped Aubrey to her feet. "So what are you in the mood for? We can eat here or if you want we can go into town or we can…"

"Do you have the ability to special order whatever you want for lunch like you do for dinner?"

He nodded. "Of course."

She considered it for a moment. "What do you normally have?"

"Well…" Friday was normally a turkey club, but again, he wasn't going to lock her into his crazy food OCD. "You know, a sandwich. Nothing major. Why? What were you thinking?"

"Quiche."

"Quiche?"

She nodded.

"Those take a while to make, don't they?"

Again, she nodded.

"Um…sure. We can call over to Jacques and ask him to get started on it, and we'll be in there in around… what? Thirty minutes? Forty-five?"

Aubrey stepped in close to him and took his hands in hers. "Or…" she began, "we can give him the order and have it delivered to your room." She closed the distance between them and looked up innocently. "Your choice."

"You really do come up with the best ideas," Hugh replied. Reaching over to his desk, he grabbed his cell phone and quickly led Aubrey from the room. "I'll call him on the way and tell him to take his time."

Chapter 7

THEY LEFT WEST PALM BEACH EARLY SATURDAY morning and made their way up the coast to Hilton Head Island. It was the weekend, and the weather was beautiful. They found a bed-and-breakfast just outside of St. Augustine and impulsively decided to stop.

The decision had been prompted by a fairly innocent comment while they were driving. She'd mentioned her dancing schedule had left very little free time when she was growing up. Then she'd dealt with the cancer and chemo that dictated just about every part of her life. After she'd gone into remission, it was all about school and graduation, then college.

"The day we met, when I climbed out the window? That was the most impulsive thing I'd ever done." Then she laughed and smiled. "And it felt great!"

Hugh had laughed with her. They'd shared their compulsion for living fairly regimented lives and that's when it hit her—she was tired of playing it safe. Of always being cautious. She wanted to experience all the things she was too timid to try out of fear of disapproval from her parents.

With her upcoming travel schedule, Aubrey knew she had been essentially handed the opportunity of a lifetime.

When they arrived at Hilton Head, Hugh took her around and introduced her to the staff before heading to his office and his meetings. Lisa McKay was the on-site event person assigned to show Aubrey around.

"Mr. Shaughnessy sent over a packet for me to look at with all the information regarding your project," Lisa began, "so I think I'm up to speed on what you'll be doing. I want to start by giving you a tour of the resort. Feel free to ask me anything that comes to mind to help you."

"I appreciate that," Aubrey replied, already excited at the possibilities the new resort represented. "Tell me, what kind of activities do you offer here?"

"We offer some amazing pools for swimming, tennis courts, spas…"

"What about something for the people who are a little more…active?"

Lisa smiled. "Ah, the adventure seekers who really don't want to relax."

"Exactly."

"We have a nice variety of offerings right here on the property, and there are also a lot more to choose from in town. What were you thinking of?"

For a minute, Aubrey felt shy—and a little silly— about mentioning her desire to try some of those activities out for herself. But if she was ever going to break out of her rut, now was the time to do it. "I was thinking along the lines of parasailing or zip-lining. Does the resort offer either of those?"

Lisa's smile grew. "They are two of my favorite activities! And yes, we have them both. Would you like to check them out?"

"Oh…um… Well, I haven't ever tried either of them before. I just thought…maybe…"

Reaching out, Lisa placed a hand on Aubrey's arm. "Not to worry. We'll walk around and check out the property, and then we'll go down by the water and see if we can get you a lesson or two at either the zip course or with our parasailing team. How does that sound?"

Aubrey's heart did a little happy dance. "Absolutely perfect!"

Two hours later, she wasn't so sure.

Standing on a platform much higher off the ground than Aubrey had thought it would be, she looked nervously from the ground to Lisa to the operator who was getting her harness secured.

"You don't have to do it if you don't want to," Lisa said.

"No, no, no… I want to." *Maybe*, she thought. No, definitely. Aubrey felt she had to do it.

"We can do a tandem harness if you want," Lisa suggested. "It just means we do it together if it makes you feel a little more confident."

Aubrey shook her head and took a steadying breath. "Thanks, but I really need to do this on my own. I knew it would be a little intimidating, but I can do it." She looked around and felt a wave of uncertainty. "How high up are we again?"

"Seventy-five feet," the operator said, tugging on her harness to make sure it was secured.

"And…" she gulped, "how far is it to the other side?"

"This one is a straight run of twelve hundred feet," he said. "Once you hit the other platform you can either move on to the next line or you can get down. The choice is yours."

"How many lines are there?"

"We have a total of six. They're all of varying heights and offer a couple of different views. We're small compared to some of the major zip-line parks, but the guests really enjoy it." When he noticed Aubrey was still looking a little green, he placed a reassuring hand on her arm. "It goes pretty fast. You'll be at the next platform in no time and you can be on the ground not long after that."

With a nod, Aubrey slowly turned and got into position. "I can do this," she said more to herself than anyone else. "I can totally do this."

"Are you ready?" Lisa asked.

Her mouth was suddenly too dry to speak, so she nodded again and looked over at the operator. He gave her the final instructions, and before she could have another round of second thoughts, she was soaring across the line.

With her heart racing and the wind in her hair, Aubrey screamed. Quickly enough, she realized it wasn't fear she was feeling, but joy. Pure, unadulterated joy! She let out a squeal of delight and let go of the harness with one hand to feel the wind blowing by. It was the most exhilarating feeling of her life! And it was over way too soon. Her feet hit the platform and she felt the operator of the next line steadying her.

"That was amazing!" she cried. "Can I go on the next line?"

The young man chuckled. "Absolutely, miss," he said with a smile. "Step over this way and we'll get you hooked up."

When she stepped off the platform, she knew she would never forget this day or this feeling for the rest of her life.

—◠◠—

Four days later, Hugh was feeling a little insecure.

In the last week, he had thrown caution to the wind more times than he had in the last seventeen years. It wasn't bad, per se, but it was a bit unnerving. Aubrey had a way of making him forget about his schedules and his plans. She must have sensed his unease, because she had teased him about it.

At the time, he'd laughed with her, but he was starting to see a pattern develop. When they'd arrived at Hilton Head, he had a schedule and thought she did as well. Next thing he knew, she was calling him to say she was going zip-lining and parasailing.

She was doing her job, but since she was superefficient, she didn't require an eight-hour day to get it done. And in all fairness, she wasn't asking him to foot the bill for her excursions; she was just going out and trying things she had never done before.

But she was doing it all without a plan.

Whenever he'd ask her what her plan was for the morning, the afternoon, or whatever, she would shrug and say something like, "I'm waiting to see where the day takes me."

She was killing him.

Several times he had attempted to get her to schedule these excursions, so he'd know where she was and he could make sure she had the most experienced guides with her, but she had balked at the idea.

"I don't know what I'll feel like doing today," she told him with an impish grin. "I'll just see how it goes."

Yeah, she was killing him.

His staff loved her. By the end of the first day, she'd pretty much mapped out her entire plan for the launch gala, and it was magnificent. Now she was simply getting a feel for the local activities and offerings to put together packages for their VIP guests. Apparently experiencing it all for herself was part of her plan.

Again, nothing wrong with it.

Except he never knew where to find her or what she was doing.

They were scheduled to leave the island tomorrow and Hugh had yet to get an answer out of her about whether she was going to fly home as originally planned or if she wanted to spend a couple of work-free days with him.

Of course, it could be because he hadn't asked her yet.

Normally, Hugh wasn't an indecisive man, but trying to keep up with Aubrey these last few days had him feeling a little out of his element. When he finally got her alone, they were almost frantic to be together. He blushed at some of the images running through his mind—Aubrey in the shower, in his bed, on his desk…

"I'm seriously losing my mind," he muttered and looked at the clock. He was done for the day and their time together was running out. True, they could cancel her flight reservations, but then what? He was scheduled to go home and see his family. And as much as he was ready on some level to bring her home to meet them all, he wasn't sure if Aubrey was ready for that.

The only thing that made the idea of letting her go home tolerable was the fact that she only lived three hours away. Even if he went home for a couple of days, he could easily make the drive to see her in Raleigh.

There hadn't been any formal talks about where she was traveling with him next. If it were up to him, he'd take her with him on all of his stops. He could easily fit in each of the resorts within the next month and then... well, then he wouldn't have to miss her. She'd get to know him and how he worked, and he'd get to know her better. It was the perfect plan.

Reaching for the phone, he called Dorothy. She was based in California, but she was his go-to person for all of his travel and scheduling needs.

"Hey, boss!" she said cheerily when she answered the phone. "What can I do for you today?"

"I know we had me down for a certain schedule with the resorts, but..." He paused, knowing his assistant was going to think he was crazy. "But...I think we need to change things around."

Silence.

"Dotty? You there?"

"What? Oh, yes. Sorry. I just... I just thought I mis-heard you. It sounded like you wanted to change your travel plans."

"I do." It was fun to throw his unflappable assistant a curveball.

"Oh. Okay. Um...let me pull up your schedule and see what we have."

For the next twenty minutes they talked about all the possibilities and Hugh had her pencil everything in. "Let me talk to Aubrey and run this by her. As soon as I have an answer, we'll move forward. Is that all right?"

"You're the boss," she said with a nervous chuckle.

"Do you think it's too much? Is the schedule too tight?"

"No. No, that's not what I'm saying at all."

He waited for her to elaborate and when she didn't, he prompted her.

"I'm just wondering if Aubrey is going to be comfortable with all this traveling. It's all happening so soon. It…well…personally, I would have a problem packing up and being away from home for a month. But that's just me."

"So it's too much," Hugh said, feeling a little deflated.

"Hugh, I'm just stating my own opinion. You're giving her ten days at home now, so that should be plenty of time for her to prepare for the trip, but you have to remember she had a life before coming to work for you. She may have prior commitments that will hinder her ability to stay away so long. Remember to keep that in mind when you're throwing this schedule her way."

He sighed. "I'm not throwing it, Dotty. I'm going to discuss it with her and make sure she's comfortable with it." He paused. "And I don't do that. I don't…throw things at people."

"Um…boss?"

"Yeah?"

"You do. A lot. Like, all the time."

"No, I don't."

"I'm not going to split hairs with you," she said pleasantly. "You have a tendency to work something out in your head and automatically think everyone is going to be able to read your mind and fall in line with what you want. Sometimes it just doesn't happen that way."

There was no point in arguing. She was right. "Fine. I promise I won't throw this at her and I won't get angry if she cannot simply hop on board and go with it. I'm willing to be flexible."

She laughed. "I guess there's a first time for every-thing!" When Hugh would have commented, Dotty made a quick excuse and hung up.

Hugh stared at the phone for a long time, thinking about what she'd said. For years, Hugh had believed he was organized and efficient, when the reality was he was inflexible. It was as if meeting Aubrey had suddenly brought all of this behavior to light and everyone was jumping up and making sure he saw it.

Dammit.

He put the phone down and sighed. How had his entire world turned upside down in such a short amount of time? How had…?

There was only one other time in his life it had. And just the thought of it brought a stab of pain. In his mind, this kind of upheaval was a bad thing, but right now it didn't feel wrong. It was uncomfortable and a little unsettling, but it wasn't like his world was coming to an end.

He just didn't want things to spiral too much out of his control.

The light knock on the door interrupted his thoughts, and he knew by the sound that it was Aubrey. She opened the door, stepping inside with her hair windblown and her face glowing, and he began to wonder if control was completely overrated.

———

"I wish we had another week here," Aubrey said later that night over dinner. Hugh had taken her out to eat away from the resort. It was nice not to have any of the distractions of work, and as a live band played in the lounge, she secretly hoped they'd get to spend at least part of their night dancing.

"Funny you should mention that," Hugh said, quickly taking a sip of his wine. "I know you have a flight back to Raleigh tomorrow and I'm heading out to see my family, but I was wondering what you had planned. Do you need to get home right away? Or could I drive up next weekend to see you? I mean, I completely get it if you already have plans or if you're looking forward to finally having some time to yourself and relaxing without thinking about work…you know…that's fine."

Aubrey reached across the table and put her hand on top of Hugh's. "You're rambling. What's going on?"

He let out a breath and turned his hand over so he could hold hers. "I'm trying—and failing—to see what your plans are for when you go home tomorrow."

"Oh." She couldn't hide the disappointment in her voice. For a minute there, she'd thought he was going to ask her to go with him to meet his family. It was crazy, really. It was too soon for all of that, and yet she couldn't help but feel let down.

Hugh must have picked up on it, because he gently squeezed her hand. "I'm not on any kind of schedule to go home. I mentioned to my dad I'd be coming in, but I didn't give him an exact date."

Aubrey looked at him as if she doubted his story.

"Okay…I gave him an exact date, but I can change it." He looked at her and added, "We can stay for a few more days if you'd like."

It was so sweet of him to offer, and if he was doing anything other than going to see family, she would be tempted to accept his offer to stay and play a little longer. But if there was one thing she had learned about Hugh, it was how important his family was to him. She might not have firsthand experience of what that was like, but she knew enough to realize it was special and wonderful, and she didn't want to interfere with it.

Finally, she shook her head. "No. But thank you. You need to see your family. But I will take you up on your offer of coming to see me. Then maybe, you know, you could stay with me for a couple of days."

"Are you sure? Because it wouldn't be a big deal for me to call my dad and—"

"Hugh," she interrupted. "Go see your family. I don't expect you to change all your plans for me."

He chuckled at her words.

"What? What's so funny?"

"Just something Dorothy said earlier."

Behind them the band started to play an old Motown classic and Aubrey's eyes lit up. "Ooo…I love this song!" She looked toward the trio playing and then back to Hugh. "I like the bluesy, jazzy spin they put on it, don't you?"

Hugh didn't answer. Instead he stood and pulled Aubrey to her feet, leading her over to the lounge area. Gracefully, she spun into his arms as they began to sway to "Under the Boardwalk."

Aubrey sighed as the music washed over her. When was the last time she'd danced for pleasure? Sure, she'd gone to her share of events where everyone danced, but whenever she gave in and agreed to dance, it was normally with an agenda. She had to schmooze the donors and dignitaries in order to convince them to write big checks.

But this? This slow, intimate swaying? It was so good it was almost orgasmic. She heard every word being sung. Felt every note being played. And her body naturally responded to it all.

Hugh's arm banded possessively around her waist, his large hand splayed across her back while the other held her hand. They moved together as if they'd been dance partners for years. It felt so good, so perfect. One song played into the next and he never let her go. She thought it was sweet that he sometimes hummed to the music, and when he didn't, he rested his cheek against hers or kissed the shell of her ear.

She made a mental note to go through her music collection when she got home because she was going to want to do this again — when they were alone.

The band announced one final song before taking a break and Aubrey felt a pang of disappointment. She wasn't ready for this to end. When the song ended, they'd stop dancing. Then soon they'd leave the restaurant. It was getting late and she knew that soon the night would be over and she'd be heading for the airport.

Alone.

Pushing that depressing thought aside, she was just settling into the new song when suddenly Hugh started to sing it softly in her ear. His voice was deep and gravelly and mesmerizing as he sang of her being his completely.

Oh my.

They swayed together and Aubrey knew she was going to be adding the Shirelles to her music collection. She wanted to always remember this moment and Hugh singing "Will You Still Love Me Tomorrow."

As he spun her around one last time, Aubrey knew her answer.

Yes.

—w—

Hugh pulled into his father's driveway and parked.

Home.

So many emotions coursed through him that he took a few minutes to get himself under control. This was his childhood home. He'd go inside and it would be like stepping back in time. He'd sleep in the same bed he had for the first half of his life, and he'd eat his meals at the same table he and his siblings always had. It was comforting. It was soothing.

It was exactly the way it should be.

No changes.

No surprises.

Taking a deep breath, he climbed from the car and stretched. He was used to the four-hour drive, but this time he did it in one straight run, no stopping. His original plan had been to take Aubrey to the airport himself, but she had argued that it would be out of his way, and she didn't want to say good-bye while sitting in the car at the curb while people rushed by all around them. She wanted their good-bye to be private.

And it had been. After they had gotten home from dinner the previous evening, they had made love well into the night. She was like a drug to him—he craved her. When they had exhausted themselves, they had fallen asleep in each other's arms.

And Hugh had never slept better.

That morning, they'd shared breakfast in bed and

he'd helped her pack. In his head, he'd kept up a running dialogue where he would ask her to stay. Ask her to come home with him and meet his family. At one point, he'd even made a joke about it.

"Come on…why go home when you can come and meet my family? We can share my twin bed."

Aubrey laughed. "Only if the Spider-Man sheets are still there too."

"Please, I'm more sophisticated than that. They're Ninja Turtle sheets, and they're still wildly popular."

She laughed harder. "The sheets?"

He rolled his eyes dramatically. "No…the turtles." He shook his head. "Such a girl."

And that had been it. He hadn't said any more because he hadn't wanted to come off as desperate and needy. Even though it was exactly how he felt. And Hugh wasn't sure what to do with that. This was a completely new sensation—he was used to women chasing after him, and even though he'd chased a girl or two in his life, it had never been like this.

Watching Aubrey climb into the cab that morning had been harder than he'd expected. She'd kissed him softly and promised she'd see him soon, yet he'd stood there like a sap, watching the cab until it was completely out of sight.

"I need to get a grip," he mumbled, turning to open the trunk so he could get his luggage. This trip home was exactly what he needed. A peaceful time to visit with his family—to get caught up on their lives and hang out in the one place Hugh could count on to never change.

Slamming the trunk closed, he stopped and looked at the house. The exterior had been painted over the years, but it was always white with red shutters. His mother had loved the combination and it really did look nice. The shrubs were in need of trimming but he supposed it went with the territory. His father wasn't getting any younger, and with a full-time job and a budding social life, Hugh imagined trimming bushes wasn't the way his dad wanted to spend his free time. He made a mental note to do some yard work while he was here.

Walking up the steps to the porch, Hugh felt some of the tension finally leave his body. It was always like this when he came home. With a smile, he opened the front door and was about to call out when he froze. "What the hell?"

"Oh... Hugh!" Ian Shaughnessy said. "I wasn't expecting you until dinnertime."

Hugh stood there speechless. His father was sitting—rather closely—on the sofa with a woman. His gaze narrowed and he realized it was Martha Tate—Zoe's boss and resident interior decorator. And by the looks of all the fabric swatches and books open on the coffee table, she was looking to decorate *this* interior!

"Oh, hey, Hugh," Martha said with a big smile. "It's good to see you!"

He grunted some sort of response, but his attention immediately went back to his father. "What's going on?"

Ian walked over and hugged him, choosing to ignore his question. "Why didn't you call and let me know you were getting in earlier? Did you call your brothers? I'm guessing they'll all be here for dinner."

"Dad, I don't really care about dinner at the moment. What's going on here? What's Martha doing here?" He dropped his suitcase down beside him but didn't move any farther into the room.

A nervous smile crossed Ian's face. "Well…um… Martha is here to help me with some…uh…"

"Oh, for crying out loud, Ian Shaughnessy, I'm here to help spruce this place up!" Martha said, coming to her feet. "It's a beautiful home, but it's stuck in a time warp. We're going to freshen everything up!" She smiled at Hugh.

Looking at his father and doing his best to ignore everything Martha had just said, Hugh frowned, completely at a loss for words.

Ian turned to Martha. "How about I give you a call next week?"

With a wink, Martha began collecting her things. "No problem, Ian." Once she was done, she made her way to the door, smiling at them both. "I hope y'all have a nice visit."

Hugh waited until the door was closed and he heard Martha's car start before speaking. "You're freshening everything up? What does that mean?"

Ian chuckled and walked back into the living room and sat down. "I didn't raise any idiots, Hugh, so stop pretending to be one. You know exactly what it means."

A growl of frustration came from Hugh as he followed his father to the sofa and sat down beside him. "Fine. I know what it means. I guess my question is… why? Why are you changing anything? This house is fine just the way it is."

"No, Son, it's not. Things are worn and faded, and it's time to do something about it."

Hugh shook his head. "I don't think so. And I'll bet when Quinn and Aidan come here tonight, they'll agree with me."

"They're all on board with it. Aidan's going to replace the cabinets in the kitchen for me and Quinn's going to help with the painting." He laughed. "I'm sure there's going to be a lot of fighting over who's in control. I'll probably end up breaking up quite a few scuffles."

For a moment, Hugh was too stunned to speak. His brothers were all for this? "I…I don't understand how this happened. Last time I was home, everything was good. No one was talking about redecorating or ripping out the kitchen. Mom loved—"

Holding up a hand, Ian stopped him. "Your mother loved this house and everything in it, Hugh. But you cannot honestly believe if she were still here she wouldn't have changed things up over the years. Do you remember how many times we changed the color of this room alone when you kids were little?"

He hadn't until just now. Then he couldn't help but laugh. "She kept going with darker colors because the twins kept drawing on the wall."

Ian nodded. "Exactly. So many times while you kids were growing up, your mom wanted to do things with the house, but we couldn't afford it. And then after she was gone, I didn't want to change anything. I felt like I had to keep it all the same for her." He sighed. "It wasn't until Zoe started coming around and helped Darcy redecorate her room that I realized what a rut we were in."

Annoyance at Zoe instantly flashed through Hugh's mind, but he quickly realized it wasn't her fault. It was what she did for a living and it came to her as naturally as breathing. He just wished she hadn't been so good at her job.

"I can hear you thinking from here, Hugh. I know you enjoy coming home and having everything in its place. I know it's how you live your life—you're regimented and you don't like surprises. Unfortunately, life is full of surprises. And believe it or not, not all of them are bad."

Hugh sighed and threw his head back against the sofa. "I know, Dad. I'm not stupid. I just don't believe in fixing what isn't broke."

Ian laughed. "Now you sound like an old man. That's my job."

Looking at his dad, he laughed with him. "You'll have to get used to sharing it then."

"You're far too young to be this set in your ways. You travel all over the world for your business and even though I've never seen most of them, you can't tell me each and every one of your resorts are all the same. It's not possible."

"No, they're not. But my apartments all are."

The laughter stopped. "You could do anything you want with those spaces. Why wouldn't you take advantage of that?"

He shrugged. "I like what I have. It's comfortable and familiar and no matter where I am, it always feels like home. My home. I know some people think it's odd…"

"Probably more than some—"

"But," Hugh interrupted, "it's the way I want it. Not everyone wants a dozen different homes that are all…different."

"Then you haven't met most women," Ian said.

"Mom wasn't like that. She knew what she liked and stuck with it. I must get it from her."

Wordlessly, Ian got up and went to the kitchen.

Hugh watched him leave, not sure if he was supposed to follow. Two minutes later he was back, beers in hand. He handed one to Hugh and opened the other for himself.

"When your mother and I got married, we knew we wanted kids right away. Luckily, she got pregnant immediately. We lived in a tiny, one-bedroom apartment close to the beach at the time. When Aidan was born, we were so head over heels at being parents, we knew we didn't want to wait too long to have another baby."

"Dad," Hugh said, "what does this have to do with redecorating?"

"Just listen," Ian said. "Anyway, we got pregnant with you right away, and having two babies in the house was exhausting. And expensive." He shook his head. "We said two was enough. We bought this house. It was more than we could really afford, but your mother was a whiz with budgeting and if we were really strict, we could make it work."

"Why didn't you buy a smaller house?"

"Because your mom fell in love with this one. It was bigger than what we needed, but she was adamant that it was perfect for us. It needed a lot of work, but we wanted to tackle those projects together."

Hugh looked around the room. "And you did. I always remember the two of you working around here. You loved it. Mom would sew curtains, you painted… You made a great team."

"No, we made each other crazy."

"What? How is that possible?"

"We never argued in front of you kids, but we always

wanted to do more around here. We simply couldn't afford it. I didn't want to spend my weekends painting or fixing the roof, and your mother was exhausted from chasing after kids all day. We were always living paycheck to paycheck. Things didn't stay the same because we wanted them to, they stayed that way because they had to. Big difference."

"Okay, I can understand that. I do. But…there's just something comforting about the familiarity. It's not a bad thing."

"You're right, it's not. But it should be the people in your life and the feelings they invoke that make you happy, not a structure. You think it's the house that gives you a sense of security, but it's not. It's the feelings that come with being here. You can't let changes like this throw you for a loop." He patted Hugh on the knee. "Wait until you meet a woman and fall in love. You'll see how often she'll want to change the wall color or the drapes or the comforter on your bed. Hell, your mom used to want to change everything with each season. I had to put my foot down on that one."

Why hadn't Hugh remembered that? "I can't believe that's really a thing."

"Well, it is. Zoe tells me it doesn't have to be such a big transition, but I don't believe her."

"I bet she's making Aidan crazy with it," he said with a grin.

"Yeah, but he's loving every minute." Ian paused. "Which brings us to you. It's been a while since you mentioned seeing anyone."

Crap. He'd expected this conversation, but his feelings for Aubrey were so new he feared his father would see right through him if he tried to downplay them. Shifting uncomfortably in his seat, he took a long pull of his beer and frowned when his father started to chuckle. "What? What's so funny?"

"On anyone else, the silence wouldn't mean anything. But with you, I can tell you're trying not to tell me something. So? Out with it. Who is she?"

"How do you do that? How do you know what I'm thinking?"

Ian shrugged. "I'm your father. It's my job."

Hugh sighed. "Yeah, well… You don't have to be so good at it all the time." He couldn't help but smile at his father, who was still watching him expectantly. "Okay. Fine. I met someone."

"You don't sound happy about it."

"I am. I just… I wasn't expecting her."

"Ah…"

"What? What does 'ah' mean?"

"It means after everything we just talked about, I can see why you're a little out of sorts. So tell me, how did the two of you meet?"

Hugh relayed the whole story—from finding Aubrey climbing through his office window to watching her drive away this morning—staring at the beer in his hand the entire time.

"And she lives here in North Carolina?"

Hugh nodded.

"And you didn't bring her home with you?"

Hugh gave him a wry look. "Do you see her anywhere?"

"Careful. You're not so old I won't smack you for being a smart-ass." His words were firm but his eyes twinkled with amusement.

"Sorry. I thought... I just... It's going so fast and I know she had a life before I met her. Hell, she had a fiancé before I met her."

"Yeah, but she explained all of that to you. I don't particularly understand it." He shrugged. "You kids today... You don't get married for the right reasons. Back when I met your mother, people married for love. End of story."

"You don't really believe that, do you? People have been getting married for convenience for centuries. It's great that you and Mom married for love, but it doesn't mean everyone did."

"Maybe. The important thing is she didn't marry the guy. That tells me she's got integrity. She may have gotten a little off-track for a while, but she came to her senses. You can't hold it against her."

"She's impulsive," Hugh stated quickly. "It was an impulsive decision to marry that guy, and it was an impulsive decision to run away. She jumped at the job opportunity Bill presented to her and since coming to work for me, she's been trying new things. Scary things." He raked a hand through his hair and almost growled. "She went parasailing the other day, for Pete's sake!"

Ian's loud bark of laughter filled the room.

"Now what's so funny?" Hugh demanded.

"You."

"I don't follow..."

"I'll admit Aubrey seems a little impulsive, but you make it sound like a crime. It's not. Some people just lead with their heart."

"Yeah, well, it wouldn't kill her to slow down and

think things through a little." He snorted with disgust. "Parasailing. Pfft. People get hurt doing those things. If she had researched it and looked at the statistics and—"

"Oh, for crying out loud," Ian said and stood. "Did she get hurt?"

"Well…no."

"Did she have a good time?"

"I think so. She was smiling when she told me about it."

"Then what's the problem, Hugh? She didn't make you do it."

Hugh sighed loudly with frustration. "She could have gotten hurt," he blurted out. "The lines could have gotten tangled, there could have been a strong wind. The driver of the boat could have been inexperienced. Take your pick. I don't see the need to rush in and take risks that could get you hurt."

Ian walked up to Hugh and slapped him upside the head, grinning. "Bet you didn't plan on that, did you?"

"Ow! What was that for?"

"You can get hurt anywhere, Hugh."

"Yeah, but—"

Ian held up a hand and cut him off. "I know where this is coming from. I do. But you can't base everything in your life on what happened to your mother." His voice caught on the last word. "She'd made that trip to the pharmacy hundreds of times without one thing happening. It was an accident."

Ian's eyes held all the sadness Hugh felt in his heart. "But if you can prevent…"

"You can't. People get hurt in their own homes. They get hurt doing the things they do every single day. There's no rhyme or reason. And if you spend your entire life trying to avoid situations where you might get hurt, then you're missing out. Is that really what you want?"

Hugh couldn't speak. His throat felt tight and his eyes stung with unshed tears. He simply shook his head.

"I can guarantee you, your mother would not want her legacy to be that you were afraid to live your life. She was a woman who enjoyed life and made the most out of every minute. You kids meant the world to her and she took joy in everything you did." He squeezed Hugh's shoulder. "Think about it."

Aubrey was curled up in bed with the TV remote, flipping through the channels, trying to find something to watch. Honestly, with hundreds of channels, it shouldn't be this hard, she thought.

It was late for her. The eleven o'clock news was over and all of the late-night talk shows were starting up. It had been so long since she'd watched any of them, she wasn't sure which channel to go to or what she'd find.

"Maybe I should read," she muttered, looking around for her Kindle. She was a one-click addict—there had to be something on there to pique her interest. Shutting off the TV and reaching for the nightstand drawer, she let out a squeak of surprise when the phone rang. A slow smile crept across her face when she saw Hugh's name on the screen.

"Hey," she said softly, relaxing back onto her pillows.

"I didn't wake you, did I?" Hugh asked.

"Nope. I was just sitting here trying to figure out

what to do with myself. It was a toss-up between late-night TV and a book."

"Book. Always go for the book. You'll sleep better."

She chuckled. "I'm not too sure about that. I found I sleep better when you're next to me. And we didn't read a single word."

He groaned. "You're killing me."

"Okay, sorry," she said. "So tell me how your first day at home was. Did you get to have dinner with everyone?"

"Oh…yeah," he said sourly, and Aubrey knew something was up.

"Out with it, Shaughnessy. What's going on?"

He told her about his father's plans for the house and why he wasn't particularly thrilled about it. "What about your brothers? Do they feel the same?"

"Hell no. They spent a good portion of the night telling me why I was wrong."

She could hear the pout in his voice and her heart went out to him. "I'm so sorry. What can I do? Do you want to come here for a few days?"

"I do…but if I leave it's just going to give them more ammunition."

"You're entitled to feel the way you feel, Hugh. They don't have to agree with it or even like it, but you don't have to change for them. Chances are they do things you don't like or agree with. Right?"

He sighed. "What's your point?" There was no animosity in his tone, only curiosity.

"Just because they think or do things differently than you, do you love them any less?"

"Well…no."

"So don't let this bother you. You're probably the

only one still thinking about it. Take this time to enjoy your visit with your father and your brothers. If they give you grief about it, just shake it off."

"Easier said than done. And you should know that. Weren't you on the receiving end of family grief only a week ago?"

Aubrey was quiet for a moment. "That's different, Hugh. Your brothers aren't being mean to you or belittling you for the sake of being cruel. They're probably doing it more out of good old-fashioned sibling teasing."

"You're right. I'm sorry."

It still stung. "So," she began cheerily, "what are your plans? Anything exciting?"

He outlined his plans to help his dad with the yard work, to see his brother Aidan's house, and to look at some property for a potential new resort.

"Sounds like you're going to have a lot to do."

"I suppose."

There was that tone again. "Hugh? Come on. There's something wrong. I can hear it in your voice."

He was silent for a long moment, and just when Aubrey thought she'd have to prompt him, he said, "I miss you."

Her heart melted at his words. "You just saw me this morning," she said quietly.

"I know, but this last week we've been around each other all the time. And now…now I wish you were here with me."

An idea flashed in her mind and she had to stop before she simply blurted it out. Aubrey had a feeling Hugh would agree to it, but she had to take a minute to make sure she was offering for the right reasons.

Hugh broke the silence first. "How was your flight home? Was everything all right? I got your text saying you were home but you didn't elaborate."

"There really wasn't much to say. Everything was on time, my car was parked exactly where I left it, and when I got home, my refrigerator was empty so I went food shopping. All in all, it's been a very exciting day."

He chuckled. "Sounds like it. I wish all I had to do today was food shop," he grumbled. "I'm telling you, Aubrey, I don't know if I can stay here and watch the house get torn apart. Aidan's planning on starting this weekend. Had anyone bothered to tell me this beforehand, I probably wouldn't have come home."

That was her cue. "What if I drove down to you this weekend? You could show me your hometown and we can go look at the property together. We can find someplace to stay so you won't be in the middle of the construction zone. What do you think?"

"I thought I was going to drive to you? That was the plan, wasn't it?"

She laughed because she was beginning to notice a pattern with Hugh—he did not accept change easily. "We talked about it, yes. But you have a lot going on there and it would be just as easy for me to come to you as it would be for you to come to me. This way you're not missing out on any of the things you need—or want—to do."

"I hate to ask you to do that, Aubrey. You're already traveling so much because of me and my schedule. I would think you'd like to sleep in your own bed for more than a handful of nights."

"I imagine I'll sleep just fine—as long as you're right beside me."

He made a sound that was part growl, part groan. "You're amazing, you know that, right?"

"So you keep trying to tell me."

"It's true." He paused. "Does it... Do you ever feel like..." He stopped. "Never mind."

"No. Come on. Tell me," she urged him. "What were you going to say?"

"Does it ever feel strange to you that we've only known each other for such a short time and yet...?"

"And yet it feels like we've known each other forever?" she finished for him.

"Yes! That's exactly what I mean." He waited a beat. "So...does it?"

Aubrey had been thinking about that very topic all day. When she'd left Hugh back in Hilton Head that morning, she'd thought it would be no big deal. Their new romantic relationship was wildly exciting and she loved every minute of it, but it was time to get back to reality.

Boy, had she been wrong.

In the short amount of time they'd been together, Aubrey felt as if her entire life had changed. She felt out of sorts in her own home and hadn't known what to do with herself most of the day. She knew she'd had a fairly full life before going to Napa and yet now...she couldn't remember what had filled her time.

Maybe she didn't want to remember. She was normally given busywork from her father or Paul, and it bored her to tears. Since meeting Hugh, Aubrey felt truly alive. It was wonderful and invigorating and...she missed him. Not just the work and the way her days filled her with joy, she missed talking to him, bouncing ideas off him.

And it had been less than a day.

"Um…Aubrey?" he asked, and she realized she'd gone silent for a long time.

"Sorry. My mind wandered for a second."

"And…?"

She smiled at the hint of uncertainty in his voice. "I feel the same way, Hugh. I mean, I know it's only been two weeks and I know we shouldn't be this comfortable with one another and yet, we are."

"Does it freak you out?"

"No," she replied honestly. "It just feels right." Then she thought about it. "Why? Is it freaking you out?"

"I'll admit I may be feeling a little…unsettled. I don't want to feel like I'm rushing you or like we're acting…"

"Impulsively?" she teased.

Hugh must have noted her tone because he grumbled, "Yes."

Aubrey was certain Hugh had his reasons for being so cautious in all areas of his life—and she'd find out what they were. Eventually. For right now, however, she was content to just let the topic go.

"If it's any consolation," she began silkily, "I really enjoy being impulsive with you."

She could hear the smile in his voice when he said, "I enjoy it too."

"Well, good. Now how about we both get some sleep and plan on me driving down on Saturday."

"Aubrey, I was serious. You don't have to. I really don't mind driving to you."

"Do you want to get away from your family already?"

"Why?"

"Because if that's why you want to come here, then

we'll do it. If you want to do all the things you were
telling me about, then let me come to you. I don't mind.
I haven't been to the Carolina coast in years. I would
love to see it."

"Only if you're certain…"

"I do have one stipulation."

"Name it," he said.

"I'm not sleeping on Ninja Turtle sheets. I have to
draw the line at that."

Hugh burst out laughing. "I think we can work something out. We'll find someplace else to stay. My brother
Aidan has an apartment over his garage I've stayed at
before. Or if you'd prefer something a little more private, I can get us a hotel room."

"You live out of hotels all year long. I think your
brother's apartment sounds perfect. We can food shop
and cook meals together and lock the world away if we
want to."

Hugh chuckled.

"What? What's so funny?"

"Wait until you meet my family. They're not going
to give us much privacy no matter where we stay, but if
we're staying at Aidan and Zoe's place, I have a feeling
they'll be just as intrusive as housekeeping at any resort."

The idea didn't bother Aubrey. No one bothered her
much in her everyday life. At least not because they
loved her and wanted to spend time with her. It was
normally about work and obligations. It would be nice
to see how a loving family behaved with one another.

"I don't think it will be so bad," she finally said.
"But I'll leave the choice up to you. I'm just happy to be
seeing you—it doesn't matter where we stay."

"Oh, don't do that. Which would you prefer?"

"Surprise me." Aubrey yawned loudly. "I hate to hang up but I really am exhausted. It's been a long day. Can I call you tomorrow?"

"You can call me any time you want, sweetheart," he said softly.

"Mmm…" she purred. "I like that. I'll talk to you tomorrow, okay?"

"Okay. Good night, Aubrey."

"Good night."

———

Hugh lay in bed staring at the ceiling for a long time after he and Aubrey got off the phone. She was coming to meet his family. Was that good or bad? Was he ready for it? Was his family?

Great, now he had a headache.

While it would be great to whisk her away to some exclusive resort for a long weekend, Aubrey was right—he lived his entire life out of hotels. It could be nice to be a little more domesticated and stay at the apartment Aidan had over his garage. It wasn't much— just a two-room apartment—but they wouldn't need much more. Just a roof over their heads, a bed…and for his family to keep their distance a little bit.

Hugh had a feeling with work beginning on the family house, he was going to be expected to pitch in since he was in town. He couldn't do it. It was one thing to mow the lawn or prune some trees, but there was no way he could willingly start stripping wallpaper or tearing down cabinets.

His brothers were welcome to it.

Aubrey would be the perfect distraction. Not that it was his only reason for wanting her here—he just... wanted her here. His father and brothers would take pity on him, he'd take their good-natured ribbing, and in the end, he'd get to have his time alone with Aubrey.

Not a bad plan.

Of course there was the potential for things to go wrong. Once he asked Aidan about the apartment, he'd get the third degree. Then Zoe would want to meet Aubrey. There would probably be a family dinner and the equivalent of the new-relationship interrogation.

Crap.

Hugh stopped himself. He was doing it again. Plotting. Planning. Trying to work everything out in his head rather than just waiting to see what happened. Old habits and all. Not that Hugh thought he had to change his habits—just tone them down a bit.

He sighed. This was exhausting.

As his eyes began to drift closed, Hugh made a promise to himself. Tomorrow he was going to let everyone know Aubrey was coming to spend the weekend. And he'd see how they responded. Hopefully Aidan would offer the apartment, and he'd accept like he hadn't already thought of it.

Then he'd reiterate that he was going to be in charge of the landscaping part of the renovations. Nothing more. No painting. No demolition. If pushed, he'd play the girlfriend card and hopefully it would shut everyone up.

Maybe.

If he was lucky.

If not, he'd have a plan B ready. He just needed some sleep first.

Chapter 8

"So the refrigerator is stocked and there are clean linens on the bed. If you need extra towels, they're here in the linen closet." Zoe walked around the small apartment with a wide smile on her face. "We have cable and there are extra pillows and—"

"Zoe?" Hugh interrupted.

"Hmm?"

"We've got it. The place isn't that big. If it's not here, we won't need it."

She made a face at him. "I'm just making sure you're comfortable. So sue me."

He put his arm around her and kissed her on the forehead. "That won't be necessary. But seriously, we'll be fine." He looked at Aubrey. "Right?"

She nodded. "I can't thank you enough for letting us stay here. I know we could have gone to a hotel, but this is much cozier."

Zoe seemed to visibly relax. "It's a great little place. And we don't get to see Hugh nearly enough. He's normally globe-trotting someplace."

"Well, you won't be seeing too much of me this time either. I've got some property to look at and I plan on helping Dad out with the yard. I want to show Aubrey around town, too."

"Just make sure you make time for dinner tomorrow. It's my only request. I'm forcing everyone to take tomorrow off to come here for dinner."

"Who's everyone?" Aubrey asked.

"Ian, Aidan, Quinn, Anna, the two of you…" She stopped. "If you were going to be here next weekend, you could have met Darcy and Owen. They're both going to be in town."

Hugh looked at her quizzically. "I didn't have any idea. Why didn't anyone tell me? I would have put off my visit for a week."

"It just sort of happened that way. Darcy wasn't due to come home, but when she heard about all the work going on at the house, she got anxious to see it, and Owen didn't need much prodding when Aidan told him what was going on."

"Oh dear Lord," Hugh said with a chuckle. "Don't let him use any power tools."

"Why?" Aubrey asked. "He's not handy?"

"My brother is a brilliant scientist. His brain works in ways that constantly baffle me. But he's got two left hands and he overthinks everything. He'll end up hurting himself without lifting a finger."

Zoe chimed in. "Owen has his own skills."

"Oh, I completely agree. And as long as he sticks to pencils and paper, typing on the computer, and looking through a telescope, we're all going to be fine. Trust me, Zoe. Give him simple tasks—raking leaves, picking up lunch—but don't let him actually do anything."

She sighed. "Fine. I'm sure Aidan is aware of this already, right?"

Hugh nodded. "Just tell Aidan to have extra helpers on hand while Owen's here so it looks like he's really not necessary. No need to make him feel bad."

"Aww…look at you being all concerned for your

brother's feelings. That's very sweet." She stood on tiptoe to kiss his cheek. "You are amazing."

"And that is my cue to leave." Zoe made her way to the door. "You have my number if you need me. I have to head into town to check on a job. Aidan won't be home until after five. If you want to join us for dinner, text me. But no pressure. Enjoy yourselves." And she was gone.

It was funny—for a man who thrived on being in control, he felt anything but. No sooner had the door clicked shut than he had Aubrey in his arms, his lips on hers. "This is madness," he growled as he reacquainted himself with the taste, the feel of her.

"I know," she panted, doing her share of exploring.

The thought of making love to Aubrey had been in the forefront of Hugh's mind pretty much since he'd last seen her. He'd lost count of the fantasies that had run through his mind in the few days they'd been apart.

Sex on the living room carpet wasn't one of them, but as he and Aubrey slowly sank to their knees, kissing ravenously, it seemed like the perfect way to start.

They rolled, they kissed, they touched.

"I need you," Aubrey sighed, her nails raking his scalp as his mouth nipped and kissed her chin, her throat, the vee of her blouse. "Now."

His brain wasn't functioning. It was the only thing Hugh could say to excuse the fact that he was behaving like a horny teenager alone in the house with the girl of his dreams. He wasn't civilized. He wasn't gentle. Hell, he barely remembered where they were. The only thing that mattered was feeling more of Aubrey's skin.

"Now works for me just fine," he growled as he sat up and quickly began to undress. Aubrey did the same.

Then, there were no words. Only sighs.

———⁓———

"The breeze feels wonderful, don't you think?" Aubrey asked. They were walking hand in hand around the semi-cleared property Anna Hannigan had brought them to see. They'd been wandering around in silence for several minutes and the quiet was starting to get to her. She had a feeling Hugh was simply mulling things over in his mind. She would have given him some space, but he wouldn't let go of her hand.

Looking over her shoulder toward Anna, she noticed her shrug.

"So." Anna cleared her throat. "This tract of land consists of 236 acres. I know it's a lot larger than your other properties. But depending on where you build the main resort, you could definitely ensure privacy for your guests. There is approximately fifty acres of buildable uplands with an additional ten-acre island." She paused. "The island could really be a selling point."

Aubrey gasped as inspiration struck. "Oh, you could build a spectacular venue on the island for weddings or other high-profile events. Just think of all the possibilities. Glass enclosures, beautiful lighting, the sense of being someplace far, far away…" She sighed.

"What was the land previously going to be used for, Anna?" Hugh said, seemingly unfazed by Aubrey's exuberant plans for the island.

"The previous developer had an approved plan for eighty residential lots with accompanying boat slips on the river."

"And why did it fall through?"

Anna began to furiously scan through her notes. "Um…it looks like it was a financing issue. The city was on board with the plans, but the developer couldn't come up with the proper financing to make it happen."

"If the city was on board with a residential plan, what makes you so sure they'd be on board with this being used for commercial development?"

With a confident grin, Anna pulled a sheet of paper out of one of the folders she was carrying. "I've already been in contact with the city to secure the necessary paperwork, and talked to the local businesses. It looks like everyone agrees with the type of project you would be doing. Had you wanted to come in here and do a theme park or some sort of monstrosity, they probably wouldn't have been on board. But your reputation speaks for itself, Hugh."

He smiled as he took the paperwork from Anna's hands. "You're good, Anna," he said. "And confident, too."

She shrugged. "I don't know about that. You're really my first commercial client." Her hand flew to her mouth and she blushed. "Sorry. I probably shouldn't have said that."

Hugh smiled. "Knock it off. We're practically family. I know you're just starting out. If anyone else had brought this property to my attention, I probably wouldn't have given it much thought. But when Quinn called and told me about it…"

"Quinn called you?" she asked. "When?"

"I don't know. A week ago? Maybe two?"

She muttered under her breath.

"Why? What's the problem?" Hugh asked, confused. "I thought he mentioned it to you when you got here.

He didn't say he'd jumped the gun. I told him to wait until I was ready with all of the research before saying anything, and he just went ahead and did whatever he wanted anyway." She rolled her eyes.

"Well, it still worked out, right? I mean, he told me about it, but we didn't talk until this morning so…no harm done."

She glanced at him. "I know you're right. I just wish…"

"Quinn would listen to someone other than himself?"

She laughed. "Exactly. I know he wants to help me. He's a good friend. I just think sometimes he doesn't really pay attention to what I say."

"If it's any consolation, he doesn't listen to anything anyone says. It's not just you," Hugh said softly. Reaching over, he put an arm around Anna and pulled her into a brotherly embrace, planting a loud, smacking kiss on her head. "He'll catch on eventually."

"Sure he will," she grumbled, stepping away from him.

Aubrey stood back for a moment and watched in fascination. What had just happened here? What had she missed? She knew Hugh's and Anna's families had been friends for years, Hugh had told her that much. But clearly there was some sort of thing going on with Quinn she hadn't been brought up to speed on. She made a mental note to ask Hugh about it later when they were alone.

They came to a stop. Aubrey had lost track of where they were or how far they had walked. She looked around and saw a whole lot of nothingness around her, but one look at Hugh and she could almost see his mind at work.

It was fascinating.

"I have an information packet for you as well,"

Anna said. "Demographics, information on local construction—you know, just in case working with Aidan isn't a possibility—and things like that." She hesitated. "I made a small PowerPoint presentation that we can look at back at my office if you're interested. Or I can send it to you."

He smiled at her, the breeze blowing his hair slightly. "That would be great." Looking around one last time, he grabbed Aubrey's hand and gave it a gentle squeeze. "It's a lot to think about."

Together, the three of them began their trek back toward the car. Anna had picked them up at Aidan's place earlier and given them a quick tour of the area on their way in. It wasn't the type of decision that could be made on the spot. Aubrey knew that, and yet she had a feeling a commission like this would mean a great deal to Anna.

"You coming to dinner tomorrow?" Hugh asked after a few minutes.

Anna nodded. "Wouldn't miss it. Zoe's an amazing cook."

"Says the woman who makes some of the best burgers in the world. Just say the word, Anna, and I'd set you up in any one of my resorts," Hugh joked.

Aubrey looked over at Anna. "You're a cook? I thought you did real estate."

Anna gave Hugh a playful shove before answering. "I used to manage the local pub. They had a kitchen and I helped them change up their menu from barely edible to somewhat enjoyable."

"She's being modest," Hugh interjected. "It used to be a run-down greasy spoon, and when Anna came in, she cleaned the place up and took on the kitchen. People come from miles around for her burgers. She won't tell us the secret to them, but I'm telling you, they're borderline addictive."

"Now I'm intrigued," Aubrey said, smiling brightly. "I do love a good burger."

"Well, maybe while you're in town I'll have you over for dinner. Which reminds me, how long are the two of you going to be around for?"

Aubrey hesitated. "I was really only planning on staying the weekend. Hugh and I will be traveling more and I haven't been home much. I've got to get my stuff in order and get packed before we hit the road again."

Beside her, Aubrey could feel Hugh stiffen slightly. They hadn't talked about how long she was going to stay. She'd just thought it was a given. No doubt they'd talk about it tonight.

"I planned on being here through next weekend," Hugh said pleasantly. "But plans can change."

"Well, if either of you are around, my schedule is pretty flexible and it's never a hardship to light the grill and whip up a meal, so let me know."

"Any idea what Zoe's making? Does she have a specialty?" Hugh asked.

"Oh, you are going to love it," Anna said as they approached the car. She unlocked it remotely and they climbed in. "She's really gotten into your mom's cookbooks and has been coming up with something new every week—dishes everyone says they haven't eaten in years. I don't know what's on tomorrow's menu, but the last couple of weeks have been a real treat. She made your dad cry that first Sunday." At Hugh's horrified look, she quickly corrected herself. "In a good way! Honestly! Sorry! I meant it was just a good memory and he hadn't realized how much he missed some of those dishes."

Aubrey patted Hugh's shoulder from the backseat. "I'm sure it's going to be wonderful. I can't wait."

"So about those demographics," Hugh said, effectively changing the subject.

———

Mindlessly, Hugh's fingers played with Aubrey's hair as they watched a movie. It was late. They'd had dinner and were relaxing, but his mind kept going in a bunch of different directions.

The property.

It was a fabulous piece of land and the potential was more than he'd ever let himself think about. It would give him the opportunity to expand in ways he hadn't thought he wanted to and yet… Maybe it was time to do something a little different. He knew he wouldn't stray too far from the formula that had proven successful for him in the past, but he could expand on it.

Aubrey.

She'd only planned on the weekend? Why hadn't they discussed it? It made sense. He knew that. And yet…dammit. Just the thought of watching her drive away again was already eating away at him. He had no idea why he was struggling with it so much. It had never been an issue before. There had to be a way to overcome it and get a grip.

Then he remembered they were going to be traveling together for the better part of the next month. There'd be no need to worry about it because she wouldn't be driving away from him. Just the thought made him relax a bit. And then he remembered...

The dinner.

So Zoe was breaking out his mother's old recipes. He wasn't sure how he felt about it. Hugh had gotten used to the way he lived his life in regards to honoring his mother. He stuck to the schedule she had lovingly made for her family—it didn't matter if it wasn't new and exciting, it brought him comfort. Of course, he had a business to run and business dinners to go to, so he wasn't completely faithful to the schedule.

Somehow he doubted Zoe would be able to completely re-create all of the recipes exactly. It wasn't possible. So he'd go and he'd eat and he'd thank her. It wasn't that he didn't appreciate her effort—on some levels it was very sweet. But those were his mother's things. Not hers. Maybe if Darcy had taken an interest in it he'd feel differently, but she hadn't.

He sighed loudly and Aubrey turned to look at him. "You okay?"

Great. How did he explain the ridiculous conversation he was having in his head? "Yeah. Sure."

She rolled her eyes. "Out with it."

"Don't you think it's weird Zoe's making my mother's recipes? I mean, why? It's not really her place, right? Shouldn't my sister be doing that sort of thing?"

Pulling away from him, Aubrey straightened and faced him. "Why? Why should it fall on your sister to do it? I think it's kind of sweet Zoe would try to do this for your family."

"You do?"

She nodded. "Of course."

Now he straightened, curious to get her input. "Tell me why."

"Why what?"

"Why do you think it's sweet? I mean, it's not her family. Shouldn't she be cooking some of her family recipes for us?"

Aubrey laughed. "Hugh, do you hear yourself? The Shaughnessys are her family now. She's marrying your brother. I think it's sweet that she wanted to do this for him—for all of you!"

"Yeah, but…"

"I don't think she's trying to take anyone's place. You shouldn't look at it as a bad thing. It's not."

"But maybe Darcy would have liked to have the chance to do it."

She leveled him with one look. "Your sister is in college and I doubt she's sitting around thinking about making traditional Irish dishes in her spare time. Don't get me wrong, I don't know a thing about your sister, but I'm going to go out on a limb here and say she's got other things on her mind."

"Maybe," he grumbled.

"It's okay, you know," she began hesitantly.

"What is?"

"For things to change. Your family is going to grow and change, and traditions may start to look a bit different, but it doesn't make any of it bad. You shouldn't go into this meal tomorrow with a negative outlook. Maybe with a hint of anticipation. Like 'Oh, I wonder which dish she's going to make?' I know I'm as curious as all get-out!"

He chuckled. Couldn't help it. "Have you ever eaten traditional Irish food?"

She considered the question. "I've had corned beef and cabbage."

He laughed again. "So has everyone. I have no idea what Zoe will be making but it's not all good."

"I'm sure your brother gives his input before Zoe decides on a recipe. At least…I hope he does."

That made Hugh feel better. He and Aidan had very similar tastes, and no doubt he would encourage Zoe to make something the family had enjoyed at some point. "One can only hope." He looked at the hopeful expression on Aubrey's beautiful face and sighed.

"What? What was that sigh for?" she asked softly.

"You," he said huskily. "I look at you and I'm just blown away." His hand reached up to caress her cheek. "You're so soft and beautiful and every time I look at you, I can't help but want to touch you."

She purred and moved so she was stretching out on top of him. He reclined on the sofa beneath her until they were perfectly aligned. "Mmm…this is nice."

"Yes, it is."

Leaning forward, she placed a chaste kiss on his lips. "I don't feel like watching any more TV. How about you?"

One arm banded around her waist as he shook his head. "No. No more television. I'd much rather sit here and watch you as I touch you," he began as his lips met the slender column of her throat. "And kiss you." He nipped at her collarbone. "And make love to you."

Aubrey all but melted against him at his words. "You have a way with painting a picture," she whispered.

His hand wandered down and cupped her bottom. He squeezed, pressing her firmly against his growing arousal. "I don't want you having to picture anything, sweetheart. I want you to see it. Feel it." The other hand cupped her nape and brought her lips to his. "Want it."

He kissed her with a hunger that was becoming all too familiar. His lips slanted over hers again and again, and he growled when her tongue darted out to mate with his.

It would have been easy to take her right here, right now, on the sofa. But they'd already made love on the floor once in this very room and Hugh was determined to get them to a bed and make love to Aubrey properly.

Carefully, he sat up and smiled when Aubrey moved with him, her legs gracefully coming around to circle his waist, her arms looped around his shoulders. He was on his feet and carrying her through the tiny apartment to the bedroom, heedless of the lights he was leaving on in their wake. He'd deal with them later.

Laying Aubrey down on the bed, he contemplated following her down and taking his turn stretching out on top of her. But instead, he disentangled them and began to slowly undress her.

Funny how he'd never taken the time to simply enjoy that activity. This time, he looked at her as if she were a present. She squirmed under his touch and it was all he could do to slow himself down. "Patience," he murmured as he slowly pushed her shirt up over her breasts. The pink lacy bra she had on was of the barely-there variety, and his throat went dry at the sight of it. But rather than lean forward and feast on her, he continued his task of slowly unwrapping her.

The shirt went over her head and onto the floor. Next he skimmed his hands across her ribs, down to her waist, and then let them softly trace the line across her belly until they rested on the button of her slacks. Hugh's eyes never left hers as he unclasped them, slid the zipper down, then gently tugged them over her hips, down her legs.

Aubrey licked her lips and Hugh had to stifle a groan.

The pants hit the floor and he took a minute to massage first one foot, then the other. When Aubrey moaned with appreciation, he lifted her foot and placed it on his shoulder. Tilting his head, he kissed her ankle and then journeyed downward—over her shin, her calf, her knee. His fingers teased her, tickled her gently right behind her knee until she started to squirm again.

"Hugh," she sighed with a hint of urgency.

"Soon," he murmured, but he was in no hurry.

Softly, gently, slowly, his fingers skimmed her thighs. Aubrey's hips slowly rocked off the bed, but Hugh forced himself to keep moving. Instead of steadying her, placing his hands on those hips and gripping them like his hands twitched to do, he kept them on the move. Back up her rib cage and to the lacy pink bra.

Now it was his turn to lick his lips.

"So pretty." His hands traced the swells of her breast. "So soft."

And then he lowered his head and smiled when Aubrey cried out his name. Her hands went to his head, raking through his hair and holding him to her.

His tongue followed the path of his hands until he reached behind her and unhooked the bra, pulling it from her body. Aubrey's back bowed, her breasts offered up like some sort of feast.

And he readily took advantage of it.

His mouth and hands were everywhere. Aubrey did her best to pull Hugh down on top of her but he wouldn't budge. He wanted to bring her pleasure—wanted to prolong this feeling, this anticipation. Beneath him, Hugh could feel her hips still rocking, still seeking, and when she whispered "please," his restraint broke.

Straightening, he quickly removed his shirt, his jeans, and his boxers, and stared down at her. "What do you want, Aubrey?" he said, his voice raw.

"You. Only you," she said.

With a slow grin, Hugh reached out and skimmed her panties over her hips, down her legs, and tossed them over his shoulder.

"You have me," he said as he stretched out on top of her. "Always."

⁓⁓⁓

"Hugh? How about it? You want the last slice?" Zoe asked, her smile knowing.

He was so full he could barely speak, and yet he waved his future sister-in-law on. He couldn't help but smile—his response clearly pleased her. The meal had been spectacular. She hadn't made anything outlandish and she wasn't trying to reinvent the wheel. She had simply chosen a recipe from his mother's collection and made it for the Shaughnessys to enjoy.

Mission accomplished.

"What did I tell you?" Aidan asked, looking at Hugh with a grin on his face. "It's like we're kids again and Mom made Sunday dinner."

"You were right," Hugh said after a minute, taking

the time to savor another bite of the Guinness- and honey-glazed pork. "I can't remember the last time I had something like this."

"Too long," Ian chimed in, his tone wistful. "I never claimed to be a cook and didn't want to try and risk ruining anything. When Zoe was helping me design the new kitchen and we found your mother's recipe box, she asked if she could go through it. I told her she could have the whole thing on the condition she made some of the dishes that were in there for us."

The room went silent. Aidan, Ian, Hugh, Quinn, and Anna—who was practically a Shaughnessy—all seemed lost in their own memories of growing up under the loving care of Lillian Shaughnessy.

Quinn broke the silence, raising his glass to Zoe. "My compliments to the chef. You would have made Ma proud." They all toasted.

Hugh looked at Aidan, his arms wrapped around his bride-to-be, and couldn't help but feel envious. His brother had it all. He didn't begrudge Aidan his happiness. The dynamics in the family were beginning to change; that had become obvious once Zoe had come into their lives. Hugh knew how much Aidan fought against the change and had even made fun of him for it, but now that it was moving forward, Hugh couldn't help but feel a little overwhelmed.

Zoe, Aubrey, and Anna all began clearing the dishes. It was funny how none of the men offered to get up and help, but none of the ladies seemed to mind. Hugh had his suspicions. He figured Anna and Zoe were anxious to get Aubrey alone and talk to her. Or maybe they were just letting the four clueless Irishmen sit and commiserate on how much they missed Lillian.

Hugh opted for number two.

"Zoe's a hell of a cook, Aidan. If I closed my eyes, I would have sworn that was one of Mom's roasts."

Aidan smiled. "Yeah, she's been having a good time going through all that stuff. Not all of her re-creations have been successful though," he said with a laugh. "Either that or I've really lost the taste for some good old-fashioned Irish stew."

They all laughed. "It's cool that she wanted to do it," Quinn said. "I mean, I know we ate a lot of regular stuff—Mom's weekly menu rarely changed unless it was a special occasion or holiday—but I didn't realize how much I missed some of those meals until Zoe started doing this."

"Darcy might have wanted to check those recipes out," Hugh said, looking to his father.

Ian shook his head. "Your sister loves to bake. If I let her, she would fill every inch of our kitchen with cookies and cakes, but she doesn't have the connection to these meals the way you boys do. She was too young."

They all nodded solemnly. Darcy hadn't even been a year old when Lillian Shaughnessy died. Mother and daughter never had the chance to spend afternoons in the kitchen together cooking or baking. Hugh had to wonder if Darcy ever thought about it, and then cursed himself for not taking the time to talk to his sister about such things. Maybe he'd have to rectify that in the future. Maybe on her next break from school he'd arrange for her to spend some time with him at one of the resorts.

Aidan was the first to sit up straight, clapping his hands together loudly as if to break the somber mood.

"So I hear you looked at property yesterday," he began. "What did you think of it? Was it any good?"

Hugh nodded. "The property was amazing. I think there's a lot I can do with it. It's probably more than I need, but I don't have to develop it all. I can accomplish what I want with it resort-wise and maintain some of the natural landscape around it to ensure privacy."

"So you're going to buy it?" Quinn asked, sounding a little anxious.

"I'm not sure yet."

"Why the hell not? You just said it was amazing!"

"For crying out loud, Quinn," Hugh huffed, relaxing back in his seat, "do you buy the first building you look at for your shops?" He didn't wait for an answer. "No. You don't. You look over several properties, gather information, and take the time to figure out if it's the right fit for you."

"I just bought property here for the new shop," Quinn said smugly, crossing his arms over his chest.

"Oh really?" Hugh asked. "So…what? That means I have to buy property here too?"

"Boys," Ian warned. "It's been a nice afternoon and we've just finished dinner. No fighting."

"I'm not fighting," Quinn said, leaning his arms on the table now. "All I'm saying is Hugh was presented with a great piece of property at a reasonable price. He's willing to build everywhere else in the damn world, why not right here?" He looked around the table, expecting an argument. "I mean, you've already got a realtor in Anna, a builder in Aidan, a decorator in Zoe…it would be a real family endeavor. Hell, I would even consider investing in it if you were open to it."

Hugh raked a hand through his hair. Working with his family? Having them invest in one of his businesses? He hadn't considered that. His father had helped him out with the very first resort he built, and that had been kept between the two of them. He sort of liked that the resorts were all his. "I already have investors—"

"So?" Quinn snapped. "You can't have more?"

"I don't think that's the point," Aidan interrupted. "Hugh's entitled to take some time to think about this. Just because the property is available doesn't mean he's ready to take on another project. Did you know what he had planned for upcoming developments before you pitched this site to him?" he asked Quinn.

"Well, no. But—"

"So that's a pretty big assumption on your part. What if I found a place in, say...Phoenix right now that would be great for one of your auto shops? Would you be willing to drop everything to make it happen?"

Quinn slouched in his seat. "No. I'm working on this new site here."

"Exactly," Aidan said evenly. "So cut Hugh some slack."

"It would...it would be great for Anna to make this commission, that's all," Quinn said quietly, looking over his shoulder to make sure none of the girls heard him. "This real estate thing is new for her. She's not confident in her skills yet and no one's taking her seriously. They tease her in the office, ask her to go get lunches and whatnot, and I think it would be a good thing for her to land a deal like this."

Ian smiled at his son. "While that's commendable, Quinn, you can't expect your brother to buy over two hundred acres of land simply for Anna's sake. It wouldn't be a smart business move."

"What's not a smart business move?" Zoe asked, walking back in with a platter of assorted cookies.

Aidan waited until she placed it down before snagging her around the waist and pulling her close. "Is the coffee ready yet?" he asked instead of answering, and Hugh marveled at how they seemed to know without speaking this wasn't a subject that needed to continue right now.

"Anna's bringing it out."

For the remainder of the evening, the family stuck to safer topics—Quinn's new shop, how Darcy was doing at school, and local events. When those topics were exhausted, everyone seemed to turn collectively toward Hugh and Aubrey. "So I hear you're going to be doing quite a bit of traveling over the next month," Zoe began. "What's this big project?"

Hugh looked to Aubrey, but she smiled serenely and deferred to him. He gave a very brief description of his business arrangement with William Bellows and what Aubrey was bringing to the table.

"Basically, I need her to get a feel for each of the resorts so she can customize these events. It's why we're taking this whirlwind trip. I don't have any major expansions or happenings going on right now, so my schedule was flexible."

"And there's no time like the present," Aubrey chimed in.

"Do you do this sort of thing for a living?" Zoe asked.

"Oh…um…" Aubrey stammered, looking to Hugh before answering. "I…I used to do a lot of charity work and fund-raising for my father's company. I'm used to coordinating those kinds of events, and after talking with Bill while I was in Napa, I threw in my two cents out of habit. I was kind of surprised he was listening and took me seriously."

"Why?" Anna asked as she came to sit back down. "From everything you've told me, they sound like great ideas. Why wouldn't he take you seriously?"

"He didn't know me," Aubrey replied. "He had no idea what my qualifications were, and for him to not only listen to my idea, but to more or less force me on poor Hugh... Well, it was far from your typical job interview."

Without thinking about it, Hugh placed his hand on top of hers and squeezed before smiling at her. "I think it all worked out for the best."

Conversation picked up on neutral topics while they ate dessert, and by the time they were done and everything was cleaned up and put away, Hugh was anxious to get Aubrey alone. He walked over to Aidan and Zoe and thanked them for dinner.

"Everything was amazing, Zoe." He kissed her on the cheek. "I wasn't sure how I was going to feel about the whole thing, but this was a pleasant surprise."

She swatted him away playfully. "I'm glad you enjoyed it. Aidan said you'd probably be the one to give me grief about it, but I figured I'd win you over."

Hugh looked at his brother in mock annoyance. "You think you know everything?"

Aidan smiled broadly. "Yup. Sure do. You're a stick in the mud who likes everything done a certain way."

Hugh laughed out loud. "Um...pot? Meet kettle."

"Yeah, yeah, yeah," Aidan replied. "But I got my

head out of my ass. Yours is still firmly rooted there. When you feel like taking it out and joining this millennium, let us know."

"Smart-ass," Hugh grumbled, saved from saying anything else when his father came over to wish them a good night.

"When are you heading home, Aubrey?" Ian asked.

"I was planning on leaving tomorrow, but…"

Hugh looked at her anxiously. "You think you'll stay a few more days?"

She shrugged. "I'm not sure. We'll talk about it," she said with a wink. "Either way, Mr. Shaughnessy, it was so nice to meet you. You have a wonderful family."

Ian smiled. "I certainly do. I hope we get to see more of you too, my dear." He leaned in and kissed her on the cheek before heading off to find his jacket.

Quinn and Anna were the last to say good-bye, and Hugh decided to take a minute to speak with Anna in private. They were out on the front porch when he turned to her. "I'm sure you're wondering what I'm going to do about the property."

Anna's eyes went a little big before she could stop them. "Oh…um…well, I know you need some time to think about it. I mean, of course it would be great if you just said yes, but I'm not *that* inexperienced, Hugh. I know how things work."

"It's a very big decision, Anna, and I don't want you to get your hopes up. I don't want to let you down. You know that, right?"

She smiled at him. "Hugh, I don't expect you to build a resort you don't want just so I don't look like a loser to my colleagues. If you want the property, I'm here to help. If you don't, that's fine, too. Either way, we're friends, right?"

He pulled her in for a hug and kissed her on the top of the head. "Always, kiddo. Never doubt that."

They pulled apart when the door opened and Quinn and Aubrey stepped out. They all wished each other good night and Hugh took Aubrey by the hand, leading her across the yard toward the two-story structure that housed their guest suite.

They silently walked up the stairs in the moonlight. Once inside, Aubrey gently pulled her hand from his. "Your family is really great, Hugh. You're very lucky."

He nodded. "I know. I don't always remember it when I'm away, but when I'm with them I realize how great they all are. It's not often we're all together, but even when it's just a few of us, it feels good."

"So you're feeling good right now?" she teased.

"I am," he said evenly, taking a few steps toward her. "But I could be feeling better."

She smiled knowingly. "Really? You think?"

He continued to move toward her and noticed for every step he took, she took one backward, heading for the bedroom. Nodding, he said, "Oh yeah."

"Hmm… Anything I can do to make that happen for you? You know, with feeling better?"

Hugh knew he would never be bored with Aubrey. It didn't matter what they did or where they were, he loved her teasing ways, her smile, their bantering. Rather than rush the moment and simply scoop her up as he'd originally hoped to do, he continued their game.

"What are you offering?"

Aubrey pretended to think about it. "Well, I suppose I could…give you a shoulder massage."

"Interesting. But my shoulders feel fine."

Another few steps.

"I could fluff up the pillows and we can watch television in bed," she suggested. "I'll even let you pick the movie."

Hugh shook his head. "I'm not in the mood for a movie."

A few more steps.

"Boy oh boy," she sighed dramatically, "you are a *very* difficult man to make feel good. How about I just… oh, I don't know…" She stopped and pulled her shirt over her head, shaking her hair out. "Why don't I just get naked? How would that make you feel?"

The bark of laughter came out of nowhere and Hugh felt lighter, happier than he could ever remember. "It would make me feel like the luckiest man alive."

He closed the distance between them, but didn't touch her until she was standing before him in nothing but white lace panties. Her breathing was ragged as her eyes met his. "How are you feeling now?" she whispered.

"Ready to take on the world," he growled as he picked her up and tossed her on the bed.

———

The next morning, Aubrey awoke with a smile on her face. Hugh was wrapped around her—a favorite sleeping position for them both—and she could already see the first rays of sun coming through the blinds. She sighed with contentment. Maybe she didn't need to leave today. Maybe one more day…

"Don't go home today," Hugh whispered sleepily from beside her, as if reading her mind.

"I thought you had all kinds of yard work to do today. I saw the list you left on the kitchen table." The man certainly enjoyed making lists. It was detailed almost down to the minute how he was going to accomplish getting his father's property cleaned up.

"I don't have to. Not if you're here. I can put it off until tomorrow. Or the day after." He nuzzled her neck and Aubrey couldn't help but stretch to give him better access.

"Oh please," she said lightly. "No doubt you have tomorrow and the day after already planned out, too. If I stay, you won't get anything done and then you'll be grumpy."

He lifted his head and looked at her. "I don't get grumpy."

"You sound pretty grumpy right now."

He silenced her with a kiss. "Stay. We could go have a picnic on the beach or drive along the coast and find someplace nice to have lunch."

She gave him a mischievous smile. "Or we could find someplace secluded and go skinny-dipping."

"What?" he choked. "Why? Why would you even suggest that? It would be light out. The beaches around here are all pretty public."

She shrugged. "I've never really done it. I thought it could be fun."

"I don't know about that. The last thing I want is to be caught naked out in public." He shifted so his arm was around her, her head was nestled on his chest. "Can I ask you something?"

"Anything."

"Well, I'm curious. How did you end up working for your father?"

Lifting her head, Aubrey looked at him oddly.

"We never talked about it. From everything you've told me, it seems you never had a good relationship with your parents, so I was wondering why you'd work for him."

"We really need to work on your morning-after conversation," she said with a giggle, placing her head back on his shoulder.

"I'm sorry. I shouldn't have brought it up."

She sighed. "No. It's fine. It's just... Well, I don't come off very well in this particular scenario."

"What do you mean?"

"I did it out of guilt," she said simply. "He and my mother never let me forget how I let them down with my dancing..."

"You had cancer, for crying out loud! How could they blame you?" he demanded, but she ignored him.

"When I graduated and was looking for a job, my father told me they were looking for someone within his company." She wrinkled her nose at the memory. "It wasn't even like he was offering the job as much as he was silently telling me he'd paid for my education and now it was time to pay him back." Then she shrugged. "I didn't mind it so much, but it wasn't my dream job."

"I don't think many people get to work their dream job."

"Yeah, but most people get to have the freedom to choose. It took a while for me to realize he was controlling pretty much every aspect of my life. I'm not proud of that."

"What would you have done differently?" he asked softly.

"Other than not working for him? I would have moved away, found another job, experienced life! They kept me in a protective bubble for so long I forgot what it was like to do anything. That's why the things I've been doing these last few weeks have been so amazing. To some people they may seem normal or tame, but to me it's all an adventure. I've never felt so alive!"

Hugh hugged her close. More pieces of the puzzle were falling into place. He couldn't begrudge her recent escapades. She'd needed them. It didn't mean he wasn't going to worry about her or wish she'd choose safer hobbies.

"So…skinny-dipping, huh?" he joked.

Her entire face lit up. "Really?"

He shrugged, trying to sound as if he were completely comfortable with the idea. "Sure. There's a small lake we used to go to back in school. It's pretty private."

"Hugh, you don't have to. I can tell you don't really want to. We can have a picnic or I can even help you with your dad's yard—"

"No, no, no," he interrupted. "I mean it. I don't want you to have to work on your time off. Especially not around my father's yard."

"It's really not that big of a deal. Once I go home, I'll just be running errands, getting ready for our trip, and doing some stuff around my house. One is as good as the other."

"Tell me about what you have to do when you get

home," he said smoothly, trying to change the subject a little bit.

"The usual. I'll stop the mail, check in with my neighbors to make sure someone looks in on my place. I'm going to try to have lunch with a friend on Thursday, and I have a doctor's appointment on Friday…" She stopped and thought for a minute.

"Doctor's appointment? Everything okay?"

She nodded. "Just a routine physical. No biggie. I figure with all this traveling, I might as well get it out of the way. I was due for my annual next month but when I called to make the appointment, they said I could come in this week."

He sagged with relief. "Oh. Okay. You have your passport and everything you need for the trip to Sydney?"

"Oh, yeah. I have to admit, that's the leg of the trip I'm looking forward to the most. I've never been there but I've always wanted to go."

"You may feel differently after the long flight. I still wonder what possessed me to build there because every time I go, the travel time almost always does me in."

"Just more time for the anticipation to build."

He laughed. "We'll see."

"I know it's going to be quick…"

"And most of the time will be spent getting to and from there…"

"You're really killing this for me," she admonished playfully. "Hush."

"Fine. But don't say I didn't tell you so. I don't want you to be disappointed."

Honestly, Aubrey thought it was sweet he was so concerned. She kissed his chest. "So it's settled then.

I'll head home tomorrow to get everything in order and today we'll spend the day helping your dad out together."

"I guess," he grumbled.

Now that they'd effectively discussed her—and her family—she felt like it was her turn. There were a few things Aubrey wanted to know and figured now might not be a bad time to bring it up. "So...last night wasn't so bad, right?"

"What do you mean?"

"Well, I know you were having some issues with Zoe and the recipes. But everything was great. Everyone enjoyed themselves."

He shrugged. "I know it seems weird. Or maybe I'm just being ridiculous. I don't know."

"It seems to have evoked a lot of good memories for everyone. Surely that can't be a bad thing."

He shrugged again. "Maybe."

"How long has she been gone?" Aubrey asked softly.

"Too long," Hugh replied. His voice was raw.

She hugged him close. "Tell me about her."

"I was mad at her."

That wasn't the response she had been expecting, and Aubrey's heart broke for him. "I'm sure that's a normal response when you lose someone you love. You're angry at them for leaving you."

Hugh shook his head. "No. Before the accident. I was mad at her. I was grounded and I did everything I could to avoid being around her when I was home. I wanted to punish her for grounding me." He gave a mirthless laugh. "She died knowing I was mad."

"Oh, Hugh...no. She knew why you were lashing out. You were her son. She probably knew you better than you think. You can't honestly believe she thought you were seriously angry with her. I imagine she figured you'd get over it and she was giving you space."

He took a steadying breath. "But I'll never know. I'll never be able to make it right. There will never be a time when I can go to her and say I'm sorry for what I did and how I acted and how disrespectful I was. And because of me…" He stopped.

Aubrey raised her head and saw the anguish on Hugh's face. She stroked his cheek as tears began to fall down her own.

"I should have been the one in the car," Hugh said, his voice cracking. "It should have been me."

"What are you talking about?"

Sitting up, Hugh climbed from the bed. "It's nothing. I…I don't want to talk about this anymore." He reached for the jeans he'd discarded the previous night and pulled them on. "I'm going to make us some coffee and see what there is for breakfast, okay?"

More than anything, Aubrey wanted to call him back and say the hell with breakfast. But she stared at his retreating back, knowing the moment was gone.

Flopping back on her pillows, she sighed. In all her life, Aubrey couldn't recall ever losing anyone. Her parents and grandparents were all still alive. She couldn't imagine what it must have been like for the Shaughnessys to lose their matriarch so tragically and so young. The fact that Hugh somehow felt responsible seemed unbelievable. If he wasn't willing to talk about it, Aubrey had no idea how she'd find out what had really happened—or how she could help Hugh deal with it.

More than anything, she wanted to help him have some

peace. Was that why he was so regimented? So careful with the way he lived his life, because of his mother?

"Eggs or cereal?" Hugh asked, popping his head back into the room as if they hadn't been discussing something earth-shattering just moments ago.

"Cereal is fine for me," she said, pasting a smile on her face as she sat up. "I'm just going to throw on a robe and I'll be out to join you."

Hugh smiled and walked away, and Aubrey wondered what she could possibly do to draw the man out and help him face what was probably the biggest demon anyone should have to face.

Chapter 9

SIX WEEKS LATER, SHE STILL DIDN'T HAVE ANY ANSWERS.

Or a clue.

After her time visiting with the Shaughnessys, Aubrey had gone home with every intention of coming up with a way to draw Hugh out. During her short time at home, she had devised multiple ways to bring up the topic of Lillian Shaughnessy's death, and had even gone so far as to do some research on how the death of a parent affected their children.

None of her knowledge came in handy.

When she and Hugh had met up again to begin their whirlwind resort tour, she had all the confidence in the world about how she was going to rescue him—much like he had rescued her.

Never had the chance.

They had traveled, they had worked. Aubrey had met more people than she could remember and creatively, it was the most exciting trip of her life. Every place they traveled to, all of Hugh's resorts seemed to bring out a side of her she couldn't believe existed. For so many years, she had allowed herself to be content to blend into the background, and now it was hard to keep out of the spotlight.

Not intentionally, however.

There was something about Hugh and the people who worked for him that brought out this side of her. For the first time since her days studying dance, Aubrey felt like she fit in with a group of people.

She became engrossed in learning about all aspects of running these luxury resorts. They would arrive and she'd meet up with the team of people Hugh had assigned to help her, but once she had her plans mapped out for the galas, she would find herself getting involved in other things—cooking, menu planning, directing activities. At one point in Vermont, she even jumped in when they were short on housekeeping staff!

Hugh had a fit at that one, claiming she did not need to be cleaning rooms or filling in for his staff. But he thought she looked cute in the uniform and they made a game out of it as soon as they were alone.

Aubrey blushed at the memory. The man was magnificent in so many ways. He took her breath away on a daily basis—in and out of the bedroom—and yet there was a side of him he kept closed off from everyone.

Even her.

So many times over the course of their trip, she would be laughing and joking and an idea would hit her, and while Hugh would always patiently listen, he didn't get excited about it or make any sort of commitment. The only time he would comment one way or the other was if she talked of changing something.

It didn't take long for her to catch on to the fact he didn't enjoy making changes at his resorts, no matter how inventive or exciting the idea.

Then there were times she'd finish work early and go to seek him out in hopes of getting him to play hooky and go sailing or swimming or—on one particularly adventurous day—jet skiing, but he never went. There was always a very reasonable excuse, but it was as if the man didn't want to have fun.

She sighed and shook her head. No, that wasn't right. Hugh could be a lot of fun. They laughed more than she thought humanly possible whenever they were together, and they had eaten at some of the finest restaurants and gone dancing together, but it was just…controlled fun. Wait, was that even a thing? Something like structured playtime? The thought made her laugh out loud.

Or maybe she was just seeing things that weren't there.

Hugh was a good man. Hell, she'd even call him a great man. So he didn't like to do anything remotely adventurous. So he was a little reserved and lived his life by his day planner. It wasn't a crime.

Boring? Yes. Criminal? No.

She was back at home, working out of the small office she had made for herself there. Hugh was down in Florida. He had offered Aubrey the chance to go with him, but she felt tired and a little traveled out. Going from one luxury resort to the next had been great at first, but living out of a suitcase had quickly lost its appeal and she missed being home in her own space. Hugh had grumbled and done his best to persuade her to join him, but she'd held firm.

Next week was Ian Shaughnessy's birthday and they had made plans to join his family for the celebration. Aubrey was definitely looking forward to it, and as she looked at her calendar, an idea hit her—Zoe and Anna. Maybe the key to figuring out Hugh could be found in those two. Anna had known the family for forever and Zoe was marrying into it, so there was a chance she'd get some insight from them.

Maybe she could drive down a day early under the pretense of having a girls' day out. Lunch, mani/pedis, that sort of thing. And she could do her best to draw out some information on why Hugh felt responsible for his mother's death.

A small pang of unease hit her.

Should she be doing this? Would it be better simply to leave it alone?

No. If Aubrey had learned one thing as of late, it was that life was too short. It wasn't until she had met Hugh and began this fabulous new phase of her life that she'd realized everything that had been missing from hers. She'd been content to let others make her feel small and to accept the way they treated her, but after meeting Hugh, she saw there was another world out there. Another way.

And she wanted him to find his new world and his new way, one where he could relax and enjoy life and maybe, just maybe, they could move forward together.

"Might as well get the ball in motion," she muttered to herself as she scanned through some of her files until she found Zoe's phone number. Taking a deep breath, she dialed and crossed her fingers.

And prayed she wasn't making a huge mistake.

———∾∾∾———

"So a bunch of us are going out tonight. You in?"

Hugh looked up from the pile of mulch he was carefully spreading out along the flower bed in front of his father's house and stared blankly at Quinn.

"Dude? Come on. Every time you come home, you pretty much just...you know...sit. Let's go out tonight, grab a couple of drinks, play some pool. You know, like we used to."

"I never used to do that." Hugh moved the rake through the mulch pile again.

Quinn rolled his eyes. "All the more reason to come out and do it tonight. Come on, Hugh. Aidan's going, Bobby's going, Riley and his shadow are going. Hell, I think we're even going to get Owen to go if he gets here in time."

Hugh chuckled. "What exactly do you think Owen's going to do in a bar?"

"Laugh if you will, but he's a whiz at pool. He spouts all kinds of geometry crap and he's a little slow making his play, but when he does, it's a thing of beauty. We made a killing last time he was in town."

"That's just wrong."

"No," Quinn corrected, "it's fun."

Hugh supposed some could call it that. "Thanks, but I think I'm just going to hang back. By the time I'm done here in the yard, Aubrey should be back. I figured I'd take her to dinner."

Taking the rake from his hands, Quinn shook his head. "Uh-uh. Nope. I already took care of that too. Anna's taking the girls—including Darcy—to her place for a continuation of girls' day. She's making them dinner and they're going to watch a movie and do whatever it is girls do at those things."

"You mean like having pillow fights in their underwear?"

"Dude. Gross. Our sister is going to be there. Don't make me stab my own eyes out."

Hugh shuddered. "You're right. Sorry. I wasn't thinking."

"Anyway, I think Dad and some of his friends may meet up with us too, so you have to go. Everyone will be there. Don't be all…you know…you. Be like us mere mortals for a night."

There was no way he was going to win this argument. Quinn was the most tenacious of all his siblings, and when he wanted something—or thought he was right about something—he'd keep the argument going all night. Not what Hugh was in the mood for.

But the thought of going out—especially without Aubrey—wasn't appealing.

"Stop it. Stop it right now," Quinn snapped.

"What? Stop what? I don't know what you're talking about!"

"God, you are so whipped! I can't believe it. You've been dating Aubrey for, what? A month? Two? I can already see it. You're standing here with a look on your face normally reserved for thirteen-year-old girls looking at the latest teen magazine and fantasizing about dating Justin Timberlake or a member of One Direction. Knock it off!"

Hugh grinned. "I think it's adorable you know who One Direction is."

"Screw you. You know I'm right. You're all sad and a little depressed because you're not going to see Aubrey tonight. Stop being such a chick! Why are you even dating anyone?" He took the rake from Hugh's hand and tossed it aside. "You have the perfect life! You and Riley—I swear—I don't know how you got to be so lucky."

"You've lost me. Again, might I add."

Quinn rolled his eyes and began to pace. "You travel

all over the country—sometimes the world. You have no ties to any one place. Why would you tie yourself to one woman? You could literally have a girlfriend at every damn place you own and be living the sweet life! Why are you tying yourself down? And so damn fast! Hell, Hugh, you barely know this girl!"

Rage started to slowly build inside of Hugh. It wasn't often he shared his personal life with his family. Primarily because he didn't have much of one. But right now he really resented the fact his brother was talking like this about Aubrey.

"First off," he began with a deadly calm, "it's none of your damn business. If you have a problem with Aubrey—"

"That's not it," Quinn quickly interjected. "I just don't get why you—careful, always has a plan—are suddenly so committed and deeply involved with a woman you just met. It doesn't make sense."

Hugh guessed he could understand. It didn't fully make sense to him either. He'd never felt like this before and no matter how much he analyzed it, there weren't any clear answers or explanations. All he knew was he and Aubrey simply fit.

He scrubbed a hand across his face and sighed. "I didn't expect it either," he finally said after a minute. "If anyone had told me the woman breaking into my office was going to turn my world upside down, I wouldn't have believed them. But she did. And I'm not sorry for it either."

"Well, shit," Quinn muttered. "You're gonna do it too, aren't you? You and Aubrey are going to be trailing along just like Aidan and Zoe. It's just wrong."

"Why is this bothering you so much? Maybe you

need to find someone and settle down a bit. You know, stop hanging out at bars till all hours of the night, still trying to act like you're twenty."

"I don't do that," he pouted.

"I think you do," Hugh chuckled, walking over to pick up the rake. "Or maybe you're just running from what's right in front of your face, figuring if all of us keep running, no one will notice how much you're screwing up a great thing."

Quinn looked at him as if he'd started speaking a foreign language. "I have no idea what you just said. What the hell are you talking about?"

Hugh shrugged. "It's nothing. Don't mind me."

Hugh continued to rake, and Quinn walked around the yard picking up stray twigs and branches and hauling them off to the yard waste pile. They worked like that for several long, silent minutes, and when there was nothing left to do, Quinn finally stopped and looked at Hugh.

"So? Are you in for tonight or not?"

"Sure."

—*~*~*—

It wasn't that Aubrey wasn't a social person, because she was.

She just hadn't realized how boring all of her relationships with her friends were until right now.

Sitting in Anna's living room with a fruity virgin cocktail in her hand, she was laughing so hard she thought she might pee. "Oh my goodness!" she cried through the laughter. "I can't believe you did that!"

"It's true!" Anna yelled from across the room,

laughing hysterically. "I'm sure if I dug through my closet right now, I'd still have the picture!"

"Oh, come on, you guys," Darcy finally said. "Stop! Those are my brothers. Can't we talk about other guys?"

"Sorry, doll," Zoe said as she plopped down on the sofa beside her soon-to-be sister-in-law. "You wanted a night out with the girls, and we're all girls who are involved with your brothers."

"Yeah, but...gross."

"Gross or not," Anna said, walking across the room and taking her own seat on the floor, "all of your brothers have very fine butts."

"Please, you don't think I hear that at school all the time about Riley?" Darcy said with a hint of annoyance. "I guess I didn't realize how lucky I was growing up around here. Everyone knew us—knew Riley—and it wasn't a big deal. But at school now? As soon as people find out I'm related to the great Riley Shaughnessy, suddenly I'm bombarded with questions and requests for autographs, pictures, and private concerts."

"Give me a few minutes and I'll find the picture of his naked butt," Anna said with a laugh.

Darcy made a gagging sound and Zoe finally took pity on her. "All right, all right, all right. No more talk of Shaughnessy butts, okay? Why don't you pick the next topic, Darce?"

"It's fine," she said. "I get it. You're all into my brothers. I still don't get why—they're all jerks most of the time—but I suppose it's okay." She turned toward Aubrey. "You got the most normal one."

"Oh really?" Aubrey asked. "How do you figure?"

"Hugh's like an old man in a young guy's body."

"That's not true," Aubrey tried to argue, but her three friends immediately cut her off. "What? I don't see it."

"Oh, come on," Zoe said with a grin. "You mean you haven't noticed how careful Hugh is? How stable and calm and…"

"Boring," Darcy supplied.

"Yeah, boring," Zoe said, but with love. "Hugh's great, but for a guy who travels the world, he's really stuck in his own little rut. We're all hoping you'll break him out of it."

Here was her opening—the perfect opportunity to get it all out in the open. But one look at Darcy and Aubrey wasn't sure if this was really the time or the place.

Well, in for a penny…

"I've been trying. But every time I try something new, he balks at it."

"Have you gotten him to do anything new?"

Aubrey told them about the parasailing, the zip-lining, the jet skiing… "He never goes with me." She shrugged. "So I go without him."

"Good for you!"

"I really wish he'd come with me at least once and try…something. Anything! I always have fun and I've met some great people, but it's not the same. I want to experience these new things with him." She sighed. "I have no idea how to get him to engage, you know?"

Aubrey had to hand it to herself—it was the perfect segue to get the conversation going.

Darcy straightened beside her. "Okay, here's something you have to know about my brother—he's been

like this his whole life. He just doesn't know how to
have fun."

"No, no, no," Anna interrupted. "That's not true."

"It's how he's been my whole life!" Darcy argued.

"Yeah, well…believe it or not, he was the rebel of
the family at one time," Anna said, and if Aubrey wasn't
mistaken, she looked a little uncomfortable with sharing
the information.

"How is that possible? Did he get hurt? Did something happen to him to make him so straitlaced?"
Darcy asked.

Anna looked at the youngest Shaughnessy and then
to Aubrey and Zoe.

"It's okay," Aubrey said, unwilling to make Anna
break a confidence. "We don't have to talk about it
right now."

"No," Darcy demanded. "I'm curious."

"Maybe now's not the time," Zoe said as she stood
and walked over to the kitchen. "Do you want me to
light the grill? I'm getting hungry."

"Anna…?" All three women looked over at Darcy as
she whined.

Aubrey held her breath as she waited to see what
Anna was going to do. While she would completely
understand if Anna opted to change the subject—and
possibly spare Darcy's feelings on what was probably a
very sensitive topic—she hoped they were going to get
to the heart of the matter.

"Okay, but just remember you asked," Anna warned,
her gaze firmly set on Darcy. "What we talk about here,
Darce? It stays here."

"Fine, fine, fine. My lips are sealed." She made a

zipping motion over her lips and got comfortable on the couch.

Zoe slowly made her way back to the sofa and sat down close to Darcy in a silent show of support.

Anna sighed and sat down on the floor. She looked up at three pairs of wide, curious eyes. "Just so you all know, I've known those guys since I was six. I spent almost every day growing up hanging out with them, but that doesn't mean I know everything about them. So all I'm saying here is what I've heard or talked about with either my mom or Quinn."

"Oh, for the love of it, Anna," Darcy said, "no one's going to hold you to anything." Then she smiled. "My brothers don't share anything with me and they're all so much older, it's hard to imagine them as kids or different than who they are now."

"Aidan was always serious," Anna began. "He was the sweetest and most polite boy I'd ever met. He made sure everyone was taken care of and all games were played fairly."

Zoe smiled. "Sounds like Aidan. Some things never change."

Anna nodded. "And I'm not just saying it because you're sitting right here and he's your fiancé, he was just always a great guy. Never got into trouble, good student, and willing to help out anyone who needed it."

"And that's why I love him," Zoe said and took a sip of her drink.

"Now, Hugh was a completely different story."

Aubrey perked up—they all did—and leaned a little forward as if Anna was about to reveal the secrets of the universe.

"He was a lot rougher than Aidan. He played harder, talked tougher, and I know Lillian was exhausted from keeping up with him."

"So he was like…bad?" Darcy asked. "Like, a problem?"

Anna shook her head. "No, sorry. That wasn't what I meant. He was just the opposite of Aidan. Hugh would be the one making the bike ramp in the yard or taking things apart to build something bigger and better. He was always on the move. He played a bunch of different sports."

"So what happened?" Zoe asked. "That's a far cry from the man he is now."

"It is. By the time he hit high school he was hanging out with a group of guys who weren't the best influence. He was staying out late, got caught drinking a time or two, and even though he was maintaining good grades, he was butting heads with Ian and Lillian at home."

"I can't imagine my dad tolerating that sort of thing. All of my brothers have an almost scary respect for him. It's hard to picture Hugh being the one to disrespect him."

Anna gave a slight shrug. "It goes with the age, and believe me, they all did it to some extent. It changed after your mom passed away but they all had a bit of a rebellious period."

"Even Owen?" Zoe asked.

"In his quiet way, yes." She chuckled. "But his rebellion was about wanting to go to the museum on a Saturday when there was yard work to do." They all laughed.

"I can't imagine Aidan being rebellious," Zoe said.

"Yeah, well… He was a bit older so I don't know

much, but I do know he fought hard to drop out of college after Lillian died. He wanted to be there for everyone. Ian held firm, though."

Silently, they all nodded.

"So…what do you think changed for Hugh? Why such a drastic change?" Aubrey asked, unable to help herself. "I know losing a parent is completely devastating, but from what you're saying, he did a complete one-eighty. Why?"

Anna looked around uncomfortably. "I can't say with any great certainty…"

"But…" they all prompted.

Anna sighed. "Hugh got in trouble a few days before the accident. He broke curfew a couple of times, gave Lillian a bunch of attitude." She looked over at Darcy sadly. "I remember her having tea with my mom and saying she didn't know what else to do. She couldn't understand why he was being so difficult and why he couldn't accept the rules she and Ian gave them."

"I imagine it's frustrating for any parent when your child breaks the rules or lashes out," Zoe said.

"My mom said the same thing and shared how frustrated she got with me and Bobby and how much we always fought with one another. They used to get together and talk a lot. They were really good friends."

Darcy looked around the room and then back at Anna. "I feel like there's something you're trying not to say." She gave a little huff of annoyance. "You don't have to be afraid to say anything in front of me, Anna. I don't remember anything about my mom. I wish I did, but I don't. So if you're trying to spare my feelings, don't. I love my mom. I always will, but…I don't have a connection to her other than what other people tell me about her."

"I wish you could, sweetie. I really do. She was an amazing woman."

"I know," Darcy said with a hint of wistfulness.

"Well, Hugh was giving her the cold shoulder with his punishment. She said he would barely talk to her and when he did, he was belligerent." She paused. "She died the next day. I think Hugh knew he was being a brat and it's always been there—like he knows the last time they talked, he was rude to her."

Zoe shifted on the sofa. "Okay, so I can see him dealing with some guilt then, but to completely change his life?" She looked around the room for confirmation. "It doesn't make sense."

"Yeah, we all thought the same thing. My mom and I have talked about it a lot over the years and the only thing we can come up with was that Lillian's death was like some sort of wake-up call for him. The day of the funeral, Hugh just…shut down. He became a different person. He was quiet and withdrawn."

"That sounds normal considering the circumstances," Aubrey said.

Anna shook her head. "It was different. He suddenly morphed into a model citizen and son. It was a little weird. He stopped hanging out with the friends he'd always had, stopped going out, and focused on helping Ian out."

"Wow," Darcy said.

For a minute, Aubrey wasn't sure if she should bring up what Hugh had said to her those many weeks ago, but she was in too deep now. "Hugh mentioned once that it should have been him," she said quietly. "Do you know why he would say that?"

Anna considered the question for a long minute. "If I had to guess, I'd say it's because normally Lillian would have sent him on that errand. She used to love how she could send Hugh and Aidan out to pick things up for her. Aidan was away at school, but Hugh normally would run to the store if she needed him to. Maybe he felt if he hadn't been grounded and had been allowed to drive, he would have been in the car instead of Lillian."

You could have heard a pin drop in the room and Aubrey felt her heart break even more for him. Could that be it? Could that be why he felt the way he did?

"Do you…" She stopped and cleared her throat. "Do you think he made such a drastic change because he felt guilty? In his own way, he's trying to make up for how he—"

Anna cut her off. "I honestly don't know. I would imagine—based on what you just said—he's got a certain level of guilt. He's never talked about it with anyone and as far as I know, no one else looks at it that way. Over the years Quinn and I have talked about it, my mom and I have too, but none of us ever blamed Hugh."

"I wonder if he knows that," Aubrey said. "I wonder if he's carrying around all this guilt—keeping it bottled up inside. Maybe if he'd just talk about it…"

"You have to be careful," Zoe said. "Trust me. I've learned a thing or two in the time I've been with Aidan. They are fiercely loyal to one another and they don't take too kindly to anyone getting involved with family matters."

"I think that was just Aidan's issue," Darcy said.

"Maybe," Zoe replied, then looked at Aubrey. "But if you're going to have a relationship with Hugh, take my advice and tread lightly in this matter. It was one of our biggest obstacles when Aidan and I first started dating. And yes, part of it had to do with his mother. So if I were you, I'd take my suggestion and don't push."

"But it seems crazy he's so cut off from everything!" Aubrey cried. "If I can get him to just open up and deal with…"

"I'm with Zoe on this one," Anna said. "The Shaughnessys are a very tight, close-knit family and very private. Hugh takes it a bit to the extreme, but everyone deals with loss in their own way. Knowing what I do about him, I don't think Hugh would be able to handle it if you forced him to talk about it when he wasn't ready. He's very careful, very in control of his life."

"No one can control everything that happens around them," Aubrey argued lightly. "Things happen. Surely he doesn't think because he hasn't written it down it can't happen."

"Oh, but he does," Darcy said. "And if he can't control it, he won't talk about it." She went to refill her glass. "He's the king of sticking his head in the sand when he doesn't want to deal with something unpleasant. If I want to plan something for my future, I go to Hugh. If something is going on right now that's uncertain, I pretty much go to anyone else."

Anna stood and stretched. "I don't know about the rest of you, but now I really am hungry. I'm going to go and light the grill."

Everyone began to move around, but somehow, Aubrey had lost her appetite.

———

"You know you're not the designated driver or anything," Riley said, coming to sit beside Hugh at the bar. "Marco's got you covered."

Hugh lifted his ginger ale in a toast. "Thanks. I'm good."

"You can at least pretend you're having a good time."

With a quirked brow, Hugh looked at his brother. "So now there are rules for how I need to behave while we're out?"

Riley laughed. "Normally, no. But we're all hanging out and relaxing. Hell, even Dad's playing darts over there, laughing his ass off. Stop being the grandpa of the group and participate in an activity or two."

"Look, it's been a long day. I worked all day on Dad's yard, and if Quinn hadn't been up my ass about it, I'd be home right now."

"With Aubrey?"

"Hell yeah," Hugh said without giving it a second thought. "I had planned on taking her out tonight, but somehow I got wrangled into this."

"Seems to me it all worked out because she's out with Anna, Zoe, and Darcy. It's okay for the two of you to go out separately once in a while. It's not a crime."

Hugh glared at his brother and took a sip of his drink. "We spend plenty of time apart, and that's why when we have the chance to be together, it's what I want to do. I'm not like you, Ry. I'm not into the club scene."

Riley laughed harder now. "Dude, if you think this is a club scene, then you are severely out of touch. There are fifteen people here and our group takes up about half of that. It's just a night to kick back and relax. We never do that. We're always together for a celebration—like for Dad's birthday tomorrow night. Tonight was just for fun. Can't you just do that?"

"Do what?"

"Have fun?"

"I have plenty of fun!" Hugh snapped. "Seriously, why is everyone on my case about this?"

"Fine, I'll get everyone—whoever that is—to lay off if you come over and play a game of pool. Come on. Aidan's getting cocky over there and Owen's up about a hundred bucks already. I think you and I can take them on."

Riley started to turn away, but Hugh reached out and stopped him. "Hey," he began reluctantly. "Can I ask you something?"

Riley sat back down. "Yeah. Sure. What's up?"

"What do you think about...you know...me and Aubrey?"

"Wow. Okay. Um...I think she's great. You know I think she's great. Why? What's going on?"

There were too many things going on in his mind. That was the problem. "You know what...never mind. It's not important."

"No, no, come on. What's up? What...did Quinn give you shit today?"

Hugh frowned. "Quinn gives everyone shit, that's not anything new."

"Okay, then what's this about? Are you having second thoughts and it's awkward because she works for you?"

"No. Hell no!" Hugh replied adamantly. "If anything, things are getting better. It's just...damn. I can't wrap my brain around how fast it's happening. I mean, it's been a couple of months but…I want her with me all the time. When I'm traveling and she's home…I miss her."

Riley shifted uncomfortably. "Maybe you should be talking to Aidan about this. Or Dad."

"Yeah," Hugh grumbled. "Don't worry about it. I'll figure it out."

"Okay, fine." Riley sighed. "No need to get all dramatic about it."

"I'm not—"

"Yeah, you are." He signaled the bartender to bring over another drink. "So you're in love with her."

Was he? Hugh had been careful to not put a label on what he was thinking and feeling but when Riley said it, it felt right. He couldn't force himself to say it so he nodded instead.

"Okay. So…good." Riley took a pull from his beer and looked around carefully to see who could possibly save him. "Do…do you think she feels the same way?"

"That's the thing. I have no idea. We have a great time when we're together and we're completely in sync in almost every way, but I don't want to push her. I don't want to say anything to make her get skittish or scare her off."

"Like telling her you love her?"

"Well…yeah. Some people get freaked out by that sort of thing."

"I know I would."

"Good thing we're not talking about you, jackass."

"Look, I didn't ask to be part of this conversation so

let's not start with the name calling," Riley teased. "If you want my opinion, you're going to have to realistically put yourself out there."

"But…"

"Yeah, yeah, yeah. It's not who you are. Got it. But for whatever reason, you refuse to live your life without a constant safety net, and you're going to have to let that go. Are you willing to do that?"

"What if I wait? See if she says it first?"

"What if she's just as stubborn as you and is waiting for you to say it first? How long do you think it will take before that kind of game drives you batshit crazy?"

"Good point."

"Look, Hugh. I wish I knew what to say here, but I don't. I'm not trying to pawn you off or blow you off, I just think this is a better topic for Aidan."

"Or Dad."

He nodded. "Or Dad. It doesn't make me a bad person, you know."

"Yeah, I know. I guess I thought you might have something different to say."

"What do you mean?"

"Dad and Aidan? They're going to tell me to take the risk—it's worth it."

"And?"

"And I guess I was looking for another way."

"Dude, you have got to get over this obsession with playing it safe. It's borderline crazy now."

There wasn't anything he could say. It was the truth. But right now wasn't the time to let his brother know he was right.

Once more, Riley motioned for the bartender. "A

beer for my brother." He looked at Hugh as if daring
him to argue.

Yeah, that had been another part of playing things
safe but for tonight, he'd let his brother have this other
victory and he'd be a good sport about it.

"Come on. Let's see if we can help Owen part with
some of those winnings."

—◦◦◦—

It was late when Aubrey arrived back at the little apartment over Aidan and Zoe's garage, and she was surprised to find Hugh wasn't back yet. It was a happy
surprise because it meant he had relaxed enough to stay
out and have a good time with his brothers.

Or they were refusing to let him leave.

She chuckled at the thought as she got herself ready
for bed. The space was small and cozy, far from the
luxurious hotel suites she and Hugh normally stayed
in, but she loved it. She'd choose a place like this any
day of the week. The more she got to know Hugh, the
more she understood his logic in designing and decorat-
ing them all the same, but it was still a little…cold. No,
maybe that wasn't the right word. Maybe it was…nope,
cold. It was still a glorified hotel room—lacking any
real personality. And after visiting his childhood home,
knowing his feelings about it, she couldn't understand
why he didn't want something a little more like it.

"Just another layer to Mr. Hugh Shaughnessy I'd love
to figure out," she murmured as she slipped her nightie
on over her head. Although she wasn't tired, the thought
of curling up in the bed with her Kindle was very appealing. Sliding beneath the sheets, she grabbed the device

from the bedside table but didn't turn it on right away. It had been a very enjoyable night, she thought.

Conversation with the women who were quickly becoming very near and dear friends was never dull. They had laughed and joked around all night long and even after their very serious conversation about Lillian Shaughnessy, they were still able to go back to the easy bantering they'd been having. It was a nice feeling knowing she had found these friends. They were coming to mean more to her than some of the people she had known most of her life. They accepted her. Encouraged her. And if she wasn't mistaken, they genuinely cared about her—and not just because of her relationship with Hugh.

And boy, was everyone right about Anna's cooking skills. Sheesh. That girl did more with a burger than some of the five-star restaurants she and Hugh had dined at. She placed a hand over her still-full belly and smiled. Yeah, that was going to become a habit whenever they came here to visit. Or maybe she'd have to invite Anna to come inland and hang out with her for a weekend. Now there was a plan.

"Aubrey! I'm home!"

Looking up, she saw a very happy and relaxed-looking Hugh standing in the doorway. If she wasn't mistaken, he might even be a little bit tipsy. She almost giggled at the thought. Men didn't get tipsy, did they? "Hey, you," she said, smiling up at him.

"Whatcha doin'?" he asked, walking slowly across the room until he could plop down on the bed beside her.

"I was just going to read for a bit while I was waiting for you." His hair was tousled, his shirt was untucked, and he looked completely adorable to her. Reaching out, she ran a hand through his hair. "How was your night?"

Hugh stretched out beside her as he kicked his shoes off. "I took fifty bucks from my brother. It was awesome."

She chuckled. "Which brother?"

"Owen," he said around a yawn. "Served him right. Trying to trick me up with math."

Her brows furrowed. "Math?"

"Yeah. Such a smarty-pants. Thinks he knows everything. But I beat him. He may know about angles and lines and spots but I know how to provide a good distraction," he said with a silly grin.

"So you cheated."

"Ha! That's a good one! No, I did not cheat. I just happened to notice how Owen kept sneaking looks at this girl standing over by the jukebox. So while he was doing his geo…geolo…geomethology…"

"Geometry?"

"Yeah…so while he was doing that stuff in his head, I went over and introduced myself, then brought her over to meet Owen." He laughed. "Then he forgot all about how to do…you know…and Riley and I were able to kick his and Aidan's butts. It was fun."

Yeah, he was definitely a little tipsy and it was adorable. It was nice to see he could unwind and have fun with his brothers. "I'm glad you had a good time."

"How about you, darlin'? Did you have fun tonight?"

"I did. Anna made burgers and—"

"Oh man! And I missed it?" He sat up and looked around for his phone. Pulling it from his pocket, he began scrolling through his contacts.

"Hugh? What are you doing?"

"I'm starving. Do you think she'll make some more?"

"Who?"

"Anna," he said with a huff. "Sheesh."

"Hugh Shaughnessy, you cannot call Anna now and ask her to make you a burger!" She tried to sound firm but couldn't stop laughing at the confused look on his face. "Give me the phone."

"But...do we have any burgers here?"

She shook her head. "Nope. Sorry. No burgers."

"Well damn," he muttered, flopping back down on the bed. Looking over at her, he smiled sleepily. "They were good, right?"

Nodding, she said, "Yup. They were." Aubrey knew he was going to be asleep in a matter of minutes, but figured she'd humor him for a little bit longer. "Do you want me to make you something to eat? Or maybe just a little snack?"

"Mmm..."

Turning on her side to face him, she nudged him around until she got him undressed down to his boxers and even managed to get him under the blankets. He made several sloppy attempts to kiss her but she kept it playful to distract him. By the time he was settled, she was exhausted.

"Sweet dreams, wonderful man," she whispered, kissing his cheek.

Hugh smiled sleepily. "Love you," he murmured in response. Aubrey was glad his eyes were closed and he was already snoring softly, because she was certain the look of shock on her face would have been hard to explain.

Did he really mean what he'd said? Was it possible

Hugh was really in love with her? It was hard for Aubrey to wrap her head around. No one had ever said it to her before. And to be honest, Hugh really hadn't said it to her either—not consciously, anyway.

But now that it was out there, she had a feeling it was going to be pretty hard to forget.

Chapter 10

SOMETHING WAS DIFFERENT. HUGH COULDN'T PUT HIS finger on it, but he was certain he wasn't imagining that Aubrey was looking at him like he was a ticking time bomb. What could possibly have happened last night to cause that reaction? Sure, he got home after her, and he'd had a little more to drink than he usually did, but he remembered them talking and getting cozy before he fell asleep.

Was that it? Was she upset he'd had too much to drink and fell asleep before he could make love to her like he'd promised? He had to admit, the thought of her being disappointed about not being intimate made him smile with male pride. Then he looked at her and realized maybe he was patting himself on the back a little prematurely.

"Good morning," he said with a tentative smile.

"Good morning," she replied a little hesitantly. "How are you feeling?"

Ah, so it was the drinking. Good to know. "I'm fine. I'm sorry if I freaked you out last night. Riley convinced me to break my one-drink rule. I'm a bit of a lightweight now because of it. I hate that I fell asleep so fast. You know I had big plans for us."

Aubrey only nodded, then turned to look at the bedside clock. "Um…it's getting late. Do you want some breakfast?" She started to rise from the bed but Hugh reached out a hand to stop her.

"Last I checked we didn't have any place to be this morning," he said smoothly. "No need to jump up. Why don't we ignore the clock and take advantage of having time to ourselves." He gently tugged on her arm until she was reclined beside him.

Her eyes scanned his face, as if she was still uncertain of his well-being. Hugh couldn't believe she was being this cautious over one night. "Aubrey, sweetheart, I'm fine. You can stop looking at me like I'm not of sound mind."

"What? Oh no...that's not it. Sorry. It's just... Do you remember what happened last night?"

"You mean when I got home?"

She nodded.

He thought for a minute. "I came in here and you were already in bed—and looking incredibly sexy," he said with a wink. "Then I joined you and we talked about...me beating Owen at pool and the fact you had a good time with the girls." He looked at her for approval.

She nodded again.

"And then I got undressed and fell asleep. Why? Did I do something embarrassing?"

She chuckled. "No." Then she paused. "No."

He groaned. Dammit. The last thing he wanted to do was look like an idiot in front of Aubrey. Or anyone. "What did I do?" She told him about his near phone call to Anna and he burst out laughing. "Is that it? Whew! I thought I maybe groped you inappropriately or drooled on you. Trust me, Anna is used to Shaughnessy men calling her at ridiculous times of the night in search of food."

She arched a brow at him. "What exactly does that mean?"

"Quinn," he said with a smile, stacking his hands behind his head. "Anna's been spoiling him for years and he takes advantage of it. We all see it—hell, I think Anna even sees it—but she caves whenever he asks. She's been known to bake cookies at all hours of the night and bring them to him. With milk!"

"No!"

Hugh nodded enthusiastically, still thrilled this was all over his wanting to call Anna while mildly inebriated. "I really wish she'd cut him off. I think it would be good for him."

"Stop feeding him?"

"All of it. She's too good for him. Like I said, she spoils him. He doesn't appreciate her and he's too self-absorbed to realize she's in love with him."

Aubrey looked at him with wide-eyed shock. "Are you sure? How do you know?"

"Like I said, we all see it. Except Quinn. He treats her like she's his pal, his buddy. His best friend. I think she needs to play a little hard to get and wait for him to chase her."

"What if he doesn't?"

With a shake of his head, he replied, "Uh-uh. I know my brother. He's just clueless. I think if nudged in the right direction, he'd see Anna is the best thing that's ever happened to him, and he'll kick himself for wasting so much time."

"I don't think it's that simple," Aubrey protested.

"What? What's the matter?"

"I can't believe I didn't pick up on it. I'm normally really good with that sort of thing. I just thought they were good friends."

"Well, you haven't had a lot of time to observe them together."

"Yeah, but...damn."

"It's not that big a deal," he said lightly. "Come on. You're taking this a lot more personally than I thought you would. Why?"

She shrugged. "I don't know. It's...last night when I got back here, I started thinking about how much fun I had with the girls and how much they were starting to mean to me. I feel closer to Anna and Zoe...and even Darcy...than I do to some of the women I've been friends with for years. And to realize I missed out on a pretty key element of Anna's life? That just makes me feel like I'm not very good at this friend thing."

Like lightning, Hugh rolled over, pinned Aubrey beneath him, and kissed her hard. They were both breathless when he raised his head. "You are amazing at everything you do. Don't ever doubt that."

Unfortunately, she didn't seem convinced. "I pay attention to all kinds of details when I'm planning events and anything work related, but I'm so out of touch dealing with people I'm missing things," she said with dismay. "That's a huge character flaw, Hugh! What if I'm missing out on some key things with this campaign I'm doing for you?"

"Hey, hey, hey...come on now," he soothed. "I don't think the two are remotely related and you're getting yourself upset over nothing. Seriously." He pulled her into his arms and could feel the slight tremor in her body. Tucking a finger under her chin, he gently nudged Aubrey to look at him. "I'm sorry I upset you. I didn't mean to." He kissed her temple. "And I'm sorry I made a bit of a spectacle of myself last night. That's why I try to be more in control. It won't happen again."

Aubrey groaned and pulled out of his embrace before rolling from the bed. "Oh my God, Hugh! Enough!" she cried and stormed around the room looking for her robe. Pulling it on, she faced him. "I think it's great you went out last night and let your guard down! Hell, it's hard to sit back and watch someone be so damn perfect all the time. It's nice to see you can be human!"

His eyes went wide at her words. Seriously? She didn't think he was human? Carefully sitting up, he held a hand out to stop her. "What's going on here? I don't understand what you're upset about."

Rolling her eyes, Aubrey paced the confined space a few times. "I'm not upset you went out. I'm not upset you had more than your standard one beer. Hell, I'm not even upset you were going to call Anna."

Now he was really confused. And getting more than a little pissed. "Then what the hell is this all about?" he said, louder than he intended.

She huffed. "You don't remember, do you?"

Shit. What could he have possibly said to upset her like this? Racking his brain, nothing immediately came to mind, and he could do nothing but look up at her helplessly. "Aubrey, I...I seriously don't remember what I could have said."

She made a small sound of frustration and stormed from the room, muttering about how alcohol clearly muddles the brain. Rising from the bed, Hugh quickly donned his pants from the night before and went after her. He found her in the kitchen angrily pulling a box of cereal down from the cabinet. Stepping up behind her, he grasped her shoulders and spun her around.

"What did I say?" he asked with a slight shake. "If I'm going to be condemned here, at least have the decency to tell me the crime!"

"You said you loved me," she said quietly after a long moment.

"O-kay," he said slowly, not sure what the correct response was to diffuse the situation. On one hand he was relieved he had obviously said those words to her, while on the other he was pissed he couldn't remember saying it and it wasn't with some grand romantic gesture.

Nope. His first "I love you" would forever be remembered as drunken, stupid, and sleepy.

Great.

Once again she pulled out of his grasp. "That's it? That's all you have to say?"

"Aubrey, I'm kind of afraid to say anything at the moment," he said with a nervous chuckle.

For some reason, that had a calming effect on her. She waved her hand around as if to dismiss the whole thing. "Let's just forget about it, okay?"

"No. No, it's not okay," he said firmly, walking over and pinning her against the counter. "I'm not going to lie to you, I don't remember saying it." She tried to move away, but Hugh held her securely in place. "But that doesn't mean I didn't mean it."

Aubrey's eyes went wide.

"It's true, you know," he said, his voice and his eyes softening as he looked at her. "I do love you. I didn't think it was possible for it to happen so fast but...I love you, Aubrey Burke."

The transformation of the woman standing before him nearly took his breath away. Everything about her seemed to relax and soften. Her eyes went from wary to dreamy. A slow smile spread across those lips he longed to kiss. Ever so slowly, her arms wound their way around his shoulders.

"Say it again," she whispered.

"I love you, Aubrey Burke."

"I really like the sound of that."

So did Hugh.

Of course, he'd like it even more if she responded with her own declaration, but he could wait. Securing his arms around her, Hugh tugged her in close and lowered his head to kiss her. It was slow and sweet, better than anything he could remember. When they finally pulled apart, he felt Aubrey's shaky breath leave her body.

Taking a small step back, Hugh smiled at her. Her hair was rumpled, her robe was gaping slightly in the front, and her lips were glossy from their kiss.

She was a living, breathing wet dream.

But rather than take the obvious route by scooping her up in his arms and taking her back to bed, he decided to take things slow. He didn't want her to think his saying he loved her was a way of getting her back into bed.

"How about some coffee?" he asked instead.

She shook her head.

Looking over at the forgotten box of cereal, he moved toward it. "I could make us some eggs if you'd prefer?"

She shook her head again.

Placing the box back in the cabinet, he looked at her once more. "I need you to say something, sweetheart. You're making me nervous."

Now it was her turn to close the distance between them. Once again her arms went around him, and she got up on her tiptoes and kissed him. This time it was hot, wet, and it promised all kinds of things.

Hugh's body immediately got on board.

And just as soon as it started, it stopped. He looked at her in confusion, but she took one of his hands in hers and led him back to the bedroom. When they were next to the bed, she slowly pulled the sash from her robe and then let the garment slip to the floor. It left her in nothing but a tiny slip of caramel-colored silk and his mouth went dry.

Keeping her eyes locked on his, she lowered the slim straps from her shoulders. Stepping in to him, Aubrey pressed her naked body up against his.

"Had I known you were naked under that nightie, I wouldn't have let you out of bed earlier," he said, his voice rough and gravelly.

She nibbled on her bottom lip and gave him a small, sexy smile. "I need to tell you something."

"Anything."

"I love you too."

Hugh had never been happier or felt more complete. "I wanted us to say that for the first time in a much different way." His hand came up and caressed her cheek. "I wanted to do something romantic. I had planned..."

She shook her head and placed a finger over his lips. "This was perfect. No planning. No schedule. This is how it's supposed to be, Hugh."

At the sincerity in her voice and her eyes, Hugh knew she was right.

—///—

The party was in full swing when they arrived. Music and laughter filled the room, and Hugh could only think this was the greatest day ever. He and Aubrey had spent the day wrapped up in each other. Surrounded by his family and so many friends, Hugh felt a sense of peace.

It had been a long time coming.

Not that he'd been at war with himself. Much. But for far too long he'd been cautious and careful, doing everything just so. He'd forgotten how to just live.

Aubrey had helped him to live again.

Pulling her close to his side, he placed a kiss on her temple. "Ready to mingle?"

"Absolutely," she said with a big grin.

She was stunning. Her beautiful long hair was pulled up in a messy kind of twist that somehow managed to look both sexy and elegant. The dress was the same color as the silk nightie she'd worn this morning, and it brought out the golden tone of her skin and the shimmery makeup she wore.

His golden beauty.

And she loved him.

For the next thirty minutes, they made their way around the room together. The Shaughnessys had always enjoyed spending time together and celebrating life's accomplishments, but this was the first time Hugh could remember there being so many friends. In Hugh's mind, he always associated large groups like this with his mother's funeral. He knew those friends and neighbors had been there that day to offer comfort and support, but he had seen them as intruders. But now?

Now he saw smiling, laughing faces, saw how happy his father looked, and it managed to push the bad memory further away.

"You're looking awfully cheery tonight," Aubrey said from beside him.

"I'm feeling very cheery." He grinned.

"Any particular reason?"

Adjusting her so they were face-to-face rather than side by side, he pulled her in and kissed her thoroughly. "I've got the woman I love with me and we're here to celebrate my dad. Doesn't get much better than this."

She chuckled. "I think you need to have more than one beer a little more often."

He looked at her quizzically. "What?"

"Ever since last night, you've just…I don't know… mellowed. You look rested. Happy. At peace." She combed a wayward strand of hair from his temple. "Even a little unkempt. And I like it."

"Just like?"

She blushed. "Okay…love. I love it." Then she sighed a little dreamily. "And I love you."

"That's good, sweetheart, because I love you too."

"Are we ever going to get tired of saying it?"

He shook his head. "Never." Then he rested his forehead against hers.

"Oh, for the love of it, get a room, you two." They turned their heads to see Riley walking over. Once he reached them, he kissed Aubrey on the cheek and shook Hugh's hand. "Glad you could finally put in an appearance."

"We weren't late," Hugh grumbled.

"Thirty minutes. Dad was ready to send out a search

party. You're never late. You're anal like that." Then
he chuckled. "So I reminded Dad that you happened
to have a beautiful distraction and we should just let
you be."

"You're a prince, Ry," Hugh said, relaxing.

"Thank you, Riley," Aubrey added. "Everything
looks great."

They all looked around the room. "This is Dad's
favorite restaurant and they know us here—the owners
treat us like family. We knew they'd make everything
just right for him."

Aubrey scanned the room until she spotted Zoe and
Aidan. She was about to excuse herself when she heard
Riley curse under his breath. "What's wrong?"

"Look at that," he said in a low tone, pointing to a far
corner. "I need to put a stop to it."

Hugh put a hand on his brother's arm. "Put a stop
to what?"

"Quinn. He's over there in Anna's face, and she's
either ready to punch him or burst into tears. Either way,
I'm not having it tonight. No way is he going to ruin
Dad's party."

"What's his problem?"

"Does there need to be one? Really? He's just being
himself." Riley took off through the crowd, and Hugh
grabbed Aubrey's hand and followed.

Once they were within earshot, it wasn't hard to
figure out what was going on.

"Why are you being so difficult? Just put the damn
sweater on!"

"I don't want to put the sweater on! There's nothing
wrong with what I'm wearing!"

"Oh really? So you think going around practically topless is fine now. Is that it?"

Anna rolled her eyes. "It's a strapless dress," she said wearily.

Riley put his hand on Quinn's shoulder. "Hey, bro, can you come and give me a hand by the bar?"

"What? Why?"

"Because I need your help, that's why." And before Quinn could argue further, Riley was leading him away.

Hugh and Aubrey stepped in. "You okay?" Hugh asked.

Anna shook her head. "I swear he gets more and more ornery the older he gets." She nervously fidgeted with her hair and smoothed a hand down the front of her dress. Looking at the two of them, she asked, "Seriously, is there something wrong with this dress? Should I run home and change?"

"You look beautiful," Hugh said, and Aubrey nodded. "Don't listen to him."

"It's hard not to when he keeps getting in my face. I had to send Mark on a fool's errand just to keep things from getting out of hand."

"Wait…who's Mark?" Aubrey asked.

"My date," Anna said distractedly, looking around the room.

"Your date? When did that happen? You didn't mention a date when we were hanging out last night."

Anna shrugged. "It was an impulsive decision. He's a nice guy. I met him at work and he's asked me out a couple of times. I thought this might be a good ice-breaker. You know, no pressure. Just hanging out."

Aubrey and Hugh exchanged looks. "Did Quinn know you were bringing a date?" Hugh asked.

"It didn't come up," she said, still looking around the room.

"Hey," Hugh said, reaching out and gently cupping her chin, forcing her to look at him. "I'm proud of you."

"You are? For what?"

He pulled her into a brotherly embrace. "Stick to your guns, kiddo. Don't let my brother get to you."

She sagged slightly against him. "I can't keep waiting around," she said quietly.

"I know." He kissed the top of her head before releasing her. "I'm going to go snag us a couple of drinks," he said to Aubrey, nodding his head in Anna's direction.

Once he was gone, Aubrey squeezed Anna's hand. "You okay?"

Anna nodded. "I didn't think it would be a big deal. I really didn't. I've brought dates to things before. But for some reason, Quinn just sort of…I don't know… He was instantly hostile. I felt really bad for Mark. He had no idea what he was getting into. I wouldn't blame him if he didn't come back."

"Where did you send him?"

"I told him I forgot Ian's birthday card. He was running to Walmart to grab one." Then she shook her head. "I'm telling you, he's probably twenty miles from here and not looking back."

"It couldn't have been that bad," Aubrey said.

"You heard how Quinn was talking when you came over. It's been like that since I got here. Once he saw Mark leave, he got on me to cover up with that stupid sweater." She touched her dress again. "It's not a bad little dress, and other than it being strapless, it's kind of tame."

Aubrey had to agree. It wasn't a figure-hugging dress at all—more of a loose-fitting sheath. But the colors were bright and vibrant, very different from anything she'd seen Anna wear. "Well, his brothers are on to him so I'm sure you won't have to deal with any more of his comments."

"One can only hope." Then Anna got a good look at Aubrey. "You look different tonight," she said cryptically. "Something's different—you're all…glowy." Hugh stepped back over and Anna looked at him. "You too."

"Me too what?" Hugh asked, slightly confused.

"You're both all glowy and have sappy grins on your faces. What's going on?"

They looked at one another and Aubrey was about to speak when Hugh beat her to the punch. "We're in love."

"Aww…you guys." She gave a happy little squeal before hugging them both. "Thank God. Some good news!"

Aubrey couldn't help but smile. She took the drink Hugh held out and thanked him. "Why don't you go and mingle? Anna and I are going to talk for a little bit until Mark gets back."

"If he gets back," Anna grumbled.

Hugh took the hint. He kissed Aubrey before walking away into the crowd.

"I knew you would be good for him," Anna said, pulling Aubrey toward a quiet table in the corner. They each took a seat. "He needed someone like you."

"I needed someone like him, too."

"I felt bad after we talked last night. I can't really say for sure what's going on in Hugh's mind. It was all speculation, you know that, right?"

Aubrey nodded. "It was great to have a little insight, though. And what you said made a lot of sense. I think he's turned a corner. He's so much more relaxed than he was two months ago. I'd like to take some of the credit for it, but I think he just needed a little nudge."

"He needed more than a nudge," Anna said with a smile. "And it came in the form of a good woman."

"I just want him to be happy, you know?"

"From your lips to God's ears." Anna raised her glass in a toast. They clinked glasses.

"We're happy, his family—for the most part—is happy, and he's looking at some pretty impressive business expansion in the next year. He has plenty of reasons to feel good right now."

"I really am glad, Aubrey. I'm sorry if I'm being a downer. I guess I let Quinn get to me more than I should have."

"What are you going to do about it?"

"I don't know. I thought bringing a date would be a good thing. A good distraction. All I managed to do was kill my good mood."

Aubrey noticed Anna's brother Bobby towering over Quinn menacingly. "Uh-oh…"

Anna followed the direction of Aubrey's gaze and chuckled. "Don't worry. It happens all the time."

"They don't get along?"

"That's an understatement. Bobby won't tell me why, but he can't seem to help himself. If the two of them are in a room together, Bobby's all over Quinn."

"He's looking out for you," Aubrey said simply.

"Maybe. Or maybe he just doesn't like Quinn."

"Like I said, he's looking out for you."

"Okay, enough about me. Tell me about you and Hugh. Was it romantic? Did he do it over candlelight? He looks like the type who would say it over candle-light. Were there flowers? Roses?"

Aubrey laughed and stopped her. "You have a very overactive imagination. It wasn't anything like that. It just slipped out."

"Really?"

Aubrey nodded. "He said it as he was falling asleep last night."

With an exaggerated sigh, Anna slouched in her seat. "Wow. I'm bummed. I thought for sure it would have been more romantic than that." She shook her head. "Very disappointing."

"Sorry. I didn't know there were going to be points awarded," Aubrey teased.

"Well, now you know. I'll be expecting something much more romantic at the next milestone." She paused. "Did you guys talk about the future? Getting married? Kids? Settling down? Any of that good stuff?"

Aubrey glanced down at the drink in her hands. "Not really. I mean, we talked about our feelings and the future in a general respect. But nothing specific. Nothing about marriage, that's for sure."

"Do you want to get married?"

"To Hugh?"

"No, to Diego, the dishwasher in the back. Of course Hugh!"

Aubrey couldn't help but laugh. "Okay, okay. Sorry." She thought about it. "I really do. I can't believe it. I mean, two months ago I was willing to marry a man I didn't like—let alone love—and now I can't imagine my life without Hugh. When he said he loved me, it was everything I ever wanted to hear. No one's ever said it to me before."

"Ever?" Anna asked incredulously. "Surely your parents…"

Aubrey shook her head. "Never. My parents aren't the warm, fuzzy types. Honestly, Hugh was the first."

"Wow. I don't know what to say to that."

"Yeah, I know. It's weird."

"Well, I'm sure it won't take long for you to get used to hearing it. From everything Zoe's shared, Aidan tells her all the time how much he loves her. And when Lillian was still alive? She and Ian were very affectionate with one another. It was very sweet to see."

"Aww…"

Anna nodded. "So what about kids? Do you want to have a bunch of kids? I imagine Hugh wants to. Out of all of the Shaughnessys, I picture both him and Aidan with a bunch of kids."

Aubrey paled. "Why do you say that?"

"Because deep down, those two are the most nurturing of the family. Plus, they had the most years watching Ian and Lillian raise their family. Zoe's excited to get pregnant and already said she wants at least four. And a dog." She stopped and chuckled. "Aidan said he was completely on board with it—including the dog—but wasn't sure he'd want any more than that."

"I didn't think people had big families anymore." Aubrey quickly finished her drink.

"Well, for them it's more about Zoe not wanting to have an only child like she was and Aidan coming from a big family. They're sort of on the same page.

So what about you? How many do you want? Three? Four? Seven?"

"Dogs or kids?"

Anna rolled her eyes. "Seriously?"

"I…I don't…" She cleared her throat and looked around for a way to snag another drink.

"So? What are you thinking?" Anna asked excitedly.

"I really haven't thought about it."

Anna made a bit of a face. "Really? I thought everyone thought about stuff like that. I know I want at least two but no more than four." She took a sip of her own drink. "Two is very manageable but it could be fun to have a few more."

Aubrey nodded, scanning the room distractedly. "I suppose."

"Hey," Anna said, reaching out and touching Aubrey's hand. "Are you okay? Did I say something wrong?"

"What? Oh…no. It's nothing. I guess it just hit me that kids and marriage and all those things are going to start coming up. I'm barely able to believe someone like Hugh is in love with me and it's hard to wrap my head around anything beyond that."

Anna looked relieved. "Oh. Good. Whew! I thought I'd upset you." She relaxed in her seat for a minute before asking, "What are you thinking right now?"

"Tell me again how lucky I am," Aubrey said, smiling and pushing the negative thoughts that were creeping in aside.

"You are the luckiest woman I know. Well, next to Zoe." Anna's gaze landed on the woman in question. "I look at what she and Aidan have and I can't help but be envious. Now I'll have to look at you that way too."

"And someday, we'll both look at you like that. Deal?"

"Deal."

———⁓———

"Mmm…this is nice," Aubrey murmured as Hugh held her in his arms and swayed to the music.

"It certainly is," he agreed, pulling her just a little bit closer.

"Your family knows how to throw a party. Believe me, I know. I've done dozens of parties for my father's company and never have I ever seen so many smiling faces."

Hugh chuckled. "Probably because everyone here is just happy to celebrate Dad's birthday. No one's hitting them up for money or business deals."

"Maybe." She sighed and lifted her head from his shoulder. "Your dad is enjoying himself."

The sight of his father dancing with Martha Tate was a little much for Hugh to process so he put his focus back on Aubrey. "He deserves it. Normally we have a family dinner to celebrate his birthday, but as he's getting out and socializing a little bit more these days, we all thought we'd try this. I guess it was a good call."

"I'd say it was definitely a success."

They swayed until the song ended and then made their way off the makeshift dance floor. Looking at his watch, Hugh saw it was nearing midnight and the crowd was starting to thin. It would have been easy to make the rounds and say good night to everyone, but he wanted to wait until it was just the family left.

His eyes scanned the room and he saw Aidan and

Zoe sitting in the corner talking with Owen. Darcy was standing with a small group of ladies from the neighborhood—no doubt talking about how she was enjoying college. Riley was over by the bar talking with one of the waitresses. Hugh realized it was Tina Kay—a girl his brother had dated in high school. He couldn't help but smile and wonder if it was awkward for Riley when he ran into old girlfriends.

Anna and Mark were talking with the rest of the Hannigans, and Hugh was relieved the earlier tension had died down. But where exactly was Quinn?

A loud bark of laughter rang out from across the room and Hugh breathed a sigh of relief when he spotted Quinn talking with a few of his father's cronies. They were all interested in the classic cars Quinn specialized in, so there was probably a heated debate going on.

"You're smiling," Aubrey said softly beside him.

"This is good." He wrapped an arm around her waist. "I'm looking around the room and it's filled with all the people who mean the most to me. They're all here for Dad and they're all having a good time." He kissed her temple. "In my book, that makes it a good night."

"A great one," she said.

For the next hour the crowds continued to thin until it was only the Shaughnessys along with Bobby, Anna, and Mark. Even though the restaurant's waitstaff was cleaning up, everyone lent a hand. When the room was completely put back together, everyone began to herd toward the door.

Ian stopped in the entryway and turned to everyone. "You all have no idea how much this night meant to me. I know I'm not usually the party-going type, but I really think that could change. You made this old man feel like a king tonight and I love you all for it."

"Oh, Daddy," Darcy said, walking over to hug her father. Soon the rest of the family piled on.

They stayed like that for a solid minute before Ian called out, "Of course I'd love to try it again sometime if I don't suffocate first!"

Everyone laughed and moved back, making their way out the door to the parking lot. Within minutes, Hugh and Aubrey were in their car with Aidan and Zoe in the backseat, watching the other cars pull away first.

"Thanks for driving us home, Hugh," Aidan said. "We came with Dad but he and Darcy were anxious to get home. You're saving him the stop."

"I don't know why we didn't come together earlier," Hugh said, pulling out of his spot.

"Because I wanted to get here early and make sure everything was set up as we wanted it," Zoe replied. "I think it was an amazing night. Yay us."

Aidan leaned over and kissed her on the cheek—a move Hugh witnessed in the rearview mirror. It made him smile.

"So," Aidan said, clearing his throat, "I know it's late but...do you guys think you could hang out a bit back at the house?"

"Sure. What's up?" Hugh asked.

"We wanted to pick your brain about wedding locations," Zoe said. "I know Aidan called a while ago and we said no rush, but..."

"Is there suddenly a rush?" Aubrey asked, turning around with a broad grin.

"What?" Zoe croaked. "Oh dear…no. No, no, no, no, no."

"Oh. Well, darn." Aubrey turned back in her seat. Hugh reached over and squeezed her hand.

"Yeah, we can hang out for a little while if you'd like," Hugh said.

The rest of the ride was spent talking about the party and how happy Ian had been. By the time they pulled up at Aidan and Zoe's, everyone was starting to mellow.

"You sure you're up for it?" Aidan asked.

Truth be known, Hugh had other plans he'd rather be following up on right now. Aubrey had looked like a fantasy come true all night, and his fingers were twitching with the need to peel her dress off her. One look at her and he saw she was reading his mind.

"Later," she whispered.

Hugh made up his mind to give his brother thirty minutes to describe what he wanted, and if they hadn't decided by then, they'd pick up the conversation another time.

There was a lot he wanted to do to Aubrey—with Aubrey—tonight. Seeing her with his family after having declared his love for her sealed the deal for him. He wanted to talk about their own tomorrow—their future.

And he wanted them to start right now.

Chapter 11

Something was off.

Hugh couldn't put his finger on it, but for the last several weeks, things hadn't been quite the way he'd hoped.

After the night of his father's birthday, he and Aubrey had begun to talk about the future but she always pulled back a little. Hugh didn't doubt she loved him—he knew it. He felt it. But talking about planning their future seemed to make her uncomfortable. She wanted to take it slow, enjoy the moment…and normally it would have been fine for him, but lately? It wasn't enough.

And for a guy who normally thrived on taking things slow and planning them out, that was saying something.

Sitting at his desk in his Napa office, he looked over the list for the final preparations for the first gala launch in Montana this weekend. It was hard to believe it was already here. He had to hand it to Aubrey, she had outdone herself. Even if he wasn't already in love with her, he'd be blown away by her skills and the way she had taken on this project and made it her own.

On a typical work day, Hugh would read reports like this for hours on end, but right now he couldn't quite concentrate. He needed to know what was going on with her and how to break down her defenses where their future was concerned. He'd been willing to ride the wave, so to speak, but he wasn't used to this feeling of being in limbo.

While he thought they'd been on the same page, lately he'd been a bit bold—talking about marriage, children, settling down. Aubrey had seemed like she was on the same page at first, but the more Hugh talked about it, the quieter she became. For the life of him, he couldn't imagine why and he'd hoped she'd share her concerns with him, but as she'd remained mum on the subject, he knew it was going to be up to him to find out what was going on.

Glancing at his calendar, Hugh calculated he would be seeing Aubrey in a little less than forty-eight hours. He had wanted them to fly in together, but she had told him she had some things she wanted to oversee at the resort for the party and would be arriving before him, and to please not change his schedule for her.

She was considerate like that and normally he appreciated it, but he had a feeling not wanting him there was more personal than business.

But why?

There was a war raging within him. Hugh was torn between respecting Aubrey's request and getting to the bottom of things. She had turned his life upside down from the moment he'd first seen her, and he'd come to realize not all unexpected surprises or spontaneous events were bad. While one spontaneous act had led to something horrific, Hugh had realized he had gone to extremes to avoid making that mistake again.

It would have been easy to wallow and obsess about missed opportunities, but what was the use? No, right now all Hugh could focus on was how he was going to change—how he was going to live his life. Starting right now.

And that meant going to Aubrey and finding out where exactly they stood, and what was obviously scaring her about marriage.

Picking up his desk phone, he called through to Dorothy.

"Yes, boss?"

"I need to get a flight to Montana for today," he said, his pulse racing with anticipation.

"Today?"

"As soon as possible." He felt the tension of only moments ago easing from his body. "I need to get to Aubrey."

"Why? Is she all right? Did something happen?" she asked nervously.

Hugh chuckled. "No. I just... I need her, Dotty." And although he couldn't see her, Hugh could have sworn he heard his assistant smile.

"Give me ten minutes. Go pack," she said before hanging up.

———◦◦◦———

"Liza, I think we need to get the electrician to add more twinkly lights in the east corner of the room. What do you think?" Aubrey was studying the lighting inside the large party tent, nibbling on her lip. Everything was coming along exactly as she had planned it, and now they were just fine-tuning.

"He just stepped out to grab some more. I'll let him know." Liza was the on-site assistant at the Montana resort and, as far as Aubrey was concerned, an angel.

From the moment Aubrey had arrived on site, Liza had been by her side. She seemed to anticipate what

Aubrey was going to need before she realized she needed it. She was making things flow far easier than Aubrey thought possible and it was wonderful.

And right now, Aubrey was all about needing things to go easier because her mind and her heart were in total chaos.

Ever since her conversation with Anna, she had been a complete mess. It was one thing to tell Hugh she loved him, and to say she wanted to marry him—even though she'd only shared that last bit with Anna. But beyond that? The thought of kids and forever scared the hell out of her.

Her parents had never had a happy marriage, and having Aubrey had only seemed to make things worse. She'd had no idea what a happy family looked like until she'd spent time with the Shaughnessys, and that wasn't enough for her to feel confident having a family of her own.

Instinctively, her hand rested on her flat belly as she sighed. Maybe if…

"Okay, the electrician is good with setting up more lighting in the east corner. The sound system is ready for a test drive. Any requests?" Liza asked with a big smile.

Aubrey looked at her oddly. "Requests?"

"Yeah. Music. Any favorite songs? Something fast? Something slow? You name it, and he'll play it."

Somehow Aubrey doubted the DJ had any classical music or jazz on hand. "Ask him to play something by Riley Shaughnessy."

Liza's smile grew. "An excellent choice." Then she walked back over to the DJ.

Standing alone, Aubrey pushed all thoughts of Hugh

and marriage and children aside. There was so much to do, and she knew tonight—just like every other night since Ian's party—she would lie in bed while her mind raced with thoughts of what the future with Hugh would look like.

Suddenly music blared all around her. She had always disliked large parties—they were always so loud. Walking over to where Liza stood, she leaned in close. "We don't want our guests having to talk in each other's ears all night. The music needs to be soft—even if it's upbeat music, we need the volume down. This isn't a dance club."

Liza nodded. "Got it." She hopped behind the music podium to speak to the DJ. Moments later, the volume softened and she looked at Aubrey for approval.

With a smile and a thumbs-up, Aubrey turned and did a slow tour of the room while the song played.

> *I swear we're one as I get lost in your eyes,*
> *Forever in my heart, your soft hand in mine.*
> *You'll whisper in my ear, I love you*
> *And I'll sleep better than I ever have.*
> *I always see you in my dreams.*
> *I'm never without you…*

Tears welled in Aubrey's eyes at the lyrics. So beautiful. They described how she felt about Hugh. Emotion threatened to overwhelm her, and she knew if she didn't get some fresh air, she'd be a weeping mess in front of the staff. One last glance around showed everything was under control and she turned to head for the exit.

And there he was.

As if she had conjured him up, Hugh stood in the entryway of the tent looking all kinds of sexy. Aubrey suddenly felt shy, almost afraid to go to him. Mainly because of how she felt over listening to Riley's song, but partly because she loved him so much it scared her.

Hugh's eyes locked on hers and he stood still, waiting for her to come to him.

As if she could stay away.

Slowly, she walked toward him. Her heart raced and her eyes burned with unshed tears but once she was standing in front of him—so close she could feel the heat of his body—Aubrey forced herself to come off as light and breezy, pushing aside her fear and anxiety for the time being.

"You weren't supposed to be here yet," she said teasingly.

"Are you mad I'm here?" Aubrey could tell it was taking every ounce of his control to not reach out and touch her.

"That depends… Are you checking up on me? Afraid I'm going to mess up this event?"

Hugh smiled warmly. "Never. I know you could do this sort of thing with your eyes closed and still make it spectacular."

"So then what brings you here? I distinctly remember your schedule keeping you in Napa for another two days."

Lightning quick, his strong arms banded around her waist as he pulled her close. "I didn't want to wait that long to see you." His eyes scanned her face, his smile slowly fading. "I needed to see you. To be with you."

And Aubrey's heart did a little flip in her chest.

Would it always be this way? How was it possible this man had the ability to make her anxious and overwhelmed one minute and then a complete puddle the next? Why did being in love feel so much like an emotional roller coaster?

Hugh tucked a finger under her chin to force her to look at him, seemingly distressed when she didn't respond. "I should have called first."

"No." She shook her head. "No…I was just surprised, that's all. I'm so wrapped up in fine-tuning everything around here and I wasn't expecting to see you until Friday. I'm sorry."

He didn't look like he believed her. "Are you almost done here? Can we have dinner?"

Aubrey looked at her watch. "Oh my goodness… I didn't realize it had gotten so late." With a look around, she spotted Liza and stepped from Hugh's arms. "Just give me a minute and we can go."

"Aubrey," he called after her. "I don't want you to change things on my account. If you have things to do, I completely understand."

And she knew he did. But she also knew it was time to call it a day. Her stomach rumbled, and she realized she had never stopped for lunch. "Just give me one minute," she said with a smile and made her way across the room.

———

They had dinner.

They toured the resort so Aubrey could show him how everything was unfolding for the event.

Now they were back at Hugh's suite and they were

both quiet. Standing back, Hugh simply observed her for a few minutes. She had come in, kicked off her shoes, and seemed a little tense. They had talked about work and the gala over dinner but had stayed away from anything more personal.

Hugh walked to the kitchen and poured each of them a drink before going to the living room and inviting Aubrey to sit with him. She smiled at him over her shoulder and joined him. Once she was there and they were comfortable, Hugh reached for her hand.

"It's so good to be here with you," he said, marveling at the softness of her skin. "I missed you." It had been less than a week but that didn't make it any less true.

"I missed you too," she said, then went silent again.

"Aubrey, what's going on? I feel like you're pulling away from me and I don't know why. I don't understand what happened."

Her eyes went wide for a moment and she shifted in her spot before looking away. Hugh knew whatever she was going to say, it wasn't going to be what he wanted to hear.

"I'm just trying to focus on these events," she said a little quietly. "We've been working on them for what seems like forever and I don't want to let you down."

Reaching over, he cupped her cheek in his hand. "Sweetheart, you could never disappoint me. Ever. I've seen how hard you've worked, and walking around here tonight, seeing your vision come to life, has been amazing." He caressed her face. "But I think it's more than that. I think something else is on your mind."

Aubrey sagged a little in her seat. "I'm feeling a little overwhelmed," she finally said.

"With the work or…with us?" he asked cautiously.

"Us." Her voice was barely a whisper.

Even though Hugh had known this was a possibility, he still wasn't prepared for the kick in the gut he felt at her confirmation. Slowly, he lowered his hand. "Why?" It seemed like such a small word, yet it was so full of emotion he almost choked on it.

Her eyes met his. "You once asked me if I thought everything was moving too fast."

"And you told me it felt right," he countered, anxious for her to remember that fact.

Aubrey nodded. "I know. And it did. It does," she quickly corrected. "But I look at you and your family and, I don't know how to explain it, Hugh, but it scares me."

"My family scares you?" he asked incredulously. It was the most ridiculous thing anyone had ever said to him.

Rolling her eyes, Aubrey faced him. "I come from a very different world, Hugh. I'm an only child. My parents are divorced and I'm not close with them. They're not warm or loving people like you grew up with. I don't know how to be like that!"

Now his eyes went a little wide. "Aubrey, I love who you are. I don't want you to be like anyone else. And I don't think I ever implied I did." He took her hands in his again. "I love you. And I know we haven't talked about it much but…I want to marry you. Have a family with you. Every time I look at you…I feel like I'm home. I know everything's going to be okay."

Tears filled her eyes as she lowered her chin and shook her head.

A trickle of panic began at the base of his spine. "Aubrey?" he whispered. "Tell me. Tell me what's wrong."

She looked up at him and his heart broke for the pain he saw there. "You can't know that," she said, her voice shaky. "You can't possibly know everything's going to be okay. What if something happened? I see how your mother's death still affects you even though you won't talk about it. There are no guarantees, and I don't know if I can handle that kind of pressure."

"What are you talking about? What pressure?"

"You look at me with hope. You look at me like I can guarantee you this wonderful life and I can't!"

"Aubrey, I'm not looking for a guarantee—"

"Yes, you are," she interrupted. "You always are. It's what you do. You don't take risks. You don't stray from the schedule. You play it safe."

"There's nothing wrong with playing things safe, Aubrey. Not everyone needs to take risks or be irresponsible."

She pulled her hands from his as she stood. Moving away from the sofa, she paced. "Taking a risk doesn't mean you're being irresponsible. Sometimes life is about the risks! Sometimes you have to take a chance, break free..."

"Like climbing out a window?" he asked, shocked at his own sarcasm.

She laughed mirthlessly. "Are we back to that?" In an instant she was standing right in front of him. "You may look at that one act and judge me, but let me tell you something, Hugh Shaughnessy, it is no different from what you've done with your entire life. Yes. I climbed out a window to get out of doing something I knew was going to be a huge mistake. But your whole existence since your mother died is one big open window. You refuse to take the chance. Or the risk. Why? Because you're too afraid to."

Now he stood. "It's not the same thing at all!" he shouted. "Do you realize there are consequences for some of those risks? Some of those chances? I was an irresponsible, selfish jackass at seventeen! I broke the rules more than I followed them, and because of that, because I didn't give a damn, my mother is dead!" He raked a trembling hand through his hair. "You ran away because you knew you were making a mistake, and rather than just own up to it, you shimmied out a window. I chose to stop making the mistakes. Big difference."

"Hugh, what happened to your mother was an accident. It wasn't your fault!" She reached for him, but he pulled away. "How long are you going to keep carrying that guilt?"

"Forever," he said grimly. "If I had followed the rules, I wouldn't have been grounded. If I hadn't been grounded, I would have gone to the pharmacy for her that day and she would still be alive right now."

"Hugh…"

He held up a hand to stop her. "I don't want to talk about this anymore." His voice was quiet and calm. "I don't want to look back anymore, Aubrey. Not with you. I want a future with you. A life. I love you. I don't care that you came from a home where your parents didn't express their love. You're one of the most loving people I've ever known. I know you love me and I know you're going to be an amazing mother one day. Don't be—"

"No. Just…please. Just stop."

"I don't understand."

"Can we please not talk about this right now? Can we please just get through the weekend and through the gala before we talk about this again?"

"Aubrey, sooner or later we're going to have to talk about it. I don't want to live in limbo with you. I want us to start planning our future."

She smiled at him sadly. "Please."

And he nodded. He had no choice. He wanted Aubrey, and if that meant giving her a little more time, then he'd do it.

———

"I've got to hand it to you, Aubrey, you outdid yourself. Everything was amazing."

Standing a little straighter and smiling through the pain from her stilettos, Aubrey looked over at Bill. "Thank you. Everything turned out even better than I had hoped."

"Seriously, kid, you rocked it. The food is delicious, the room is gorgeous, and everyone is having a great time and talking to me about my wines." He motioned to a spot across the room where Hugh was talking to a reporter. "And your man has never looked more relaxed and comfortable in his own skin. That's because of you."

Aubrey's eyes went wide at his words. "What…? How…? Why would you say that?"

A loud, hearty laugh escaped Bill and he finished off his glass of wine. "Sweetheart, I've known Hugh for a long time and he's never been like this. The two of you aren't exactly a secret, you know. And personally, I think it's great. You're good for him."

"Thank you," she murmured, wishing the conversation had stayed on the gala.

"So have the two of you set a date yet?"

"Excuse me?"

He nodded toward Hugh again. "A date. A wedding date," he said to clarify. "Hugh comes from a large family and he's not getting any younger. I imagine the two of you are ready to start settling down, making babies. What's he got, six, seven siblings?" he asked with a laugh.

"Five," Aubrey said as her stomach sank just a little.

"Damn. I couldn't imagine. His poor mother, right?"

Rather than reply, Aubrey decided to change the subject. "So did the food complement your wines?"

But Bill was no fool. He gave her a glance and reached for another glass of wine from a passing waiter. He nodded and took a sip. "Nice deflection," he murmured. "Yes, the chef really hit it out of the park. Everything was perfect."

"Good." She almost sagged with relief. "I'm glad. For the party next month we're—"

"Aubrey," Bill interrupted. "Relax. Enjoy the party. There's no need for you to be talking business anymore. You're a success! This party is awesome! Just go mingle and enjoy yourself, okay?"

And without another word, Bill walked away, leaving Aubrey alone. Unsure what to do with herself, she began to wander the room, making sure everything was all right. Technically, she wasn't working, she was observing. Liza was more or less running the show and handling any issues that came up.

The music played at an enjoyable level, and when a slow song came up, Aubrey gasped as strong hands landed on her waist and spun her around.

Hugh.

"Dance with me," he softly said as he wrapped her

in his embrace. Together they swayed to the music, and Aubrey couldn't help but sigh and relax into him.

If nothing else, she was so thankful for moments like this—for the way Hugh had made her love dancing again. Right now, as her body moved against his, she felt peace. The music. The man.

If only it could be like this all the time.

"You're tensing," Hugh whispered in her ear. "No tensing. We're dancing and it's a beautiful night."

Damn, she hadn't realized she was doing it. One second she was relaxed and the next…? Never mind. She let her body ease back into that relaxed state and let the music wrap around her again.

"Would it be terrible if we didn't stay to the end?" he murmured.

"Yes," she said with a light chuckle. "This is your night, Hugh. This is a big deal for your resort. You need to stay until everyone leaves so they can tell you how fabulous you are."

"I don't need the praise. What I need is you."

She sighed. They hadn't made love since he'd arrived in Montana. After their argument that first night, they had been cautiously circling one another, each afraid to say anything to upset the other. While Aubrey was used to living that way—she had for most of her life—she knew it was bothering Hugh. She had asked for him to wait until after the gala, and time was quickly running out.

They danced.

They mingled.

They graciously accepted the compliments on the success of the event.

It was after two a.m. when they finally walked through

the door of their suite. Aubrey immediately kicked off her shoes and reached for the pearl choker she had been wearing to take it off. Hugh's hands gently brushed hers aside as his fingers and lips grazed her neck. "Let me," he whispered.

After such a long night and a hectic week, his touch felt glorious to her. Leaning back into him, she purred. "That feels nice."

"It's going to feel a whole lot better. I promise."

Aubrey let the rest of the world simply melt away. For tonight, she would luxuriate in Hugh's love and not give tomorrow a second thought.

The sun had barely started to break through the curtains when Hugh found himself wide awake. Aubrey was curled up against him, her hand on his chest, her head on his shoulder, and he smiled. It was the perfect way to wake up.

The first gala was a success and now it was behind them. The next one wasn't for another six weeks, so they had some downtime coming to them and he was anxious to get to it. With no more distractions, Hugh was confident Aubrey would be open to their finally planning their future. So far, he knew he hadn't handled it well—at least judging by Aubrey's reactions—but he was going to rectify that today.

This morning.

Now, if he thought he could pull it off.

Unable to help himself, he placed a gentle kiss on the top of her head and pulled her close. Aubrey purred and snuggled closer. Images of the hours they'd spent making love flickered through his mind. Looking over at the clock, Hugh saw he'd only slept for two hours and yet he'd never felt more invigorated.

It would be mean to wake her up. She had worked so hard for so long and he knew he should let her sleep, but he couldn't stop from whispering her name. She barely stirred. Maybe he should try to go back to sleep himself. After all, two hours wasn't enough sleep for anyone. Forcing himself to relax, Hugh closed his eyes.

"Hugh?" Aubrey whispered, and when he opened his eyes, he was shocked to see four hours had gone by since he'd last looked at the clock. She smiled at him. "Good morning."

"Good morning to you," he murmured, lowering his head to kiss her. "Did you sleep well?"

She nodded. "I could probably stay here in bed all day, but I really want to go downstairs and make sure everything got cleaned up last night and check in with Liza to see what kind of feedback we received."

He couldn't help but chuckle. "There is time enough for that tomorrow. You worked hard all week and today is for resting."

"But—"

Placing a finger over her lips, he shushed her. "No arguments. I'm the boss and I say no work today."

Aubrey pouted. "That doesn't mean I'm not going to be distracted thinking about it."

"Maybe I'll have to distract you myself," he teased as he rolled over and tucked her body beneath his. "I can think of several ways to do that, you know."

She giggled. "Oh, I know you can," she said, "but I'm starving. I promise to let you distract me after we have a bite to eat."

It wasn't quite the way Hugh imagined spending the morning, but he realized he was a bit hungry himself. Besides, maybe they could do some talking over breakfast and he could finally convince Aubrey to overcome her fears of marriage.

"I'll order some food for us if you want to use the shower first," he suggested.

"Perfect!"

Thirty minutes later, Aubrey sat next to him in his dining room wrapped in her robe, her hair up in a towel. And she still managed to take his breath away.

He listened to her observations about the previous night and how successful she thought it all was, and Hugh had to agree. He already knew their guests had had a wonderful time and Bill was pleased as well.

Finishing off his omelet, he reached over and took one of her hands in his. "I don't know if I've said this already, but thank you."

She looked at him quizzically. "For what?"

"I know I was a real jackass in the beginning when this all started and you had every reason to not want to take this job, but you did and you did an outstanding job on the whole thing. So thank you for putting up with me." He kissed her hand.

Aubrey blushed. "That's very sweet of you, but I think it was a team effort. You may not have been happy about it in the beginning, but you came around to it quickly and gave me all the tools I needed."

"We do make a great team," Hugh said, happy to have the perfect lead-in to their discussion.

"Yes, we do," she smiled serenely as she finished the last of her breakfast.

"I know we started to talk about this the other day and…" He paused. "I think we need to talk about it some more." Instantly he noticed the wary expression on her face. "Aubrey, I love you. I never expected to find you or to meet someone like you." He squeezed her hand.

"Hugh…"

He wasn't ready for her to stop him. "I don't want to compare ourselves to your parents or mine. We're us. We're who we are and we don't have to be like anyone else. We've had a unique relationship from the start, and together we can build a unique life."

Carefully, Aubrey pulled her hand from his. "I don't understand why you're pushing so hard on this right now," she said quietly.

"Because I love you," he said simply. "I thought I was happy with my life—I was living the way I wanted to. But once I met you, I knew I was wrong. I hadn't been truly happy in a long time. You make me happy, Aubrey. You've shown me what it's like to really live."

"I wish that were true." She rose and walked over to look out the window.

"What do you mean?"

Turning back toward him, Aubrey took a steadying breath. "Hugh, you're still too cautious. You say you want to marry me and have a life with me, but there's more to a life together than what we've been doing."

For a moment he could only stare at her. "I don't follow."

She sighed. "We travel together. We work together. We spend a lot of time together doing those two things. But what do we do besides that? Do you really think we're going to spend our lives living like nomads? Once this whole thing with Bill is done, I'm going to need to get a job. It's going to require me putting down roots somewhere."

"Why? Why can't you work for me? With me?"

"Because I need to know I can do something on my own! For years my father dictated where I worked and what jobs I took, and it would be no different going from that world to yours. I'm enjoying experiencing new things, trying new things." Then she looked at him sadly. "I wish you would try some of those things with me."

"I've been with you all this time and—"

"No," she interrupted. "You've been in the same area with me, but you've kept yourself safely ensconced in your office. You live under your protective bubble of the resorts and refuse to venture out and try something new."

"So because I won't…what? Go skydiving or jet skiing, that means you can't marry me? That seems like a flimsy excuse, Aubrey."

She rolled her eyes. "That's not what I'm saying and you know it! All I'm saying is I think you have an unrealistic view of what settling down means."

"I don't think I do. That's why I've been trying to talk to you about it. When we have kids, I know we'll have to settle down more and find a place of our own so we can—"

"What if I don't want kids?" she asked flatly.

"What?"

"You heard me. What if I don't want kids? We never discussed it. You never asked and yet everyone has just assumed we're going to get married and start popping out a big family."

Hugh stood and walked over to her. "Is that what you're saying? That you don't want to have a baby?"

His heart sank. In his mind the two went hand in hand—you got married, you had children. Even though in the past he had always envisioned a marriage based more on practicality than love, he never once imagined it would exist without children.

Aubrey stared hard at him before taking a shaky breath. She nodded her head. "Yes. That's what I'm saying."

For a moment, time stood still. Hugh felt like he was going to be sick. "Wow. Um…okay. I mean, maybe in time…"

She shook her head. "No. Time isn't going to change anything. I know you grew up in a big family and…"

"I'm sure it wasn't easy being an only child," he said quickly, "especially when you were sick and dealing with unsympathetic parents, but it doesn't have to be that way."

"You're not getting it, Hugh," Aubrey said with more than a hint of frustration. "If you want to marry me, then you need to accept this. I'm not going to change my mind. I'm not going to wake up one day and go 'Okay, let's have kids.' It's not going to happen."

He raked a hand through his hair and began to pace. "Aubrey, I…hell, I don't know what to say."

"I'm sorry," she said, her tone flat again. "I probably should have told you this a long time ago. I guess I never thought it would be an issue."

"Meaning what?" he asked, his voice like gravel.

"Meaning, I didn't think we'd ever talk about marriage. A future."

She was killing him. Who was this woman? Where had the loving woman he had spent the last several months with gone? "How could you say that? After everything we've shared. I don't understand."

She shrugged and then he noticed a stray tear rolling down her cheek. "I never thought you'd be the guy to change so much you'd want to settle down. You're so regimented and don't like change… I just figured we'd happily go along like this." She fidgeted with the towel around her head. "You seemed content to stay in your own world and let me do my own thing."

He shook his head adamantly. "No, I wasn't content. That's what I'm telling you. I…"

"Hugh, you fight every opportunity to be spontaneous. I have a better understanding now about why you're that way, but I can't live like that. I won't live like that. I'm finally learning it's okay to break free from the restraints others put on me and…and I'm afraid…"

"I'm going to be the one restraining you," he finished for her, his voice grim.

"I'm sorry," she whispered.

There was nothing he could say. Nothing he wanted to say. There was no way he could make promises and guarantee her that he could suddenly unclench and be the kind of free spirit she clearly wanted. And as for the issue with kids…? Well, that was really more than he could handle right now.

"Me too," he forced himself to say.

And then he had to stand back and watch as Aubrey went into the bedroom alone. Without him. Deep down he knew she was packing. She was leaving. And he was too numb to stop her.

—⁓—

Aubrey read the text on her phone for what was probably the hundredth time in the last week. She'd never talked to Hugh about it. Never talked to anyone about it. It was too painful. Now, as she sat in the airport lounge waiting to board her flight back to North Carolina, it was the only thing she could manage to do.

Test results are in and they're not what we were hoping for. Please call me. Dr. G.

Aubrey had been going to Dr. Pamela Gabbert for more than ten years. They were more like old friends than doctor/patient, so the rather unconventional text wasn't unusual to her. The only problem was she wasn't ready to make the call. Maybe after she got home and dealt with having to walk away from Hugh, she could do it, but right now, she couldn't handle any more bad news.

On some level, Aubrey had known it would end like this. Who was she to believe that she would get a happy ending? Nothing about her entire life had been happy.

Except when you were with Hugh.

Yes. He had made her happy while they were together, and more than anything, she wanted to be the one to make him happy. But that wasn't going to happen and he didn't deserve to have to suffer any more in his life.

Especially if it could be avoided.

So she left. Some would say she was running again, but this time it wasn't for selfish reasons. Self-less, yes. But not selfish. The only way she could give Hugh the safety net and let him continue to live in his careful world was to walk away.

No matter how much it hurt.

"You know you disappoint me, Runaway Bride."

Aubrey didn't have to look up to know Bill Bellows was standing in front of her. With a sigh she put her phone away and forced herself to look up.

"I figured you'd be basking in the glory of your successful event," he said, taking the seat next to her. "So imagine my surprise when I heard you handed over your files to Hugh's people and stepped down from the remaining events." He made a tsking sound. "Not cool, Aubrey."

"Now's not really a good time, Bill," she said wearily.

"Yeah, yeah, yeah," he said. "I'm sure. But let me just say this—I don't know what went on with you and Hugh, and personally, I'm fine with that. It's none of my business. You're damn good at what you do, and our agreement was you would be the one working on this campaign."

Her eyes flew to his. "Don't take this out on Hugh, Bill. I just... I can't work for him anymore. It's not his fault, it's mine. Please."

He nodded. "I wouldn't do that to him. He told me you had everything taken care of for the remainder of the campaign and I'm cool with it. But know this...you were good for him. I've known Hugh Shaughnessy for a lot of years and I've never seen him as happy as he's been since he met you."

She willed herself not to cry. "Please..."

"I saw it that weekend in Napa. I wanted you for this job not only because I knew you would kick ass with it, but because I knew you would also be the one to breathe a little life into Hugh." He put a hand on her shoulder and squeezed. "When the dust clears, if you need or want a job, give me a call."

Aubrey didn't respond. She couldn't. Bill walked away and all she could do was sit and stare at her hands clasped in her lap. When her flight was called a few minutes later, she forced herself to get up and move. She stared out the window the entire flight home and somehow managed to make it all the way to her house and inside to her bedroom before she completely collapsed and cried.

She cried for her past.

She cried for her present.

But mostly, she cried for the future that wasn't going to come.

Chapter 12

Two weeks. Three days. Nine hours and twenty-three minutes.

That was how long it had been since Hugh had watched Aubrey walk out of his life. And every minute of it had been hell. Now, standing in the driveway of his father's house, he felt ready to collapse. The front door opened and there stood Ian Shaughnessy. Hugh knew he must look a fright, and his father's expression confirmed it.

Gone were the designer suits, the perfectly styled hair, and the sleek professional he once prided himself on being. In its place was a man in faded jeans and T-shirt, with a face that hadn't been shaved in two weeks.

In a word, he looked like hell.

It pretty much fit.

Neither spoke a word as Hugh picked up his suitcase and walked toward the house. Ian held the door for him. Once inside, Hugh simply kept walking until he reached his childhood room and put his luggage down.

"That's a new look for you," Ian said quietly and Hugh turned. He hadn't heard his father follow him.

"I'm trying something new."

Ian gave a sad smile. "I like your old look better." They stared at one another for several moments. "I was just getting ready to have a bite to eat. It's just leftover chili, but Anna made it. Care to join me?"

Hugh nodded and followed his father down to the kitchen. They worked in silence as they reheated the meal. Ian pulled two beers from the refrigerator and placed them on the table. When everything was ready, they sat down. Ian said grace and then dug into his meal. He was three spoonfuls in before he spoke. "It's never easy."

"What?" Hugh murmured, focusing on the bowl in front of him.

"Being alone." He took a pull from his beer and waited a moment. "It doesn't matter if it's by choice or not. It doesn't matter who walked away or how. It hurts."

Damn. Hugh knew his emotions were too raw and he was seriously close to breaking down. He wanted to change the subject. He wanted to beg his father to talk about something else, but no words would come out.

"And the thing is, I don't think you're ever prepared for it," Ian said, breaking the silence. "I know it's not the same—me and your mom versus you and Aubrey—but it still hurts." He looked at his son. "It's okay to let it hurt, Hugh."

Hugh nodded. "I know," he finally said. "I just can't help wondering what I could have done different. What I could have said...or done."

"There may not have been anything. Sometimes things don't work out. I know it's painful but..."

"She wanted me to be more spontaneous. To...to go out and do things. Try things."

"Well, you should have told her to join the club. We've all wanted that for you. You shut down after your mother died, and although I held my tongue about it, I never agreed with it. You were too young to simply stop living like that."

"I had to," Hugh said sadly, his voice breaking. He knew it was time. There was no way he could ever move forward if he didn't confess to his father why he did the things he did. Looking up, his eyes welled with tears, and rather than cursing them, he embraced them. "How could I continue to live the way I had when I'm the reason Mom's gone?"

To his credit, Ian's expression only went wide for the briefest of seconds before it went neutral. "Hugh, what are you talking about? A drunk driver is the reason your mother is gone."

Hugh vehemently shook his head. "No. It's my fault. I should have gone to the pharmacy that day. I should have been driving. Not Mom. Don't you see? She'd be here right now — Aidan, Quinn, Riley, Owen, and Darcy would all have their mother here with them if I had been a more responsible person!"

The last reaction Hugh expected was for his father to resume eating, but sure enough, Ian picked up his spoon and took a few more bites of his chili and another swig of beer.

"Dad," Hugh finally said, "aren't you going to say anything? Doesn't what I said mean anything to you?"

Placing his spoon down, Ian picked up his napkin and wiped his face before looking at Hugh. "Do you remember how your mother normally was around dinnertime?"

"What do you mean?"

"She was normally tired, a little scattered, and mostly she was ready for a break — especially after Darcy was born."

Hugh thought back and could see Lillian exactly as Ian was describing. Her long hair was normally pulled back in a ponytail, and by dinnertime half of it had broken free from its clip. She always made sure to keep the conversation going over dinner and asked everyone about their day, but she was tired—she looked tired."

Finally, Hugh nodded. "I remember."

"That day," Ian began, his own voice catching, "she called me at work. She told me about Darcy and the ear infection and how she needed to pick up the prescription. I offered to go for her because of the weather. After all, I could have easily done it on my way home. Do you know what she said to me?"

Hugh shook his head.

"She said, 'Ian, if I don't get out of this house for a little while, I'll go crazy.' You see, Darcy had been crying all day and the trip to the doctor had been exhausting because there was some sort of illness going around so she had to sit in the waiting room longer while listening to your sister—and about a dozen other kids—cry." He let out a small chuckle. "One of the many things I loved about your mother was her honesty. She wasn't a martyr and she didn't pretend to be the perfect mom. You kids made her crazy a lot of the time, but she loved you all. And that day, Darcy was making her crazy. She wanted to get out and get a little air and just be alone in the car for a little while."

Hugh didn't know what to say, so he waited to see if his father was done.

"Even if you hadn't been grounded, Hugh, she wasn't going to ask you to go on that errand. And if she had, then you and I might not be here talking right now."

It was one thing to have tears in his own eyes; it was quite another for Hugh to see them in the strongest man he knew. "Dad…she had so much to live for. It would have been better—for everyone—if it had been me and not—"

Ian reached over and grabbed Hugh's arm. "Don't say that! Don't ever say that! God almighty, Son. Is that what you think? Is that what you've been thinking all this time?"

"How could I not?" Hugh cried. "At any other time, she would have asked me to go! I ran errands for her all the time!"

Shaking his head, Ian moved to take Hugh's hand in his. "You listen to me. I know how many times you ran errands, but that day, you weren't going to no matter what you think. I know! You don't think I struggle with the same thing? If I had insisted I be the one to go to the pharmacy on my way home, she'd still be here!" And then he openly broke down in tears. "Every day I curse myself for not doing it. For not putting my foot down," he sobbed.

Hugh's tears flowed openly now. "Dad…"

Ian wiped his eyes. "The thing is, Son…we'll never know. Sometimes things happen and we don't know why and don't understand how God lets it happen. But I know your mother would not want either of us living like this. We're not so different, you and I. I stayed close to home not only because I had you kids to take care of, but because I became afraid of living. If something like that could happen to your mother, it could happen to any of us."

Hugh nodded. "I thought I could control everything. I thought if I stuck to my structured routine and played everything safe I'd be okay." He wiped his eyes. "But

I'm not. I missed out on a lot of things by being so cautious and in the end, I lost Aubrey because of it."

They sat in silence for a long time, each lost in his own thoughts as they finished their dinner. While they were cleaning up, Ian finally spoke. "I think you're wrong."

"Excuse me?" Hugh asked in confusion.

"I don't think you lost Aubrey because you were cautious, Hugh. I think there's more to this than she let on."

"She didn't want kids."

Ian let out a sigh. "And that's a deal breaker for you?"

"It kind of is. I always knew I wanted kids, a family. She apologized for never mentioning it before but...I don't know. It seemed weird the way she told me." Hugh relayed all of the details of their last morning together. "It all seemed to come out of nowhere. It was almost like she wasn't herself."

"Have you talked to her since then?"

Hugh shook his head. "I can't. Just hearing her voice... It's too much. I hate feeling like this. I hate knowing I'm that weak and yet...there it is."

"You're not weak, Hugh. You're hurting. And it's okay."

Maybe.

Hugh just wished it didn't hurt so damn much.

The knock at the door brought Aubrey out of her thoughts.

Every day she got up. She ate. She breathed. But more than anything, she missed Hugh. So many times she simply wished he would call or that she was brave enough to call him, but in the end, neither happened.

She knew she wasn't expecting anyone, but her heart

skipped a beat in hopes that he was on the other side of the door, coming to make her see some sense.

Instead she found her mother.

Clearly the universe hated her.

"Mom?" she said, cursing the fact that her hair was a mess and she was wearing yoga pants and yesterday's T-shirt. "What brings you here?"

Angela Burke walked in, looking impeccable as usual. "I haven't heard from you in weeks, so I figured I better come and check." She took a good look at Aubrey and frowned. "And it's a good thing I did. Good grief, Aubrey. What is going on?"

Where did she begin? "You could have called," Aubrey murmured as she shut the door and walked toward the kitchen. "Can I get you a drink?"

"No, but you can go take a shower and get dressed. We're going to lunch."

"Mom," she sighed, "I'm really not in the mood for lunch. Maybe next week…"

"Aubrey, I drove all the way over here, and from the look of things, you aren't eating much. Please go take a shower. We'll go to the club for lunch. You know they do some amazing salads."

At that point, Aubrey's stomach growled, and she wanted to look down and call it a traitor. That's when she knew she was losing her mind and really did need to get out of the house. "Fine," she said. "Give me thirty minutes."

Twenty-eight minutes later, they were in Angela's car and on their way. They made small talk on the drive—the weather, current events. It was exactly how things usually went when they were together, and Aubrey found some comfort in it. It wasn't until they were seated in the restaurant and had ordered that Angela took her daughter by surprise.

"Okay, who died?"

Aubrey's eyes went wide. "Excuse me?"

"I asked who died. Seriously, you look like you haven't slept in weeks, your house was a mess, and you're moping. You really need to stop doing that. You'll get wrinkles." She reached out to touch Aubrey's forehead, but Aubrey swatted her hand away.

"Mom, stop," she hissed.

"Well then, tell me what's going on," Angela said, smiling at the waiter who brought her sweet tea over.

For two weeks Aubrey had kept to herself, not wanting to burden anyone with her problems. But for some reason, now seemed the perfect time to unload a bit. "Do you regret having me?" she asked before she lost her nerve.

Her mother's eyes went wide with shock. "For goodness' sake, Aubrey! Why would you ask such a thing?"

Feeling more than a little invigorated—and rebellious—Aubrey leaned back in her seat, crossing her arms over her chest. "For starters, you've never said you love me." She stared at her mother, almost daring her to deny it. "I know you and Dad didn't have a great marriage, but it seems like I made it worse."

"Aubrey," Angela began, her voice low, "is this really the time for this discussion?"

"I don't see why not," Aubrey countered. "You wanted us to go out."

Angela frowned and took a sip of her tea. "I don't regret having you. I don't know why you would say that."

"I believe I already answered, Mom. If you don't regret it, why were you always so distant? Why wasn't anything I did ever enough?"

There was a long silence. "I knew from the beginning I never should have married your father. We had dated for a long time but we weren't in love. And then I got pregnant with you. We both thought it was a good thing and that, in time, we'd fall in love. But we never did. We had differing parenting styles. He was always working and always criticizing me."

"Why didn't you leave?"

Angela shrugged. "I was young. I didn't want to be divorced. I didn't have a lot of skills and I just figured things would eventually get better."

"And then I got sick."

"Yes. I wanted to yell and scream and choke the doctor when he gave us the news."

Aubrey straightened. "No," she said fiercely, all her anger suddenly more than she could bear. "You asked if I could still dance in that damn recital!"

"No," Angela said sadly. "Doctor Mason had given your father and me the news before we all came into your room. He sat your father and me down and told us what they found. I can't remember ever crying more. When he saw how distraught I was, he gave your father and me some privacy and I just cried harder. Then your father told me to pull myself together, that seeing me upset wasn't going to help you. I needed to be strong. To prove this wasn't going to stop you from living."

"But—"

"So we agreed we were going to look at your diagnosis as if it wasn't a bad thing—like there wasn't a chance you weren't going to recover." She shook her head. "He drilled it into me daily. 'Don't let her see you be weak, Angela.' 'Don't get all emotional, Angela.' Ugh, I wanted to smack him."

The explanation did little to ease Aubrey's ire. "And what about afterward? He wasn't around all the time, you know. What would have been the harm in being kind to me? Do you have any idea how much I needed someone to show a little compassion?" she cried.

Angela's face softened to a sad smile. "You have no idea," she said quietly. "You have no idea what it's like to look at your child and wonder if she's going to live or die. I would lie awake at night praying for you to get better, and there were times when you got worse. I was angry at God and I was angry at you. After a while, I detached myself because it was the only way I could handle it. If you hadn't survived…"

"So you were preparing yourself for my death?" Aubrey asked incredulously. "That's horrible!"

"I'm not proud of it, Aubrey! I can't begin to describe what it felt like to sit there and watch you suffer in pain, knowing there was nothing I could do! I saw how your father wasn't engaging either and I realized it was a coping mechanism. And I had to do the same."

"But what about when I went into remission? Why—" Her voice cracked. "Why couldn't you let yourself show me that you were happy? Or relieved or…anything?"

Angela sighed. "Because that fear never goes away."

"What fear?"

"The fear that it will come back," she said, her voice barely audible. Her eyes held Aubrey's. "You sat there and heard everything the doctors said along with me.

There's always a chance and…and I had a hard time dealing with it. I still do. What if…what if something…"

"Don't you think I struggle with that, too? Every time I go to the doctor, I have that fear! And no one will sit there and hold my hand! No one is there to let me cry on their shoulder! Do you know how *that* feels? It's my life—my body—we're talking about!"

"I wish… I wish I could be different. I wish I had handled things differently. I don't know how, Aubrey! I'm not a perfect person and I know I failed you as a mother but I can't be someone I'm not!"

"Well, I can't either! This is who I am. I'm Aubrey and I had cancer and I may get it again! I'll never be a dancer. I'll never have children, and I—"

"Wait," Angela interrupted, "why did you say you'd never have children? Where did that come from?"

Well, crap. She was momentarily saved from responding when the waiter returned with their lunches. "Thank you." She smiled and immediately dug in to her French fries.

"Honestly, Aubrey," Angela admonished, "they have healthier choices than that."

Her inner child won out and Aubrey picked up another fry, dipped it in ketchup, and happily ate it. "I wanted this," she said and reached for her burger. "And I don't know why you're acting so surprised. You heard me order it."

"I didn't think it would be so…big. And messy."

"Here, try one." She held out a French fry to her mother. "Have you ever just let go and done something just because you wanted to?"

Indecision warred on Angela's face. "That's

ridiculous. Of course I have. Now put that down, people are staring."

Aubrey looked around. "No, they're not. Come on. Eat this one fry."

"Tell me why you mentioned children."

"You know what? Never mind. Don't eat the fry. More for me."

Angela took the fry out of her daughter's hand. "Oh no. You started this, you need to finish it." She delicately ate the lone French fry and smiled. "Well...that was really quite good."

"Most of the things you refused to let me eat are," Aubrey said, taking a huge bite of her burger.

Disappointment marked Angela's features as she looked down at her salad and then at Aubrey's plate. "Is the burger good?"

"Yes, it is," she said with a knowing smile. "I have a friend who makes the best gourmet burgers and even though this doesn't come close, it's still pretty good."

"I know most of your friends and none of them cook. Who's the new friend?"

"No one you know." She nodded toward the salad. "Eat up."

"Oh, for crying out loud. You're acting like a child. You won't tell me who your friend is. You won't tell me why you're living like a bag lady. You won't tell me why you think you can't have children. I mean..."

"I don't think, I know. Big difference."

"What did Dr. Gabbert say? Have you seen a fertility specialist?"

Aubrey put the burger down, her appetite quickly fading away. "I've known for a long time that the chemo meds they used on me meant my chances of having children were slim to none. The doctors have said it almost since the beginning. And then, not that long ago, I went in for my annual. Long story short, my ovaries aren't in great condition. She sent me to a radiologist for an ultrasound, and those results, combined with my sporadic cycle, confirmed that it's pretty much hopeless."

And in a very uncharacteristic move, Angela Burke slid her chair close and embraced her daughter. "I'm so sorry, sweetheart. I think you would have been an amazing mother."

Tears welled in Aubrey's eyes. "I once thought so, too."

They sat like that for a few minutes before Angela pulled away. "You know, getting pregnant and giving birth does not make you a mother." She laughed awkwardly. "I should know."

"It's okay, Mom. Really. I'm…I'm dealing."

"I don't think you are," she said thoughtfully. "There are so many children in this world who don't have parents. You could adopt. Or you could find a surrogate. I mean, there are so many options out there. I don't want you to lose hope."

For a minute, Aubrey felt as if she couldn't breathe. "I…I never really gave those options a thought. Dr. Gabbert's mentioned them but…" She shrugged. "In my mind, if I couldn't get pregnant then I didn't get to have children."

"Oh, sweetheart. Always remember, where there's a will there's a way. You're a very loving and giving woman, Aubrey. I wish I was more like you."

"Mom…"

"It's true! You're an amazing person. So beautiful. So talented. I hate to think of you selling yourself short. You can have and be anything you want to be." She looked at her daughter and studied her seriously for a moment. "What is it you want, Aubrey? What do you want to be?"

I want to be Hugh's wife.

She didn't say that, though. Instead she said, "I don't know."

"It's okay. You can keep your secrets. For now," Angela added with a wink, and then waved the waiter over.

"Is everything okay, ma'am?" he asked.

"I believe it is," she said. "But please take this salad away and get me what my daughter's having." And when he was gone, she smiled broadly. "If I'm going to give you the 'climb-every-mountain' speech, I might as well follow it myself."

Rather than answer, Aubrey cut her burger in half and handed half to her mother. "Just to hold you over." And then she held up her side and toasted, "To a new beginning."

Angela smiled. "For both of us."

———

A week later, Aubrey found herself sitting in another restaurant waiting for none other than Bill Bellows to meet her.

Her lunch with her mother had been very eye-opening, and it made Aubrey realize not only did she have options, she also had hope. It took a little time to come up with a plan to achieve what it was she wanted out of her life, but once she got the ball rolling, the obvious step had been to call Bill.

"Hey, R.B.," he said as he sat down across from her and got himself situated.

"R.B.?"

He rolled his eyes. "Runaway Bride. I was being cute," he said with a wink. "Have you ordered yet?"

She shook her head. "I just got here five minutes ago so I figured I'd wait."

Bill immediately called the waitress over and gave her their drink orders. "I know what I want because I eat here all the time. Do you mind if I order for us?"

"That's fine. Go right ahead," she replied.

It took Bill a solid five minutes to get through the order and Aubrey was certain she'd misunderstood him. Once the waitress was gone, Bill turned back to her and smiled. "That's an awful lot of food for just the two of us, Bill," she said with a chuckle.

"I promised my assistant I'd bring her back something."

"Oh, okay."

He folded his arms on the table and studied her. "You doing okay? Everything going all right?"

She shrugged. "I'm getting there," she said honestly. "I think I'm done wallowing around and ready to get back to work." She cleared her throat. "You mentioned you might have some work for me when we last saw each other."

"Always," he said. "After seeing the kind of work you do, I know I can find a position for you. I like what you did for the campaign with Hugh's resorts and I think I want to try the same thing with other clients."

"But…you can't."

"I'm pretty sure I can," he countered.

"No. You can't. Not until Hugh is done with all of his events. It wouldn't be right. It was our idea and it was supposed to be exclusive to him. All the rest will fail if you're doing them with all your clients."

Bill leaned in across the table slightly. "First, it was never exclusive. It's not in the contract. Second, it was primarily my idea, so really…that means I say whether we can do it with one client or fifty."

Aubrey shook her head. "I'm telling you, Bill, it's wrong. Wait until Hugh gets done with all of his. Let the momentum keep building and by the time we're done there, everyone will want something like it. Stay aloof for a while and then watch all your clients beg you for the chance to do one."

"Or they'll go to somebody else."

She wouldn't be swayed. "And they'd fail because they weren't getting the best."

Bill leaned back, crossed his arms, and smiled. "That's the girl I remember. There's the fire I remember!"

She blushed. "I know. I forgot about it for a little while, but I'm back."

"I'm glad, Aubrey. I'm really glad. And for what it's worth, I agree with you. We'll wait until all of Hugh's events are done and then we'll work on making this a package I offer to my clients—present and future."

"I think it's a great idea. We can really take our time and put together something special. You can start making a list of clients you want to work with, and we can really do our research and be able to present them a highly customized event package from the get-go."

"You mean walk into their offices with my ace in the hole?" he said with a smirk.

"Exactly."

"Damn, Aubrey, I really like the way you think." He clapped his hands loudly and rubbed them together. "I can't wait to get started. I think…" His cell phone rang and interrupted his train of thought. "Excuse me a minute."

Aubrey looked around the restaurant in appreciation. It was one of the fanciest steak houses in Raleigh and one she'd always wanted to go to. The lunch crowd was out in full force and yet the noise level was very agreeable. The waitress put their drinks on the table as well as a basket of warm bread, smiling before turning away.

Bill stood, phone in hand. "I have to take this outside because I think I'm going to have to really yell to get my point across. Give me five minutes, okay?"

"No problem," she said and waved him off. Thank God he had the good sense to wait until he was outside before pitching a fit. She knew from experience how loud he could be when he was happy; she couldn't imagine how much worse it would be if he was angry.

Reaching for a roll, she couldn't help but smile. She had stood up to Bill and he had listened to her. She had a potential job. Things were starting to fall into place for her and maybe, just maybe, once she got settled a bit, she'd be able to pick up the phone and call Hugh.

Deciding to check her email, she bent down and reached into her bag for her cell phone. When she straightened, it fell from her hands.

Hugh.

He was there.

Sitting across from her, looking better than she ever remembered seeing him.

"Hi," he said softly.

"Hi." Her heart was hammering wildly in her chest as her eyes hungrily drank in the sight of him. "I…I like your beard. It looks good on you."

Hugh ran a hand over his jaw and smiled. "Thanks. Although up until a couple of days ago I looked more like a homeless man. I finally figured out how to trim it back so it's not so out of control."

She nodded. Words escaped her.

"It's good to see you," he finally said. "How are you?"

"I'm okay," she said honestly. "And you?"

"I'm okay," he said. "I've missed you."

And everything in her melted. "I've missed you too." She blushed. "I wanted to call… I should have called, but…"

"No, I should have," he said. "I shouldn't have pushed so much. It wasn't fair to you and I'm sorry. I was putting my unrealistic expectations on you."

She shook her head. "I was doing the same thing to you! You had your reasons for how you lived your life, Hugh. Who was I to try to tell you it was wrong?" A mirthless laugh escaped. "My life has been a mess and there I was trying to tell someone else how to live theirs. Who does that?"

"Aubrey, we can go back and forth about this all day, I think. Let's just agree we both handled things poorly. Okay?"

She nodded. "I can do that."

He smiled. "Good." Discreetly, he motioned for the waitress to come over. "How about we order?"

"Um...Bill already did and..." She stopped and gasped and looked around. "Bill! Does he know you're here? He went outside to take a call and he should be back any minute."

A waiter appeared next to the table with a large carry-out bag just as Bill returned. "Perfect timing, Robert," Bill said to the waiter as he took the bag from his hands. Stepping close to the table, he gave a mischievous grin. "Just call me Cupid," he said as he leaned over, kissed Aubrey on the cheek, and shook Hugh's hand. "Call me, R.B. I see big plans in our future!" But before Aubrey could respond, he was gone.

"R.B.?" Hugh asked.

"Don't ask," she said with a laugh. "So...did you know I was going to be here?"

"Not until I arrived. I met Bill outside and he told me." He paused. "Did you know I was going to be here?"

She shook her head. "Not until I sat up and saw you sitting here."

The waitress discreetly cleared her throat and they both laughed with embarrassment at how they had forgotten she was there.

"Sorry," Hugh said, taking the menu from her hand. Aubrey did the same and they continued to laugh quietly until she walked away.

After a few minutes, they placed their orders, then simply sat and smiled at one another. "I can't believe you're here," she finally said.

"I should have come sooner."

"I think this is another one of those situations," she teased. "Let's just enjoy our lunch and we'll talk after, okay?"

"We'll have to talk during or it will be awfully quiet," he said with his own teasing grin.

So for the next hour, Hugh caught her up with what was going on at the resorts and the feedback they'd gotten on the Montana event. He shared how he'd finally found a replacement for Heather and even caved and hired a few more event planners and coordinators for most of the resorts so he'd never be in that position again.

"I think you made a wise choice," she said.

"I foolishly thought no one would ever quit," he said sheepishly. "Lesson learned."

Aubrey knew he wasn't only speaking about Heather's leaving. "I'm glad you've got it all covered."

"What about you? What have you been doing?"

She shared with him how her very short meeting with Bill had gone. "I thought about calling my father and going back to my old job, but I just couldn't do it. I'm done with that part of my life."

"I'm proud of you."

"Thank you."

Their lunch arrived and they continued to talk about everything and nothing, each doing their best to keep the conversation light until they could be alone. By the time they were finished and the bill paid, Aubrey felt like running from the restaurant dragging Hugh behind her.

They walked casually together outside and Aubrey waited anxiously for Hugh to ask to come home with her.

"Thank you for lunch," she said, hoping to prompt him.

"It was my pleasure." He paused, hands in his pockets. "I was hoping I could see you tomorrow."

Tomorrow? He was asking about tomorrow when

it was barely two in the afternoon today? What in the world?

"Um…sure. I mean, yes. Of course. I'd like that." She took a breath, reminding herself to be calm and not throw herself at him. "We could have lunch at my place. I don't cook as well as Anna or any of your chefs but I can make us some…"

"Would you mind if it was later in the afternoon? Maybe around three?"

She was so confused. All she wanted to do was get Hugh alone and beg for his forgiveness, but obviously he wasn't quite as ready. Resigned to waiting, she nodded. "Sure. That would be fine."

"Great." Leaning in, Hugh kissed her on the cheek, much like Bill had earlier. "I'll see you tomorrow."

Aubrey watched him walk away, torn between sighing with pleasure at the sight of him and screaming in frustration.

———

By two the following afternoon, Aubrey was ready to go crazy. The house was clean. She'd changed clothes four times, and now all she could do was wait.

And pace.

It seemed to be a good way to kill the time. Until she realized she was walking all over the nice vacuum marks in the carpet.

So she vacuumed again.

The clock read two fifteen.

Her mind raced with possible ways to apologize to Hugh and how to ask him for another chance. She wasn't opposed to begging. The last couple of weeks without him had been awful and she didn't want to be without him anymore.

She only hoped he still felt the same and he wasn't coming here to thank her for breaking it off with him. That would be terrible.

Forcing herself to sit, she picked up her Kindle and began scanning for something to read, and ended up playing several games of Solitaire on her tablet to kill the rest of the time. When the doorbell rang at two fifty-five, she almost wept with relief.

Opening the door, she found Hugh looking just as nervous as she felt. "Hi," she said a little breathlessly. "Come on in."

He stepped inside but he didn't touch her or kiss her hello. "Thank you."

Motioning for him to have a seat in the living room, Aubrey made sure she sat on the opposite love seat, facing him but keeping a safe distance. Suddenly she felt a little insecure.

After several long, awkwardly silent minutes, Aubrey finally spoke. "Can I get you a drink?"

"What? Oh, no. Thank you, I'm good."

"Oh. Okay. Good."

Silence.

Hugh chuckled quietly. "I'm so nervous. I thought I'd be able to come in here, look at you, and say what I had to say, and now that I'm here, I can't seem to do it."

Yup. He was cutting her loose. There was no way she could let him know how devastated she was, so she went for light and breezy. "It's okay, Hugh. I…I think I know what you're going to say and really, it's all right. I get it. We were moving too fast and things got out of control.

It's a good thing we found out what we did before we went any further."

He looked at her oddly. "Aubrey, what are you talking about?"

"Us," she said simply, hating the quiver in her voice. "You're relieved I broke things off. Now you can have the future you want and I won't hold you back. I'm okay. Really."

"That's not what I came here to say."

"Oh?" she whispered.

"No. I...dammit," he muttered, raking a hand through his hair. "You were right about everything. I was scared to live. I was afraid to do anything that might not end the way I wanted. I wanted to always play it safe. And then I met you." He stopped and smiled. "And suddenly I realized everything that was missing from my life. You gave me hope. But even then I couldn't break the chains I put on myself. You have to know that I wanted to...but it was hard for me."

"Hugh, I do understand. It wasn't fair of me to expect you to do it."

"No, I needed that, Aubrey. I needed someone to nudge me. To force me out of my comfort zone, make me see that I wasn't really living."

"It's not an easy thing to see. Everyone comes to the realization in their own way," she said. "Just because I realized it for myself didn't mean you had to at the same time. I'm sorry I wasn't more understanding."

"I love you, Aubrey. I love you and I still want to marry you." His gaze held hers steady.

Her heart rate picked up again and her stomach twisted in knots. "Hugh, I... I need to explain something to you." She shifted in her seat, wishing she was closer to him. "About the…you know, having kids thing."

"Wait, before you go any further, let me ask you something."

"O-kay," she said hesitantly.

"I know you said you didn't want kids and I'll be honest with you, that was a shock for me. I guess I thought everyone wanted to have kids. I'm sorry I didn't handle it well. I respect your feelings and if being with you means we don't have children, I'm fine with that. At the end of the day, I'd still have you. And you're what I want more than anything."

Her heart ached now. This man, this sweet, generous man, was willing to give up on his dream of a family for her. It was almost enough to make her cry. The tears were already welling up. "Hugh, I really need to explain to you why I said that."

"Can I just interrupt one more time?"

She nodded.

"At any time in your life did you consider having kids?"

She smiled at him, her vision a little watery as she nodded. "When I was younger, I thought someday I'd get married and have two kids." She was a little taken aback as she watched Hugh pull out his phone and type something in. "Is everything all right?"

"What? Oh, yeah. Dotty had texted me about one of the new hires. I'm sorry. That was rude of me to do that while you were talking."

It was, but she chose to keep silent about it.

"So…two kids." He nodded. "I think most people think that. It's a good number."

"Hugh…"

"Aubrey, you mean more to me than anything. I'd be lying if I said I didn't want to have kids. I can't help it. I grew up in a big family and I always thought I'd have one of my own. But I don't need to. I have enough siblings who are going to do that one day—I can be the favorite uncle. It's not a bad thing. I just… Please tell me I'm not too late."

She was just about to answer when there was a knock at the front door. Frowning, she stood. "Excuse me a minute." The last time she'd had an unexpected visitor, it was her mother. Aubrey silently prayed it wasn't going to happen a second time.

Pulling the door open, she was a little surprised to find no one there. She was just about to shut the door when she heard a faint whimper. Looking down, she saw a basket with a balled-up blanket in it.

And then the blanket moved.

"What in the world?" she whispered as she crouched down and gingerly pulled the blanket up.

And stared into two pairs of puppy eyes.

"Oh my goodness!" she cried softly. "Look at you!" Turning the basket slightly, she looked for a card or some sort of identification. "Where did you two come from, huh?" She sensed more than heard Hugh come up behind her. "Hugh? Do you see this? Aren't they precious?"

He smiled and crouched down beside her. "I see you've met Cocoa and Abercrombie."

"Cocoa and… Wait…you know these puppies?"

"You don't think they got here all by themselves, do you?"

"But…" She looked from the puppies to Hugh. "I don't understand."

And then he shifted onto one knee before reaching over and picking up the puppies—one in each hand. "Aubrey Burke, we love you. All three of us. We want to spend the rest of our lives with you, being a family. You see, these little guys left their family so they could be part of ours. We can't promise we'll be perfect or that we won't make mistakes, but that's what makes life interesting, right?"

Tears flowed down her cheeks. The sight of the man she loved and the things he was saying would have been enough. Throw in the two adorable puppies and she was a goner.

"Say yes, Aubrey. Say yes to loving me and marrying me and making the four of us a family," Hugh said, his eyes so full of love.

"Yes," she whispered. "Definitely yes."

Then they kissed. She wanted to pull him close and be held in his strong arms but the squirming puppies wouldn't allow it. They whimpered and did their best to break free. Finally Hugh put them down and, as if reading Aubrey's mind, embraced her.

Nothing had ever felt so good. Over and over his mouth slanted over hers, and soon she found herself pinned beneath him on the foyer floor. She lost track of time because everything she'd ever wanted was right there in front of her—loving her.

When Hugh finally lifted his head, he immediately began looking for where the puppies had scampered off to. "Uh-oh," he murmured and stood up. "Um…Aubrey?"

"Hmm?"

"I think Abercrombie just christened the carpet."

Chuckling, she stood. "It's all right. He's just nervous and it's a new place. Besides, he's marking his territory. His home." She walked over and found the pup sitting, looking a little ashamed. "It's okay, sweetie," she cooed, picking him up before going to the kitchen for cleaning supplies. Hugh took them from her hand and went to take care of the mess. "They are just so sweet! How many were in the litter?"

"I'm not sure. When I went to get them, there were three left. I took him and Cocoa."

"Oh, Hugh!" she cried. "You left one there all by himself?"

"Well, I…I didn't want to assume. I mean, two dogs are a handful. Three might be a little crazy. It's like raising triplets!" He laughed.

"But that poor baby. Left behind without his brother and sister." She nuzzled the puppy and went to sit on the floor beside Cocoa, who was happily watching Hugh clean. Aubrey reached over and pulled her into her lap too.

Hugh disappeared into the kitchen and soon the doorbell rang again. Carefully putting the dogs down, she made her way to the door. "I don't think I've had this many visitors in all the years I've lived here," she said as she opened the door.

And found a tiny black lab puppy sitting on her doorstep, looking up at her curiously. "Hugh Shaughnessy," she called as she crouched to pick up the puppy, "what have you done?" She turned and found him grinning from ear to ear, Abercrombie and Cocoa at his feet.

"This is our family. Unique, like us." He crouched down beside her.

The giggle came out before she could help herself. "You're crazy, you know that? Three dogs? Puppies? How did you get them to come to the door like that?"

"I had a little help," he said sheepishly, and as if on cue, a big pickup truck pulled out of the driveway and drove away.

"Who was that?"

"Cupid."

That just made her laugh harder. "Wow. He really is something," she said as she pulled all three dogs in close. "You guys are too damn cute!" The newest pup stood up and began to furiously lick her face.

"Careful, Bill's a little excitable. The wild man of the group."

"Bill?"

Hugh shrugged. "I kind of promised…"

Pulling back a little, Aubrey picked up the tiny black puppy and watched as he squirmed furiously in her hands. "It's perfect. I love it." Then she looked at him. "Abercrombie, Cocoa…and Bill."

"Not the most traditional kids' names, but that's not what we were going for, right?"

"I love you so much," she said as she put the dog down and reached for Hugh. "And our unique little family." She kissed him.

When they broke apart, Hugh cupped her cheek. "It's not so little. These guys are going to grow. Fast. They're not small dogs either, you know."

"I guess that means we're going to need a bigger place."

"Funny you should mention that." There was a

twinkle in his eyes as he stood and held a hand out to her. "Are you ready for another surprise?"

———

Three hours later they pulled up to a house on the outskirts of Wilmington. Hugh knew Aubrey was beyond curious but he refused to tell her exactly where they were going. It had been a lot of fun teasing her along the drive while dealing with the three puppies in the backseat. They had to stop multiple times for their sake so the drive took even longer.

"Are we here? Is this it?" she asked excitedly as he parked the truck.

She took his breath away. Her beautiful eyes were wide with wonder, her smile was stunning. He couldn't speak so he simply nodded.

Aubrey jumped out of the car and immediately went to the backseat for the dogs. "Come on, guys. We're here!" There was a bit of commotion and some tangling of leashes, but she handled it like a pro as she walked toward the large house. "This is amazing. Is that the surf I'm hearing?"

Hugh came up beside her and took two of the leashes from her hand. "It is. We're a little far back but we have a direct path through the dunes."

"Wow," she sighed, as she made her away around to the back. "So...you bought this?"

"It's just a rental I took on for the short-term. I wanted us to pick where we wanted to live and I thought you might appreciate having a little more space and a great view while we were deciding."

"Hugh, it's amazing! And I haven't even been inside!"

"The inside is equally impressive. I haven't spent

a whole lot of time here, but it's furnished and I made sure we have everything we'll need for the dogs, so we're good to go."

For the next thirty minutes, they walked around the inside of the house and got the puppies settled, putting up a baby gate to keep them corralled in the laundry room. Hugh took her hand and gently tugged her away.

"But they're so small," she protested. "Maybe they'll be scared to be alone."

"That's why they have each other," he said. "Besides, they're exhausted. Come on." He pulled her along until they reached the master bedroom.

"This is the best room in the house," Aubrey said, immediately going to the French doors that led out to a private balcony where she could see the ocean. Hugh came up behind her and wrapped his arms around her waist, holding her close. "And now it's even better."

He sighed with contentment. "Do you really like it?"

"I do," she said dreamily. "The house, the view…" She turned in his arms and faced him. "You. I love it all." Standing up on her toes, she kissed him slowly, languidly. "It's perfect."

"Not yet," he said and took a step back, taking her hands in his again as he led her to the bed. "But it will be. Soon."

He had hoped they would go slow. He had looked forward to seducing her. But when she slid the straps of her sundress off her shoulders and let it slide down her body to pool at her feet, the only thing he could do was reach for her and think…*mine*.

~~~

The sun was setting as Hugh walked back into the bedroom. "They've been walked and they're eating."

"And they weren't traumatized from their nap in the
laundry room?"

He chuckled as he stripped off his jeans and shirt and
crawled back into the bed beside her. He kissed the tip
of her nose. "No one needs therapy yet."

She relaxed against him. "Well, that's a relief." They
were content with the silence for a little while, but
Aubrey knew she had to bring up one last ugly subject
before she would be able to fully move forward.

Rising up on her elbow, she looked at him.
"Everything's been so perfect today, I hate to bring up a
subject that may ruin it."

Hugh's expression was serene. "Then don't."

She chuckled. "I think we really need to talk about it."

He folded his hands behind his head on the pillow
and took a deep breath. "Okay."

"I wasn't fully honest with you." She waited to see
if he'd say something, but Hugh remained quiet. "That
day, that last day in Montana, I said I didn't want kids.
It wasn't true."

"Aubrey..."

But she didn't let him finish. "It was a coping mechanism I'd taught myself a long time ago. It was easy—
after watching my dysfunctional family, I used them as
an excuse, but the truth is..." Her voice was shaky and
she was close to crying.

Hugh sat up and instantly placed a finger over her
lips. "Don't, okay? I know, sweetheart. I understand."

She looked up at him in confusion.

"Back in the beginning, when you told me about the cancer and all you had gone through, I did some research of my own. I didn't want to make you talk about it because I knew it was hard for you. I knew— even back then—that there was a good chance you wouldn't be able to get pregnant. I was devastated for you. Not for me. And when we started talking about the future, I figured we'd talk about options. But I didn't express that very well. Aubrey...I don't care if we don't have kids that are biologically ours. If you wanted to, we could adopt or...or...take in foster kids...or have a dozen dogs... It doesn't matter to me. I hope you know that."

She was quietly crying now, wiping her cheeks. "Oh, Hugh...you have no idea..."

He pulled her into his embrace. "I'm so sorry for everything you suffered. For all you lost. I want to give you all I have. Everything. I know I can't make those years go away, but I promise to make all the ones coming for us better."

Unwilling to move from the security of his arms, Aubrey whispered, "You know there are no guarantees, right? The cancer could come back."

Tucking a finger under her chin, Hugh gently forced her to look at him. "And I'll be there to take care of you. Always."

Aubrey felt everything in her soften and relax. She was about to say something when a loud crash sounded from the other room.

"Uh-oh," Hugh said as he moved from the bed and quickly donned his jeans. "That can't be good."

Aubrey stood and pulled on her dress. "Brace yourself, Shaughnessy, we're about to go on a wild ride."

He smiled at her, understanding the multiple meanings to that one simple statement. Taking her hand in his, they went in search of the pups.

Epilogue

"Everyone's going to be mad, you know."

"They'll get over it."

"It was kind of selfish of us."

Hugh shrugged. "Nah. I think it was just right for us. Perfect, really."

"It's just... Cocoa, stop," she said with a laugh as she playfully pushed the puppy from her lap. "I knew letting them in here was going to be a mistake."

"What was I supposed to do? You saw their faces. I'm only human."

"You're a softie, you know that, right?" she teased.

"Not just me, sweetheart. We're both weak where these guys are concerned."

"Fair enough." The three puppies were scampering around on the king-size bed. "They really are adorable and I think they did very well today."

"You trained them hard," Hugh said. "Plus the treats every thirty seconds really seemed to do the trick."

She swatted at him. "You weren't supposed to notice that."

"Hard not to notice when the bride keeps reaching into her bouquet and throwing things behind her."

Aubrey laughed. "Fine, so I wasn't particularly discreet. It worked."

"Yes, it did." He kissed the top of her head. "But this is our wedding night. I think we deserve a little privacy."

Aubrey still couldn't believe it. They were married. They had opted to have a simple ceremony on the beach. Originally they'd wanted it to just be the two of them, but they'd needed two witnesses. Aubrey had asked her mother and Hugh had asked his father—who had shown up with Martha Tate.

They had gotten married in the early afternoon on the beach and the dogs had been their bridal party— each adorned with a white bow. Afterward, they shared a light lunch and then sent everyone on their way.

"Your siblings are going to be offended you didn't invite them and that you made your father keep a secret."

"He loved it. And we'll have a party later if we want to. This was the perfect way to go. No circus atmosphere. No months of planning."

"I seem to remember you looking down at people who did this sort of thing not so long ago," she reminded him.

"That was before I was the one figuring out what I wanted. Besides, I didn't want to take away from Aidan and Zoe. Their wedding is only two months away and they've been planning it for a while. If we decide to do anything, I think it's only fair to wait until after theirs."

"I agree." She sighed happily and snuggled up against her husband. "I'm glad they're going to do it close to home. I just wish they had let us help a little more."

"They're no different from us. They wanted something small and intimate and yet a little away from home."

"Hilton Head Island really is beautiful. We could have done something spectacular at the resort."

Hugh shrugged. "After coming here and seeing this

house, they decided they wanted something like that for themselves. Besides, it's not about the ceremony."

"It's a little about the ceremony," she corrected.

"Maybe for the bride. For the groom it's all about the wedding night," he said with a growl as he nuzzled her neck.

"Hugh!" she cried out with laughter, and soon the dogs were all barking and jumping around them.

"Okay, I can see we're going to have to take a pause in the action." He stood and pulled on a robe before calling the dogs. "Let's go!"

Aubrey watched, laughing the entire time, as Hugh led the dogs from the room like the Pied Piper. Five minutes later he was back. He shut the door, stripped off the robe, and climbed back in the bed beside her.

"Thank you," she said to him, her tone softer, more serious.

"For what? Putting the dogs away?"

She shook her head. "No. For loving me. For accepting me. For being willing to take on this adventure with me."

He smiled slowly, seductively. "Sweetheart, there is no one else in the world I would rather be with. You're my everything."

Aubrey knew their lives would never be dull. Never predictable. They were truly starting a new life.

Read on for a sneak peek at the next brand-new book in The Shaughnessy Brothers series

Always My Girl

ONE LOOK AT THE MASSIVE BEACH HOUSE HAD QUINN Shaughnessy shaking his head. Why this wedding couldn't just be a normal event—at a hotel—he couldn't understand. It would be easier. It would be more practical.

And it would mean there was a bar on the premises for him to go to and get away from his family for a little while and maybe pick up an attractive woman.

Not that he didn't love his family—he did. But three days with everyone back under one roof was a little more togetherness than he was in the mood for. No matter what the occasion.

Ever since moving out of the family home at eighteen and going to college, Quinn had never looked back. There were the occasional trips home for school breaks, when he was forced to go home and share a room with one of his brothers, but for the most part, he found excuses to stay other places. He enjoyed his space, his freedom, and he'd never felt the need to make excuses about it.

Being one of six kids in a four-bedroom house growing up had been less than a dream. When he went to college—even though he shared a room there with one other guy—living in the dorm felt different. No one was looking over his shoulder or trying to get him into trouble or trying to tell him what to do.

It was like nirvana.

After graduation, he'd lived on his own while on the race-car circuit. When his career came to an end—sooner than he'd anticipated—Quinn still managed to land on his feet. And with a place of his own...rather than going home.

The large house loomed in front of him.

Aidan and Zoe were getting married this weekend, and because Zoe didn't have any family left and Aidan was a private kind of guy, they'd opted for a small, intimate wedding. On the beach. With only the family and a few friends in attendance.

All under one roof.

He cursed under his breath and sighed. It was only one weekend. It was the chant he kept repeating in his brain as he climbed from the car and stretched. Why they had to choose a beach four hours from home when they lived at the beach in North Carolina was beyond him. And to make it worse, they'd chosen a location that wasn't all that far from Hugh's Hilton Head Island resort! They could all be in their own rooms at a luxury resort right now, having drinks served to them by the pool instead of this.

"Clearly, being in love makes you an idiot," he muttered and opened the trunk to grab his luggage.

"You've been here less than five minutes and you're already calling people idiots?" a voice said from behind him. Turning, he saw his brother—the groom—walking toward him with a big, sappy grin on his face.

Quinn straightened. "Not people, just you," he teased.

"Aww...you say the sweetest things," Aidan teased right back before grabbing Quinn in a bear hug. "Glad you made it."

"Like I had a choice."

Aidan sighed good-naturedly. "This makes Zoe happy. So I'm happy."

"You could have picked a place closer to home. Or Hugh's place."

Aidan shook his head. "The resort was beautiful and everything would have been taken care of, but Zoe and I aren't like that. We wanted a place where—"

"You can be in control?" Quinn interjected with a laugh.

Aidan couldn't help but laugh with him. "Something like that. Either way, the house is great—six bedrooms—and we snagged the place next door for the rest of the guests."

"How many people are coming? I thought it was just us."

"No, we couldn't do that. We do have friends we wanted to have here, you know. Some of them had to travel a lot farther than you, so we wanted to have them close by and give them a place to stay."

"Makes sense. So who's on the guest list? Any single friends of Zoe's?" he asked with a lecherous eyebrow waggle.

"Keep your hands to yourself," Aidan chided. "Three of her friends from Arizona are flying in for the weekend. They'll get one of the bedrooms next door. Then Aunt Rose and Uncle Ryan will have one, Uncle John and Aunt JoAnn will have one, the Hannigans will be over there, and Bobby snagged the last bedroom. It's a kiddie space and we've all gotten a good laugh at that one. Can't wait for him to get here and see his reaction."

"Man, that's going to be good," Quinn laughed. "So everyone else is over here? In this house?"

"Yup. It will be like old times."

Quinn groaned. "Oh…good."

"What? What's wrong with that?"

"I'm sure it's not a big deal for you—you get to share a room with Zoe. But I'm going to have to share a room again with Riley and Owen. It's like I'm twelve again."

"Actually, you're sharing a room with Dad."

His eyes went wide. "Why?"

"Riley's people didn't want him traveling alone—he's made the news lately with his plans to take an extended break from singing and the press is hounding him. They're sending a bodyguard with him."

"So the bodyguard gets my space in the room?"

Aidan nodded. "So you'll be spooning with Dad."

Quinn groaned even louder. "Oh, man, come on! Why me?"

"Because you've always bitched about sharing a room with the twins. Your entire life! So I figured you and Dad would be a better fit. It's only a couple of nights. You can handle it."

"Dad snores."

"Trust me, bro, so do you. It's like a match made in heaven."

Turning, Quinn picked up his suitcase and slammed the trunk shut. "Screw you. This sucks. Please tell me there's at least some beer in the fridge."

Aidan nodded. "Go around back. Zoe's out by the pool, and she'll give you the grand tour and show you your room—and where the beer is."

"Where are you going?"

"I'm picking up Riley, Owen, and the bodyguard from the airport. They're landing at one of the smaller ones to try and avoid some of the drama and bypass the press."

"Well, just give me a few and I'll go with you."

Aidan shook his head. "It's going to be tight in my car as it is and I have no idea what kind of luggage any of them are bringing. You hang out here and get settled in. Hugh and Aubrey should be arriving in about an hour, and Dad and Darcy shouldn't be too far behind."

"Fine," Quinn grumbled. "I'll stay and be the welcoming committee. Thanks."

"It's that sparkling personality of yours that helped make the decision." He gave Quinn a friendly pat on the back. "Keep on smiling, sunshine."

Quinn cursed a little more colorfully this time and gave his brother the one-finger salute before turning and heading for the house.

"If this whole situation didn't suck before, it certainly does now." He stepped away from his car and made his way toward the gate on the side of the house. Aidan said he'd find Zoe back there. Maybe he could convince her to give him a sofa to sleep on rather than sharing a room with his dad.

It held little to no appeal.

Okay, fine, he'd share the room with his father and smile when he was supposed to and be nice to people. It was only three days and there were going to be three single, out-of-town girls here for him to entertain.

Maybe it wasn't going to be such a bad weekend after all.

"This is how life was meant to be lived."

"You got that right."

"Why don't we live this way?"

"Because we're poor and have to work."

"Oh yeah. I temporarily forgot about that. Thanks for the reality check." Anna Hannigan stretched out on her belly on the chaise lounge by the pool and simply sighed with happiness. Her best friend was getting married, she had the weekend off, and the sun was shining. Life didn't get much better than this.

"It's what I do," Zoe said from her chaise beside her. "Although, all this sun is going to give me a very freckly look soon."

Anna raised her head and looked at her friend. "You've got on a hat with a brim as wide as a UFO, and we've coated you with enough SPF one million to keep you safe. And, might I add, you're practically in the shade thanks to that giant umbrella."

Zoe sighed. "You have no idea what it's like to be a fair-skinned redhead. I just want to look perfect for tomorrow."

"Zoe, you could be freckly, blotchy, and have no makeup on, and you'd still be stunning."

"Ha! Clearly you have not seen that look on me before. Trust me. It's not pretty. And honestly, neither has Aidan. I'm saving it until after the wedding, when it's too late for him to turn tail and run."

"Good plan." They sat in companionable silence for a few minutes. "I love this."

"The beach?"

"The peace. It's so quiet and relaxing. I just feel all of the tension of the workweek rolling away."

"I thought things would be a little less intense for you since quitting the pub. Real estate isn't quite the same frantic pace."

"No, but it's a different kind of tension. It's all on me now, you know? Before, I collected a paycheck whether the pub was busy or dead. Now, I have to earn a commission and that means getting sales. I'm still settling in to the whole thing."

"Yeah, I know the feeling. Working essentially for yourself is never easy. But you had saved up enough to carry you through all this in the beginning, right? We went over your budget."

"I know and I appreciate you helping me with it." She paused and then looked at Zoe. "Can you keep a secret?"

Zoe nodded.

"Part of me really misses the pub. Maybe…maybe I made a mistake."

"Why would you say that? You just got started. It could just be nerves."

Anna shook her head. "No, it's more than that. You see…I didn't really make the career change for the right reasons."

"Uh-oh…"

"Yeah," Anna sighed. "I…I wasn't getting anywhere. I was meeting the same people and doing the same thing day in and day out. I want what you and Aidan have—to be in a relationship, to be in love, to know the rest of my life is just getting started and there's a future to it that includes a husband and kids and a happily ever after."

Zoe was quiet for a moment. "Why didn't you tell me any of this before? And you think leaving the pub and going into real estate is going to help you achieve that dream?"

"I don't know." Anna shrugged. "But at least I'm getting out and meeting new people. Everyone who came into the pub has pretty much known me my entire life. I was never going to find my future husband there."

"Maybe you already know him and you just haven't realized it yet."

Anna made a face. "Please. I think I would know by now. It's the same old crowd in there, and they all still look at me like I'm the tomboy they knew in high school. They come in and talk sports with me and want to relive a little of their glory days. It's kind of sad."

"Quinn doesn't do that."

"Yeah but…maybe not to all of it. Quinn likes to talk about himself mostly. But at the end of the day, he still sees me as Anna, the girl he grew up with and played baseball with and who kicks his ass at basketball. I'm one of the guys to him."

"Maybe because it's all you let him see."

Anna put her head back down and sighed. "There isn't much more to see. This is who I am."

Zoe started to say something but cut herself off. "Um…I'm going to get something to drink. You want something?"

"Some water would be great."

Standing, Zoe took her oversized hat off and placed it on the back of Anna's head. "Watch this for me, will you?"

Anna laughed. "Sure. Whatever." She wasn't sure why Zoe tossed the hat on her, but it didn't matter—she was too relaxed. Wiggling slightly, she got more comfortable and sighed. This was good.

"Hey, you made it," Zoe said quietly to Quinn as she approached him. "I didn't expect you here so early. I figured we'd have to send out the search party to get you."

"Yeah, well…I decided to skip work today and head down here and see if you needed help with anything." He looked past Zoe's shoulder and spotted someone lying on one of the chaises.

Zoe followed his gaze. "Well, why don't you come inside? I was just about to grab a couple of bottles of water and then I can show you your room."

Quinn shrugged. "Sure…yeah. Um…is that one of your friends from Arizona? Aidan didn't mention anyone being here yet." He took a couple of steps past Zoe, a grin slowly appearing on his face as he appreciated the curvy, half-naked woman on the chaise. She was wearing a tiny blue bikini and was all tanned limbs.

"Uh…Quinn?" Zoe began.

"You go and grab the drinks. I'll go and introduce myself." He continued to walk.

Rather than do as he suggested, Zoe followed slowly behind him, anxious to watch what was about to unfold.

Quinn sat down on the chaise Zoe had vacated and cleared his throat. "Hey," he said smoothly. "I'm Quinn, Aidan's brother. Zoe's going inside to grab some drinks and I thought I'd come over and…"

Anna turned over, the large, floppy hat falling behind her.

Quinn quickly stood and stumbled and fell backward over Zoe's chaise. "Holy shit! *Anna?*" He slowly came to his feet. "What the hell?"

She shaded her eyes and gave him a sour look before looking over at Zoe. When Zoe started to come forward, Anna held up a hand to stop her. "I got this." Once her friend was gone, she returned her focus to Quinn. "Is there a problem?"

Quinn helplessly looked around and grabbed the towel from Zoe's chaise and threw it at Anna. "For crying out loud, what are you doing?"

"Um…sunbathing? Lying out? Getting a tan? Really, take your pick."

He straightened the chaise and sat down, but his eyes stayed focused on the ground. "Well, maybe you've had enough sun for today and should…you know…put some clothes on."

A small laugh escaped before she could help it. It would seem she had finally managed to get Quinn Shaughnessy to notice she was a girl. Well…a woman. Great. It only took her being practically naked for it to happen.

When she stayed silent, Quinn lifted his head but kept his eyes firmly on hers. "I'm serious, Anna. You need to go and get dressed."

It was the tone that did it. Anna was used to him being bossy and condescending most of the time—it was who he was—but right now, all of her good humor and thoughts of teasing him went right out the window. "No," she said firmly and made herself more comfortable by rolling over onto her back.

He said her name again. This time it was nearly a growl.

She turned her head and looked at him. "If you have a problem, maybe *you* should go inside. I'm staying right here."

A stream of curses was his immediate response. "Any minute, my brothers are going to be showing up here. Is this how you want them to see you?"

Now she reached for her sunglasses that were tucked away under the chaise and put them on. "They've all seen me in a bathing suit before, Quinn. Why is this such a big deal?"

He stood angrily. "Because it is! This…this isn't a bathing suit," he stammered, waving his arms over her. "This is indecent!"

Zoe came sauntering back over with a huge grin on her face. "I know, isn't it fantastic? Who knew Anna was hiding such a rocking figure under those T-shirts and jeans?" She handed Anna a bottle of water and then a beer to Quinn. "I figured you might appreciate one of these."

Quinn took it from her silently and opened it, muttering the whole time under his breath about people being stubborn. He took a long pull of his beer before turning to Zoe. "Would you please tell her to go and put something on before everyone gets here? I mean, she's being stubborn."

"Aidan was here with her earlier and everything was fine. I don't think anyone's going to have a problem with her," Zoe said evenly and gently moved Quinn out of her way so she could resume her position on her own chaise. "Can you hand me my hat, Anna?"

"No problem," Anna said sweetly and smiled at Quinn as she picked up the hat and handed it over to Zoe.

Quinn rolled his eyes and looked around for a place to sit. "At least roll back over. Or put on more sunscreen or…something!"

"I just got comfortable, Quinn. Now either be quiet, or go away. Go unpack or watch TV or just…stop being annoying."

"*I'm* annoying?" he asked sarcastically. "I ask for one simple request and I'm the one being annoying." He huffed. "When does your brother get here? I bet he'll back me up on this."

Anna lifted her sunglasses and glared at him. "I wore this exact bathing suit to the beach with Bobby last week. No issues. So why don't you unclench and…again… go away." Putting her sunglasses back in place, she wiggled a little—unnecessarily—and got comfortable. Was that a groan she heard coming from Quinn? She smiled to herself.

"You know, Anna," Zoe began, "it really has been a while since you've put on some sunscreen. You're probably due." Then she picked up her phone and began to furiously type something.

Anna looked at her quizzically.

Zoe nodded while Quinn wasn't looking and then nudged her head in his direction with a thumbs-up. "Yeah. I definitely think it's time. Especially on your back. Your shoulders are getting a little red." More typing.

Anna still wasn't sure what Zoe was up to. "Oh…um. Okay. Can you help me?"

"Sure, let me just grab…" And then her phone rang. "I really need to get this. Quinn? Can you help Anna? I need to take this inside. Wedding stuff." And then she was on her feet and walking away.

If Anna wasn't mistaken, Quinn was actually blushing. "You don't have to help me," she said quickly.

"No…no," he grumbled. "It was my suggestion,

so…" He came and stood beside her. "I don't know… roll over or something."

She rolled her eyes and did as he requested. Why was he being such a jerk? And why did it only seem to make him more appealing? Clearly she needed to get her head examined. Or get a boyfriend. Or just get some relief from the sexual frustration that was dominating her life right now.

She'd always been in love with Quinn. Ever since they were kids. She just…she knew. He was the one for her. Her soul mate. The only problem was Quinn didn't feel the same way. She was his pal. His buddy. There'd never once been anything romantic between them, and if he even suspected how she felt, he'd never let on.

With a sigh, she relaxed back on her belly with her arms folded under her head. And now, even if he did suddenly notice she was a woman, it still didn't make a difference. He was still surly and difficult and not impressed. Lying here in next to nothing, rather than making him maybe be a little more charming—like he always got with other girls—he was angry and trying to cover her up.

Quite the ego boost. *Not*.

And then his hands were on her and…*oh*. Slowly, those big, work-roughened hands started at her ankles and began a journey upward. *Oh my…*

She almost wanted to turn and watch him work. With his sandy-blond hair, blue eyes, and rough hands, he was her every dream. All the Shaughnessys had dark hair except for Quinn. It used to bother him, and by the way he normally wore some sort of hat or beanie, Anna could tell it still did. But he wasn't wearing one now, and with all the sensations he was creating in her, she wanted to roll over and rake her hands through his hair and pull him down toward her.

It was never going to happen, but the imagery kept her smiling while he touched her.

Quinn was completely silent and Anna seemed unable to breathe. She couldn't move, couldn't breathe...she could only feel. And, boy oh boy, was Quinn making her feel. His hands skimmed the backs of her knees, and when they hit her thighs and one finger came close to her bottom, she had to stifle a moan of pleasure.

His hand stopped for a moment as if he realized what he was doing—and what he almost did. Anna almost lifted her head to look at him but thought better of it. And then his hands were on her again—this time on the small of her back. And then upward—circling, rubbing, massaging. She wanted to purr.

When they hit her shoulders, his motions seemed to slow as he went into what could only be described as a deep tissue massage. All of the tension from a few minutes ago completely faded away as his hands—those magnificent hands—worked on her. On any given day, Anna was all for a good massage, but this was beyond good. It was almost a religious experience. And this time she couldn't stop herself from purring.

His hands instantly were gone.

She didn't bother to look up. Didn't bother to question it. No good would come of turning around and seeing the look of horror on his face at her reacting the way she just had to him.

Idiot.

Beside her, Quinn cleared his throat and stood, the bottle of sunscreen hitting the ground. "Um...yeah, so...

that should do it," he croaked. "You should be good for now. I'm going to go and find Zoe and get settled in. I'll see you later."

Again, Anna didn't bother to respond. The man was clearly running away because she had been foolish enough to let her guard down for a minute. She waited until she heard the sliding doors to the house open and then close before she allowed herself to lift her head and look around.

Out of the corner of her eye, she saw Zoe stepping back outside shaking her head. When she got closer, she said, "What did you do to him?"

"*Me?* Nothing! I just laid here and let him put sunscreen on me. Why?"

Zoe laughed as she sat back down. "He ran in the house as if he were on fire and demanded to know which room was his. I offered to show him, but he was already halfway up the stairs yelling for me to just tell him which one!"

"So weird."

"Tell me about it." Zoe relaxed back in her spot. "So…he didn't say anything to you? Not even while he had his hands all over you?"

Anna glared at her. "Yeah, thanks for that. The only time Quinn ever touches me is to give me a high-five or to punch me in the arm when I beat him at something."

"Ah…so this was the first time he like…really touched you."

"What are you doing, Zoe?" Anna asked wearily. "Why are you stirring up trouble?"

"Because it's so obvious you're into him."

"Well…duh! It's no surprise. We've talked about this. A lot."

"Yeah we have, but you never do anything about it. I was merely…prodding things along."

"Yeah…well…keep your prodding to yourself. In case you didn't notice, your little attempt failed. Big time. Now I know what it feels like to have his hands all over me, and while I'm sitting here in a puddle of my own drool, he's running and hiding in his room to escape. He couldn't get away fast enough."

"Oh, I don't think I'd count this as a fail, my friend," Zoe said sweetly. "I think you made him nervous. I think we prodded him just enough for the blinders to finally come off."

"What are you talking about? He was horrified. He was…he was massaging my shoulders and I…" Anna paused and cringed. "I moaned."

"Like a sex noise?"

Anna shot her a look. "Yes, like a sex noise. Like a big, loud 'I'm on the verge of an orgasm' sex noise. There. Are you happy?"

Zoe threw he head back and laughed. "Oh my gosh! That's awesome!"

This time Anna twisted and sat up. "How is it awesome? He's going to avoid me like the plague from now on! It's bad enough he only sees me as a friend and now I'll lose that! Dammit, Zoe."

"Okay, hold on. You're freaking out over nothing. I'm telling you, that man just got the shock of his life. When he spotted you over here, he didn't realize it was you, and he was practically salivating."

"Yeah, and it all stopped as soon as he got a look at my face and saw it was me."

"Anna—"

"Forget it," she said and got to her feet. "I...I can't talk about this anymore. I'm going for a quick dip and then I'm going inside. Maybe *I* need to hide out in my room for a while." And then she took the few steps to the side of the pool and swiftly dived in.

———

Quinn slammed the door behind him, threw his suitcase on the bed, and then cursed a blue streak. Hands raking through his hair, he paced the room from one side to the other, unable to see anything except Anna in her tiny bikini. Where did she get off having a body like that?

He cursed again.

Why had he never noticed that about her? He saw her almost every day. Okay, maybe not *every* day, but he'd seen her enough over the course of his life where he should have noticed she had...curves. Lots of them. Stopping, he racked his brain for what he normally saw when he looked at her.

Short blond hair. Brown eyes.

Jeans. T-shirts.

No curves.

"Man, was I way off base there," he muttered. Even now, he could close his eyes and see them, feel them.

Finally taking a moment to look at the room, he groaned. Twin beds, dresser, nightstands, closet. Small. The walls were closing in on him already. At least the beds were long twins. There was no way he and his father would be able to fit in anything smaller and even that was going to be pushing it.

Eyeing his suitcase, he contemplated unpacking but

couldn't summon the will to do it. Instead he flopped down on the mattress and closed his eyes.

Big mistake because there she was again. Except now he was horrified to find his hands twitched with the need to touch her again. Her legs had been firm and soft at the same time. He knew Anna had always been athletic— hell, she competed with him in almost every activity and most of the time could kick his ass.

But the things he normally loved on a woman—the small of her back, her grabbable ass—now he noticed on Anna, and it felt…different. Not wrong, exactly, but definitely different. Thank God Zoe was going to have her single friends here this weekend. Quinn had a feeling he was going to need a distraction or he'd end up pouncing on Anna, and he couldn't allow himself to do that. They were friends—*best* friends—and there was no way he was going to ruin that over a great ass.

Or long, tanned legs.

Or… He groaned. The list was now endless. How the hell was he supposed to survive the weekend like this? They were going to be together the entire time and Quinn had no doubt Anna was going to be in his face if he ignored her. No doubt she'd call him out on being a jackass and tell him to grow up. And in any other situation, he'd gladly take it and admit she was right. But now? He had no idea how he was going to look her in the eye without letting his eyes wander and wondering what she was wearing underneath her jeans and T-shirts.

Damn wedding.

Why couldn't he be at work right now? If he were working on a classic car, everything would be right with his world. When he was working on a project, it held his attention from start to finish—no distractions. Sure, he went out and socialized. Hell, he even dated. He was a guy after all. But it was all superficial—a quick stop at the pub, a quick bite to eat, and some hot sex. But for the next three days, there was nothing but family and…Anna.

He seriously hoped Zoe's friends were hot. It would be a welcome distraction. It would quite possibly be the only thing that would save him from any awkward interactions with Anna. Then at night, he'd have to deal with the other awkward situation—sharing a room with his dad.

A shudder wracked through his body. He knew it was only for three nights, but the only person Quinn wanted to share a room with was Anna. *NO!* Wait… Oh hell. A woman. He only wanted to share a room with a *woman*! Damn Anna and her bikini. Now he was going to have to be even more careful for the rest of the weekend, or it wouldn't only be Anna getting in his face about his behavior. Soon his brothers would be in on it and eventually…Bobby.

Crap. It was no secret there was no love lost between Quinn and Bobby. He wasn't even sure when it started. They were all friends when they were kids, but somewhere along the way—probably around high school or maybe even as early as middle school—Bobby had taken a disliking to Quinn, and that, in turn, had made Quinn dislike Bobby. They'd had more than their share of brawls, but whenever Quinn would come out and say, "What is your problem?" Bobby would just throw his hands up in disgust and walk away.

And it got worse when Bobby became a cop. Not

to say he was harassing Quinn, but Quinn knew he got more tickets than the average citizen and it was normally over nothing. You'd think Quinn would just call it in and set up his business's home base someplace else. But no. Not only did he set up one of his shops in his hometown, but he'd seriously expanded and made it his crowning location.

Idiot.

Okay, so now he was up to three awkward situations on tap for the weekend. Maybe he should just stay in his room and fake being sick or something. Luckily there weren't any medical professionals in the bunch. Riley wouldn't come near him for fear of getting sick and missing out on being with the public. Owen was a bit of a germaphobe and would definitely stay away. Darcy would poke her head in just to be nosy, while Hugh wouldn't want to risk getting Aubrey sick. And Aidan…well, it was his wedding, there was no way he'd risk getting sick for his wedding day.

But could he really do it? Just to get a room to himself and not have to face Anna or Bobby? Was he really so completely selfish that he'd risk ruining Aidan and Zoe's weekend?

Maybe.

"No," he growled and sat up. He wasn't a coward. And hiding out implied he was. "I can face all of them and tell them each to go to hell if they have a problem with me." Well, except his dad. There was no way he'd say that to his dad. Ian Shaughnessy was the best dad a guy could ever ask for, and even though Quinn wasn't looking forward to bunking with him, it wasn't an attack on his father.

Just his snoring.

Outside, he heard a couple of car doors slamming. Walking over to the window, he saw Hugh and Aubrey had arrived. Another car pulled in behind him and Quinn didn't recognize it. It wasn't particularly unusual—there were guests coming that he didn't see on a usual basis. For all he knew, it was one of his aunts or uncles, the Hannigans, or even Zoe's friends. It could be…

Wait a minute…

Squinting a little, Quinn leaned closer to the glass and felt an impending sense of doom. Rising from the driver's side door of the second car was Martha Tate. Nothing wrong with that; she was Zoe's boss. She was laughing and smiling, and she waved at Hugh and Aubrey like they were old friends. But she wasn't alone. Stepping out from the passenger side was… Oh dear Lord.

Ian Shaughnessy.

About the Author

New York Times and *USA Today* bestseller/contemporary romance writer Samantha Chase released her debut novel, *Jordan's Return*, in November 2011. Although she waited until she was in her forties to publish for the first time, writing has been a lifelong passion. Her motivation to take that step was her students: teaching creative writing to elementary age students all the way up through high school and encouraging those students to follow their writing dreams gave Samantha the confidence to take that step as well.

When she's not working on a new story, she spends her time reading contemporary romances, playing way too many games of Scrabble or solitaire on Facebook, and spending time with her husband of twenty-five years and their two sons in North Carolina.

I'll Stand By You

by Sharon Sala

New York Times and *USA Today* bestselling author

———

When no one ever takes your side...

Dori Grant is no stranger to hardship. As a young single mother in the gossip-fueled town of Blessings, Georgia, she's weathered the storm of small-town disapproval most of her life. But when Dori loses everything within the span of an evening, she realizes she has no choice but to turn to her neighbors.

All you need is one person in your corner

Everyone says the Pine boys are no good, but Johnny Pine has been proving the gossips wrong ever since his mother died and he took over raising his brothers. His heart goes out to the young mother and child abandoned by the good people of Blessings. Maybe he can be the one to change all that...

———

Praise for *The Curl Up and Dye*:

"A delight...I couldn't put it down." —*Fresh Fiction*

"One of those rare treats." —*RT Book Reviews*

"Engaging, heartwarming, funny, sassy, and just plain good." —*Peeking Between the Pages*

For more Sharon Sala, visit:

www.sourcebooks.com

Every Bride Has Her Day

Magnolia Brides

by Lynnette Austin

—⁓—

Cricket O'Malley can't wait to plant roots back home in Georgia, where she's returned to restore an abandoned flower shop to its former glory. The only blemish? Her neighbor's house is even more neglected than her old flower shop, and its occupant seems as surly as he is darkly handsome.

Devastated body and soul after a tough case went south, New York City detective Sam DeLuca thought he'd have no trouble finding solitude in the quiet Georgia town of Misty Bottoms, but his bubbly neighbor seems determined to shine happiness into Sam's life. Sam is equally determined to close himself off, but his heart says otherwise…

—⁓—

Praise for *The Best Laid Wedding Plans*:

"Entertaining…the push and pull of emotion
feels real." —*RT Book Reviews*, 4 Stars

"An intriguing premiere…well-developed characters
and sensual romantic tension." —*Publishers Weekly*

For more Lynnette Austin, visit:

www.sourcebooks.com

Missed Connections

by Tamara Mataya

New York Times and *USA Today* bestselling author

———— ᴧᴧᴧ ————

Missed Connection:
I saw you standing there,
and I was struck by your eyes.
Gorgeous, but not as gorgeous as your smile.

Thanks to her job at a crazy New Age spa, what should have been a sizzling New York City summer is hijacked by demanding hippie bosses. To unwind, Sarah spends her nights cruising Missed Connections, dreaming of finding a romantic entry all about her. Of course, the moment she finds it, real life comes crashing down around her in a night of unbridled passion with someone completely different: totally off-limits Jack.

Best. Hookup. Ever.

Gorgeous and wealthy, Jack can give Sarah everything she needs—except an emotional connection. That she gets from her Missed Connection, the romantic stranger who never fails to make her swoon. Torn between the bad boy she can't keep and the sensitive stranger who bares his soul online, her heart and body are soon in two very different relationships…or are they?

For more Tamara Mataya, visit:

www.sourcebooks.com

Trouble Walks In

The McGuire Brothers

by Sara Humphreys

New York Times and *USA Today* bestselling author

He could be the man to rescue her

Big-city K-9 cop Ronan McGuire loves women, loves his dog, loves his job—but when old flame Maddy Morgan moves into his jurisdiction, he can't think about anyone else. Ronan knows she's way out of his league, but he's determined to help Maddy live life to the fullest.

In more ways than one

With tragedy in her past, Maddy has immersed herself in work and swiftly made a name for herself in the hot New York City real estate market. She's looking for safety, not love, but Ronan McGuire is as persistent as he is sexy, and his crooked smile is hard to resist. But all other concerns are wiped away when Maddy goes missing and Ronan and his bloodhound K-9 partner are tasked with finding her and bringing her home.

For more Sara Humphreys, visit:

www.sourcebooks.com